1.00

LADIES' OWN
EROTICA

*Two Bestsellers
from the Kensington
Ladies' Erotica Society
Together in One
Volume*

KENSINGTON LADIES' EROTICA SOCIETY

MJF BOOKS

NEW YORK

Any similarity to real persons, places, and events is in the eye of the beholder.

Published by MJF Books
Fine Communications
Two Lincoln Square
60 West 66th Street
New York, NY 10023

Library of Congress Catalog Card Number 96-76474
ISBN 1-56731-139-3

Copyright © 1984, 1986 by the Kensington Ladies' Erotica Society

Book Design by Nancy Austin
Illustrated by Pat Adler
Copy Edited by Estelle Jelinek

This edition published by arrangement with Ten Speed Press.

Manufactured in the United States of America on acid-free paper   ∞

MJF Books and the MJF colophon are trademarks of Fine Creative Media, Inc.

10   9   8   7   6   5   4   3   2   1

Ladies' Own Erotica

Tales, Recipes, and Other Mischiefs
by Older Women

THE KENSINGTON LADIES'
EROTICA SOCIETY

ILLUSTRATED BY PAT ADLER

Here are a group of unassuming women who can teach us men much. In their statement addressed to penis owners (page 23) there is a significant lesson . . . a profound insight that men will do well to read . . . and re-read . . . and profit from. But there is more . . . much more . . . in the tender art and sensual joy of love and sex. It is much more than fucking. Much that men can learn from these women, and tens of thousands like them all across the nation, if only we will take the courage to put aside our macho arrogance, and learn to touch and feel and ride with pure emotion. Let us men take up their challenge and make the sexual revolution complete.

—JUDD BOYNTON

Contents

We affectionately dedicate these pages
to the memory of our patron saint, Judd Boynton.

The Kensington Ladies

Introducing the
Kensington Ladies

We are an improbable group of women over forty, for whom dashing off an erotic story was one more task to be sandwiched in between trips to the supermarket and visits to the dentist. Some of us scribbled erotic tidbits on the backs of envelopes during lunch hours while others lavished whole weekends on a story. We regard ourselves as women who embarked on an experiment and, as a kind of afterthought, wrote and published. We met at one another's houses, prepared and ate hellishly good meals, and confided our sexual fantasies like pajama-clad schoolgirls.

It was Sabina who, seven years ago, gave birth to the group. Always the instigator as a child ("I'll be the witch and you . . ."), her questions to us were: Do you think women and men agree about what is erotic? Are our experiences different from theirs? Do we really know what turns us on, or do we just go along, accepting and acting out what male writers proclaim to be erotic?

Our first meeting, a potluck dinner, was at Sabina's house. Only a handful of women came — not quite knowing what it was they were coming to but clearly pulled in by the word "erotica." Right off, we discovered that we shared an unbridled passion for food. To establish a feeling of safety, Sabina assured us that this was not to be an encounter group and that no private revelations were demanded. We then took a dutiful look at Anaïs Nin, Henry

Miller, and Nancy Friday and even glanced at the technicolored vaginas and muscled playboys of *Penthouse, Chic,* and *Playgirl.* We were not amused!

Our writing began, at Sabina's instigation, as an "assignment." Drawing on our love for food she asked, "If you could concoct a recipe for the perfect lover, what ingredients would you use?" (For many of us cooking has always been a safe expression of our erotic selves.) In response we turned to our adolescent awakenings, then to our movie star idols from those years, and finally to enchanting strangers from exotic lands. These confrontations reminded us how seductively we had been sold on women's helplessness and victimization. Out of this recognition came our one rule: no victims. Our efforts to shelve sexual stereotypes have not always worked, but as we became more aware we were able to play with them.

We continued to meet every month. Each home was different, but the ritual remained the same. We began our Erotica evenings with chilled wine and, of course, hors d'œuvres: crackers, sly and salty, crusty French bread still warm from the local boulangerie, Brie spreading dreamily across the cheeseboard to mingle with the sturdy Gouda and the owlish Swiss, smoked salmon, rosy and pungent, and black olives glinting with a hint of malice from a glass bowl. Like ceremonial swords, these offerings allowed us to carve out the slice of time we needed for transition.

The presence of our men at these preliminaries added a particular flavor. The resident husband or lover, by mutual consent, was there at the outset — graceful, suave, polite, supportive — but, we noticed, his knuckles tight on the wineglass stem, the area about his mouth a little drawn. We would smile, loving smiles. We would grow remote, eager for the coming experience. We felt ourselves slipping beyond a tangible boundary: we were mysterious, powerful, eminently desirable — ready to cast our precious domestic bread upon the wine-dark waters of our fantasies.

And then the moment arrived, exquisite, wordless, inexorable — the moment for the man to withdraw. And that was when the fun began! Erotica!

I. AWAKENING

Reminiscing about our sexual awakenings, most of us recall a vivid time that passed with glacial slowness. We gathered information randomly—poring over pulp magazines, clandestinely comparing our anatomies, blundering in upon lovers locked in stolen embraces, or overhearing conversations not meant for our ears. We consulted the dictionary, which thwarted our search with rebounding synonyms and glaring omissions. We puzzled over the meaning of ambiguous phrases like "he took her" or "she came," knowing there was more to these familiar words than we understood.

Our awkward revelations left us unsettled and aroused. We took our cues from friends and older relatives and learned to disguise our naïveté with sophisticated trappings: stockings, lipstick, earrings. We spent eternities sunbathing, shampooing, grooming for that first kiss. What a relief when it finally came, even though it fell far short of the delirium of "movie star kisses"! In the recollections that follow, we allowed ourselves to be carried back into childhood's sensual drift.

Summer Rain

There are experiences that have no age, even when the people in them are children and one of them is you. The image remains with you just below the conscious level, and nothing that's happened to you since in any stage of love seems to equal it.

A summer rain in the dry San Gabriels causes a lot of excitement. The dusty pine needles drain off into powdery earth, and there is the expectant feeling of a very special event; even the smell is special. I am in a cabin in those mountains when the rains come, and I am thirteen and in love with a genius of fourteen. Of course his family is there with us, and I'm their guest, so I hide my feelings.

While the rain falls, sentimental songs play on the ancient phonograph. The words are as foolish as the mannered voices singing them, but the world *love* occurs frequently, and it has recently become a powerful word to me. So I gaze dreamily away while everyone else is laughing at the quaintness of the music, and they tease me about it. I long for older times when thirteen-year-old girls were thought marriageable women and could be dead in childbirth at fifteen. That short, intense life could be richer than dreams of roses, but I'm expected to live a long time and not to discover my sexual self for many more years — maybe when I'm twenty-one it's supposed to happen — and at thirteen that seems like another century.

In the stormy evening when his parents and his sister go off to bed one by one, leaving us to lantern light and the fire burning down to glowing ashes, our eyes want to meet and detonate the charged air. But we are both suddenly afraid of something, so we agree without words to dance. We dance very well together as a result of our lessons, and we take pride in that, careful not to let it degenerate into an embrace. Still his fingers at my waist feel like misplaced fireplace coals, and when the phonograph winds slowly to a stop, neither of us moves to rewind it. The rushing of the rain water down the dry gullies outside is now very loud. All the earth's messages seem to tell us to come together, and our eyes finally engage in that long-deferred glance.

But there are stirrings of late-night activity from the family, and we are reminded that the planet is not solely our own. A spark has fallen on the Navajo rug, and I rush to put it out while he restores function to the phonograph. The electric moment is gone.

We make hot chocolate and discuss the meteorology of the rainstorm. After all, he is a science prodigy, and rain cannot be regarded as merely romantic. The phenomena of nature occupy much of our daily discussions and contemplations, believing fervently as we do that everything man can perceive in the cosmos will someday be understood. When we are both very sleepy, we part at his bedroom door, and our goodnight kiss is as soft and sensual as it is brief. Even young love wearies and needs rest more than fulfillment.

When I awake alone and lost at 3 A.M., I know something cataclysmic is happening. There is a dense blackness and silence in my room, but I'm sure some loud sound awoke me. Then I feel the earth buzzing and humming through the planks of the floor, up through the old iron bedframe and into my very bones. There is an immense cracking sound and a sizzle of the most intense light I've every dreamed of: every object in the room has its halo. Instantly, a roar of sound shocks my bed and floor and room and roof. Outside, crashing reverberations roll up and down the mountainside and out into the valley, echoes reinforcing echoes.

I am terrified and fascinated and leap out of bed to witness this judgment day, padding barefoot to the window. As I stand there in my child's flannel pajamas, which have somehow crossed over into my adolescent wardrobe unnoticed, I am suddenly aware of someone behind me. I'm prepared for a ghostly presence on this night, but it is a familiar newly deep voice that whispers: "Lightning may have struck the cabin — there was no time-lapse before the thunder." His arms come around me, and his dear warm body snuggles against my shivering frame. There is a long wait for the consequences of either the lightning or the illicit embrace, but nothing happens. "Let's get into bed — you're cold," he whispers.

Without another thought the icy bedsheets are breeched, and we lie shivering together in the tangle of old wool blankets and tired feather pillows. Once only we look toward the door — it is firmly closed and bolted, and no further thought of intrusion crosses our minds through the rainy night. Our total embrace of arms and legs, cheeks and temples, hands and hair, begins immediately. The comfort of our mutual presence is overwhelming. My seizure of shivering stops, and a sweet warmth begins to spread.

The outer storm still crashes, but it is less threatening now, moving slowly along the mountain range and out into the valley. Our lips touch and draw apart. "You know we will not do the corrupting things," he says. We know, because we have discussed it long and philosophically: love is the universe and its suns; lust is the dark side of the planets. We are not sure how the drenching desire we both now feel fits into the cosmos, but we know it must have a place this side of corruption. We trust completely and that trust cannot be betrayed.

As the hours pass, we lie entwined, shifting slightly for comfort, pajamas unbuttoned so the warm flesh of each embraces its counterpart. There is drowsing and waking and drowsing again. Lips brush and cling in infinite kisses. Tongues flicker over eyelids and earlobes and touch tongues. Toes caress toes. Knees and arm joints work past each other to meet at smooth places. Hands cup and fondle. His arousal brings my fingertips to stroke and release. His fingers run the rapids of my warm caves and hollows, lingering while I lapse into sleep. We awake to resume the caress interrupted by sleep.

When dawn lightens in gentle shades, the storm is only a faint echo in the far distance, and our own world is dripping, quiet, and serene. For a long time I watch his dear face sleeping, then slip into sleep to wake and find him watching me. Then suddenly he is disentangled and gone. Now I sink into the sound sleep I have not had all night, and it takes the whole family surging in my door at ten o'clock to awaken me. Only one question is asked: "How could you sleep through that incredible storm?" And "Ahhh, to be young!" from his mother.

Later I learn that we had experienced a landmark summer storm for those mountains, one which became local history of fallen trees, crushed cabins, and washed-out roads. But in my personal history the image remains one of embraced bodies, a depth of closeness in our intertwined forms, the absolute trust and visceral intensity of our happiness together. Long after I've forgotten how the love ended, the memory keeps an ephemeral presence that mocks all future moments of abandonment and ecstasy. Nothing, nothing, has been like that summer storm at thirteen.

Retreat

He stalks the corridors of the school, a magnet in black Jesuitical clothing, virile, comminatory, physical, remote. Terence Trumpington, S.J., visiting priest to the convent where I am being educated: celibate, sexual, imported from God knows where to guide us — two hundred reluctant virgins, ages thirteen to seventeen, and our fragrant, fluttering potpourri of wimpled jailers — through this year's Retreat. For six days we withdraw from the world of schoolbooks and schedules. We embrace prayer, silence, meditation. We confront our souls. The younger pupils and that race apart, the "non-Catholics," inhabit a parallel pedestrian universe. For them, business as usual: black marks, blotters, rule and rote. For us the devout, the white-veiled, life has become the realization of a page torn from an illuminated manuscript. We are lambent, we are sanctified, we are obsessed. We are a group of willing sacrifices. Since the initial shocks — his white-blond mane like deadly exposed wires, his voice, his resonance electrifying our liquid flesh — we are ready at the flash of a blunt white hand to hang up our girdles on the nearest bush. Every one of us, now, answers to the name of Heloise, hears the name whispered like a summons down every corridor of vaulted dark. Drawn by invisible gold threads, which he holds in his hands, we are tugged toward him into his magic circle of mystery. He is a charmed particle in our shadowy, flickering universe of rules. Normally, we rarely see men; those we do see have already been transliterated and have lost their enchantment. They are flat cutouts of their particular functions: gardeners, altar boys, visiting siblings. Occasionally, one of us will roll up her purity into a tight ball of rage, hurl it in a high arc across the pierced light of a painted window, and get pregnant.

And now, among us, is a most passionate priest. Padding across our hidden consciousness, he is tawny, magnificent, feral. He circles us, growling softly, brushing our skins with exhalations that have the same blood scent as the flood of our own moontides. His movements are fluid, released in distributed tension along his limbs and throughout his body. The early sun strikes bent bars across his brow at mass; his vestments flash like jewels, like plumage; his body snaps the brittle morning air. He crackles; bowing, bending, spinning, he performs before the tabernacle his love dance to our waking souls. Later, in his talks with us, his sensual intellect splinters like gold leaf the sequestered, swooning chapel air. Soft now, the air, and pliable; the incense hangs in stale tatters above our heads. Breathing the brocaded atmosphere, refulgent, odorous, we sense our suffocation amid white waxen flowers and votive lights that flicker crimson in their pots of oil. We watch the flames dancing on fat thrusting candles and feel the aching weight of burgeoning breasts that throb, rosy and tumescent, beneath our stout viyella blouses. Our veils bestow a furry bloom to our hair; every shrouded cheek holds the pale polish of desire, reflected in the snail-track smears we find each night on the cotton crotches of our panties. Some of us are menstruating; the rich marine smell of monthly blood communicates our restive longing, and our periods spread like a medieval mania as we watch our fantasies take shape behind bound volumes of *The Lives of the Saints*. Orgasmic Theresa, drooling Damien, raving, quivering John of the Cross: our thighs are sticky with the fluids of our crepuscular dreams. Possessed, our lives saturated by our moist imaginings, we move uneasily on our hard wooden chairs. From the swollen convolutions of our sex slide the glistening, undulant whorls of our desire. Carnal longing crawls from our groins and, groaning, prowls restlessly in search of Terence Trumpington, S.J.

Imperceptibly, we have changed. We are alien and suspicious, haughty and challenging to one another. The schoolgirl canter along the corridors has slowed and stopped; now we flow from the base of our spines, arms slack in rhythm to the superb pelvic sway. We ripple; we surge with high breasts and throats arched. Our breath comes hard; in our nostrils we feel the tight dry tingle of desert air; we follow the rumor of the crowd, swarming barefoot along the Way of the Cross in pursuit of the sweating, bleeding figure in the scarlet dust ahead of us. And our Magdalene hair, red and rampant down our backs, lifts and stirs in the sour yellow breath of a Galilean afternoon. We follow our lover over rocks and bones to the place of the stark triple trees, and we are gulped like draughts of air and water into the cavern behind the rolled-back stone.

Alone with him at last, dusky, murmuring; lips a whisper away from his ear, from his hand resting against a pallid temple. Like a stripper he will see my soul, he will look at me at last. A touch, just one touch! Like this, below the belly, where the pubis thrusts out curling copper tendrils (ah!) and here, on the nape, quickly, between the braided ropes of hair (ah!) and down over the shoulder, between the breasts, here beneath the jutting stone. . . . There's time, yes, there's time, before it's all over and you have to go. . . . I will hold you softly in my hand, like velvet, and lick the shiny dewdrop from the tip, like this. Ah, love, now you're nailed, expiring with a scarlet wound. They've stripped you to a loincloth, but I will draw it aside, like this; I will join you on your gibbet and straddle your body and slowly change the groans that wrench from you to murmurs of ecstasy. . . . *Agnus Dei, qui tollis peccata mundi,* don't let me die, touch me, save me. Sweet cleric, leaning across the altar to pronounce the darkling words of the Transubstantiation *(corpus Domini nostri, Jesu Christi),* I have stripped you of every stitch, all off, chasuble, stole, alb, soutane, stripped you to your loincloth and bent my face to your groin, inhaling the scents of yeast and leaf mold.

"Have you committed any sins against purity, my child, in thought, word, deed, or omission?" *Mea culpa, mea culpa, mea maxima culpa:* impale me, my censored one. I shall unfold to you, petal by petal, a veritable rose of sins. I pass before you in my veil, murmuring my trespasses into your dusky confessional ear. Body and blood; body and blood; my adolescence drips from me, pricked by crimson thorns; roses burst from the nail wounds in your feet, and I pluck them and wind them in my long red hair. *Et te, Pater:* inhale me now, as you pronounce my penance; bless my petals, my vices, my inward, salivating womanhood just recently declared in blood. *"Ego te absolvo."* Am I dying? "Go in peace, my child, and sin no more." I smell of earth and flowers and sweat and dew; and for gazing with impurity upon the crucified figure of Our Lord, Terence Trumpington, S.J., stern, austere, glittering with the white light of grace, pronounces sentence: three decades of the rosary and twice around the Way of the Cross. We are dazed, vacuous, blundering into one another, for the chapel is very crowded this Friday afternoon. Oh Father, forgive us, for we know now what we do.

Bedtime Story

I can still see the three narrow beds, each with a chair at the end where our underwear is neatly folded beneath our skirts, our blouses draped smoothly over the back. After thirty years I still shiver when I remember that unnerving coolness that clung to the bare white walls even in summer. It had nothing to do with the climate, but with the absence of love that left me terrified from the moment my parents abandoned me at my aunt's house.

"It will be good for you to live in such a large family," they said in parting. I violently disagreed. There were four boys and two girls. Although Sigrid was ten like myself and Ursula only a year older, I did not know my cousins well. The girls wore identical dresses, and even their shoes and socks matched at all times, for my uncle owned the clothing store on the ground floor of their rambling old house. My parents had told me about their good manners and about the discipline that my aunt and uncle exercised in running both store and family. "They will teach you to keep order," said my father, who thought that my mother had spoiled me while he was away in the war.

I soon learned that the store was the heart of the house; it compelled everyone to live by the hours it opened and closed. We children received our orders at breakfast, and every chore was checked on schedule by Tante Gerda, whose eyes were everywhere. Although she never punished me for my negligence, I was terrified of her.

I was also terrified of the dark and of losing my mother. As soon as I closed my eyes, I would imagine all kinds of things that might happen to her. Ever since the bombing of our apartment house, I was afraid of airplanes. I dreaded that she might get hurt by an airplane or by falling out of a moving train. Every day on the radio the Red Cross listed the names of all the parents and children who had lost each other. I imagined the crowded train and my mother telling me to hold onto her hand. But then somehow I had to let go, and she fell out.

I wanted to read before going to sleep, but Tante Gerda did not allow us to turn the light on. My favorite book was *Arabian Nights*. She took it away because she found it unsuitable for children.

I marked my calendar, counting the days until my mother would return. "I'll be back in time for your birthday," she wrote. But then she sent a telegram that she could not get away. My father was still looking for a place to set up his business.

"She promised to be back for my birthday," I cried. My cousins teased me that she would never come back and that I would have to stay with them forever.

"Now, now, one might think you are homesick," frowned Tante Gerda. She was the only person in the house who did not know that I cried every night. Even Onkel Johann occasionally brought me a piece of candy to help me go to sleep.

On my birthday he pulled a handful out of his pocket, but I pushed him away and flung myself out of bed toward the window. I banged against the shutters screaming: "I want to get out of this prison! I want to get out of this prison!" They all came running, Tante Gerda, the boys, and Anna, the maid, who took me into her arms: "The poor little dumpling; I know just how she feels." Anna too was homesick for her native Rumania where people spent all their life dancing and kissing. Tante Gerda insisted that Onkel Johann should give me a spanking, but he gently picked me up and carried me back to bed. Then he shooed the family out of the door, proving that he was after all the master of the house. Sigrid and Ursula were enthralled. I had finally won their admiration. "She'll punish you tomorrow for sure," they agreed. I didn't care. I knew that I had to stop crying. I decided to try to keep myself from thinking about my mother.

"You want to hear my story from *Arabian Nights*?" I asked. "It's about Harun-al-Rashid and the slave girl Suleika. It's a forbidden story."

Naturally, the girls wanted to hear it. Like Scheherezade, who kept alive by telling the sultan a story every night, I managed to keep myself from crying night after night as I cast my magic spell over Sigrid and Ursula. They even joined my game eagerly when I suggested we act out our stories. Sigrid was the new slave Suleika, and Ursula the sheik's favorite wife Rahmoon. From then on I was no longer a scared little girl but the mighty sheik Harun-al-Rashid.

We began with Suleika dancing the dance of the seven veils. While I told the story, she removed them one by one: first the brown, earth-colored veil signifying that she was a slave, then the orange veil that revealed her noble birth; the blue veil showed that she was a virgin, and the red veil told about her joy of becoming a woman. Finally, only the gold veil covered her skin because gold was the color of the royal harem. In this veil she danced her bridal dance while the other wives beat their cymbals and tambourines. Many of the wives hoped that she would make a wrong move and be sent back to the orphanage, especially the sheik's current favorite, the clever and beautiful Rahmoon, who had not yet produced a son and needed to keep Harun-al-Rashid's nightly favors. But Suleika danced perfectly until she fell exhausted to the ground.

"I shall visit her tonight. Bathe her in donkey's milk and rub her with oils and perfume," ordered the sheik.

"But I hoped you would spend the night with me," chimed Rahmoon. "I have prepared a special dance for you." Only his favorite could dare to speak without asking for permission, but Harun-al-Rashid allowed her to perform for him. She moved so seductively, shaking her diamond bracelets, that he once more succumbed to her spell and promised her the night, but not until he had greeted Suleika, the newcomer, as befitted a noble sheik.

When I crossed the room to Sigrid's bed, my bare feet did not walk on linoleum but on marble. My pajamas were studded with diamonds, and Sigrid's nightgown was a golden veil. Gently, I touched her face and removed the last veil. I told her how beautiful she was and how she must not be afraid because from now on her life would be given only to dancing and loving. Suleika remained still, but when Harun-al-Rashid took her into his arms, she nestled closely against him.

"I will now make you a woman." I pressed my naked belly against hers. Shyly, she felt my buttocks, and a warm glow spread from my secret place between my thighs urging me to explore her forbidden parts.

"Open your loins for me, sweet love and receive my seed, the seed of the royal house of Rashid."

"I hope it will be a prince like you," whispered Suleika.

Then I hurried over to Ursula's bed.

"I kept my promise, favorite of my heart."

"But you went to the newcomer first, master."

"I was only performing my royal duty. You must try to understand."

"Yes, my master, as long as you love only me."

"You know how much I love you, my queen, my jewel."

"I belong to you, take me in your arms."

"Open your loins for me, sweet love, and receive my royal seed."

I looked at her body, which seemed like a mirror of my own, intimate, yet strangely exciting. Together we rocked, overcome with the sensation of each other. It felt so soft and warm and moist down there. My skin tightened as it rubbed against her pubis. "I can hear your heart beating, my love."

"And I can hear yours."

"Now we are one flesh," said Harun-al-Rashid. "Wherever I am, wherever you are, when I call, you must come to me. Nothing can keep us apart. Remember — we are one flesh."

Ursula and Sigrid giggled. I ran back to my own bed and fell instantly and soundly asleep.

Sabina's Sauerkraut

My craving for sauerkraut in the raw goes back to when I was six years old. Propped up in bed (I had the flu), I spent my idle and listless hours watching the cows outside my window. Although they spent the whole day doing the same thing over and over, they never showed the slightest sign of boredom. On the contrary, their satisfaction showed with every mouthful of fresh green grass. I watched them circle clumps of grass with strong, fleshy tongues, then pull up a tasty bunch and munch steadily, without haste. Every so often they looked up dreamily just to chew, totally absorbed, totally content. Knowing my mother would not let me out to graze, I begged her to get me a plate full of raw sauerkraut. I still remember how I masticated the tangy shreds, feeling very much in tune with the cows' intense eating experience.

Unfortunately, I never found a partner willing to share my passion for eating sauerkraut in bed. My husband finds it disgusting, so I do it secretly.

If raw sauerkraut is too kinky for the common tongue, I recommend this cooked version. Although not as elemental, it is equally earthy. Since the ingredients are ordinary kitchen staples, rather than fancy French delicacies, all the credit goes to the imaginative cook, not the gourmet grocer. It satisfies a voracious appetite, which usually follows vigorous exercise and therefore is best served at the conclusion of a seduction. Only hardy eaters will be able to consume this hearty meal before lovemaking. If, for reasons beyond the control of the cook, the food has to come first, I suggest a brisk walk in the woods as a transition, possibly an al fresco setting for the post-sauerkraut event.

Drain and rinse one pound of sauerkraut (or a twenty-seven-ounce can) in cold water. Place in a casserole with large smoked sausages or ham hocks. Add two lean pork chops, and top with a can of diced pineapple including the juice. Sprinkle with chopped walnuts, coarsely ground pepper, a bay leaf, and a dash of salt. Cover and simmer in a moderate oven for at least two hours. This should leave plenty of time for an unhurried erotic encounter enhanced by the tantalizing aroma from the kitchen. As soon as you are ready to return your attention to cooking — there are no exact time limits — brown four small breakfast sausages in a skillet, drain off the fat, and arrange them on top of the sauerkraut with the other pieces of meat. Serve with fluffy mashed potatoes, garnished with fried onions. (Smoked beef and veal frankfurters can be substituted for a kosher version, and dried fruit with small white beans instead of meat can turn this into a vegetarian meal.)

Recommended for active couples who are seeking a nourishing relationship. The flavor increases with reheating.

II.   BODY LANGUAGE

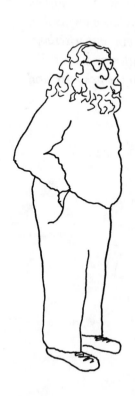

Although our bodies, in art and in life, are capable of inciting passion merely by being stripped of clothing, the excitement of the male body is less in the way it looks than in the way it does. In our stories, the male hero may be paunchy, stoop-shouldered, pale, or thin; his appeal lay elsewhere — in the way he looked at us, the way he moved or spoke, how he explored our body. It is in his body language, we realized, that we revel, and in this sense we found that hesitancy could be as appealing as sureness and playfulness as tantalizing as heavy breathing. When we did focus on his body as object, it was usually a detail — a head of thick, sensuous hair (and gray hair, at that) or a massive hand. Notably, none of our heroes is described as "well endowed."

In describing our own bodies, most of us found it fun to indulge in the narcissism so freely granted (even encouraged) in our own gender. At the same time, we felt comfortable in exposing our imperfections, without resorting to Felliniesque ridicule of our shapes and sizes. We particularly delighted in moving from the beheld to the beholder and from the prone to the predatory.

Address to a Penis Owner

We are not anti-penis. In the feminine experience the penis can add the finishing touch to satisfaction, but it is not *sine qua non*. No, indeed. We have been brainwashed into paying more homage than is due this particular attachment of the male anatomy, and far too much has been made of its rise and fall. The fact that we admire a Greek statue no less when the penis has crumbled off should be sufficient proof that male beauty does not depend on this unique feature. Freud, of course, was wrong when he claimed that women suffer from penis envy — it is the men who do. Sadly, a man without a penis is no man at all in our culture, and in male mythology the penis distinguishes a valiant man from a timid one.

We do appreciate a lusty penis when it knows its place. Penis owners should keep in mind that a well-trained penis is a joy to hold and cuddle. If it knows a trick or two, so much the better. A well-behaved penis is indeed woman's best friend, but we object to those mindless penises that indiscriminately push their way in and out of our folds like sewing machines.

We suspect that the penis culture is a male invention from an earlier age when fertility was tantamount to the survival of the race. Understandably, then, the penis is still an important showpiece, and while it also adds much gratification to its owner, it offers comparatively less to the fulfillment of female desires.

If this comes as a shock to you, penis owner, please look at yourself from the female point of view. What is natural to you, who handle your penis many times a day, is quite unnatural to us. To us, the penis is a foreign object. I think that no man knows how alien his rod is to the girl who is confronted with it for the first time, when she is told to stroke it, to lick it, to like it. We know neither the power that comes with owning this tool nor the fear of losing it. Since we don't have anything as obvious and as embarrassingly untrustworthy in our love-making paraphernalia, we share your concern for its ups and downs, so much so that we have obliterated our own needs for gratification. We are not trying to diminish your appendage, but we want to enlarge upon those parts of you that have been unjustly ignored. These are the parts that are essential to our pleasure: your hair, your eyes, your lips, your tongue, your chest, your thighs, your voice, and — most importantly — your hands. It is no accident that our stories have celebrated these greater assets.

DON'T WORRY, HAROLD, SIZE DOESN'T MATTER TO ME.

Hands

The hostess had arranged the dinner table so that "significant others" faced each other, and she had seated us on each side of her at the head of the table. We had settled into the first course when she asked him the triggering question: "How is your house coming along?"

Whenever he described the house he was building, he became extremely animated. He talked a little faster than usual, his voice rose in pitch and decibels, and his eyes became laser-bright. His "dream house" (as he unabashedly called it) had become a total preoccupation—if he could not be on the site, pacing it out or poring over his plans, the next best thing was to talk about it. To anyone who asked, whether casually or seriously, he turned with eager gratitude, immediately reaching into his shirt pocket for the little notebook he carried, or accepting a proffered scrap of paper, or seizing an unused paper napkin to sketch whatever aspect of the structure intrigued, baffled, or delighted him at the moment. If paper were not available, the open air became his chalkboard as he cupped his hands and fingers around an imaginary piece of chalk and lost himself in passionate drawing—almost but not quite oblivious to the presence of his catalyst, at the moment, our hostess.

From my vantage point across the table from him, I was in a perfect position to watch, yet one more time, his metamorphosis from the man, the dinner guest, my lover, to Master Builder. As always, his face brightened as he began rapidly filling in answers to increasingly sophisticated questions he urgently wanted to answer but she didn't know to ask. Words like "joists," "beams," "lath," "subflooring," and "plenum" darted in and out, and soon became an auditory blur. All I saw were his hands, gesticulating in the air in front of my eyes.

His hands were massive, the fullness at the base of the thumb and the matching column of flesh from wrist to little finger creating a deep, sensuous bowl of the inner palm. His fingers were not long and sinewy — the romantic conception of the piano player's fingers — but, rather, thickly gnarled, each one a study in "finger-ness." My eyes followed the movements of his hands — coming together, breaking apart, clasping each other momentarily, making sudden twisting motions, freezing for a split second, and then starting their frenzied dance all over again. It was as though I were seeing them for the first time, these hands my body knew so well. I suddenly remembered that they had once fabricated larger-than-life kinetic sculptures which responded to movement and light — intellectually wrought pieces that once out of his hands carried on a life of their own, needing only the passing of a body in front of them to come alive.

As I stared, transfixed, I felt their soft and gentle thickness grip my shoulder, then encircle the back of my taut neck, knowingly and insistently searching me out, discovering each hollow, curve, and subtle shift in skin texture. The warmth of splayed fingers cupped my breasts and trailed downward to my navel, traced the in and out of my hip bone, groin, inner thigh. Beneath his touch, my body became a mound of clay, satin-smooth, moist, elastic. Now yielding, now resisting, twisting, turning, stretching, curling up in feline pleasure, I became the center of an exquisite dance between his hands and my flesh. I shuddered as his hand pressed its heat into my belly and let its fingers slip down quickly into my meadowland, stroking me tenderly, dancing one dance and then another, playing hide-and-seek, disappearing into the cave of me for a split second and then emerging to roll around in the now wet, slippery, pungent grass that sung of spring and wildflowers. From some faraway exotic land I heard the rustle and moan of the wind coming closer and closer and suddenly swelling into a thunderous, piercing cry. Two giant hands reached under me and pulled me upward while a thousand fingers burst into the deep, dark tunnel whose walls endlessly shook and sobbed.

"Darling. You look a bit strange. Are you feeling all right?" The hostess turned to me in concern.

"Yes, I'm fine . . . just fine."

I smiled reassuringly at him and reached across the table to take his hand in mine.

Aerobics

I work out in the back of the studio
knowing that you usually come
late, arriving after the leg lifts and arm rotations,
but always in time for the pelvic thrusts.

You weave your way
past flailing limbs that flash
in metallic tights like thresher blades.

Flat on my back, knees and buttocks
raised, I watch you spread
your legs and join the unison:

> Push, push, squeeeeeeeeze,
> push, push, squeeeeeeeeze.
> 1,2,3. 1,2,3.
> Now one leg up:
> flex and point, flex and point.
> One more set,
> come on now.
> Don't stop.
> Pelvic tuck.
> Add the head.
> Lift and reach, lift and reach.
> For God's sake, BREATHE!

You are framed between my thighs
and with each head lift, from where I lie,
I can see you strain, eyes shut
tighter than fists,
press, release, press, release,
again and again and again.
With each exhalation
your head alights atop your pubis
like some Aztec god
giving birth to itself.

Da Capo

It has always been his hair, from the beginning, from the first day we met. That day I stared and stared at his hair, which was an exuberance of close-cropped, metal-colored curls, smarting and resentful from the barber's rigorous corrections. His hair was what made him "distinguished-looking," but that first day, at the beginning, it was a magnesium flash that shocked me and violated my safety: it made me see myself. I thought I saw my own face ricochet off that gasp of refracted light — lucent, perturbed, vigilant, sly. His name was a label pinned to his lapel. I understood that I would be working for him.

I barely knew him when I started watching my fantasies. These had to do with my hands, which would float to his temples and come to rest, the lacquered fingertips quivering, somnolent as lepidopteral specimens transfixed on a collector's tray. And then, their printless, palpitant, indefatigable caresses, across and through and around the spangled silver wire that shone around his ears and strayed toward the collar of his starched clinical coat.

As we grew less shy with each other, working late on an agenda or collaborating on a report, I found myself becoming more obsessed. The determined boundaries between fantasy and fact began to sag. I noticed that my attempts at disciplining my hand were growing more lax, my movements more languid, more fluent in his company. The phantasmagoria of my dreams, those luxuriant plant forms of milkweed, flax and blowing prairie grasses, began to assume the rigid boundaries of probable fulfillment. I saw that our shadows flowed ominously together when we met to work; entwining, rending, flooding back into merged stains upon the walls and ceiling even as we sat demurely apart, our bodies serenely isolated from each other's touch. An embrace was thickening the air between us. After five months of collaboration we each knew enough about the other's body signals to wonder who, finally, would make the choice to shed the heavy mantling of reserve lying along our limbs like a refugee's blanket.

One afternoon, standing behind him at his desk while he frowned at the typescript of some minutes I had drafted for him, I made the choice. He leaned forward across his desk to stub out his cigarette in the overflowing ashtray. As he straightened, marking a note in the margin and grunting approval, I moved closer and, stretching out a hand that felt flayed, gently passed the palm across the top of his head. The steely argent of his hair flattened and sprang back like the blazon on a shield. My first sensation was one of complete surprise. I had been expecting tin, sharp, resistant; instead, I found silk. My other hand flew down to join the first for a second opinion. I joined them on top of his head and drew in my breath. I wondered how I would explain my behavior.

With my hands resting on the crown of his head I stared thoughtfully at the enormity of my boldness. What if I were wrong? "You have a cinder on your head," I could say, or, "Just hold still a moment while I remove this lint from your hair." And I could brush, vigorously, with both hands. The words were stillborn on an exhalation. They had no reason for being. I could not pull my hands away. My skin, I found was as subservient to his hair as if it were wet and in contact with live, naked wires. I submitted, then, and let my hands weigh upon his crown.

Dreamily, I began to stroke his brow and temples with my fingertips, the back of my hand, the inside of my wrist. My skin began to tug against my flesh, against my bones. I wanted to feel his hair against all the unexpected surfaces of my skin, against my ankles, under my arms, across my spine where it flares at the base, beneath my chin, around my ears, the nape of my neck. I felt I might weep with temper.

He was so still, so petrified in the amber wash of my obsession that I wondered if time had telescoped, fossilizing us both in the fire and ice of eons precipitated by the force of my agitation and my desire. He was as still and as silent as a mollusk on wet sand, and I thought my breath would stop. Then, in wordless response to the minutest hesitation in my caress, his hands crept around behind his chair and held my legs. I felt my body begin to droop with languor, and I brought one hand down to his shoulder, drawing it softly up the side of his neck and across his chin, which was abrasive from the lateness of the hour. His eyes were closed, and I saw the dark fan of his eyelashes resting on a glint of tears. I brought my cheek down to his marvelous contradictory hair and gently started pulling his head back against my breast. Still he did not open his eyes, and I stared at his face, wondering if my heart would burst my body.

I brought my lips to his brow, to the place between his eyes where they say there is a third eye, the eye of all knowledge. I parted my lips and let the tip of my tongue slide across his eyelids. He jerked back his head and our mouths fell together with an exhalation that rose up from the deepest part of our being, full fathoms five, and still I could not separate my hand from his hair. My fingers writhed and swam like eels trapped in a seine net. I could move among the meshes of his hair but not away. Above us the bars of fluorescent light that lit his office flickered blue as ice.

His face, when I lifted my head to gaze at him, was ashen. His eyes, open now, were like brown, washed pebbles. He watched me with bright hunger and no small distrust. I pressed my face to his hair, nuzzling the silver phosphorescence, and my hands moved down to rest on the lapels of his name-tagged coat. But then my nerves began an agonized appeal that, could it have been heard, would have been a whimper. I had to hold his head, had to feel the live velours of his cropped mane beneath my hands.

And so we remained, beneath the frostlight of the flickering lamp, entwined in that sculptured space while the evening fog lapped the mirrored blackness of the window, speechless, remote. The glittering silence of inanimate objects — the sink and the microscope, the telephone and silver-framed family on his desk — filled the room and illuminated our joined figures at its center as if we, too, were fixtures. Our kisses had pierced the quilted, sterile air like splinters from a smashed bottle of ammonia, and there was no withdrawing.

Later that evening we went to dinner; then we went to bed. We became lovers: luxuriant, inflamed, experimental, preoccupied with the minutiae of voluptuous exchange. Later still we inhabited the same house, embarked upon the manipulation of money and domestic detail. We talked and laughed, wept and lied, fought and felt shame, and made up and always made love. And it's still the same. When I divine his desire, now, after so many years, when he eyes me in a certain way — across the kitchen, emerging from the shower, feeding the cat, on the beach, at the theater — and I move toward him through the folded air, it's still the same. At the moment of contact my hands fly up to his hair, which is white now after all these years. I hold his head in my hands and stroke his hair. I know discovery and reward. The night recedes, my soul escapes, and my body knows good.

Moon Bosoms

How much I dislike hospital banquets, I realize, as I settle into the chair dear Sidney holds out for me. In recent years I have been avoiding these events as more and more staff wives are becoming doctors themselves. Strangely enough, I miss the old days when wives had the freedom of outcasts and clustered together to laugh over common woes. Now, with so many earnest lives focused on medicine, it is almost impossible to escape the medical patter.

The table looks as neat as a hospital bed and is draped with as much linen. I have to lift the tablecloth to make room for my knees, and the large white linen napkin feels as heavy as a folded sheet upon my lap. Gleaming rows of cutlery foretell a long and ponderous meal.

The group at our table look younger and more ostentatiously coiffed than ever before. A frizzy permanent obscures the male Asian intern at my left. Two seats beyond I discern that my husband's old rival, now chief of medicine, has sprouted a crown of hair transplants that look more stubborn and painful than thorns. Thank God, Sidney is content to be bald with dignity and resignation!

The spangled ochre jacket of an approaching waiter catches my eye. Carefully lowering a tray of steaming soup bowls to a nearby serving station, he begins serving the guests across the table. I peer anxiously over the chrysanthemum centerpiece, hoping the soup will be madrilene or, better yet, mock turtle.

The woman opposite me is being served, and I strain to get a better look at the shimmering golden liquid. Before I can determine what it is, the woman dips the broad base of her spoon into the soup and drops it with a resounding splash.

It happens so quickly and unexpectedly that the woman springs back in her chair with a quick gasp. Her hands rush to her breasts that rise majestically from the pectoral arch to summits barely concealed by folds of blue chiffon. The sight fills me with awe. Each globe nestles blissfully beside its twin, compressed into a deep cleavage that I have always wanted. How warm and reassuring it must be to have them so close together! I try to imagine how their weight and fullness would feel if they were mine. How gently they would jostle each time I moved. They would absorb embraces differently from anything I have known. I want to reach out and touch each smooth, peach-soft creamy moon. How totally unlike my own small sinewy body.

The bearer of the bosoms is taking her napkin in her right hand and, with infinite care, slips her left hand under a blue-chiffoned breast and gently cradles it. With the napkin wound around her forefinger, she dabs tenderly at the bulging sphere. I stare transfixed. Has the perfect skin been scalded? My view is obstructed by the hand that wipes and dabs with deliberate and unhurried care.

At last, the hands settle in the woman's lap. The pale alabaster moons glow luminescent. I lean closer to inspect the damage to the left breast, which seems to be of most concern to its keeper. It looks just as perfect as the right one; in fact, I have never seen a more symmetrical pair. Miracles like that, I know, seldom occur in nature.

Sidney, my devoted husband, sitting beside me, has obviously been as spellbound as I by the silent drama that has just unfolded. His years of medical experience tell him that those exquisite breasts probably belong to a nullipara. Their nipples will be pale and pink and the skin light enough to reveal a filigree of veins beneath. During pregnancy these breasts will swell and harden painfully and may be plagued by cracked nipples, engorgement, and possibly infection when nursing commences. The perfect smoothness of the skin may even now conceal lumps of various sizes and textures that will have to be watched and charted in future years.

All this knowledge does not lessen Sidney's desire to lower his face into that delicious cleavage and inhale its natural perfume. He wants to lay his cheek upon those breasts, close his eyes, and float suspended; to lift them from the gown, one by one, and let them hang liberated above the steaming soup; to watch them while she dances, swaying slowly at first, then jiggling as the tempo quickens, until they toss wildly in a tempest of passion. He can feel his hands moving slowly over and around them, marveling at their pliant abundance. He will sink to his knees and gaze up at her twin moons looming overhead and feel protected. The warm underside of each breast will shield his baldness and restore his flagging energy. He wants to lie down and be blatantly seduced.

Sidney glances at me. I stare motionless, tightly coiled, like a cat ready to pounce. My pupils widen, and, had I a tail, it would be twitching. Sidney sees a faint blush rise from my throat to my cheek. He loves the way my color changes when I am aroused. He looks back across the table.

The young woman has a face that is a little too vapid for his liking. She would benefit from some of my intensity. Sidney has always managed in public to quash any sudden lustful feelings, but tonight is different — not because of her but because of my obvious captivation that joins us in sexual conspiracy. I put down my soup spoon and pat his knee. Our eyes meet.

"I caught you!" I whisper triumphantly, moving my hand up his thigh and finding his erection.

You certainly did," he whispers back, "and I caught you!"

We laugh and squeeze hands.

"I was afraid your glasses would fall into your soup," he confides.

"I know," I laugh. "I nearly had to climb the chrysanthemums to get a decent look!"

"For a minute, I thought she was going to feed them some soup. Didn't you?"

I stifle a laugh.

"Of course," he adds loyally, "she won't look as good as you when she's your age."

"Oh, come now. I wish I had them."

"They'll sag pretty soon."

"Fine! I'll take them!"

Sidney slips his hand under the folds of tablecloth and fondles my thigh appreciatively. Keeping his hand on my leg, he turns slightly to answer a question about medical politics that issues from his side of the table. As he speaks, I feel his hand begin to creep under my skirt. His long fingers close over the inside smoothness of my thigh and begin tracing small circles. His cool fingertips undulate over my bare skin, and I am thankful that I haven't worn stockings.

At my side of the table the conversation remains on marathon running. I try to look attentive, shifting my gaze from speaker to speaker and laughing on cue with the rest, but all my senses focus on the long fingers that stroke me, slowly advancing from my knee toward my crotch and back again.

The waiter is passing dinner rolls. I draw my legs together abruptly as he approaches, but Sidney does not remove his hand. He refuses the bread with a wave of his other hand and continues to argue the inequities of the present system of medical reimbursement. His little finger wiggles dangerously close to the elastic binding of my panties, and I shift self-consciously in my chair.

Through the remainder of the soup course the pressure of his hand increases. By the time I finish my soup, he is at my panty line, fondling the stray hairs escaping from the lace trim. The waiters are now clearing the soup plates, and I cross my thighs, trapping Sidney's probing hand to keep it still. Not to be thwarted, he keeps his hand locked in place. With infinite patience and unrelenting pressure, he slowly slides his fingers beneath my panty and confidently seeks the secret place he knows so well. My resistance is crumbling.

Waiters start to bring in the entrée, which, to my great alarm, is roast beef. Sidney will need both hands to cut it. I will have to act quickly. Calmly rearranging the large napkin in my lap, I lean closer to the table and begin to butter my dinner roll. As I do, my pelvis rocks forward to increase the pressure of his hand against me. The fingers begin to move more quickly as I bear down more heavily upon them. The room seems suddenly very hot and full of motion, as though it swirls around me. I am a ravenous vortex, recklessly . . .

"Excuse me . . ."

Sidney's fingers freeze. I look up breathlessly and peer through the chrysanthemums. The bosomed woman is addressing me!

"Excuse me," she repeats, "but would you please pass the butter?"

Backstroke

It was a sultry day. There was a liquid quality to the air that clung suggestively to my skin, and whatever birds had the strength to chirp did so with a throatiness that reminded me they were creatures after all and knew the joys of mating.

It was with these thoughts, barely formed and a little mad, that I had awakened and kicked off the covers — except for the sheet, which I grabbed in my fists and shook up and down so that its white, billowing waves would send cooling jets of air to my sticky flesh. I knew it was no use to shower; clearly, I would be showering all day if this heat kept up. From the closet I pulled out the sheer, gauzelike cotton tunic with its deep V neck and voluminous, pleated folds. I lifted it over my head and let the soft fabric cascade silently over my bare body. It fell to the top of my thighs, just covering the mound of pubic hair that formed a puffy shadow beneath its ivory-colored sheerness. I stood there, not moving, aware of how strangely sensual was the soft filmy fabric that whispered against my hot skin.

I moved to the mirror to see whether the thickness of its folds was enough to obscure the two dots of pink that would otherwise force their way through the flimsiness of the material enveloping me and tell the world I was braless. I twisted and turned, watching myself as if from others' eyes. Would they see? How much would they see? Could I "get away with it"? (Unlike my friends, I had never felt tyrannized by that simple strip of cloth women had flung aside as if it were a chastity belt fabricated by a jealous king protecting his "property" against enemy invasion. In this competitive and breast-obsessed society we shared, my *portobusto* was my friend, magically transforming me from small, and shyly so, to acceptably differentiated from the kings. To be liberated from this precious undergarment was to have my magic carpet stolen from me.)

Still before the mirror, I waved my arms around wildly and bent over to peer down my unfettered cleavage, again scrutinizing myself from the perspective of others. The delicate texture of the material played against my skin, teased my nipples, caressed my back. I was giddy with the myriad and discrete sensations I was feeling. Light breezes of hot air surprised my arms and flew against my armpits, awakening my flesh in fragments. No longer was my torso an undifferentiated mass of tissue, muscle, and bone. The absence of my familiar undergarment was palpable. Incongruously, Robert Frost's criticism of free verse, as being like playing tennis without a net, popped into my head.

I slipped into a pair of soft, cotton pantaloons, tucking the folds of the blouse inside the elasticized waistband. The contrast of bound and free excited me. The snugness of the band around my waist heightened the sensations of airiness encircling my upper body, and the now double-layer of fabric below clung to my moistened skin like a warm girdle of loving hands.

Throughout the morning, I walked around the house revelling in my discovered body just as the avant-garde artist delights in the "found object." At the same time, I waited for the teasing sensations to give way to the ordinariness of the body I knew as mine. Instead, I became more and more restive, more and more tantalized — it was as if I was being held in a state of excitation that would not let go. The fantasy of two massive hands pressing gently against my back quivered in me like a suppressed scream.

As if in answer to my thoughts, the doorbell rang. He was "just dropping by, hoping you'd be home." He moved to embrace me (we were still new enough to each other for that), and I threw myself into his arms with a wantonness he had never seen in me. I kissed him passionately and felt his eager response pressing hard against me. He pulled the flimsy fabric of my blouse out from under its entrapping belt and moved his hands up and across the imaginary pathway—illicit, vulnerable, and acutely conscious of where the strap was supposed to be. I sensed the startle in his hands as he hesitated a second, then quickly slid them down again as if to affirm that the border patrol forbidding entry into erogenous zones was no longer there. With the realization, his hands sped like lightning to my breasts, cupping them gently in his hands and making bumpy fistlike protrusions under the cotton fabric that hung loosely between us. The more ardently he fondled my breasts, the more I yearned to feel his warm and powerful hands on my back, sliding up and down my alert and now abandoned flesh. I reached under the teasing fabric to find his eager hands, and, ever so gently, moved them from my breasts to my back. He looked at me, perplexed. I had no answer for him—only my silent ecstasy as his hands, mindless and warm, slowly restored my body to its rightful owner.

Snake Dance

Although it was near midnight, the heat of the day still rose from the parched desert floor and warmed the blanket beneath us like an electric pad. In the absence of a moon, the desert glowed with starlight. The sight of so much unfathomable space made me feel weightless, and I was certain I would have tumbled into that cold, black void if it had not been for the closeness of Dave and Garth sleeping on either side of me.

Our long drive had left me hyperalert. I listened tensely, expecting any moment to hear the high whine of a mosquito, and immediately my exposed skin began to itch. Beetles most certainly were crawling beneath the blanket searching for crumbs while bats probably fluttered and swooped low overhead. Crickets were singing, and somewhere quite close I heard tiny feet scamper. A shiver ran across me, and I turned toward Garth's reassuring bulk. It lay slack and still, the rhythm of his breathing slow and regular.

Dave lay against my back, and I could feel him start to turn stealthily toward me. He paused, straight and taut, and lay in wait for silent minutes. Then, very quietly, his legs and arms enfolded my curled, fetal form, and his lean body pressed close. We fit together like two stacked chairs. Furtively, his hands inched under my blouse and massaged my back with soft, circular strokes. I was almost ready to be lulled to sleep like that when his hands slipped around my sides and cupped each breast. The wakened part of me shuddered with pleasure, and I straightened.

Still with his hands on my breasts, Dave rolled me over on top of him. On my back with the Milky Way above and Dave's rigid body below, I took each of his hands in mine and guided them over my hips and belly.

Garth was stirring now, attracted by the sensuous movement. He awakened with mindless readiness and turned toward us. Fingers and tongues explored the terrain of my torso and traveled its mounts and open plains, its canyons and crevices. Limbs slid over limbs like a slithering tangle of hungry boas and shed their garments like discarded snakeskins. Shutting my eyes, I imagined serpents braiding and coiling themselves into a moving maze of gleaming scales. The skein of muscled strands tied knots to no avail and tunneled in and out upon themselves. I felt myself rise and swell to their touch. Waterfalls thundered in my ears. Arctic lights swirled behind closed lids. Earthquakes shook my thrusting pelvis, and the deepest quicksand churned in my tissued core. The unguided head of a penis butted its way toward my safe, wet enclosure while another groped blindly along my thigh. Serpentine limbs flexed with a sense of destiny now and hastened toward conclusion. The multitude of predators and prey clasped each other in a paralyzing grip and, with a series of great spasmodic gulps, released. I opened my eyes and saw the entire galaxy swirling.

The Look

The look was brief,
a whisper of a glance
a breath that rustled ferns.
A look so small it
was not recorded
on galactic time.
Still in that silent glance
hardly inhabited by
a whirling electron,
I felt the crystal pinwheels
of your energy,
a bomb exploding
fragments of your space
to mine.

Eyes

She looked up and her eyes met his. They were alone in a corner, so no one was near enough to hear her. She swallowed, dropped her shoulders, and lowered her gaze for a second. Then she looked at him squarely and said: "Let's leave this boring party." His eyes opened wide. "What did you say?"

"I said, let's leave this boring, boring party!"

"What do you have in mind?" his eyes glinted back at her, his head tilted naughtily.

"I know a secret place, and there are things I'm dying to do . . . with you." A tiny blush crept up her neck, and she squirmed just a little on her chair.

His mouth opened a bit as she spoke. "Tell me, what things?" His eyes probed hers for answers.

She looked at the place where his shirt came to a V. Dark tendrils played there. Her nostrils flared, and she breathed a little faster.

"I want to touch your chest." Her eyes fixed there. She had never seen such a hairy body — lovely black curls flecked with gray, sparkling, twisting. She could almost feel the resilience of those curls pressed against her breasts and belly. "And I want to lie down next to you."

"Will you let me undress you?" he asked, without a bit of shyness. "I've got a giant hard-on. When can we go?"

"First, tell me what you want to do with me," she smiled, teasing a little now.

"My god, I want to see you naked sitting on my cock, moving up and down and sideways with your hair down around your shoulders."

"Jesus, no build-up?"

He relaxed a little. "The build-up will have to wait for the second fuck."

"Yes . . . ?"

"I'll start by oiling you up and giving you a long massage—you'll tell me where you like it, and I'll stroke and lick those places—for as long as you want. I'll roll you over on your stomach and slip into you from behind. Just when you're . . ."

The hostess walked toward them smiling. "You two must meet one another. You can't just sit here any longer not speaking—Arn, Sandy."

Sandy cleared her throat and spoke her first words to Arn: "Has anyone ever told you what marvelously expressive eyes you have?"

Hot Pursuit

Someone was following her. Now she was certain. It was very early to be out. There was no traffic to blunt her perception, no bystanders to help her either.

The footfalls, a faint pulse at first, could now be heard distinctly: soft, steady slaps upon the pavement. They didn't land with the ominous thud of boots or with the sinister click of pointed shoes with silver heel taps. The light, clean beat behind her announced a less threatening sort — someone young and quick in soft-soled shoes.

Five yards beyond, there was a side street. She decided to turn right onto it to allay her suspicion. She turned the corner, determined not to break her stride, and counted off the quiet seconds. At the fourteenth she heard the steps again. She listened for them to cross the street and to fade in the direction she had been going.

They didn't. They had turned the corner onto the narrow street. The deliberate, regular gait sounded louder now, almost matching hers, but heavier. Short exhalations, then a cough, punctuated the air. It was a man.

The next intersection loomed a half-block ahead. She would not glance back. Confidence. Stay calm. Keep moving.

The patter of their footsteps became sloppy, overlapping. They were no longer in synch. His footsteps landed faster, nearer. His breath was deep and regular, undeniable — a percussive breath that radiated desire, primitive and hot, leaving frosty puffs in the crisp morning air. The closeness of his respiration propelled her. Her ears and neck felt suddenly flushed, and she quickened her pace.

Her hair bounced loose and free as if reaching out tentacles to explore her pursuer. Her legs felt long and strong. She wanted to go on like this for miles, bounding lithe and muscled through empty city streets like a modern Atalanta with Hippomenes panting at her heels. Her pulse beat to the rhythm of his breath.

Suddenly he sprinted forward. Her thrill rose in her throat as he brushed past her left elbow and whispered a breathless "Nice goin'."

She never broke her stride and never took her eyes off his firm buttocks flashing in flimsy white running shorts until he rounded the corner and vanished.

Vegetable Love

From the beginning they had described their relationship as a kind of miracle, for so it seemed in the easy way they had moved together right from the first. It was as though they had leaped over that "period of adjustment" all couples are supposed to go through: when he discovers that she hangs wet underwear in the bathroom and she discovers that he wears the same socks three days in a row. Whenever they talked about the miraculousness of their being together, they laughed about it furtively, like children who had "got away with" something. But they also knew that miracles had a voracious appetite, demanding constant feedings of magic.

He would be home soon. It was her night to "manage" the meal, his to be "in service" — a formula they had agreed on when they first moved in together two years ago. They usually made a game of it, easily dropping the mother-to-son or master cook-to-helper roles that invaded other liberated kitchens, mostly because neither knew how to cook with any finesse. She had already decided to have the broiled herb chicken again — the one fail-safe recipe she had learned from her last lover.

She moved quickly to the refrigerator and took out the chicken breasts. She laid them side by side in a pyrex baking dish, doused them with oil, and, just as David used to do, randomly opened one herb jar after another, crumbling blossoms and stems between her thumb and forefinger and letting them fall over each breast in a warm green herbal blanket that darkened in the glistening oil. (If David *had* been making informed selections, it never showed: "Hmmmm, this smells good," he would say with his nose in the jar, and it then joined the others). She left the chicken to soak up the oil and herbs, took the asparagus and cherry tomatoes from the crisper, and placed the asparagus on one side of the double sink and the cherry tomatoes on the other.

"What now?" she said to herself as she stood in the middle of the room, looking around and making mental notes of how their meal preparation should go. They could do the vegetables together while the chicken was broiling, and then set the table. On a sudden inspiration, she pulled out an unopened box of twelve slender candles designed to fit the wrought-iron circular candle holder she used as a centerpiece on special occasions. She carefully fit each tapered candle into its ball-like enclosure, and then set the holder on the window sill over the sink where they would be standing. She lit each candle and stood back to survey the effect. They had the festive look she wanted, and there was just enough daylight left for them to see what they were doing.

As she gathered together the various things they would need — colander, salt, pepper, paper towels, cooking pot for the asparagus, serving dishes — she heard his key in the lock. She turned the oven dial to *Broil* and went to meet him in the hallway, as if he were the first invited guest to a dinner party.

He moved toward her, his arms wide open, and looked intently into her face. He slipped his hands under her loose blouse and pulled her close. She rubbed her cheek against his, kissed his ear lightly, and then pulled away. Someone watching would have said they had been together two weeks instead of two years.

"Come on," she said. "Hungry?"

She drew him into the kitchen and over to the sink where the candles twinkled down on the vegetable display. He smiled and squeezed her hand.

"Great. I love it. What's my job?" he said. Whatever scenario she created, he always joined in with gusto.

"Well, first, the chicken goes in the broiler, and then we get to play vegetables by candlelight. Okay?"

He had the chicken into the broiler in an instant and was back at her side.

"You take the tomatoes," she said, "I'll do the asparagus."

She picked up an asparagus spear and held it under running water, flicking her finger lightly over its fragile tip. She watched him pick up the first tomato, pluck out the tiny stem embedded in its navel and roll it around in his hand under the cold water. On impulse, she took it from him and placed it in his surprised mouth where he held it like a round red kiss he was unwilling to release. The saltshaker was on his side of the sink; she circled her arms around him, pressing her breast against his arm as she reached for it. He watched now as she sprinkled salt in her hand and licked it up with the tip of her tongue. She held out her salt-flecked tongue to him and he moved his mouth toward hers, gently pushing the tomato from his lips to hers. She bit into it gently and offered him the remaining bulge of its red flesh. They chewed solemnly and in unison while their eyes laughed silently at each other. Again, he pressed his half-open mouth to hers; she let her tongue play around the soft inner flesh of his lips until his eyes became cyclopean. She drew back and smiled mischievously. He placed his still damp hands on her buttocks and pulled her body tightly to his. She felt his warm hardness against her pubic bone.

"It's time to do something with the asparagus," she whispered.

"Yeeees," he said, in that slow, teasing way he had. "Shall we?" His meaning was clear.

"Right *now*?" she asked.

In answer, he started to take off her clothes and, in a scramble, they undressed each other. In what felt like one continuous motion, he pulled her over to the straight-back kitchen chair, sat down, and lowered her body onto his. When she felt him just barely inside her, she held her body taut and poised. He clutched her hips and began to move her pelvis in slow circles around him. He burrowed his head between her breasts, then let his mouth linger on one nipple, pulling in and releasing it as she sucked in and released the silken, round tomato perched on his sturdy stalk. She took his face in her hands and stared openly and fixedly at the tangle of expressions that played around his mouth, his jaw, his eyes, knowing that her own face mirrored them back to him. Pulling his head closer to her body, she buried her hands in his hair.

The ring of the telephone suddenly burst its presence into the room and, as if wired to it in some way, he pulled her body down hard and fast on his. They clung to each other through the violent spasms that shook through them. Her body finally collapsed, her head dropping into the hollow of his neck. He stroked her hair gently and mumbled softly in her ear as the phone rang relentlessly, the chicken sputtered, and the candles bravely held on to their last flickering light.

Tantric Sex

Directions for Tantric sex:

1. Man and woman sit nude on floor, facing each other. The woman moves as close to the man as possible and puts her legs over the man's legs and around his body. The man circles her body with his legs. The arms are relaxed on the partners' hips. Both take several deep breaths, rest their gaze on the left eye of the other and meditate together, eyes open, for 5 to 10 minutes.

2. The partners move closer, and the woman puts her mouth near the man's left ear. Feeling the movement of his breath, she replicates the rhythm in his ear, breathing his breath. (Do this meditation for 5 minutes.) They move their heads to the other side and the man replicates the rhythm of the woman's breath. (Do for 5 minutes.) They shift heads again. Starting with their individual rhythms, the partners slowly arrive at a common rhythm, "breathing the one breath." (Continue this meditation for as long as is enjoyable.)

3. After gentle loveplay, the woman introduces the erect penis into her well-lubricated vagina, in the same posture described in exercises 1 and 2. Through periodic contractions of her vaginal muscles and occasional slight movements by the man, both partners attempt to keep the penis erect without thrusting. Both breathe deeply and are sensitive to the flow of energy between them.*

* Reprinted with permission of Stella Resnick, Ph.D., from her article, "The Erotic Lifestyle: Being Turned On," published in *New Age,* August 1978.

I felt very lusty and the children were all gone. It was late in the afternoon. I told him I wanted to try Tantric sex.

"What's that?"

"It's when you don't move, and I'm not sure if you're supposed to have an orgasm."

So we got completely undressed, sat down on the floor, and began.

Step number one was very strange for me. The position was easy enough to assume, but "resting my gaze on the left eye of the other and meditating, eyes open, for 5 to 10 minutes" made me very uncomfortable. It was as though that eye had been disembodied and was free-floating. It could as easily have been a stranger or a statue I was gazing at. I always seek eye contact with people to whom I'm speaking, but this was different, bizarre. Maybe I could learn to like it.

Step number two started off very badly. While replicating the rhythm of his breath in his ear, my stomach kept sending little gurgles upward to my throat—it was very distracting and very unerotic. I really tried hard not to laugh. We shifted right away to "breathing the one breath." For me this was an extremely profound experience.

The sensation of being nude, sitting about as close together as two people can, arms around one another, in daylight, was novel and very exciting. We breathed together like this for a long time. I think I felt a little dizzy. It transcended any verbal communication we have ever had. It was probably the closest I have ever come to having a spiritual experience. I did feel our spirits merging together in a way that was entirely different from joining together sexually.

Then, as though in a dream, and in slowest motion, the spiritual closeness dissolved and merged into a physical union as body parts slipped together gently, quietly, and almost motionless. The feeling of transcendence remained with me. I was being taken out of my body. But the pulsing and throbbing was a reminder of our two very real bodies joined together, almost still, but with a powerful energy flowing between us. The heat and the accelerated throbbing in my groin reduced me once again (or should I say expanded me once again?) into a purely physical being. I resisted the overwhelming desire to move — to grind — but the throbbings were growing into contractions now, which were out of my control. The contractions continued to grow and swell until they were so mighty that they broke loose. My body stiffened and rocked back and forth for several long seconds, then sighed and slumped, exhausted.

I returned rather quickly to the quiet house and the afternoon.

Farewell, Fanny

I can hear your plea
for a slimmer me,
but I like my ass
although it's crass.
My powerful seat
may be fashion's defeat,
but in blaming my bottom
you must have forgotten
my lava fountain
inside that mountain,
my cradle of fire
to rock your desire.

I'm not blind
to your taboos—
feel free to choose
another kind
and leave my own
behind.

Rose's Spring Lamb

There are "leg men," and there are "leg women." As a "leg woman" nothing catches my eye faster than a well-turned leg of young spring lamb, one that tapers leanly toward the shank but bulges firmly in the thigh.

Once I am smitten by such a leg, I eye my friend, the butcher. He winks back in collusion, like Cupid arranging the perfect match, and cheerfully bones it for me. I rush home to massage it with a savory blend of curry and a clove or two of garlic. After allowing the spices to penetrate the lamb at room temperature for several hours, I barbecue it over glowing coals flecked with ash. The cooking time varies depending upon the thickness of the meat and the heat of the fire, but thirty-five to forty-five minutes is usually enough. Touch it often as it cooks. It should feel firm and springy if you want it pale pink and juicy inside.

Sometimes if the leg is very large, I will cut the tougher half into cubes for shish kebabs. Let the cubes soak for several hours or a day in a piquant marinade. For the marinade, blend two teaspoons of Dijon mustard together with a crushed clove of young garlic, a generous pinch of oregano and basil, a bay leaf, some chopped parsley, freshly ground black pepper, and a small chopped onion. Then, as if you were making a vinaigrette, whip in a quarter cup of red wine vinegar or sherry and three-quarters of a cup of purest virgin olive oil. This marinade will permeate the lamb and soften the toughest fibers.

When you are ready to barbecue, thread the lamb chunks onto skewers along with a riot of red and green peppers, button mushrooms, cherry tomatoes, zucchini, bacon, or whatever you choose. Cook close to hot coals for twenty to twenty-five minutes, basting frequently with the remaining marinade.

III.   LONGING FOR
A STRANGER

Our "stranger" stories came relatively early in the history of the Kensington Ladies' Erotica Society. Paradoxically, whatever danger they pose in real life, strangers in fiction, at least for us, served as people we could turn to safely, indulging our fantasies and longings without exposing our private lives. For some of us, the longings took an exotic turn, but for others, the escapade was on familiar turf. Perhaps what we did reveal was a restiveness with our everyday world—a yearning to have it come alive in a way it never could in "real life." In committing our "strange loves" to paper, we discovered that we had created a host of warm bodies whose presence is now very real.

My Gardener

I answered his ad in September's *Tribune,* and he came in a battered Volkswagen with Rolf, a gentle collie-shepherd mix, who greeted me like a long-lost friend. Needing no better recommendation, I immediately asked him to walk with me through the remains of a garden still clinging to life despite a two-year drought. He was full of concern and empathy for the quiet struggle taking place before him. He stood very close as we stooped over the wilted beds and droopy rhododendrons and crossed the long-dead lawn. We studied the singed remains of a great, old birch that had already dropped its leaves a month ago. He rapped the trunk with his knuckles — hard, dull thumps — and then leaned over to tear some turf from around the base. I could see the rippling flexion of his back muscles through the thin, faded fabric of his plaid workshirt.

"We should keep this cleared," he said, "and then try some deep watering. I think it can be saved."

I showed him down some flagstone steps to a lower terrace enclosed by a towering hedge of dying privet.

"Have you thought of replacing that?" he asked.

"Yes, if only I could budge them."

He strode over and with a great heave ripped one out.

"That's magnificent!" I cried. The gap revealed a shimmering view of the bay and city beyond. The late afternoon sun blazed from across the Golden Gate directly into our eyes. The shock of the glare was as startling as the intent gaze of his blue eyes, so pale that they generated a light of their own. He stood at least a head taller than me, and as he smiled down, I felt embraced. With a focus so intensely intimate, surely the plants would be healed! I hired him.

Every week he comes. Sometimes when I am home, we work side by side in the dirt. He moves with a grace and gentleness that brings the most reluctant seedlings to life. His strong forearms are tanned and covered with sun-bleached hairs. Being so close to him in the sunshine fills me with a contentment so complete that when I realize it, I become self-conscious and jump up to offer him iced tea.

If I remain indoors, he often rings the doorbell, sometimes with a question about what to do next. Other times he calls me out of the house in great excitement to show me a remarkable discovery. Just last week he led me through some brambles to a clearing where he had uncovered a hydrangea smothering a sword fern. I watched as he knelt and clipped back more of the lush hydrangea and exposed the long, shiny, serrated leaves of the fern. Then he leaned back, sitting on his heels, and said, "I like this. It pleases me. It really pleases me." It was all I could do to keep from lowering my arms around his neck and burying my face in his soft tousled curls.

Instead I returned to the house. It is my retreat and safety — clearly off-limits to him. My life here is devoted to my husband and children. Everything is as it should be. He is careful never to enter except, perhaps, to use the basement bathroom.

Usually he comes to tell me when he's leaving and what he plans to do next time. We confer long and seriously on the drafty front step. Our talk stays scrupulously focused on gardening — on color, arrangement, and natural ways to combat pests. We are both averse to sprays and poisons, though I do occasionally resort to using snail bait. He is certain that rain is imminent and wants to get the clearing and fall planting finished as soon as possible. He lingers politely on the step like a courting knight, afraid to take too great a liberty yet reluctant to leave without some small encouragement.

I stand riveted in the doorway relishing his wholehearted attention. He stands so near that I can feel the warmth radiating from his body and can detect the sweet fragrance of castile soap. The smoothness of his shave is remarkable, even in the late afternoon. He must use a straight razor, and I imagine him going through his meticulous routine with the same care that he lavishes on my plants. While we discuss the best ways to cultivate compost, I see him after his shower standing before a mirror wearing nothing but the shaving lather on his face. I imagine his razor scraping wide careful strokes around his soft lips, but I cannot bear to picture the final swaths of the razor's edge over his arched pulsing throat.

As September comes to an end, my gardener's appearances become more and more frequent. I am often suprised to find him at unexpected times — just as I am rushing out to take my youngest to nursery school or as I return from a run, all sweaty and flushed. Often in the late afternoons when I am home between car pooling, he is back, loading his Volkswagen for trips to the dump. His dog waits in the driveway to intercept me and leads me proudly by the wrist to his admiring master like a retriever delivering a prize.

When the clearing and tilling are completed, my gardener asks me to meet him at the local nursery to select fall plants. I agree, and when I arrive at the appointed time, he is already waiting. He beams at me in mock astonishment.

"My God! A skirt!" he exclaims. "I've never seen you in a skirt!"

"Really?" I blush, glad to have worn a new dress and even gladder to be able to walk the gravel path in new wedgy heels without wobbling. I love being *seen* again!

"You know what you need?" he says in a low voice.

"What?" I ask expectantly.

"Lilac."

"Oh, why yes. You're right. We don't have that, do we?" I hope my voice doesn't convey my disappointment.

"It will be magnificent near your roses next spring," he continues and places his hand on my shoulder to gently guide me to the shrubbery section.

We meander up and down the long, moist rows of shrubs. He helps me sidestep puddles, and I feel exquisitely protected. He tells me bits of esoteric information about the plants and how the different varieties adapt to the Bay Area's microclimates. I savor the gentle timbre of his voice.

We arrive at the lilacs.

"These look healthy and pretty well established," he observes. He bends over a five-gallon-sized bush and pokes the earth around its base.

"Here's one that's nice and full," I say as I wander down the row.

He looks at my selection, takes my hand, and guides me back to his. My hand feels small and cold inside his.

"Yes, but it looks a little forced. I like the root system better on this one. That's what we have to consider at this time of year." He holds my hand a little longer, and I happily concede.

With the coming of October, my gardener's weather prediction comes true: the rains come early. Storm after storm sweeps in from the Pacific. The parched ground soon becomes soggy. Permanent puddles grow into small lakes. Weeds and forget-me-nots sprout lavishly. Ivy threatens to strangle everything, and snails ooze trimphantly over all.

One drenched day I arrive home from a seminar, full of fresh thought and resolve, and find my gardener staking up rhododendrons.

"I just can't work in weather like this," he calls as I emerge from my car. Without a second thought I invite him in for coffee. After all, it is safe — my son and a babysitter are upstairs.

We run up the flagstone path to the shelter of the doorway. He unlaces his boots and lays them neatly beside the mat as I unlock the door and lead the way inside. He enters carefully, attentively, noticing everything. He strays into the living room saying that he loves the colors in the bright Moroccan rug. I am about to apologize for the clutter when he says how warm and welcoming he finds our scattered collections of shells, rocks, and other found treasures. He stops in front of an array of Barbie dolls in various stages of garish dress and undress in the middle of the room. A naked Ken and Barbie stand paralyzed in an awkward kiss. Next to them a platinum-haired rival in a tutu lies face down on a hand mirror, and the severed head of a Million Dollar Man stares glassily at the ceiling.

"Egad, what's this?" he asks.

"Just an unfinished game," I explain. "I think one day my daughter and her friends will write their manifesto, and it'll be called *Our Barbies, Ourselves.*"

He laughs and follows me into the kitchen — the inner sanctum at last! He perches on a stool at the high cooking counter and watches me make coffee.

"I've never seen you more radiant," he comments.

I tell him about my exciting morning — how I am just beginning to realize there's life after school.

"What do you mean?" he asks, leaning forward on folded arms.

I bring the coffee over on a wicker tray and sit across from him. His hair clings in damp ringlets about his face. I inhale the rich mingling aromas of his wet hair and the freshly brewed coffee.

"I stayed a student barnacle too long," I confess. "I clung to institutions. I couldn't bear to graduate so I went on to graduate school and then taught. I kept going from one incubator to another."

"I know what you mean," he nods sympathetically. "I stayed attached too long, too."

"You did? To what?"

"I was in a seminary for eight years."

I am nonplussed. He seems too physical, too much a part of the natural world for that.

"So you see," he continues, shifting slightly on his stool, "I have some catching up to do."

"That's hard," I answer. He suddenly seems so vulnerable and alone that I reach out instinctively and hold his hand.

Just then we hear the sound of footsteps pounding down the stairs. He pulls his hand back abruptly as my child and the babysitter appear.

"I'm hungry," announces my son, surveying the scene with enormous, unfaltering dark eyes. He climbs possessively into my lap. "Isn't it lunch time?"

"Yes, almost. Aren't you going to say hello?"

My child gives an uncompromising nod.

"I have to be leaving now," says the sitter.

"So should I," says my gardener. "I'll be back when the weather clears."

I usher them to the door, pay the sitter, and return to the kitchen. My small guardian stands on the counter and looks down accusingly.

"Why was the gardener here?"

"It's raining, so I asked him in for coffee."

"Why does he look at you that way?"

"What way?"

"Y'know . . . with his eyes."

"You mean he should look at me with his nose?"

"Ohhhh, Mom! Where's lunch anyway?"

Halfway through lunch the phone rings. It is my gardener sounding urgent, saying he needs to talk right away. Is this a good time?

I look at my alert companion watching from across the counter and tell him to call back in an hour.

"Who was that?" asks my son.

"The gardener."

"What does he want?"

"I don't know."

"Why does he have to call back?"

"Maybe he wants to ask for a raise," I blurt out, suddenly appalled by my logic.

I reflect on our morning visit and wonder if I was wrong to have invited him inside. Has our physical attraction grown too huge for him to bear? Perhaps he will have to find other work. What terrible revelation am I about to hear? I glance at the clock and wait.

At two o'clock exactly, the doorbell rings. I am startled because I had expected him to phone. I open the door, and he is perched on his accustomed step huddled in his rain jacket with his arms crossed over his chest. He looks down at his boots and balances carefully on one foot, then the other.

"I have to talk to you . . . ," he begins. "This thing's been on my mind a lot lately, and I just don't feel comfortable with it."

"Yes, tell me," I say, bracing myself.

He shakes his tousled hair and sighs. Then, looking sorrowfully into my eyes, he says, "The snail bait . . . I . . . I just can't use it . . . not in such quantity . . . not with your pets and children around. I just can't do it."

"Oh, that's all right," I soothe, hardly believing my ears. "Don't worry. You don't have to kill in my garden!"

"Oh, phew!" he laughs. "I've been hoping you'd say that."

Smiling at my munificence, I watch him stride down the glistening flagstone path to his Volkswagen. Snails may come and go, but a good gardener is hard to find.

IDEAL LOVER

The Leopard:
A Fairy Tale
for Responsible Adults

Doctor Bingham yawned. It was hard to concentrate in this humid, sweetly perfumed climate. The electricity was out again, and without air-conditioning the tropical heat made her fall into dreamy lethargy. The new hotel with only one wing completed in time for the conference already suffered from decay, as if termites were eating away the cheaply constructed walls. The toilets didn't flush, and the refrigerators could not keep their Western diets frozen. Like a python, the rain forest waited only one mile away to swallow up this frail hybrid of a Hilton Hotel and with it the resolutions of this international group of experts. In a few days they would all return to their temperate laboratories and scientific organizations, and the naked walls of this conference room would soon be covered with exotic fungus. Melissa wearily read over her notes. So far she had gone to every lecture. She always went to the lectures. The Global Food Fund relied on Melissa Bingham's reports.

The next speaker was Claudio Torres de Valle y Monteverde. She recognized his handsome face from a *Time* magazine article. His family had done things for the country — on horseback with swords and later with land reforms. Now, the family stripped of political power, Claudio championed the causes of the dispossessed against global greed. Melissa was prepared to distrust his flamboyant optimism about his country's natural resources. Therefore, she did not mind that he delivered his paper in Spanish. Courtesy demanded that she stay in her seat, but she would have given anything to get away.

Then, the totally unexpected happened. As soon as he took charge of the lectern, she was under his spell. Although everyone else wore shirt sleeves and rumpled khakis, he wore an immaculate suit of European cut. He was brazenly at ease in this climate. The gleaming white shirt accentuated the nutmeg luster of his skin, and the open collar revealed a heavy necklace of native onyx. In vain she struggled against his self-possessed charm, his disconcerting grace. His open smile welcomed her, singled her out from all the others as if he wanted her alone to listen, as if only she could understand him. Shifting uncomfortably on her seat, she tried to muster some scientific smugness, but she could not take her eyes from him. He looked at her as if they were alone. What game was he playing? The answer came straight from her groin. She blushed. He was undressing her, appraising her body. How dare he breach her anonymity as a fellow scientist? She was outraged. No she wasn't. She was excited, turned on.

Instead of hiding behind her notes, she decided to teach him a lesson in equality. Ostentatiously, she removed the translation phones from her ears. Boldly, she stared at his broad shoulders and narrow hips, savoring him piece by piece. Did he notice? He noticed. For a moment he seemed distracted — good. She understood enough Spanish to recognize that he was searching for words. She smiled amused. Clearly he understood that she could play her own game. Unlike the other speakers, including herself, he was not chained to the lectern. He pranced back and forth like an elegant leopard, wanting them all, forcing them to pay attention to him.

Melissa decided to relax and simply enjoy his performance. She saw a hunter who pursued his prey, devoured it lovingly, tenderly, and in turn wanted to be captured, devoured, and consumed by the huntress. His body was both soft and powerful, and so was his voice. Now and then the meaning of a word would reach her ears, but all she wanted to hear was the voice.

Closing her eyes, she saw him nude. Disturbingly seductive, his voice conjured up his lithe body, silken to the touch, vibrant, potentially wild. The language suited his voice — a melodious European Spanish, the heavy vowels of Castile, so smooth without the hissing "s" of Latin America. His language had been polished like driftwood by centuries of formal use, by poetry and courtly love. Like the flutes the natives carved of ebony, it was a well-tuned instrument, which released its secret powers slowly after years of practice. Only a master could play the haunting melodies, blending the sound of human and animal love calls. She wanted to be alone with that voice.

"I want you to cry out to me, to expose your secret life to me. I want your lips on my breast, your breath in my ears, all over me. I want soft consonants to rain over my thighs, full-blooded vowels to penetrate my inmost being. I want to taste your lips like exotic fruit. I want to see your words glisten like drops of crystal, and I want you to put them around my neck, my belly and my ankles."

When the lecture was over, Melissa filed out of the room after the others, scarcely aware of the faces and remarks of her colleagues. She wanted to bump into him, but he was nowhere to be seen. Without hesitation, she stepped inside the taxi that idled in front of the hotel. The driver said something about a restaurant at the harbor where everyone from the conference was going. She nodded. She knew he was taking her to her leopard.

The drive was beautiful along a coastal route that dipped into coconut groves and climbed over rocky cliffs. When the car stopped at a vine-covered terrace, nestled into the hillside high above the ocean, she did not flinch when she heard the extravagant sum of money that the driver demanded for the ride. Her foundation obviously knew what they were doing when they allotted a generous amount for travel expenses. But they had refused to pay for a child's ticket; how full of wisdom was the male working world to free her for his adventure. She smiled when she paid and added a large tip. Did she want him to wait? asked the driver. No, she did not care to think about going back — ever.

As if gliding on tracks, she moved among the tables crowded with people. She had seen him right away. He sat alone. Miraculously, an empty chair waited across from him.

"Excuse me," she said, "this seems to be the only seat available. Is it taken?" He gestured toward it invitingly. "It is yours, Doctor Bingham."

"I see, here we all are again. I thought I was getting away from the conference." Melissa blushed removing her name tag.

"The taxis always take the longer route. Our friends came by charter bus. This is the only restaurant within miles." He played the host, only a faint smile hinted at their conspiracy. She had counted on finding him alone.

"I suppose we are all eating the same thing," she said crossly.

"I recommend the scampi; you won't find better ones anywhere." Then he purred: "I have been wanting to tell you how much I appreciate your coming. You are one of the few Americans who understand my views. I read your article in *World Nutrition*. You know our problem here. I can show you what really goes on with American money. I wanted very much to talk to you, but—well, I expected somebody—I thought you were—I mean, I had no idea, that you were so attractive." Again she blushed, proud to be recognized, but she was running away from being Dr. Bingham. If she took back her professional identity, the magic would be gone forever. She looked at this polite gentleman who spoke English fluently. Where was the leopard? "I hope, I have not offended you?" She remained silent while the waiter stripped the gigantic prawns from the skewers. She decided to risk all.

"I find you very attractive too." She trembled inside as she forced herself to look at him. Then she boldly raised her glass.

"Salud," answered the leopard. She watched him pull off the pink shell tenderly and with mouth-watering anticipation. Deftly he lifted the plump creature to his lips holding it by its tail.

"Smell it first," he ordered. She tried to follow his example but shrank at first from snapping off the head with its delicate feelers. She was not used to smelling her food like that but did as she was told before biting into the succulent flesh. It was firm, but not tough — freshly caught, no doubt. The taste of garlic and lemon was enticing, but some other exotic flavor had been added. She asked him what it was. He explained that the special wood in the broiler made the difference. "They cure the wood; that is the secret."

"Ah, yes," she nodded picking up another tail and licking it gingerly with her tongue, appreciating the crisply stretched inner skin. To savor the flavor fully, she chewed slowly, as he did, drinking the tart local wine in small gulps.

"Very unusual, I have never tasted anything like it."

"And you never will again."

"Unless I come back."

"No — again is never like the first time." She suddenly was very much aware of his lips. They were so alive even when he was not eating or speaking. Neither too full nor too thin, they promised a feast for the senses. As if he could read her thoughts, he picked up her hand and kissed it. Her desire for his lips became even stronger. In vain, she tried to wash it away with the wine. She looked around. They had behaved as if they were quite alone. Indeed, all her colleagues had disappeared. Like locusts, they had come and gone leaving empty dishes and glasses behind.

"May I offer you a ride back?"

Melissa was ready to accept anything he offered.

"Thank you. I guess we have to get back to the panel discussion. Are you on it?"

"No, are you?" They looked at each other knowing they would not go to the panel discussion. He led her to a battered red Porsche. When the engine hummed briefly and gave up, she wished that they could be stranded, but after toying with wires under the hood, he fixed it.

"They always give me cars that don't work," he growled as he maneuvered the narrow streets of the village, past the harbor and toward the coast. They both wore sunglasses. She could stare at him without being noticed. The three seductive lines at the corner of his mouth hinted at many secret encounters with women's lips. The hands that pressed gently against the wheel told his command of whatever he touched. Relaxed, he took each curve with care and ease. Comfortable with danger, he sometimes pushed forward playfully to take a hill with daring speed; at others he held back to lean into a curb or to coast down to a steep gully. Then he would drive hard through a tunnel or straddle the edge of a dangerous abyss. The bucket seat kept her at a distance, but she yearned to reach over and caress his lips.

Impatiently he scanned the steep cliffs for access to the beach. At the mouth of a river, he followed a bumpy road down to a fine stretch of sand, protected by rocks on one side and palm trees on the other. From the trunk of the car he conjured up a bottle of wine and a large colorful scarf. Where had the scarf come from, Melissa wondered. Did he keep it in the car for such occasions? Had another woman left it behind?

He spread the magenta-colored silk over a sheltered sand pit. The bright yellow and orange butterflies woven into the fabric scintillated in the sun as if they were alive. Close to them, the surf crashed against the rocks, and the foamy waves curled toward them into the sand. Pulling her close, he slowly unbuttoned her blouse and peeled her free of her slacks. In black bikini and bra she stretched out on the silky scarf soaking in the late afternoon sun. She was proud of her athletic, trim body and her small, girlish breasts. She was glad she had put on her luxury underwear. He said something in Spanish; she squinted at him against the glaring sun. For a long time he just stood there, staring at her. No man had ever looked at her like that. Self-consciously she closed her eyes.

When she opened them again to see what he was doing, he had disappeared. Why was he behaving so strangely? What did he intend to do? Suddenly her forty years turned back to fourteen. A Greek chorus of aunts and teachers and novelists were whispering unforgettable precautions: Never be alone with a stranger— never take your clothes off— never give in to lust— never trust a man— never travel alone in a foreign country— never go to the beach by yourself.

She pulled the scarf up around her hips and reached for her clothes. Then she saw him in the water. Like Poseidon he emerged from the ocean. His nutmeg-colored skin glistened, and tiny pearls of water dropped from his thighs. She had never seen such magnificent, frightening beauty. His torso was perfectly proportioned, his limbs exquisitely balanced, and then there was his cock. It stood out straight like a weapon, clearly aimed at her — she pulled back, disturbed, yet spellbound. "I've brought on this transformation. It is me he wants. I have that power over him," she thought. He knelt down beside her, again talking to himself in Spanish as his hands moved over her breasts and between her legs. There was a blessed silence as his lips began to travel from the tip of her toes upward inside her thighs.

"Come," she cried, "come to me now." But he took his time.

"First I enjoy you, then I enjoy myself." He offered her a gulp of wine. "The first time is very special. It is a coming together of strangers, we salute each other, recognize each other. Everything about you is new, your skin, your smell, your taste. Your voice too, the voice of passion, I have not heard it. Look at me, yes, go on. Talk to me, to my body, not to my brain."

Her eyes feasted on the muscular arms, the narrow hips, the strong hairy thighs. Her hands reached around his firmly rounded buttocks — as smooth and hairless as a baby's. But she could not express that sensation in words. She did not know his language, nor could she find her own. Against her pelvis pulsated his erection with a life of its own. She had always tried to ignore this most obtrusive male appendage. Now she ran her fingers over the throbbing vein; it felt so smooth and vulnerable that she wanted to draw it into her womb. Licking its silky tip, she tasted ocean and honey and man and life.

He gasped as if in pain. She could no longer control the rolling movements of her pelvis.

"I want you, I want you!" she cried out, giving herself totally to that new sensation of lust, of shameless greed for his beautiful body. He did not launch himself at her as she expected, but penetrated slowly, deliberately giving her time to feel him inside her. Then he was tossing her about like a raft on wild water. For a time she lost her own course. Happily she bounced along with him, but then she climbed on top to ride him, driving him close to delirium until she got her full measure of delight. Exhausted and content, she put her head on his chest, bathing her skin in the dew of their lovemaking, utterly relaxed and at peace. The sound of the ocean and from time to time his voice kept her entranced until she lost all consciousness in a mysterious, dream-filled sleep.

They missed the panel discussion and they missed their planes, but eventually they returned home to do everything that they were supposed to do. Claudio Torres de Valle won the Nobel Prize. Dr. Bingham duly gave her report of the conference and filed it away. Her life went on as usual, but at the most inappropriate times, in the middle of a committee meeting or a scientific presentation, that Spanish voice would ring in her ears, that nutmeg skin would glisten seductively before her eyes, and slowly her pelvis would begin to rock. She was riding the leopard.

Sabina's Scampi à la Leopard

The very essence of this culinary treat is that you don't cook it yourself and that you taste it far away from home. The circumstances are as important as the food and are thus beyond your control no matter how well you plan ahead. Should you be lucky enough to succeed the first time, as I did, take my advice and do not try again.

I flew to Greece and found my way to the ancient harbor of Piraeus, which is an adventure if you are driving alone. When the ocean and boats came into view, I kept going higher along the edge of the cliff until I smelled the charcoal fires and saw the gigantic tentacles of octopus that hung from wooden trellises. I parked my car and strolled along the row of open-air tavernas until I found the one with the most spectacular view and the largest prawns roasting over the open fires. The tantalizing flavor of the broiled crustaceans already seduced my senses as I inhaled the smoke over a glass of ouzo.

I watched the young waiter as he pierced the plump morsels with a spit and held them over the glowing coals. The satisfaction on his face told me he knew why I had come from so far away. He put the scampi on my plate and smiled as if he had been waiting for me for a long time. He watched me anxiously as I took the first bite. Our eyes met. Yes, it was perfect! His look trailed over my face toward my body, and I appraised his bronze chest and European shorts. He looked like Achilles, but he was no prince — just a fisherman. From inside the taverna came the sound of Greek music, not Zorba for the tourists but the sad wailing of Turkish melancholia that the Greeks play everywhere because life is hard and what joy it offers comes now or never. Every-

thing in Greece celebrates the past, nothing the future. I had been given the last gift of the god Neptune. I wouldn't be back—that would be greedy—but I would remember the taste forever.

If I had been wise, I would have left it at that. But of course I wasn't. Once I had tasted the food of the gods, I wanted more, an old story. I expected to find it on the menu of our hotel at the Gulf of Corinth. The waiter smiled indulgently, shaking his head: no never, only at the harbor and even there their freshness wasn't guaranteed. They had to be eaten right after they were caught. Toward the end of our stay he confided that he knew the right place, but only for locals, not for tourists. He would take me himself because women did not go there alone. No, I couldn't bring the children; they wouldn't serve until ten in the evening. That's when I should meet him at the beach below the hotel.

By then I was so obsessed with the promise of scampi that no tourists had ever tasted, ones even better than those I had eaten before, that I deserted my two small children. I left them asleep in the hotel room and told nobody where I was going. The craving for scampi obliterated all other instincts as I crept out the door toward the abandoned stretch of sand where he was waiting.

Silently he walked in front of me. I had enough sense to stay behind, but not a soul could have heard me if I had cried for help. After about a mile, which seemed more like ten, we arrived at the dimly lit taverna. Everyone watched our entrance. I was the only woman among a motley assortment of Greeks who looked as if they had spent their lives on the water.

The prawns arrived—fifteen huge creatures in their shell, and indeed they tasted even better than the ones in Piraeus. He didn't eat but watched me solemnly.

"Very good," I said.

He nodded. His English was rudimentary. What did he expect of me? His handsome face was closed. Suddenly I felt like an American. I thought of my children alone in the room. What if they woke and couldn't find me? I thought of his wife, the old cook who wasn't all that old, but who worked twelve hours in the hotel kitchen and then some more at home, a shack in our courtyard where her children sometimes played with mine.

I couldn't finish the prawns. All I wanted was to go back to the hotel. He seemed disappointed but ate what I had left on my plate while I talked nonstop about my wonderful husband who would pick us up the next day and about my children who might wonder where I was. He understood and called for the bill. Naïvely, I had surmised that we would eat for free among his friends. But they treated him like a tourist. I offered to pay. He tossed his head back — an indignant Greek denial. I thanked him profusely — too profusely? What did he expect in return?

We walked back the same way we had come, but this time I hurried ahead, consumed with anxiety about the children. He trailed farther and farther behind. The distance between us became as great as that between our countries.

The children had not even changed their positions. I breathed a deep sigh of relief. From my window I noticed the light shining from the open doorway of the shack in the courtyard. The old cook was sitting on the step waiting for her husband to come home.

Queen of the Road

fat: in good shape; hauling a big load
— *CBer's Atlas and Dictionary* (1976)

Five more chocolates... then it would be time to go. Ava
reached furtively to the back of her desk drawer and found a
chocolate almondette, her favorite. She held it in her hand a
moment to warm it, then quietly removed the cellophane wrapper and placed the candy on her tongue, letting it linger there as
long as possible. Ava was not the sort to bite and gobble a chocolate or to eat more than one at a time. Pleasures, like chocolates,
were not to be rushed, but parceled out carefully, one by one, so
that a constant stream of taste would last forever.

Ava glanced out of her narrow office window. Far below, on
the freeway snaking out from the city, she could see the cars
already strung together like beads on a necklace. She could
hardly wait to be among them. Rush hour was her favorite time,
and Ava savored her commute as secretly as she savored her
forbidden chocolates.

Ever since Ava had bought the car of her dreams soon after her
promotion, her life had changed dramatically. She suddenly felt
part of the "Pepsi generation"—alive and sparkling just like
everyone on television. In an instant the purchase of a Honda did
everything that a lifetime of unsuccessful dieting had not. Once
inside the car she was as small and agile as anyone else. With no
effort on her part she could move with spring and zest, bounding

like a jackrabbit with just the slightest touch of the accelerator. She loved cutting through heavy traffic, squeezing in and out of the smallest parking places, and soaring the skyways like a weightless cosmonaut. How coordinated and light she had become! The Honda made her feel like a ballerina pirouetting in a size 3 tutu.

In addition to her new sense of mobility, Ava experienced an anonymity that her large size had always deprived her of. Unseen in the snug driver's seat, she was no longer the object of other people's stares, and for the first time felt free to gaze at them instead. To her amazement she saw an array of unself-conscious behavior far more revealing than anything she could watch on television or read about in magazines. Drivers seemed to think they were invisible, and Ava delighted in observing them.

Sometimes she would spot an appealing man traveling alone and would follow his car for miles, creating his life story and imagining a passionate meeting between them. More frequently, though, Ava searched for lovers, seeking some clue about what she was missing, hoping to find the kind of affectionate rapport she yearned for.

Sadly, the couples she found did not often answer her need. The well-dressed pairs in BMWs talked enough but usually sat too far apart. The wholesome ones in Volvos that sported "No Nuke" bumper stickers chatted with the most animation, but Ava guessed that their talk was too issue-oriented for romance. The entwined lovers in low-riders didn't count because they were too young and vigorous and totally beyond her ilk. The same was true for the couples huddled together on motorcycles. RV drivers were another category she excluded: the pairs in front always sat apart, pale and silent, exhausted by the effort of dragging family and paraphernalia to and from crowded campsites. If there ever was any visible interaction, it was usually one of the parents swatting a crying child.

Occasionally, though, Ava would find what she was looking for: a couple about her own age sitting close and radiating an affection that filled her with longing. Just that morning on her way to work Ava had seen such a pair ahead of her in line at the toll booth. The woman drove dreamily with her male companion sitting close. She wore only a sleeveless jersey despite the cold fog, but Ava imagined that their bed warmth still encased her. A huge barrette held her torrent of hair, and the man's left hand played with the loose curls upon her neck. Ava's own hairs had stood up aroused. Did the woman wear perfume? Underwear? The man moved closer and kissed her ear, and Ava felt a blush upon her own cheek as a shiver streaked across her shoulders.

This evening before leaving work Ava spent more time than usual in the women's room. She always groomed herself meticulously before the long ride home, but tonight she experimented with a new upswept hairdo, something like the one the woman had been wearing that morning. During lunch, she had purchased two bright plastic combs, which held her hair in soft waves away from her face. The new hairdo revealed her dangling earrings and accentuated the fleshy curve of her neck. Ava smiled and hurried for the elevator with her car keys already in hand.

In her Honda and on her way at last, Ava hoped for a traffic jam, but the cars on the freeway approach were moving normally. Suddenly a truck without its trailer cut close in front. Sparks flew from a chain that dragged from its connecting cable, and black smoke belched from its smokestack. Ava braked and honked angrily. The driver's beefy elbow hung out the window. Then his muscular arm straightened and, reaching out, motioned her to pass.

Ava gunned her engine and tore past the nuisance, cutting in this time on him. Just as she was claiming a moral victory, the cab swung out and pulled up parallel. The roar of its engine was deafening, so Ava dropped back. With a fresh toot the cab again cut in front. The big arm reached out the window and adjusted the side mirror. As it moved, she thought she saw the driver's flashing smile. Then he raised his hand and waved to her.

The traffic in the left lane was moving faster now, so Ava took advantage of the opportunity to get a better glimpse. As she came alongside the cab, she could see only the top of its huge wheels from her little Honda. She decided to cut in front and watch the trucker in her rear-view mirror. By the time she had him in focus, his head was thrown back in laughter. In a moment he was switching lanes and was overtaking her. He honked three times as he thundered past. Not to be outdone, Ava immediately accelerated, this time passing him on the right.

Their game of leapfrog continued for several miles. She was unaware of the flush on her cheek and the smile on her lips, oblivious even to the fact that she had overshot her exit. She focused only on outmaneuvering the jaunty cab, which was amazingly agile without its load. They roared neck and neck down the two center lanes, each daring the other to pull back first. Suddenly the Honda jerked roughly and grinded sharply to the right. With all her strength and skill Ava brought her swerving car to a safe stop on the shoulder of the freeway.

Ava climbed out, rather shaken, and walked to the right side of her car. The front wheel was completely flat.

"Oh, damn," she muttered. She had never changed a tire.

As she gazed at the shimmering freeway wondering what to do, she saw the cab pull off about a half-mile beyond. The trucker in his white T-shirt and jeans was running back to her. Ava beamed with relief.

"You okay?" he called.

"Yes. I just have a flat tire."

He was beside her now, panting a bit, and quite burly and tan.

"I didn't push you off the road now did I?" he asked with a wink.

"Oh, you wouldn't do a thing like that!" she played along.

"Here, I'll change it for you, little lady."

Ava almost laughed aloud. Little lady! She opened the trunk to get the spare.

"Look! It's flat, too," the trucker said cheerfully. "We'll get it filled. Grab your purse and come with me."

"Hey, thanks!" cried Ava, genuinely grateful.

"You deserve some kind of break. My God, I've never seen anyone drive like you! Now be careful in those little shoes along the side here. It's full of broken glass."

He guided her by the elbow through the garbage-strewn

rubble. Ava felt like a dainty geisha hobbling beside him. He walked with long strides. Ava liked that, even though it was an effort to keep up. The tire in his outer hand looked as small and light as a frisbee. When they reached the cab, he swung the door open for her. Ava hesitated at the insurmountable step. She would have to lift her skirt to her waist and find handholds to even attempt it. She felt panicky.

Suddenly the trucker's hands were upon her waist, and before she could scream, "Stop! You can't!" he had hoisted her to the seat. Her heart pounded. She had never been picked up like that before. She sat like a startled canary just captured and plopped in a cage. While she tottered breathlessly on her new perch straightening her feathers and trying to find her voice again, her bold handler mounted the driver's seat. She peered cautiously at him to see if he was unhurt after lifting her so rashly. He was only of average height and stocky build, definitely not a weight-lifter. He smiled back at her.

"Well, how d'ya like it?"

"I'm just amazed!" exclaimed Ava. Then, turning her wonder from trucker to cab, her eyes grew wide as she took in the confusion of knobs, switches, and buttons. "I've never seen anything like this!"

The cab was immaculate and spacious. It smelled faintly of vinyl and sun lotion. The bench seat was firm and smooth. It did not hug her like the bucket seat in the Honda. The freedom to move about made Ava a little giddy.

The trucker relished her interest.

"Just watch!" he laughed and flicked on the ignition. The dashboard lit up blue. "By the way, I'm Louie."

"Hi. I'm Ava."

"Now, Ava," he spoke her name as though he'd been using it all along, "when that light goes off you rev 'er up . . . like this." He turned the key another notch, and the deep-throated diesel began to cough and rattle. Louie gunned the motor a couple of times and shifted into a low gear. The brakes released with a hiss, and the cab quivered as he waited for an opening in the traffic. Ava's enameled nails dug into her purse. With a lurch the cab accelerated. She leaned forward and watched the pavement zipping by directly below. Strangely, the absence of a hood did not make her feel unprotected; nothing could harm her in this high seat. As Louie careened into the faster lanes, Ava looked down into the laps of other drivers.

"You only get to see knees from up here," she declared.

"You bet, and a lot of thigh! Just look at those seat covers over there!" crowed Louie. He pointed to a trim pair in cutoffs to Ava's right.

"To tell the truth," he continued, "I prefer yours. I like a curvaceous thigh."

"Why, you lousy rubbernecker! Just what I'd expect from a trucker!" she laughed.

"Oh, I'm a connoisseur of fine thighs, and I like a lady who keeps herself up the way you do."

A loud garbled voice broke in. Louie picked up a mike from the dashboard.

"Howzit?"

"Hit me one time."

"Make yer mark."

"How copy."

"Bodacious, Red Rascal. You're meltin' the voice coil."

"10−45."

"Negatory. 10−6."

"Rodger-dodger.!"

"Ten out."

Louie hung up.

"That tear jerker's been scannin' the Band all day." He glanced at Ava. "CB talk," he explained.

"I didn't get a word."

"It's a cinch once you get the hang of it."

"At least you know you're not out here all alone."

"For sure, but this ain't the time to chew the fat. I don't catch foxes in distress every day." Louie winked at her, but Ava was examining the panel.

"You like my goodies? Here, try these." Louie handed her a pair of headphones and pointed to his tape deck.

Ava laughed. "All the comforts of home!"

"Just look behind you."

Ava turned around and lifted up a curtain.

"My goodness! A bed! But where's the rest of your truck?"

"You mean that ain't enough? You want a bathroom and a TV room and a kitchen?"

Ava shrieked with laughter. "No, you know, that other part."

"My rig? She's loadin' up in Vacaville."

She? wondered Ava.

"How big is *she*?"

"Oh, about four tons and all of it cherries!" Louie exploded with mirth.

"Is it hard to move that much?"

"Naw, it's not so much the weight but the distribution. You gotta pack it right."

How true, thought Ava, and she smoothed her skirt over her generous thighs.

"Here we are," announced Louie. "I'll duck out and fill your spare."

He leaped out and was at the air hose in what looked like one simple movement. Though not a large man, Louie was compact and well proportioned. Ava admired the firm curve of his back as he leaned over the pump. In the dim twilight his T-shirt looked even whiter than before, as though it would glow in the dark. She thought everything about him gleamed with vitality, and she wondered why someone so agile would want to drive a truck.

As if to answer her own question, Ava sidled over to his seat. She took the big, flat steering wheel in her hands and placed her feet on the pedals. A sudden sense of power impelled her to blow the horn.

Louie came running back and jumped in the passenger's side.

"Okay, Ava babe, take 'er away!"

Ava broke into gales of laughter.

"C'mon, I'll show you. Here, start 'er like I showed you."

"But the gears . . ."

"Why, hon, there's only thirteen forward ones," teased Louie. "You're in neutral, so start . . . that's right. Now release the brake

and drop 'er into low ... there ... that one ... no, down more."
Louie placed his hand over hers on the gearshift and guided it to
the right notch. The cab groaned and jerked.

"Don't tense. Do the clutch just like you're used to when I say
'*now*,' and I'll help you with the stick. *Now!*"

Ava shifted into the next gear, and they crawled forward.

"*Now!*" Again they shifted.

"*Now!* Good! I knew you'd catch on fast. *Now!* Hang a left at
the corner, and you'll be on the overpass back to the freeway."

Once Ava reached a cruising speed, she began to relax. She
smiled at Louie, who watched her proudly. From time to time he
patted her hand.

"You look awful good ... just like you belong," he purred in a
low voice.

Ava grew aware of her breasts. Either the vibration of the road
or Louie's gaze upon them made them perk up. The hard ride
caused them to jiggle.

"You sure do get the feel of the road in these seats!" said Ava
trying to distance herself.

"Oh, yeah. You get a good ride," agreed Louie.

And then in her nervousness Ava accidentally ran the left tires
along the lane divider buttons, causing her heart as well as her
breasts to palpitate.

"Whoa!" she cried. "This is better than a Jacuzzi!"

Louie laughed.

"You ought to drive the whole rig. She's a real hummer! Want
to come with me?"

Ava looked at him and said in a teasing voice: "Can't you see
I'm busy driving? I don't need a man."

"Look, honey, you drive long enough and you'll *want* a man. I
can do more for you than any eighteen-wheeler."

"Like what?"

"Oh, give you a good time. I mean it. Anytime you want to
run a rig with me, just holler."

Louie took his hand off hers and reached deep into a pocket.
He brought out his card and slipped it into her hand. Ava
glanced at it and smiled at him. The laugh lines around his lips

and eyes were deeply etched, rugged and kind. She liked his expressive, smiling eyes. He was active and virile, the type of man that Ava often admired from afar.

Louie draped his arm over the back of her seat and gently touched the nape of her neck. Ava's customary impulse to deflect him with a joke suddenly left her. His touch was gentle, tender, much more refined, in fact, than his talk. They rode along in comfortable silence. Aroused by his body warmth, Ava turned slightly toward him. A road sign warned "Soft Shoulder" just as Louie fondled hers. Ava smiled to herself, remembering other cautions of the road: "Right of Way," "Yield," "Slippery When Wet."

Louie squeezed her shoulder and sighed reluctantly.

"We have to head for the next exit if you want to get back to your car. I'll help you downshift." He put his hand over hers again.

Ava smiled at him and pressed the clutch. Louie guided her hand on the stick shift. With each change of gear the cab bucked and groaned in an ever-deepening protest that matched her own. Ava felt like a helpless child again, hating the magical merry-go-round ride to end.

"Easy, easy," soothed Louie.

"I wish I could drive a rig," Ava sighed.

"Well, why don't you? It's a great living — always moving and changing. I could give you some lessons when I finish my run."

"You mean it?"

"Sure I do. But first you'll have to get a permit." While he told her how to do this, he motioned her to steer toward an overpass that returned them to the other side of the freeway. When Ava's crippled Honda came into view on the shoulder ahead, Louie helped her ease the cab off the road. It began to buck and lurch.

"Hit the clutch!" he cried, too late. The cab had already stalled with a final snort. Louie threw on the hand brake and the emergency lights and opened the door. "Good enough," he said as he jumped out and turned with outstretched arms for her.

Ava slid across the seat and allowed him to help her to the ground. This time he held her close and lowered her so slowly that she could feel her skirt riding up as it passed over his body — first rippling across the muscled bulges beneath his T-shirt, then catching on his warm metal belt buckle, before coming to rest in a rumpled heap against his rock-hard quadriceps. She thought her knees would buckle from desire and was glad that he held her a moment longer.

"Atta way," he murmured when he was sure she had found her footing. Then he took her hand in one of his, grabbed the tire in his other, and walked her back to her car. He changed the flat in no time, giving her pointers every step of the way so that she wouldn't be helpless if it happened again. He held the car door open for her as she got in. Cars flashed by behind him, so near that Ava could feel the hot blasts of air in their wake.

"Be careful," she cried.

"Don't worry," he shrugged, but he closed the door and sidled closer, hovering over the open window. "Don't you forget to get a permit," he added.

Ava laughed. She hardly needed a reminder. She squeezed the steering wheel with a surge of pleasure. Her hand still clutched Louie's card. The dampness of her palm had molded it into a tight curl.

"Wait a minute!" he continued suddenly. "How am I ever going to find you?"

The alarm in his voice touched her, and she answered, "Look under Swanson — in the Oakland phone book."

"Okay now, you be good. No more drag racing 'til I get back, hear?"

"Well, you better hurry!"

"Give me three weeks — just three weeks," he begged. Then he smiled seductively and stroked her cheek with the back of his hand before locking her door protectively and stepping out of the way. In a daze Ava took off with tires screeching. She glanced in the rear-view mirror and saw Louie waving her on. She swelled with excitement to think of taking him on in an eighteen-wheeler.

Class of '83

At the Royal Surf everything was true travel-poster Polynesian. The Pacific crashed dramatically against the black rocks. Torches illuminated the winding paths bordered by ferns and banana trees to guide happy couples from the Tonga Bar to the pool or to their authentically thatched bungalows. The Tonga Bar, like the Coral Reef restaurant and the lobby, opened on one side toward the ocean, on the other toward the tropical gardens.

The band was playing "Red Roses for a Blue Lady," and Sheila remembered that tonight was "Fifties Night" and wished that Tom were with her so they could boogie. The dance floor was full. It took her a while to realize that all the couples belonged to her parents' generation. The ladies in blue-gray curls or platinum wigs had donned flowered muumuus, and the gentlemen matched them with Hawaiian shirts. Their identical leis gave them away as a group. At the Royal Surf one walked, dined, and danced in pairs, unless one belonged to a particular constellation known as a "party." At the registration desk, single travelers were funneled into organized fun by travel agents and recreation managers to maximize the efficient distribution of money and pleasure.

The bell captain had spotted Sheila as a single guest occupying an ocean-front room with a king-size bed, and right away the Royal Surf hostess had pressed a free drink into her hand and directed her to the Aloha cocktail party where other singles were already waiting for a match.

"I am expecting my husband," Sheila had protested. Every day she fought for isolation as assorted fellow singles tried to invade her private space at the table or poolside. She soon became known as the "lady who's waiting for her husband."

Tonight, she had hoped to sit quietly in the back of the bar sipping her daiquiri, but a Hawaiian shirt was already advancing toward her. Sheila braced herself. She found it so difficult to be rude. How could she refuse an old man? Of course she agreed to dance with him. He reminded her of her father. Not only was he her father's exact age, as it turned out, but also a retired colonel. He used the same language with the same authority and moved with that familiar mixture of dash and dignity. A skillful dancer and proud of it, he pressed her close without missing a beat.

"My children have given me this trip for my seventieth birthday," he confessed, "and I'm having a splendid time. I should have done this years ago when my wife was alive, but she didn't like to travel. She'd had enough of it in the army."

Sheila told him that her children had also presented her with this trip to Hawaii, all paid for from their summer jobs and savings.

"You're just a kid yourself—class of '83?" he boldly tapped the inscription on her T-shirt.

Sheila blushed. "It's sort of a joke. My boys and I all go to college now. I never finished school." She started to tell him about Peter and Chris at college and about Kate and Kevin, the twins still living at home, when he interrupted her, nodding discreetly toward a woman who tried her best to resemble Carol Channing.

"My sweetheart," he said. "Isn't she something? She's only fifty-five and as strong as a horse. We do all the Air Force exercises together. We'll get married as soon as we get back to Long Beach. Heck, I thought my life was over, but look at me now!" His hand moved down Sheila's spine.

"Isn't your fiancée waiting for you?" Sheila asked, eager to be rid of him.

"She's mad as hell at me. You see, I make her jealous from time to time; it does wonders for her in bed." Like Sheila's father the colonel enjoyed talking, and, again like her father, his conversations always drifted in one direction like river water.

Sheila finally made her escape into the darkness of the deserted beach. She could still hear the band playing "Love Me Tender." Would she and Tom be dancing together at seventy? "I'll join you as soon as I can get away," he had promised when she left. He liked to give the impression that the business was on the point of collapse, that he was holding up the crumbling roof with one hand while keeping the wolf away from the door with the other. Occasionally he would announce his intention of starting a new life. It always sounded like a threat, as if a "new life" meant something terrible. "Let's just go away for a few days," she would suggest.

"Sure," he would say, "but not now."

She never made a scene. For Sheila, scenes were bad habits, like chewing with one's mouth open. If only she could reach out to him, but she feared that even the slightest move might cause a break. The children knew it. Romance would bring them back together, she hoped.

When she was honest with herself, she wished Tom would not come at all. What if they were to spend every night staring at their fragile marriage suspended between them — two mummies on top of a king-size bed, entombed inside their ocean-front room? Strangely, she no longer felt alarmed about Tom. Perhaps it was the air. The intoxicating perfume of the plumeria and the sound of the ocean soothed her anxiety. The warm, slightly damp atmosphere made her feel protected like a hothouse plant. Stretching out in the beach chair, she gazed into the moonlit water. Something moved in the surf. It was huge. She sat up trying to make out what it was — a fish? No, two fish, two huge creatures splashing around in the silvery crest.

"They come every night," said a voice behind her. "You can see better from over there." The boy beckoned her to follow him. Now she recognized his face. She had noticed him at dinner where he also ate alone. His white cutoffs stood out against his deeply tanned legs. His very blond hair contrasted with the tone of his skin. He could be one of the teenage crowd that spilled in and out of Sheila's house every day. He was carrying a bucket.

"Come and watch." He motioned her again toward a rocky, narrow ridge which extended like a natural pier into the ocean. Curious, she scrambled after him.

"Want one?" He offered her a piece of fish from his bucket. "Manta rays. I feed them every night. We keep it a secret, or the tourists would chase them away."

"You live here then? I thought you were a guest at the Surf."

"Well, I guess I am. I come here on holidays with my father. He has a suite. His firm built the Surf." He grinned. "I've seen you too. I like your shirt. I'm supposed to go to Cal in the fall."

"We may run into each other then."

"The truth is, I don't want to go. I don't like school. How about you? I guess nobody's making you go."

"You're right. It's something I've been wanting to do for many years."

"Why?" He seemed perplexed.

"Well, I get time to think. I get to read a lot of books that I have always wanted to read. And I meet new people who are interested in ideas, in *my* ideas. I even get a chance to write them down."

He looked at her as if she was speaking in a foreign language. Sheila was surprised to hear herself talk this way to a boy. It was the first time that she had come up with a clear statement of why she had wanted to go back to school. Maybe it was the strangeness of the situation, the balmy night, the remoteness. Maybe it was the boy's way of looking at her so directly. He tossed another fish into the water. Then she took over. By the time they had emptied the bucket, there were at least five mantas in the sea.

"Watch!" He suddenly stepped toward the edge of the rock. She gasped as he dived into the whirl of moving fins.

"The sharks," she shouted after him, but of course he could not hear her through the surf. His white shorts bobbed up and down in the dark water as he tried to take hold of a flopping saucer shape. After a good deal of splashing, he reappeared on the rock.

"There's one that lets me ride him, but I couldn't find him," he explained offhandedly.

"Isn't that terribly dangerous?" she asked.

"I've been in that water since I was four, and I'm still here, right? The sharks don't come to this cove. I don't know why, but they don't; they go over there to the harbor. Sharks hang out in the same area most of the time—mantas are like dolphins, they like to play." He obviously was showing off. Sheila was glad that he was not hers, that she had no obligation to correct him, and that she need not worry about him. She could simply watch him like another creature of the island. When he invited her to go sailing the next morning, she agreed easily.

Half expecting him not to be there, she arrived late at the marina. But he had readied the catamaran and was chatting with a group of teenagers. Casually he waved her on board as if they had done this many times before. Then it occurred to Sheila that the boy was only doing his job. She wondered how much he would charge, but couldn't bring herself to ask. Matt didn't look like the usual tourist pleaser; perhaps he would be offended. Sheila longed to be out there in the blue haze, whatever the cost.

To his surprise, she was a pretty good sailor. They took turns at the rudder until they reached the lagoon. Since she had never snorkled before, Matt showed her how to breathe through the tube and how to kick with her flippers. Then, without further ceremony, he pushed her off the side. If she was scared, she didn't show it, no silly giggles or affected screams. But when he joined her in the water, she stayed close behind him, trusting him, allowing him to be her guide.

For Sheila, the world below the choppy blue surface surpassed all expectations. Whatever she had anticipated, she did not imagine this underwater garden of black and white coral and pink and green seaweed surrounded by blue parrot fish and hundreds of small yellow butterfly fish. When Matt crumbled a piece of bread into the water, they all came toward him like pigeons in the park. The dark crags of reef scared her, especially when his finger pointed to the fierce-looking face of a moray eel, but somehow she felt accepted by nature. They were two human shapes in the seascape floating among many other shapes, curious about each other, but not threatening.

From time to time Sheila's body brushed against Matt's. It was a comforting, friendly sensation; at the same time she was aware of his maleness, his long, muscular thighs, his narrow hips. She caught herself staring at him from behind her mask as she would never have dared on shore.

Back on board she felt suddenly embarrassed as if she had seen him naked, which in a sense was true. His bathing trunks did not conceal very much. She wondered if he would try to kiss her and if she would let him. But he busied himself with a picnic basket from which he produced two beautifully wrapped gourmet sandwiches and a bottle of wine. Sheila was touched by his thoughtfulness. When had anyone made a sandwich for her? Come to think of it, when had anyone arranged a whole day for her pleasure? That was her role at home: packing picnics, arranging outings, and making everybody happy.

They grinned a little sheepishly at each other while they ate. Sex was there, she knew it and guessed that he knew it, but neither one was ready to handle that possibility. Matt pointed toward a palm-lined lagoon. "My father is trying to buy that piece of beach over there, not for himself, mind you, for his company. It has the best stretch of sand on this side of the island. It belongs to an old Hawaiian guy — to his family actually — but he lives there alone, plants taro and goes fishing. Anybody he likes can use the beach for free. He gives you fish and fruit, everything. They've offered him a million dollars, but he says he doesn't need it."

"Most people never know what they need," she replied.

"Do you?" His question surprised her. Unlike her own sons and his teenage friends he seemed to be seriously interested in her opinions. Sheila felt comfortable enough to answer him honestly.

"I thought so once. Now I'm no longer so sure. Perhaps I'm like that Hawaiian guy. I wouldn't have exchanged my house for anything in the world when the kids were younger, when I was taking care of them. Now I wish I could take care of myself. Even here, I keep looking for things to do with my husband — I mean after he gets here, things that he would enjoy."

"Like snorkeling?" Sheila could see that Matt was offended.

"What about your mother?" Sheila asked cautiously.

"She's just like my father. I don't know why they didn't stay together; they both talk money. She runs a couple of sport shops at Tahoe. She never leaves, winter or summer. Her lawyer is always after my father's lawyer; they never stop."

When they returned to shore in the evening, they knew a lot about each other. For one, he was waiting for his father, and she was waiting for her husband. Sheila could not forget what he had said about his father. It reminded her disturbingly of Tom: "My father likes the *idea* of me. He always tells me what we are going to do together, but he never does it. He always has some important deal coming up. If I didn't show, he would be upset of course." Sheila looked forward to continuing the conversation at dinner. She dressed carefully, anticipating sharing the evening with a companion.

But Matt did not show up at the restaurant. The mahimahi tasted bland. The wine was too sweet. The sun-blistered faces annoyed her. What did she have in common with them? And what did Matt have in common with her? From his point of view, she was probably just another member of the adult world that had let him down. He had told her proudly that he had plenty of friends, both haole and Hawaiian. Perhaps momentarily he had been drawn toward the mirage of a mother-friend, but his interests must lie elsewhere. She supposed he was avoiding her because he was embarrassed about the afternoon. Sheila tried to laugh at herself, but, like a slight yet persistent headache, her disappointment intruded and clouded her usual evening stroll. She ended up at the shopping mall trying on bathing suits designed for Bo Derek.

Matt saw Sheila leave the restaurant. She looked like a girl with her white slacks and dark glasses, her shoulder-length brown hair tied back with a scarf. He cursed himself for having wasted so much time shaving and picking his clothes, especially since he had opted for a pair of faded jeans and his favorite old tennis shirt. His plan had been to casually join her at the table and then, just as casually, to take her to a movie. Too late. For awhile he followed her around, hoping that she would run into him, but he knew that he no longer had the courage to ask her out. She probably took him for a beach bum or worse.

Suddenly he thought of a new tactic. As soon as she disappeared into the Beachcomber Boutique, he headed for her room. It was easy to get a master key. He knew the hotel inside out and often pitched in for the bellboy. Once she found him in her room, she would get mad and throw him out, or . . . ! In his fantasy he was James Bond. He'd search her room. He'd know all about her before he made his move.

Everything in her room was disappointingly neat and tidy. Sheila was not the kind of person to toss her shoes on the floor or leave her clothes carelessly strewn about. Only a white nightgown laid out on the bed gave her presence away. Matt picked it up and inhaled her perfume. A look behind the sliding mirror of the closet revealed an array of dresses. Orange and yellow seemed to be her favorite colors, but he had never seen her wear any of these elegant numbers. For a moment he saw her on his arm in a canary chiffon gown as they entered the exclusive King Kamehameha Club. The maître d' showed them to their table, the headwaiter stooped over Matt's shoulder with the wine list, and he ordered French champagne. Then he reminded himself that her dresses were obviously waiting for the son-of-a-bitch husband. Still he continued his investigation, opening every drawer and examining its contents: beach paraphernalia, cosmetics, some college textbooks and a lot of paperbacks by authors he had never heard of, and — of course — her underwear. He could not resist going back to that particular drawer. Running his fingers over the sheer lace, the smooth satin, he imagined his hands inside her panties.

Suddenly he heard the key in the door. Panic. He forgot all about his plan. Quickly he flicked on the television and huddled himself in the armchair pretending to watch.

"What are you doing here?" Sheila asked in surprise and a bit sternly. She turned off the set. Guiltily, Matt scrambled to his feet. "I only wanted to say good night."

"Good night." He didn't budge. She said it again, more kindly.

She realized his panic at having been caught. To help him, now that she had recovered, she kissed him lightly — maternally she thought — on the cheek. But her heart stopped, then pounded fiercely. In his hand he was clutching her panties. To her consternation, she found that sight very exciting. His hunger for her was so obvious and yet so innocent. It made him irresistible. She put down her parcels and purse and unbuttoned her blouse. Then everything happened with lightning speed. Within seconds they were out of their clothes and in bed together, and it was over just as quickly.

"My," she said, "do you always gobble everything up so fast?"

"I was afraid you'd change your mind."

"Tell you what, let me get some sleep and tomorrow we'll try again — my way, okay?"

"Can't I stay?"

Before she could answer, the telephone rang. Hastily, she pulled on her bathrobe, suddenly self-conscious of her nakedness. Matt could tell that it was her husband at the other end of the line. Still cursing himself for his clumsiness, he decided that things couldn't get worse, so he stayed in the room. The conversation was brief and one-sided.

"That's fine. Yes, I'll see you then," was all she said.

"Bad news?" Matt asked reading her face.

"No, that was my husband. He says he'll be here tomorrow night." She seemed lost in thought. Matt went over to her and brushed her hair off her face, ready to say good-bye. She pulled his head down and kissed him. He kissed her breasts, and he buried his head in her lap. She let him stay there. After a while he asked if he could look at her. Her knees opened, parting the folds of her silk robe. He could see her pubic hair between her slender thighs and touched her soft petals, gently prying her apart like a rose.

"I like that," she whispered, "kiss me there."

He felt the moist folds, the different textures of flesh and skin and hair. She shivered and moaned, telling him when to stop and when to begin again. Finally, she whispered: "You see, I am learning too. Nobody has ever done this to me before."

Sheila wondered why it was so easy to tell Matt what she wanted. In all their years together, she had never managed to tell Tom. Guiding Matt's fingers, she made him listen to her breath, to every clue in giving her pleasure. She was his teacher, but she was also a student. There was so much she did not know herself.

"Do you like this?" Matt asked again and again. His curiosity about her body never seemed satisfied. Tracing her hips and buttocks, he marveled at her curves, her finely chiseled bones, her tender skin. "Look at your nails," he exclaimed, "they are perfect, the shape, the nail polish, everything just right." And she rewarded him with a massage, proving what her fingers could do.

At some point when he was barely awake, Matt heard Sheila's voice speaking into the telephone, calmly informing her husband that it would be better if he did not come, that she needed more time for herself.

"I will be back next week," she said matter-of-factly. She hung up the phone pensively. Matt turned toward her and said, "I want to make it so good for you that you won't go."

From then on, they were inseparable. "How sweet," smiled the hotel guests, "such a nice mother and son. They do everything together."

When his friends had teased him about his affair with an "old lady," he had gotten into a fist fight. How could he explain to them what it meant to have someone who accepted him for what he was, who never put him down? Sheila had not even laughed at his art. When she had asked him why he drew only airplanes, she had sounded really interested, not critical. When they made love, she never held anything back from him. She was like no other girl he had known. She let him look at her as long as he liked until he knew every part of her. On their last night he wanted to kiss all of her good-bye. Sheila felt his tears on her shoulders. He told her that he loved her, that he couldn't bear to see her leave. Exhausted, she did not turn around. The next morning he was gone.

As the plane lifted her off the ground, her spirits soared high. "I made love, I really made love," she proclaimed to herself. The cabin was packed with returning tourists. Across the aisle sat the colonel and his bride. Hungrily they tore into a bag of potato chips. They held hands. Each wore several leis. Sheila's lei came from a meadow near the lagoon where the old Hawaiian lived. Orchids grew wild there. Matt had gathered the blossoms and strung them for her.

The whole family met her at the airport. They couldn't see Sheila right away because she followed behind the happy couple. But then Kevin ran up to her. "Hi Mom, did you have a good time? Did you bring me a piece of coral?" Tom stood back, apart from the others as if he expected to be brushed aside. She walked over to him and put the lei around his neck.

Second Opinion

Ellen Rossiter was Harvey Rostow's final office patient late on a Friday evening. He had scheduled her at the last minute because her referring doctor was a good friend. Forewarned that she was blind, he went to the waiting room himself to get her and show her to his office. This simple act of courtesy impressed Ellen and put her at ease.

"Tell me," Dr. Rostow began as he guided her down the hall, "is it worse do you think, to be blind from birth?"

"No, I don't," Ellen answered, surprised that this should be his first question. Most doctors seemed bound by their role to appear omniscient, to conceal their curiosity. "My friends who were once sighted have to learn what I know instinctively," she explained. "They translate everything from their lost sense."

"I can't imagine functioning without my sight," he confessed.

"You'd probably fare better than some, being a cardiologist. Your hearing must be well developed."

"Yes, with a stethoscope, but I'm not sure how much that would help get me around my kitchen or across a street," he laughed.

In his office now, seated on their respective sides of a massive desk, he continued in a more doctorly tone.

"Ms. Rossiter, or Ellen — which should I call you?"

"Ellen is fine."

"I understand from Dr. Lewis that you have been experiencing arrhythmias. Would you describe them, please?"

As she did, Ellen could hear his ballpoint pen making rapid notes. He enjoyed taking a history from such a bright, articulate patient. He watched her sitting across from him, calm and willowy in a soft knit dress that echoed the gray-blue of her eyes. Her hands lay quietly folded in her lap, and she looked at him with a steady, open gaze that radiated harmony and composure, a serenity that hours of primping before lighted mirrors would have destroyed, he was certain. Her finely tuned attention was so disturbing that he had to turn back to her record.

"I see that it's been almost a year since you were last examined, so I'd like to check you and then we'll talk. Let me show you to the examining room."

He stood beside her as she rose from her chair and graciously took her by the hand to a small room farther down the hall. Ellen could tell from walking hand in hand beside him that he was quite tall and thin. Her hands wanted to move across his face and hair with the quivering energy of butterfly wings to seek more information, a frequent impulse that she had grown used to stifling.

The examining room smelled of the typical hospital blend: formica, linoleum, alcohol, and iodine. Dr. Rostow cupped her hand over a metal hook on the back of the door to show her where to hang her clothes, then pressed a disposable paper smock into her other hand before leaving.

Ellen undressed nervously, knowing that it was not dread of the impending examination that undid her. Here, unexpectedly, was a man who was compassionate, kind, and self-revealing. The combination of so many rare qualities in a *man* made Ellen feel like melting. She unfolded the stiff paper gown with difficulty. It stuck together, making it almost impossible to find the armholes, and when she finally got it on and hoisted herself up on the table, she worried that the smock was upside down.

Dr. Rostow returned with an office nurse.

"Stay sitting up," he said. "We'll take your blood pressure and then examine your head and chest."

Ellen heard him go to a small sink in the corner of the room and start to wash his hands. The nurse slapped a blood pressure band on her upper arm, vigorously pumped it as tightly as it would go, and waited. With a sigh the pressure eased, and Ellen could feel her circulation return.

"120 over 80," announced the nurse, tearing off the Velcro band with a loud rip. Ellen touched her upper arm to see if it was still intact.

Dr. Rostow came and stood before her. He took her hands in both of his and held them briefly, looking at the palms and nails. Ellen found it a most reassuring gesture regardless of its medical import. Then he held her face between his hands for a moment, and when he removed them, she felt the warmth still cupping her chin like two indelible handprints. Next the warm beam of the otoscope traveled deep inside her ears, then her nose, mouth, and eyes. Afterward, Ellen heard him dismantle the otoscope and put it away in a leather case that snapped shut. There was a pause, and then Dr. Rostow's smooth, long-fingered hands probed her neck.

"Now I'll listen to your chest."

He slid the paper kimono down over her shoulders. She heard him put on the stethoscope and waited for him to touch her. There was a long pause, and Ellen stirred.

"I'm trying to warm the disk," he explained. Ellen smiled. The disk touched her upper chest and traveled back and forth across the breastbone, resting a moment at each stop, as though on an invisible track. It continued traveling down the side of each breast and deftly slipped between them. Dr. Rostow's head was bent low, almost touching hers. She could feel the warmth of his face only inches away. He smelled good with a natural sweetness not masked by aftershave lotions and hair tonics.

"Breathe, please," he reminded her. "Good. Again. Deeper. Hmm, sounds good. Now let me listen to your back."

The warm disk started its journey, but its course was not as predictable as before. It hopped more or less randomly along the outer portions of her rib cage. Ellen could feel him exhaling near her shoulder in warm, silent puffs.

"Breathe again. Good. Now deeply."

The disk rose and fell, each time touching softly and lingering like a kiss.

"Now you can lie down. I'd like to listen again in this position, but so far everything sounds normal."

Again the disk began to travel in careful unhurried circles around her breasts. Ellen relaxed with Dr. Rostow's mild pace. She felt him leaning over her, close enough again to detect his warmth.

"You sound fine," he announced straightening up. "My guess is that you experienced paroxysmal atrial tachycardia." While he went on to explain this harmless condition, Ellen felt a tear well up in one eye and trickle awkwardly toward her ear. She wondered whether it was relief or his gentleness that had moved her.

As Dr. Rostow continued through the abdominal and neurological phases of the examination, his concentration relaxed a little, and he asked her about her work.

"What do you teach?"

"English and American literature."

"Really?" he replied with interest. "You must be much better-read than I. I hardly ever read for pleasure," he admitted as he closed the paper smock over her and raised her to a sitting position. "I know I should."

"But then it wouldn't be much of a pleasure, would it?" laughed Ellen.

"True," he agreed, "but, really, I think I'd like to. Can you recommend a good book?"

Several titles immediately came to mind.

"Have you read *Angle of Repose*?" she asked.

"No. Who wrote it?"

"Wallace Stegner — he's one of my favorites." Ellen went on. "He describes the sounds and smells of places so vividly that I feel I'm actually seeing them. And he creates such believable people."

"Sounds good — maybe I will," Dr. Rostow added with a wistful sigh. Ellen wondered what else he longed to do. "You can get dressed now," he continued, "and then I'll come and bring you to my office."

"No," answered Ellen. "I can find it."

Ellen dressed quickly and noticed her heart was beating with such a strong, steady rhythm that she wondered if the arrhythmias had ever really occurred. She brushed her hair and returned to the office.

"Ellen, I'm writing a prescription for digoxin, which I would like you to take once a day. It should discourage these episodes."

Ellen heard but concentrated more on feeling the gentle vibrations of his voice wash over her. She wanted to glean all the information she could about him. Did diplomas line the walls along with photos of his wife and children?

Suddenly she asked, "Where did you train?"

"I went to Yale Medical School and did most of my postgraduate training at the University of California."

"Are there pictures of your family?"

"Yes, my two daughters."

"And your wife?"

"We're divorced. They live with her."

"Oh." Ellen stopped, blushing at her boldness. In her embarrassment, she began to fumble with her coat.

"Here," he said coming to her side and helping her into her coat. "You know, I like your dress."

"Thank you."

"How do you manage to shop?"

"With a friend usually," she replied with amusement.

As he saw her to the door, he continued: "I'm a terrible dresser. Even other doctors say my clothes are tacky, so I guess I'm glad you can't see me. Isn't that a terrible thing to say?"

Ellen laughed.

"Here's your prescription. I'd like you to make an appointment to see me in six weeks."

Ellen spent the next weeks daydreaming probably more than all her adolescent students combined. She found herself misplacing things and was impatient with her lover, Richard, who expected to monopolize her time. Ellen grew distant and secretive the more she embroidered her romantic fantasy. She rolled the name, Harvey Rostow, over and over in her mind. How well it suited his low, velvety voice. There was something vibrant, she thought, about its trochaic cadence.

Ellen constructed a patchwork quilt of wishes and memories, sensations and desires. The clever dialogues that swirled in her head sometimes made her laugh aloud. She replayed her office visit again and again, remembering the way he showed compassion and still made her feel whole and able.

In anticipation of her next appointment Ellen's daily regimen of exercises and yoga became more exciting. Because he had noticed her clothes, she shopped for something new to wear. Quite irrationally, she ended up at a small, exquisite lingerie shop, a closet of a store that always thrilled her with its exotic array of smells and sensations. Sachets hung in embroidered packets among the racks of satin and lace and flannel gowns or were hidden among the little baskets of panties and bras that lined the counters. The more expensive imports were pinned to hanging vertical panels that could be turned like pages of a huge book. Ellen's hands fluttered over the lace and ribbon trim, savoring the tiny rosettes and bows and appliquéd designs. She knew the prices would be staggering and was glad she couldn't see them; she might have spent less time adoring each piece. Finally she made her selection, a French lace bra with rosebuds in front over the clasp and a matching bikini with rosebuds on each hip.

Ellen arrived on time for her appointment to find others crowded in the small waiting room. The air was stale in the windowless room despite the circulation from air-conditioning vents overhead. It was more than forty-five minutes before the crisp receptionist called her name and showed her to the office.

"The doctor will be right in," she chirped as she shut the door.

Ellen waited. His telephone never stopped ringing. There are probably four lead-in lines, she thought, all stranded on Hold. Impulsively, she reached out to examine the telephone and groped around the surface of the desk. She collided with a stack of thick manila folders. Next to it lay a shorter pile of large X-ray envelopes and beyond that were scattered notepapers, probably memos, and stapled glossy pages torn from journals. Ellen drew back, rebuked. She hadn't counted on his being so busy. The daydream conversations she had rehearsed with so much anticipation would have no place in a rushed office visit. Just as Ellen was wondering whether he would even remember her, she heard a door down the hall open and his crepe-soled shoes approach. He paused outside the office to pick up her folder from the rack. Some pages turned, and then the door opened.

"Hello, Ms. Rossiter, uh, oh, Ellen."

The hem of his starched lab coat brushed her knees as he swept past and flung himself into the swivel chair on the other side of his desk.

"How are you doing?" he asked routinely.

"Just fine," she answered. There was a weary edge in his voice that hadn't been there before. She went on to say that not a single episode had occurred since she had been on the medication.

"Good," he answered distractedly. She heard him writing in her chart. It suddenly struck her that she would have no further reason to see him. The very thought was enough to make her heart stop. She imagined herself swooning to the floor and his leaping to her rescue. Frantic to save her, he would lean over, pressing his lips to hers. . . .

"In that case," he continued, "I think you should stay on it another two weeks and call if these episodes recur."

"I see."

"In the meantime, I'll send a report to Dr. Lewis," he concluded wearily.

"Thank you."

Ellen heard him closing the folder.

"You sound a little down," she added.

"I do?"

"Yes, your voice seems lower and slightly hoarse. Do you have a cold?"

"No," he answered contemplatively. There was a heaviness in his legs and a throbbing at his temples — all normal this late in his day. "Maybe I'm just tired."

"Is every day this busy?"

"Usually."

"Do you mind?"

"I don't question it."

He stopped, noting that her intrusive questions did not annoy him. He realized how easy it would be to drop his professional facade with this unflinching listener, to tell her anything and know that she would be there — alert, intelligent, and receptive. Censored thoughts overwhelmed him: How much I would like to be with her, maybe just for dinner, but that would be unethical, impossible. I should send her back to Dr. Lewis, wait a proper interval, six months or a year.

"Oh, I almost forgot!" Ellen opened her purse and took out a copy of *Angle of Repose*. "This is probably a terrible time to give you this; you're probably too busy to read it."

"Why, thank you! How very nice!" He sounded genuinely pleased. "I'd love to talk with you about it. Can you come back in six weeks?"

Suddenly the absurdity of his proposal overwhelmed him. Asking a patient to return to discuss a book! Did it constitute malpractice? Would he be sued? Ostracized by his colleagues? And how would his secretary bill Blue Cross? How would he ever account for this?

"Fine," Ellen was saying as if his proposal were a logical part of her therapy. She rose and began putting on her coat. He came and held it for her. She eased into it and turned toward him. She hesitated shyly and asked: "Would you let me see your face?"

"Of course," he answered in confusion.

Then, with the accuracy of someone sighted, she raised both hands to his face and delicately swept across his brow and down along the sides of his cheeks and chin. Her fingers brushed over his lips and traced his nose and eyebrows, then retreated back to his hairline, following it down over his sideburns and past his ears. She felt the throbbing pulse in his warm neck and quickly withdrew her hands, aware of his unease. She thanked him and walked serenely to the door.

Though her exploration lasted only a few seconds, it completely violated what little was left of Dr. Rostow's sense of proper doctor-patient decorum. He became breathlessly aware of a paralyzing weakness in his knees and groin. He wanted to call her back, but his throat constricted so that he could not have uttered a syllable if his life depended on it. In the doorway Ellen turned to him, smiling, and said, "See you."

It's Always Summer

It's always summer when you're around
isn't that funny?
Even when it's raining outside
and we lie on our bed shivering.
Your hands are warm
your body toasts me,
your lips are warm rivers
I drift down the Mississippi.
Your skin is golden
it shines all over me.
Your eyes are rays of sunshine
that sparkle in the dark.
Your arms are branches of tall trees
that enfold me.
Green leaves and honey bees.
Buzz around me loverboy,
I need more summer.

Prince Charming

They tell me
there is no
Prince Charming.
He is a fantasy
of the unliberated
masses.
Then why do I stroke
your silky skin
with such pleasure
and caress your
lean back with
trembling fingers?
If you aren't Prince Charming
who are you?

Ann's Hood Canal Oysters

The most sensuously delicious protein pigout I know is simple to prepare but, like caviar, hard to come by. The dish is fresh Hood Canal oysters that have been plucked off the beach at low tide and grilled on an open campfire. Slurped and guzzled with white wine and sourdough French bread, they make a soul-satisfying banquet that needs its own framework to be perfect.

Your oyster feast begins with a leisurely day at one of the protected, sand-and-rock beaches that scallop the edge of the twenty-five-mile-long finger of the Pacific Ocean called Hood Canal in the state of Washington. The opposing shores bathe the feet of the Olympic rain forest and mountain range. The sky is normally moody and changeable in summer, and the air is so different from California's that when I first arrive I feel as if I am enclosed in a warm, damp blanket. The air slows one's movements ever so slightly and is forever gently caressing the skin. There is constant activity at the water's edge — waves lapping and splashing. The water is tepid at the wading edges and tingling crisp where it's deep enough to swim. The snorkler sees water gardens of infinite blue and green beauty, and the beachcomber may glimpse herons, swallows, sea gulls, migrating geese, oysters, clams, and riffling seaweed.

Let a driftwood fire blaze for an hour to produce perfect, slightly flaming coals. Meanwhile, collect the oysters left exposed on the sand by the receding tide. It's as easy as picking overripe berries from a bush. Place the oysters on a grill over the coals. As they pop open one by one, remove them from the fire, pry them fully apart with an oyster knife, slop them with either Crosse and Blackwell's seafood sauce or lemon *juice, and greedily devour them. Cooked properly, they will be sweet, succulent, and slithery. Overcooked, they will resemble shoe leather. Feed such failures to the sea gulls. Indulge your own palate with nothing but perfection. When sated, build up the campfire again, sit cozily by it, toasting your front and chilling your back until the night gently enfolds and the incoming tide softly laps the world to peace.*

IV. FORBIDDEN FRUIT

A *few of us, especially the ones from religious backgrounds, had the opportunity to acquire a sense of sin at an early age. The ensuing war between the flesh and spirit infused sexual experience with matchless intensity and produced enough psychological fallout to taint a lifetime. The list of sins grew as fast as we did. Instead of quashing our lust, the concept of sin turned fleeting thoughts into erotic dynamite. That denial can be most arousing was borne out in the zeal with which we engaged in discussions about the forbidden. Our verbal debaucheries incited us to break lifelong taboos and to unleash censored passions in the group of stories called Forbidden Fruit. Those of us who had the misfortune to have grown up rationally in more liberal climates sometimes yearn for that which we were denied — the exotic taste of forbidden fruit.*

The Tender and the Wanton Where They Cross

Tenderness informs the fingertips and guides the blood
Beating in the hope-scarred heart
Soothes the pertinent hand from tremors of deferred desire
Loosens the searching lips for deeper quenching
Gives the hipbones softening glide
Strengthens the spine to hold back force
Hoarsens into deep the whispered voice
Cheers the sharing spirit on to share yet more
And gives the love-burst magnitude and flight.

Wantonness slips past the protest of the spoken No
Stammered through the starving flesh
Demands electric answers of the nerves
Tingling from skin-touch into visceral surge
Tongues the tender archways into caves
Pulling breath to gasp and gasp to moan
Thrusts the thighs and curves the back
Opens liquid flesh to deepest drive
And flashes purest lightning through the mind's dark dome.

The tender and the wanton where they cross
Fuse the hot bliss bringing reason's body home.

Schübling, Liebling: A Bawdy Tale

A Schübling is a sausage, definitely not a hot dog, a wiener or a frankfurter. It is fat rather than long, and it is juicy on the inside and crisply taut on the outside. To be honest, the juice is mostly fat. If you bite into a Schübling, the fat runs down your cheek and drips over your hands. This is a messy experience, sloppy and crude, but well worth losing your dignity for because it allows you to be human, to let go of your inhibitions, to smell, salivate, suck, and chew without shame.

You will, of course, hold the Schübling with your fingers—never touch it with a knife and fork. The feeling of this hot, fat piece of resilient sausage underneath its stretched-out skin, at this point still innocently dry, determines whether you will go through with the experience or not. A lukewarm, limp Schübling is not worth approaching with your lips. Push it aside and reach for another. A word of caution here: any attempt to reheat a cooled-off Schübling leads to dismal failure.

Once you have satisfied your tactile sense, bend down and inhale the aroma. Is it strong and tangy? Can you sniff out the freshness of good meat? Then it is ready for intimate contact with your tongue. You may try any of these variations, depending on your mood. Are you ravenous? Then take a hearty bite and enjoy. If you like the sensation of the dry, hot surface inside your mouth, hold on to it before you let your teeth rupture the skin. Or you may take a tiny bite first, lick off just a few drops of juice at a time, alternating between sucking and chewing. Whatever you do in the beginning, you will be drooling in the end. Your eyes will water, your nose will run, your cheeks will glisten while you smack your lips and lick your fingers, unconcerned with disapproving stares. Yes, do it in public. Schüblings are steamed in public squares and fairgrounds. Do it in front of everybody. Do it in pairs and in groups. Know that you, too, are a member of the human race.

Frau Becker stepped out onto the balcony of her brand-new Swiss chalet. She took a deep, appreciative breath of the mountain air. Once again her husband had been right when he picked this particular place. It offered every modern convenience, including a sauna next to the obligatory atomic shelter in the basement, and the view was unmolested by any trace of tourism. The ancient farmhouses clung to the steep hillside like a flock of grazing sheep protected by the shepherd, a small white church with a pointed belfry, which sat on top of the cluster as if to ward off the majestic flow of the distant glacier.

Herr Becker had bought the chalet in the winter, but now in mid-August the gleaming white caps of the mountains contrasted dramatically with the lush green slopes, while cowbells tinkled pleasantly from all directions. Frau Becker hoped that the weather would hold until September 15 when she expected friends for a weekend party. Right now the walls were bare and the rooms empty, but in four weeks' time she would fill the place with rustic furniture, dried flowers, and local color. She had done it before in Greece and in Portugal. There she had given herself more time, of course. Only in Switzerland could she be sure that the workmen would arrive on schedule and that her chairs and tables would be delivered when promised.

Before Herr Becker had made so much money in real estate, Frau Becker had stretched their budget by doing a lot of things herself; they had built their first house in Stuttgart practically with their own hands — plastering, painting, hammering, and gardening. Even now, she surprised her friends with hand-crocheted afghans, hand-woven baskets, or homemade pies. In the eyes of their large circle of acquaintances Frau Becker exemplified the German housewife of the old school who hustled and bustled all day long to keep everything clean and make everybody comfortable. Without his wife, they said, Herr Becker would never have made it because Waltraud Becker was not only industrious, or "fleissig" as they say in German, but also beautiful and charming.

She was indeed Herr Becker's "greatest asset," they would add jokingly. How sad that their only son and heir to the real estate empire had turned out so badly. As far as anyone knew, he had gone to India after doing a lot of disgusting things with his hair and his body, and was never heard from again.

On August 15, exactly four weeks before her big party, Waltraud Becker had many things on her mind other than her estranged son; but in the pocket of her apron she carried a letter signed with her son's new religious name. In it he warned her to change her diet and to turn away from materialistic endeavors. As she glanced at the clear blue sky over the mountain range, she felt closer to her son than she had in all the years of his tumultuous growing up, and more than anything else she would like to have shared this moment with him. But if she had any regrets, she did not let them surface. There were many things she did not dwell on — for instance, why she no longer loved her husband. If she could do nothing about them, why brood over them?

Better to get busy with her tasks. She returned to her all-electric kitchen, picked up her ruler, and began to measure the floor for the right-sized table. Would she prefer a butcher block? She had seen a beautiful old piece in the market; maybe the butcher would sell it to her. Her deliberations absorbed her so deeply that it took some time before the noise outside entered her consciousness.

When she went to see what was going on, she could not believe her eyes. A large bulldozer was winding its way up the narrow road, followed by a crane and a truckload of workers. The procession stopped right in front of her balcony where she now discovered the square outline of a newly started building site. She knew right away that her party was ruined, that the chalet was a mistake, and that she would have to call her husband in Stuttgart immediately so that he could get his lawyers to rescind the deal. It would be futile to buy the furniture or to do anything but concentrate on abandoning the chalet and canceling the party. Cables would have to be sent; a string of actions had to be set in motion.

But Frau Becker didn't pick up the phone. Instead, she pulled up a chair to watch the proceedings at the building site. She didn't know why, because she was not a contemplative woman. Was it because she could not bring herself to get in touch with her husband, to deal with his anger, to listen to his tirades? Was it that she suddenly enjoyed the notion of receiving her guests in a house bare of furniture, next to an ugly construction site? Or was she simply tired of buying matching towels and soaps and curtains and rugs and dishes and sectional couches?

Frau Becker had always been fascinated by building sites. The machines were so much larger than the men that they seemed to do the job on their own. Steadily, they went about their business with a great sense of purpose, like well-trained animals. The crane moved its long neck gracefully from right to left picking up large crates from the truck and putting them down gently on the grass. The bulldozer dug its heavy haunches into the ground, burrowing its head deeper and deeper into the wet earth. And the cement mixer bounced and twirled around and around until a creamy thick paste poured from its narrow opening at the bottom. The men were there, of course, patting and stroking the metal bodies to make them go up or down, forward or backward. Quite obviously they knew how to handle the truck to make it tilt its back so willingly or to get the tip of the crane to plunge precisely into such a small hole. Sometimes the men themselves joined their machines, feeding their voracious mouths with big shovels of sand or loading their backs with bricks. Sometimes they switched roles and became servants where before they had been masters, lifting and carrying large pieces of wood themselves in order to place them where the machine wanted them. All day long they worked together to the same steady rhythm, embracing rocks and balancing sticks gracefully like acrobats.

Men and machines, machines and men — their bodies in top condition, their movements in perfect harmony. To put one stone on top of another, to smooth out the edges with cement, to watch a house grow out of its foundations seemed to her a gratifying spectacle.

As the days went by, Frau Becker became well acquainted with everything that went on at the building site, almost as though she were part of the crew. Although she never thought of this herself, she identified with the workers like a spectator identifies with the characters of a play. Her day began at eight like theirs and ended with the first stroke of the bell at six. At noon everyone dropped his tools and went down to the Hotel Krone for lunch — everyone except one man, who ate his sandwich under a tree and then stretched out for his siesta until his comrades returned at two o'clock.

On the third day of her vigil on the balcony, Waltraud Becker decided to bake a cake. She felt that she had been sitting around too long without doing anything, particularly since the men were so busy all the time, and here she was — a lazy tourist with nothing to do. In order to get the necessary ingredients, she had to hike down to the village and buy everything, including a baking tin. Then she climbed back to her kitchen and made a chocolate cake. At noon she put the cake into a basket, together with a thermos bottle full of freshly filtered black coffee, and carried it over to the man under the tree.

The man seemed quite surprised. He put down the bread and the sausage he was eating and accepted a piece of her cake. In return he offered her one of his sausages — a Schübling. This local specialty was known to be especially crisp and juicy. Frau Becker declined politely but had some cake and coffee with him. He ate two large pieces, gulping the hot coffee with appreciative slurps. They both drank straight from the bottle. Frau Becker put her mouth where his had been, and he noticed it.

"Good cake, good coffee," he said with a smile. From his accent she gathered that he was Yugoslavian. She had expected this since most construction workers in Switzerland came from Yugoslavia. And like all Yugoslavian construction workers this one was handsome, strong, clean, and courteous. She guessed his age at about thirty-five. The children in the picture he showed her were eight, ten, and twelve. His wife, with her head covered by a white kerchief, was ageless like peasant women everywhere. He would go back in two years, he said. The last time he had seen them was three years ago. Frau Becker nodded. She knew more than he imagined about Yugoslavian workers because she had seen a documentary film on television. After he had shown her the picture, he offered her a drink from his bottle of schnapps. Again, she did not wipe off the rim but licked it with her tongue. He cautiously put his hand on her ankle and, when she did not object, he moved it slowly up and under her skirt. They understood each other very well.

Next to the tree was a small ravine through which tumbled a noisy little creek. The grass felt soft, if a bit wet down there, and trees protected them from all sides. Frau Becker was not disappointed that he took her very quickly because this, too, she had expected. He entered her with short, quick thrusts, but he was in no way rough or clumsy, just fast and strong like a cloudburst after a thunderstorm. Then he collapsed on top of her, mumbling "Frau, Frau, Frau," many times over as if in prayer. This moved her immensely, and she stroked his thick woolly hair affectionately while his semen trickled out of her onto the grass. What a nice feeling to lie there, next to the rushing creek with a warm young man on top of her. For so many years she had awakened at night, aroused from orgasmic dreams which left her frustrated, that now she really enjoyed keeping her excitement warm without wanting anything more.

But from the expression on her lover's face she gathered that more was to come, that he had something special in mind for her. Making sure that her skirt was out of the way, he slipped one hand under her ample backside and the other into his knapsack. She felt something soft and quivering, yet taut and subtle between her legs. Startled she discovered a Schübling in his hands, but she was too absorbed by the thrilling sensations he conveyed with this unusual tool to object to it. Quite the opposite, he was so agile with this Schübling that she found it superior to anything nature had provided. This way he could easily keep a close watch on her to adjust every turn and twist to her response. He managed to drive her wild. Occasionally, he bit a piece off from his end, eating his way to her crotch where his tongue took over until she was totally satisfied and told him to stop.

From then on Frau Becker bought a lot of groceries at the local market — she never forgot to add a Schübling or two — and every day she carried another delicacy to the building site. Sometimes there was enough left for the other workers to have a taste before they went back to their machines.

When Herr Becker arrived punctually from Stuttgart for the big party, he could not understand why his wife had never informed him about the gaping hole underneath the balcony, which by then was partially filled with concrete blocks and the monstrous steel door of the atomic shelter. After he spent hours on the telephone, Herr Becker informed his wife that he had traded their chalet for a bungalow in Ibiza and that they would leave immediately to have a look at it.

But Frau Becker refused to abandon the chalet. She applied for a job as a waitress at the Hotel Krone. The owner did not feel comfortable with a rich lady in his service, but waitresses were hard to find in such a small village, and she had agreed to work for very little. If the Krone owner had hoped that Frau Becker would bring him new and better customers from among her own people, he was disappointed. But she proved to be a good worker, the best he had ever had, and she soon took over his job as cook. And the construction workers liked her cooking so much that they never went anywhere else.

Pope Innocent XV:
Scenes from a Dream

Scene I

The pope is coming! I have been invited to a banquet in his honor by the chairman of our Twentieth High School Reunion Committee, who has reserved the private banquet room at Trader Vic's. Our class is hostessing the gala event with the kind of excitement that is fueled by short notice.

Awaiting us is the dining room swaddled lavishly in gold and white crepe de chine, a perfect camouflage for His Holiness. I approach the long white table that stretches like a satin freeway into the far reaches of an adjoining room. The brilliance of each place setting stuns me. Not only is the cutlery of pure gold, but each plate and goblet is of an original design that exactly conveys the individuality of each special guest. As I look among the place settings anxiously seeking my own, I realize that they are the work of Judy Chicago. The item expressing the unique essence of each receiver is the goblet. Starting first with the simplest, they become increasingly elaborate and ornate. The smooth, gentle lines and creamy glazes of the early goblets do not prepare me for the drama of the later ones. Great convoluted lips seethe with textured glazes and laugh defiantly at the limitations of their porcelain. One of these bold vessels draws me to it and swallows my will. I wonder how I will ever drink from its frothy folds. As I take my seat, I realize too late that this garish goblet is not meant for me. I look up alarmed and meet the amused gaze of the pope, who is seated directly across from me.

Poise. I am summoning every ounce of poise while I smile back and plot a gracious retreat. Just then another truth assaults me: all my female classmates are wearing hats. Proper black hats. Some are velvet, some have veils, but all are exactly right. I know I have forgotten mine. The thought had not even occurred to me. My hand rises tentatively to my head to confirm my fear. I pray for a hat. I touch my head, and to my amazement there is a hat! Relief overwhelms me until I look up and see that my hat is not like anybody else's. It is a sailor's hat, dirty and battered, with its rim yanked down over my eyes. Panic returns.

I scan the room. I see my Jewish friends. They are bareheaded too, and they are being seated in the adjoining room where scurrying waiters are still setting the table. I eagerly rise and join them, glad to have found my rightful place.

The dinner is about to begin. Someone at my end of the table has just shot a roll of film recording our arrival. She frees the cartridge from the camera and pulls out some already processed footage. We greedily examine the tiny still frames, searching for ourselves. The camera is a novelty. It photographs people's underwear. I look more closely at the transparent figures on the ribbon of film.

The other women wear exquisite lingerie. They have not been caught short. I see lovely bikinis, a few garter belts with stockings, and even an occasional black, strapless Merry Widow. I hadn't known they were back in vogue. Now I see a figure different from the rest. She is naked. I see the nipples, the pubic hair, and, most conspicuously, the ribs. It is I. The pope looks at me. He likes me — no, he wants me. Of all the women in the room he has chosen me. I am the chosen one. He indicates that he will come to my house.

Scene II

I am home again in my sunny kitchen. I want to start dinner, but the pope is standing in the way. His elaborate gowns cascade in brocade layers and fill the entire space between the stove and sink and the counter opposite. He seems not to notice my noisy children in their filthy cutoffs cavorting in the surf of his outer garments. I am angry with them for being no more ready for this distinguished occasion than I am. I want to reprimand them, but first I should introduce them, and I don't know how. Does the pope have a title? Your Majesty or Your Highness? No, those are too regal. Your Excellency? No, too secular. What about Sir? No, too short. Is his last name O'Neill? Mr. O'Neill? No, that doesn't sound right.

The pope is gesturing toward the dishwasher. He has never seen one before and wants me to show him how to use it. I try to teach him how to load it, but he is incapacitated by his stiff gowns and can't get quite close enough to place the dishes in their appropriate slots. Each time he bends over, his huge pointed hat threatens to fall into the sink.

He is distracted by my Princess wall phone. He has never seen one and eagerly glides over to examine it. While he is trying to place a call in Polish to the Vatican, my husband rushes in wearing sweaty tennis gear. He is not ready either, and I still haven't started dinner. I am getting frantic. I gesture to my husband, "How shall we introduce him?"

My husband finds a small piece of scrap paper and writes: "YOUR DELIVERANCE."

The pope floats back into the kitchen. Tactfully my husband withdraws. The pope is used to people withdrawing tactfully. He raises his hand majestically. I stand rapt. Slowly he begins to twirl, gradually gaining momentum so that his gowns begin to lift. I see his immaculate slippers, then his black silken stockings fastened below the knee with maroon garters. He spins faster. The robes rise above his strong, chunky thighs, and I behold him — in Excelsis Deo! He *is* Omnipotent, Infallible.

There is not room enough in the kitchen, so I lead him to the living room where the ladies are waiting. They are kneeling in parallel rows, black-laced Christians in one, naked Jewesses in another. Again he nods to me. I am to remove his garments. Carefully I expose the priceless layers, draping each one over my velvet couch, over the chairs, the desk, the coffee table. Revealed at last, the pope reclines contentedly on my deep pile carpet. His glorious erection points heavenward.

One by one we take turns paying obeisance to it. The most devout kneel before it, awed. Others beg favors in low, beseeching voices. Some mount it and glide dreamily up and down like glassy-eyed children on a carousel. When my guests are finished, I lower myself over the pope. I come instantly, again and again, electrified by his blessing. The pope winks at me smugly, then closes his eyes and murmurs: "Amen." Our audience is over. Obediently we file out, leaving him erect and glowing, the everlasting light.

Feliny (sic)

Fingers splayed, I slide my hand
through the thick furry vulnerability
of her belly.
Her legs drop open, wantonly,
and she stretches her neck,
sinking her head into the
tightly whiskered carpet,
waiting for my fingers to reach
her silken neckplaces.

From ear to breastbone to groin
I trace five sharpened fingernails,
lingering to press the heel of my hand
into the soft hollowed expanse
between her legs,
watching intently as her eyes
become glinting slits of pleasure
and her mouth quivers slightly open
as if to whisper to me in feline tongue.

Her breath is warm and sweet
as I lower my face to hers.
My fingers explore her jellied flesh
with slow insistence,
and my rings gleam through her long
black fur as I circle the trembling
moistened spot we now share.

Her tail swishes in sudden violence
and she raises her tiny head,
staring at me through enigmatic eyes,
wary, speechless.
"Hello," I purr.

Trio

"What a beautiful woman," people said after meeting Marsha. The strand of silver in her long mane of auburn hair had nothing to do with age. Age had nothing to do with Marsha. Marsha was an island. Once you set foot there, you entered her territory. You accepted her age, her language, her smell, her scenery. Bewitched, you forgot where you came from.

John was no exception. When I had invited Marsha to spend the summer with us at our cabin on the lake, I knew this might happen. Marsha had always preferred artistic men — painters, poets, actors, men who made a fuss over her, lured by her composure, her mysterious stillness, which they took for strength. But like a mountain pool that draws its water from invisible springs, Marsha nourished her outward calm from constant turmoil deep within herself. Inevitably, she attracted restless souls, who deceived themselves about her and drowned.

Yet John was anything but a restless soul. He was the solid rock in our ten-year marriage. Before I had met him, my life had been very much like Marsha's: a divorce, a series of jobs and relationships, and a lot of madcap schemes about saving enough money to start a gallery in Boston or in London or on the West Coast. Meanwhile, Marsha had made a name for herself as a landscape architect, and I had married John and ventured into motherhood at the ripe age of thirty-five. John taught math, and every summer we added another room to our cabin at the lake to house hoards of boys including John's two sons from his first marriage.

Of course he would go for Marsha, who was so different from myself, so detached, so alluringly passive. I watched his mating dance at first with amusement: his furtive glances, his intense conversations with her about casual matters, the sudden self-revelations. At night, the three of us drank a lot and swam in the moonlight without bathing suits. Afterward John and I made love. It was like starting all over again. We had both become different around Marsha, more alive, more sexy, competing for her attention. Even the boys faded into the background. When they finally left for camp, we hardly noticed their absence. Every day pushed the three of us closer together. We were like a trio of billiard balls clicking, each setting off the other. It seemed strange to me how John and Marsha avoided being alone. As soon as I disappeared into the kitchen, they trailed after me offering help. When I went shopping, they piled into the car with me. Then when John wanted us all to drive to San Francisco together, I changed the game. "Nothing will take me away from the lake," I said to Marsha, "You go with John; you haven't been to San Francisco for years." They didn't put up too much resistance; it was as if they had been waiting for my signal. So off they went.

I felt no jealousy; at least I did not recognize my own involvement in their affair as jealousy. Quite the opposite — I felt intoxicated with power. Even while they were gone, I felt elated. I saw myself in the golden glow of a magnanimous giver. I dreamed up visions of two caressing bodies on a secluded beach at Fort Cronkite or in a Victorian four-poster. Sometimes I was Marsha, sometimes I was John. Slowly he pulled back her nightgown. I saw her naked, her hair spread over the pillow like Snow White. I watched John kneel down and kiss her forehead, gently, reverently, shyly even. Her small breasts greeted his first touch. But her long, nimble thighs stayed close together. Virginal. Ophelia. Still kneeling he sucked her nipples; they were not virginal but experienced, gourmet nipples, now encouraging him to proceed down toward the auburn bush of Irish heather growing from her crotch. For the first time he smelled her woman perfume — Irish heather, Irish moss — that exhilarating perfume of a woman waiting to be tasted, yearning to open her thighs.

Marsha takes her time — a mountain lake that won't warm up until it has soaked up the summer sun. John's hands are summer sun. They singe through ice. They are patient because, in the end, they will win. Languidly, she allows him to penetrate the mossy crevices guarding her privacy even in the most intimate embrace. His lips take over from his hands until she opens herself completely to him. Even at the point of climax, she clenches her fists, fighting to keep to herself. They look at each other like adversaries in the heat of battle. For a moment her green eyes stare at him wide open, broken with ecstasy. Over and over he plunges into the mountain pool, which is no longer calm.

My tension mounted as the day came to an end. I found myself listening for the car, anticipating their return. What if they didn't come back? Watching the golden cast of the evening sun over the lake, I thought of the Greek tyrant Polycrates, who threw his most precious ring into the ocean as a gift to the gods. A fish was brought to him and inside it was the ring. The gods had refused his bribe. They took his wife, his children, his castle, and his kingdom too.

Had I tossed my wedding ring into the water? Was I tempting fate with my little game? It never occurred to me that it was their game until I heard their voices downstairs. They did not call me. They had started a life without me.

When John came to bed, I pretended to be fast asleep, but I was jumpy as a cat on the prowl. He took his time brushing his teeth and going through his regular routine. Finally, he turned off the light and slipped under the covers. His arms reached around my waist. His body felt warm and familiar pressed to my own as if it belonged nowhere else. I nestled against him.

"I love you," he murmured as if he had heard my silent question. Cupping his hands around my breasts, he began to stroke my backside with his swollen penis. In his embrace, my excitement returned. I could not forget that he had been with Marsha. I kept seeing her stretched out under him, longing for him, waiting to be touched by him. When he entered me, I was her, and my vagina throbbed greedily against his cock. It is touching me where it has touched her, I thought, and suddenly the electric charge of an orgasm jolted my body into knowing what I really wanted.

As usual, John went promptly to sleep. I cautiously extracted myself from his tight embrace. He continued to breathe deeply. A slightly smug expression lingered on his face.

Marsha's door was unlocked. She sat huddled in bed with a book on her knees. Her hair covered her like a tent. She looked up apprehensively: "Is something wrong?"

"No, everything is just right," I answered. Gently I eased her back on the bed, spreading her hair over the pillow. I sat down beside her and kissed her forehead. Slowly I pulled back her nightgown. She was snow white. She did not resist.

Voyeuses

The waitress leaned over to wipe the table, and Janet caught a glimpse inside her shirt, provocatively and deliberately unbuttoned. She caught the curve of her young breast down to the nipple before the young woman straightened up.

"Would you like a menu?" she asked brightly.

"No," Janet answered. "Just coffee, please."

Janet looked around the café. A young couple were holding hands at a table in front of a large picture window; they were clearly oblivious to the sun-speckled ocean outside. The man was a little husky with shoulder-length dark hair and rather large features that strained to be handsome. The girl was petite, full-bodied, with thick, wavy, dark hair that she repeatedly pushed back over her shoulders, revealing her bare, tanned skin and full breasts oozing up from a tight elasticized bandeau that compressed what some men would have called "a great pair of eyes." Janet winced to hear herself think that, for she hated the expression but couldn't explain why. A man in his thirties, dressed in working clothes — a mechanic? — looked at the couple from time to time and smoked a cigarette down to toke size before jamming it out in his saucer. A casually but impeccably dressed older woman was seated at the counter. She swiveled her stool around slightly, but Janet couldn't tell whether she was staring out at the ocean or at the couple or both.

No one else came into the café, and, slowly, they all began to form a strange, silent community for Janet. As she looked at the scene in front of her, it was as if a director had said: "Places everyone!" before the curtain call. The waitress brought her coffee and a check and walked away. The young man laughed softly and kissed his girlfriend on the nose. The girl smiled, almost shyly, and Janet noticed that for all of her voluptuousness — clearly appreciated by the devouring eyes of her friend — there was a sweet innocence about her.

Janet reached into her bag, pulled out the hard-covered journal she always carried with her, and thumbed past scribblings, sketches, and half-finished stories to find a clean page. Without thinking, she placed her left arm across the book so that only a minimum amount of writing space was visible to any would-be onlooker. That no one was in a position to look over her shoulder was a thought Janet did not consider; the gesture was automatic. She stared at the young couple for a second and then watched the blue ink flow as she started to write:

"The Café"

Janet hesitated. She looked at the couple again and saw him move his face close and say something. Janet couldn't hear him. She looked down at her journal and started to write again:

"You know what I want to do right now is take you out on the beach and fuck you."

"Oh Gary!" The girl looked away with a smile on her face that betrayed her mock protest.

"What's the matter? We're not exactly strangers, you and I," he teased.

"But after last night, Gary? Really!"

"Hey, I'm not one of those old farts who needs a week to recover! Whaddya think?" Gary looked hard at her for a minute, then said:

"Listen, I just can't get enough of you. You are one hot piece."

"Gary, please don't talk like that. You make me feel cheap." The girl looked down at her hands, and the smile vanished. Gary's face clouded, and he put his fingers under her chin, raising her face to his.

"Baby, hey . . . I'm sorry. I didn't mean it that way. I just mean . . . oh hell, you know what I mean."

She was obviously soothed by his sudden contriteness and answered softly: "It's okay." And then: "You are a classy lover, I've got to give you that." She smiled again, as though surprised by her own words or the admission of her feelings. Gary's face brightened.

"Come on, sweetheart. There's not a soul out there. Let's find a little spot. I've got a blanket in the trunk. I can make you real happy. You know that." He stroked her cheek.

"Yeah," she answered. "You sure can." They giggled, and he pressed his face into her thick mane of soft hair.

"Whaddya say? Let's split, okay?"

"Okay," she said, "but I don't want nobody around, you promise?"

"I promise, I promise," Gary said, jumping up quickly and taking her by the hand. She was slow to get up, and Gary tugged at her. He left money on the table and, as they pushed their way out of the swinging door, the eyes of the other customers followed them. A young mechanic, alone at a small table, jammed out a cigarette into his saucer and left on their heels; a woman in her late thirties stopped writing in her notebook; and another woman, probably in her fifties, looked up from her stool at the counter, her face expressionless.

The two women remaining looked at each other, the younger one in jeans and a thick navy sweater, her hair tied back in a ponytail; the other dressed in a casual but expensive pants suit, the then fashionable safari-olive color, with a bright red scarf tied around her gray-blonde hair. The younger of the two wore no makeup and had the healthy look of someone who was comfortable with herself yet derived satisfaction from doing rather than being. The older woman looked like someone whose monied way of life had frozen her at an indeterminate age for years to come. Her face was expertly made-up; only a woman would know how long it took to achieve the effect of ageless insouciance.

As if on cue, they got up at the same moment and waited beside each other for the waitress to take their money. The writer left first. On impulse, she didn't go to her car but, instead, crossed the street to the beach. It was quiet but not yet hot enough for beachgoers, and anyway, it was a notoriously windy spot. She stopped to pull off her tennis shoes and then dug her toes into the sand. Stringing her shoes together by *their laces, she flung them over her shoulder and began to walk. Ahead of her at some distance, she saw the couple from the café. They were walking hand in hand. Occasionally, they stopped to kiss each other, but the girl always wriggled free, running ahead and making him chase her.*

Not wanting to intrude on them, the woman dallied. She stopped to look at the water, her hands on her hips, her head thrown back. From the corner of her eye, she caught sight of a figure on the beach and turned to look. It was her companion from the café. If she had seemed out of place at the café, perched on a stool (and she had, the writer thought), she seemed even more incongruous on the beach, her sandals in her hand, her leather pouch over her arm. The younger woman turned away from her and resumed her walk in the direction of the couple, who had disappeared from view.

She saw some rocks in the distance that seemed like a good lookout spot and a perfect stopping place. (Doers need destinations, she mused — "be-ers" just walk aimlessly.) When the rocks were in clear view, she began to cut across the sand. At the base of the rocky mound, she sat down and put her shoes back on again. She saw the older woman following in her direction. She started up the rocks, an easy climb, to a flat area at the top. Once there, she stood for a moment to breathe in the salt air. Then she sat down, pulled off the heavy sweater, and hugged her knees to her chest. She closed her eyes and let the sun play on her face.

Suddenly, she heard low voices drifting up from below. "Gary, not so fast!" The voice was plaintive and teasing at the same time. She heard a giggle. Her heart raced. She felt like a child, caught in the delirium of being in a situation she knew was not meant for her eyes. She heard a noise from behind her and turned quickly, as if caught doing something inexplicably naughty. The older woman was making her way up the rocks. Their eyes met, and, involuntarily, she put her finger to her lips, motioning the intruder to be quiet, pointing ostentatiously down to where the couple were. With a knowing nod, the woman continued to climb.

The writer slid herself over to the next rock to make room for her companion and peered over the edge. There they were, in plain view, their blanket spread out in a small cove obscured from the rest of the beach. The girl's skimpy bandeau was curled up at her waist, and her breasts were exposed in all their fullness — breasts that before too many sunsets would fall helplessly to their sides, but which now seemed to reach up and out to the sun and to her lover's eager mouth.

She glanced behind her. Her friend was at the top now, and she motioned her to sit down beside her, again gesturing her to be quiet. In a second, the older woman had stretched herself out gracefully on the adjoining rock. Their view could not have been better had the scene been staged.

Gary's face was buried between the girl's breasts, and his large hands cupped their fullness on each side. He raised his head and then pressed his mouth to her breast; his head bobbed gently up and down as he sucked on her nipple. Her face was to the side, and she was breathing excitedly. Gary slipped his hand down to her waist and deftly unzipped her jeans. The girl stirred and then moved her own hands down to her hips, arching her back and raising her pelvis to push the jeans the rest of the way. Gary sprang up to yank them off her feet, and the women pulled their heads back quickly, lest they be noticed. They gave each other a conspiratorial look before cautiously returning to their vigil. Gary had taken off his own jeans now and was on top of her. His ass was milky white and surprisingly small in contrast to the broad muscular back that now obscured her magnificent breasts. She pushed her hands against him, again saying, with more vehemence this time: "Gary, not so fast . . ."

He rolled off her and lay motionless on his back, breathing heavily. His stiff penis made twitching movements, as if startled by the shock of sunshine and air. She leaned over him and began to trace a childishly nail-bitten finger in slow circles around the silken, slippery head.

The two women shifted their positions on the rock and looked at each other again. The older woman smiled, and the writer smiled back, rolling her eyes playfully. They started to laugh at the same moment, and each covered her mouth to stifle the sound before it burst out. They looked down once more.

The girl giggled. "Funny, eh?" Gary said in a playful but strained voice. In a sudden motion, she went down on him, her lovely thick hair cascading over his pelvis, her warm breasts burning their way through his skin. In a sudden motion, he pulled her head away and said: "Look, baby. You want slow, that's not the way to get it."

"You do me," she said, in that same shy voice that was at odds with her full and ready woman's body. She lay back down as he raised himself up again. He took hold of the bandeau that still encircled her waist and slowly rolled it past her belly to her thighs, where it imprisoned her legs like an oversized ponytail band. Then he sank his head into her crotch. His head moved in butterfly motions as his tongue darted in and around her pungent pink folds. She began to squirm and toss her head from side to side, arching her body up to his mouth. She was breathing heavily, her eyes shut tight. She entwined her hands in his hair and pulled his head closer to her, talking to herself and to him in an audible whisper:

"Oh, do it, baby, do it. Eat it. Oh God. Oh my god. Don't stop. Oh Jesus, God."

Her hand moved to her mouth and she sunk her teeth into her forefinger. He stopped suddenly and looked up at her, then yanked the bandeau from her, opened her legs and moved inside her — all in one swift movement. The look on his face was exultant as she cried out and encircled her legs around his back. After a quick, gasping finish, he rolled off her body and lay still beside her. She was also motionless, her legs splayed, her arms limp, her head turned away from him.

The women looked at each other, their faces now close enough that each could detect light beads of perspiration on the other's skin. The writer signaled that she was going down, and the older woman nodded. They raised themselves up carefully and quietly made their way to the bottom. They walked side by side without speaking.

After some distance, the older woman turned and said, "Well!" in a bright voice. They laughed together. "I don't know about you, but I could stand a drink," the older woman said. "Yes," her friend laughed.

"I don't live far from here. Why don't you just follow me in your car? I feel I know you already. My name is Dora. What is yours?"

"I'm Denny." The two women stood solemnly on the beach and shook hands.

Janet looked up from her notebook. The older woman was smoking a cigarette and staring out the window at the ocean. Janet sipped her coffee and returned to her story.

Dora's house was an enormous mansion around the bend and up a hill from the café. Hidden in the trees, it suddenly loomed up at the end of a long driveway. Denny pulled her car in next to Dora's. As they walked to the door, Denny commented on the house.

"What a splendid place to live!"

"Yes, I love this old house," Dora answered.

"Have you lived here a long time?"

"Yes. Ever since we first married, and that was many years ago."

"Oh, is your husband likely to be here?"

"No, he died two months ago." Dora's face looked strained.

"I am sorry," Denny answered.

"Yes," Dora answered, "I'm not accustomed to it yet. I still expect to see him every time I put my key in the lock."

"Then you live alone now?" Denny said.

"Yes. It's just me and Lady. That's our dog . . . his dog, really. I'm afraid she hasn't adjusted yet either."

"Was it sudden?" Denny asked, not wanting to be one of those people who change the subject when death is mentioned.

"Yes. It was sudden," Dora said simply, as she turned the key in the lock and beckoned Denny inside.

Dora led her through a massive dining room to the kitchen in the back of the house. It was a very large kitchen with a long refectory table in the center. Dora signaled to her to sit down and strode over to the refrigerator. In a second she was back with a pitcher of martinis and two glasses.

"Why, they're all made! You must have been expecting me," Denny said brightly. Dora laughed. "Where is Lady? Doesn't she come to greet you?"

"Not lately. She sits most of the day, sulking by Dan's chair. She won't give up her vigil." Denny wasn't sure what to say next. There was a peacefulness that issued from the house and from this strange woman.

Dora was pouring the martinis into their glasses when she suddenly stopped. "Would you mind if I were to get out of these clothes? I feel constricted."

"Of course not," Denny said. Dora paused a second and her tone brightened.

"Look, I have a wonderful hot tub in my bathroom, and a soak would be just perfect now, wouldn't it?" Denny looked back at her and thought, yes, a tub would be wonderful. They quickly poured the martinis back into the pitcher and returned it to the refrigerator. Denny followed Dora up the wide staircase, through the bedroom, and into a startlingly spacious bathroom. As Denny was looking in delight at the sunken tile tub with art deco motifs around the rim, the marble sink, the thick, black fur rug, Dora called to her.

"The hot tub is in here."

Dora explained that the circular alcove housing the tub was actually an old tower cornerstone of the building. Narrow panes of stained glass had been set high into the stone walls encircling the tub area. Denny looked up. "It's like being in church," she said.

"Yes," Dora answered.

"Is there anything above?"

"Yes, we have a guest bedroom at the top of the tower. Go ahead and take off your things while I get some towels."

Denny began to take off her clothes as Dora moved over to a tall closet, almost hidden in the wall, and pulled out two thick black towels and two white terry robes.

"I can't believe today," Denny exclaimed. "I think I've fallen into some kind of wonderland!"

Dora laughed. "Dan used to call me his 'Alice in Wonderland.' My hair was long and golden when we first married." She hung the robes on two python snakes posing as hooks and placed the towels on a curved bench by the tub. Dora disappeared into the bedroom. Denny finished undressing and quickly lowered herself into the water. Dora was walking back toward her now, completely naked. What a wonderful body, Denny thought; she displays it without a shred of self-consciousness. Dora had replaced the scarf around her head with a wide headband that held her hair away from her face and accentuated her delicate facial features and large blue eyes.

"I'm sorry you're already submerged," Dora said, as she lowered herself into the steaming water. "I'm in a terribly voyeuristic mood today. Anyway, I find women's bodies fascinating, don't you?"

Denny laughed. "Yes, I found myself entranced with that young girl's body. You know, I've never watched anyone make love before. Have you?"

Dora smiled and said nothing.

"It looks as though this wasn't your first time," Denny said when no words came from Dora.

"No, this was not my first time," Dora said, extending her arms out along the rim of the tub.

How gracefully she moves, Denny thought. "Then you've done a lot of voyeuring?" Denny smiled at her made-up word and pretended not to be as surprised as she was at Dora's response.

"Yes, I have done a lot of 'voyeuring.'" Dora acknowledged her word with a warm smile. Her face suddenly became serious, and she spoke without looking at Denny.

"I loved Dan, and when I first found out he was having other women, I was terribly upset. Terribly." Dora's eyes filled with tears. "We talked about it, of course. I really did feel that I should be enough for him, even after all our years together. In fact, our sex life had never been better," she said, looking at Denny again. "I hated the cliché of the situation and the notion that men have an insatiable lust for someone new, different. I suppose that's why I did it — to transcend the cliché." Dora was quiet again, and Denny's mind was racing ahead. Did what? she yearned to blurt out but waited for Dora, who was again staring at nothing in front of her.

After a few seconds, Dora looked at her and said: "I've left you hanging there, haven't I? I don't mean to be a tease. It's just that I've not told anyone this story, and telling it is like reliving it." Dora sighed and stretched her body the length of the tub until her toes hit the opposite side by Denny's head. Denny also stretched out until her own feet were next to Dora's head.

"Well, Dan didn't do anything foolish like promise me he'd never do it again. It was soap opera enough without that. He said a lot of things — not defensively, though. He wanted me to know that it had nothing to do with me or his love, even lust, for me. It was difficult for me to hear him out. I was afraid that at any minute he would say something I couldn't bear — something trite and inexcusable." She paused. "I used to lie awake nights thinking about the right thing to do. Through all of that, we continued to make love, and Dan was as sweet, loving, and powerful as ever. The thought of leaving him in a fit of pride, or pique, or whatever, just seemed too ... stupid and, again, a cliché. Finally, I decided on a course of action, for I had to act. I could not do nothing. 'Bring them here, Dan,' I whispered to him one night after we had made love. He was obviously taken aback but tried not to show it. 'Bring them here?' he repeated.

" 'Yes,' I said. 'let me renovate one of the guest rooms, make it something very special — an exquisitely romantic storybook world for you and your lady loves.' 'And what will you get from that, my Alice,' he had said. 'I will watch you together with them,' I answered. Dan didn't answer right away. Then he asked if that would hurt me or if it really would give me pleasure. I wasn't sure myself when I answered him, but I was able to convince him that it would give me extraordinary pleasure, and so he agreed.

"How I worked on that room! Dan left it all to me. I wanted to have it finished quickly before I could think about what I was doing. The next day would not have been too soon. Fortunately, we have money, and I have a whole crew of people I call on whenever I want something done. The next morning, after he had left the house, I started telephoning. I selected the tower room, right above us. 'Rapunzel's Tower,' I used to call it. I had the carpenters construct an inner circle of wall within the tower so that there was a circular walkway around the room. The windows start up high, just as in this room, and I had them fitted with two-way mirror glass. Everything in the room is itself circular — the bed, the rug, the tables. It was all done in rose tones. I had speakers installed, and before each lover arrived, I would put on music — Indian flute music, sitar, that sort of thing. It's extraordinarily sensual. I put a collection of body oils and incense on one of the tables. I even designed a 'sex chair' — the perfect height and width, with a railing to hold on to."

Dora's face was radiant as she described other details of the room.

"When I had finished it down to the last detail, I brought Dan up to see it. I had turned on the music so that it would be playing when we walked into the room. I could tell from his face that he approved. He looked at everything intently while I stood quietly watching him. He turned to me finally and said, 'I want it to be ours first.'

"He began to undress me very tenderly while I simply stood there. Then I undressed him. We stood there, naked, and just looked at each other for what seemed a long time. He enveloped me with his eyes, feasting on my body as I feasted on his. He stared fixedly at my breasts.

"We stood there, not touching, not speaking. I began to tremble and thought for a second I would come to orgasm. Finally, he pulled me toward him and carried me to the bed. He reached for one of the oils and began to rub my body with its slippery scent, slowly, sensuously, letting his hand linger on my breasts and between my legs. He stroked and caressed me like that for a long time — it seemed an eternity, and, to my surprise, I started to cry." She paused a second. "Then he moved into me, very very slowly, and simply waited there, quite still, as he buried his head in my neck and did exquisite things with his tongue and mouth. I felt myself losing control and struggling to hold on to the moment. I knew if I moved, even slightly, this delicious agony would end."

Dora was quiet. "I'll never forget that night," she said, and closed her eyes. Her face was the face of a woman who had been gloriously fucked.

Denny waited a few seconds and then asked softly: "What about the others?"

Dora smiled without opening her eyes. Then she shifted her body in the water, sending ripples of warmth over Denny's flesh. Dora looked at her friend again.

"The first was Annette," she said. "I liked Annette. Not a beauty, really, but she was exotic in some way. Her skin was olive-toned, and her eyes were jet dark. She had extremely short black hair, almost mannish. Her mouth was very wide and full. She was taller than Dan. She had slim boyish hips and thin arms and legs, but her breasts were low and full, and the dark coloration of her nipples spread across her breasts like bruises. She used to play games with Dan in bed. Usually, she would pretend to be a cat, growling, purring, scratching at him, then sinking her teeth into his neck and laughing wildly. Dan would just lie there and let her play. She was always on top, and it was she who did the fucking. Oh how she would scream when she came!" Dora threw her head back and laughed wildly.

"How many were there?" Denny asked softly.

"Oh many, many," Dora answered, sitting up again in the tub. "Each one is a story. The least interesting was Grace — but then, anyone with the name Grace has got to be dull as dishwater, don't you agree?"

"Did Dan tell you their names?"

"Oh no. I named them myself. Grace was named Grace because she was so Grace-like." Denny bellowed, and Dora continued.

"Oh Grace is over in a minute. She would just lie there, preening and posturing. I think Dan was determined to find a real person there, but poor Grace never did come through. I think she fancied herself in some porno flick. She always seemed to be looking for the camera."

The two women laughed.

"I don't know about you, but I'm ready for that drink," Dora said.

They climbed out of the tub and began drying themselves as they walked to the dressing room. Dora put on one of the robes and handed Denny the other. "There are some scuffs on that shelf," she said.

Once again, Denny padded dutifully back to the kitchen following this intriguing woman. Dora paused at the refrigerator door and said: "Maybe we should cool down a bit first. Let's sit out on the verandah." She led her outside to a long porch that ran the width of the house and looked out to the rocks and the sea beyond. There was a slight chill in the air now, and the sun was beginning to fade. Denny wrapped the terrycloth robe tightly around her legs and stretched out on the chaise beside Dora.

"Wasn't it painful to watch him with those women?"

Dora looked at her sharply before answering.

"It was unbearable."

Although Denny couldn't imagine any woman being able to do what Dora had done with the degree of equanimity Dora affected, nevertheless, she was surprised at her sudden admission and paused before speaking again.

"How long did this go on, then?"

"Right up until he died."

Dora's eyes clouded and she looked pensively out at the ocean. Emboldened by Dora's obvious willingness to answer her every question, Denny continued.

"How did *he die?" she asked.*

Dora got up abruptly and disappeared into the kitchen. Denny remained where she was, confused and feeling chastened for her bluntness. Suddenly, Dora reappeared carrying the martini pitcher and two glasses on a tray, which she carefully placed on the table between them.

"I brought both olives and onions. I forgot to ask which you preferred."

Denny pierced an olive with a bright red toothpick, dipped it into her drink, and rolled it over her tongue before pulling it off its skewer and into her mouth. Dora poured herself a drink, then settled back in her chaise. "Are you warm enough?" she said abruptly.

"Yes, I'm fine, thank you."

"I killed him," Dora said, and took a sip of her drink.

Denny's head spun toward her as though she had been struck. Except for a gentle sadness that played around her eyes, Dora was perfectly composed. There was the sudden cawing of a gull overhead, and Denny thought she heard a twig break under the scampering foot of some small creature in the dunes beyond the porch.

"Oh, I tried other things first," Dora said, breaking the silence between them. "I got the idea of taking another woman up there with me. I had never had a sexual experience with a woman, and because the idea frightened me, I thought surely it would affect Dan. What I wanted from him, I don't really know. I suppose it was too late even then."

"And did you—find a woman?" Denny asked.

"Oh yes." Dora sipped on her martini and reached for another olive. "Yes, indeed," she said again. "Dan was so intrigued with her, or the sight of us together, perhaps, that he asked me to invite her back for him. I felt lost, defeated. She wouldn't have done it, anyway. I knew that. Nor would I have asked her. It was then I knew what I had to do."

She was quiet again. When she looked up finally, she said: "It's quite remarkable how easy it is to kill someone. Oh, I suppose it helped that we have money, that we live in isolation, that we have few friends.

The poison was easy to obtain, and our charming nineteenth-century rituals of tea at four just made it all much simpler than I suppose it would be for someone less fortunate. Imagine working all day and then having to shop, clean the house, get the children off to bed, and, somehow, in all of that, manage to slip your husband some poison?" She looked concerned at the thought and sat quietly while Denny's mind careened around like a Ferris wheel gone amok.

It was decidedly chilly now, and the sun was setting in the sky. Denny looked at her watch and leaped from her chair. "I must go," she blurted out. "I've almost forgotten I had another life." Dora stood up and said: "Yes. I'm sorry. I would enjoy talking with you again and showing you Rapunzel's Tower."

Denny heard herself saying "Yes, I would love to" as though they were dear friends arranging a lunch date. She raced back to the bathroom where her clothes hung in the little dressing area. She forced her mind to be still as she hung the robe back on its hook and jammed her legs into her underpants and jeans. She pulled a brush out of her bag and ran it through her damp hair. She felt a sense of enormous urgency and left her hair loose instead of recapturing it in a ponytail. Dora walked Denny to her car and reminded her of how to return to the highway. With a final wave, Denny pulled away and headed back to the café.

Janet looked up, her pen poised. "Weak ending," she said to herself. Her eyes scanned the café again. Only she and the older woman remained. The sun was setting. She pushed her journal back into her bag, picked up her check, and went to the counter just as the older woman approached with her check. They smiled at each other. As they waited for the waitress, the older woman spoke.

"You were writing furiously," she said. "I've never seen such total concentration."

"Yes," Janet laughed. "I was writing a story that became very absorbing. I'm afraid my characters ran away with me."

"I'm a writer, too," the woman offered. "Gothic novels." She laughed. Janet looked at her curiously. The waitress appeared, and she paid her check. It seemed impolite to say good-bye in the midst of this unfinished conversation, and so Janet waited while the other woman paid her check. They left together and walked toward the parking lot.

"I'm so isolated from other writers these days — from anyone, in fact," the woman said. "Do you come here very often?" Before Janet could answer, she continued. "I need to come out of my cocoon. Perhaps we could meet for coffee and share our writings." Her look was open and direct, and Janet perceived that she was a woman unused to being refused.

"Of course," Janet stammered. "Yes, yes that would be pleasant." Janet had reached her car, and the woman handed her a card. Janet glanced at it.

Dora Cartwright, Woods Way Lane.
Janet looked up quizzically at the woman's face.

"Call me . . . anytime," Dora said. "I'm usually free at a moment's notice."

Janet paused before asking: "Do you have a dog named Lady?"

Dora laughed. "I have a dog — yes — but his name is Max. Why do you ask?"

Janet slid into the driver's seat and smiled. "I don't know. Writers are a little crazy, I guess."

"Yes," Dora laughed. "Call me."

Janet nodded and backed the car out of its white-lined slot. "Say," Dora was waving at her. "What is your name?"

"Denise — Denny," Janet answered. "Denny Mencken."

Janet waved, pushed her foot down hard on the accelerator, and sped down the highway to reality.

Just Desserts

They weren't in the habit of talking much — a fact that hadn't bothered Lilah before. Jed's physical presence alone had been enough to engage her. He was a large, big-boned man whose lumbering gait and relaxed slouch always reminded her of a giant grizzly. She loved his hairiness and the clay-dust aroma of his worn terra-cotta-stained clothes. The first time his gentle, over-sized hands had touched her, they had left big powdery paw-prints on her sweater. With his mark upon her, Lilah had become his in an unspoken way.

Eventually they had found a place of their own in Santa Fe where, since they both were potters, they could share a kiln. But increasingly, to Lilah's discomfort, she felt cut off and alone, more lonely, in fact, than she had ever been when she had lived by herself. As the weeks passed, the fuzzy edges of her discontent sharpened and narrowed, focusing into a critical beam on Jed.

She noticed that Jed's nightly after-dinner snooze was begin-ning earlier and earlier, overwhelming him right at the table before she even had a chance to serve the coffee. Lilah tried cooking lighter meals, drinking less, and talking more, but al-ways his shaggy head would slump forward in gradual jerks until his chin anchored securely on his chest.

Neither the discomfort of the hard kitchen chair nor the clatter she deliberately made as she cleared the dishes aroused him. In-wardly, Lilah raged, wondering why she wasn't the one to fall asleep, leaving the dishes for him to clear. She cursed the silent blackness of the New Mexico nights, the absence of traffic in

Santa Fe streets, the lack, really, of anything better to do. And, most of all, she blamed the unrelenting sameness and security of being a couple.

As summer nights lengthened into autumn ones, Jed's naps deepened, and Lilah feared that winter would bring about a full-fledged hibernation. In desperation she began inviting Alan to dinner. Alan was their best friend, a transplanted New Yorker, who crackled with the excitement of an electrical storm. Lilah marveled that his nervous, urban energy had survived intact despite the diluting spaces of New Mexico. Like a broken recorder, he seemed stuck on "fast forward."

At first, the shock of an intruder, even such a familiar one, shortened Jed's nap to a fleeting twenty-second doze that almost escaped notice. But as Alan's visits became more routine, Jed was soon back into his deep sleeps before dessert was over.

"Dessertus interruptus!" exclaimed Alan the first time it happened. "Does he ever do this during entrées?"

"Not yet!" laughed Lilah.

Unable to resist, Alan slipped a half-eaten brownie off Jed's plate and passed it beneath Jed's nose. He whispered: "I am going to eat your brownie. It's the last one." Alan paused a moment, then added in full voice: "I repeat, I am going to eat the last brownie." Jed's eyelids quivered against the weight of sleep but remained glued shut.

Alan reached across the table, lifted Lilah's hand to his lips, and noisily kissed each finger. Lilah glanced back and forth between the men, delighting in the game. Jed's eyebrows quivered, his upper lip twitched, and his cheeks puffed with each deep, regular exhalation.

Alan rose slowly from his seat and walked to her side of the table. Then, taking her chair in both hands, he tilted it back forty-five degrees and lowered his lips to hers.

His kiss was not the playful peck Lilah expected; it was soft, slow, serious. His gentle lips lingered on hers, as though deliberating, before they opened and pressed on more inquisitively. Floating in the tilted chair with her feet dangling in the air, Lilah would have felt ungrounded except for the ever-deepening kiss.

Without thinking, her tongue searched for his, wanting to make the connection stronger, and her toes curled as the kiss permeated her entire body.

Alan ended the kiss as slowly as he had started it, orchestrating a diminuendo that made Lilah want to weep. Then he set her chair upright and, quietly and deliberately, returned to his seat. Jed's head flopped too far to one side and jerked him awake with a startled grunt, bringing their game to an end.

In the days that followed, Lilah kept inviting Alan to dinner, anticipating dessert with particular relish. As soon as Jed succumbed to the nightly spell, she and Alan invented new games. Alan's ingenuity amazed her. Without leaving her chair, Lilah thrilled to new sensations. She nearly shot through the ceiling the first time he fondled her bare feet under the table. He took each foot between his hands and gently massaged the instep. Then he proceeded to caress each toe, one by one. Lilah leaned back and closed her eyes. The tenderness that Alan lavished on each worn callus made her feel totally adored. Suddenly, a velvety warm wetness engulfed her big toe, sending an electrifying jolt straight to her inner core. Lilah opened her eyes and gasped. Alan was sucking her toe.

"Oh don't!" she moaned. "That's too much."

Alan's tongue slithered over and around her toe. With an involuntary jerk, her hand flung out and knocked her wine glass into Jed's plate, shattering the ecstatic moment.

Still, the vivid memory of Alan's mouth enfolding her toe lingered for days. It reverberated with aftershocks of pleasure and even haunted her dreams. One night Lilah awoke in a sweat: she had been dreaming of chocolate fondue.

In her dream great quantities of the most colorful fruit had been arranged on a platter with the precision of a mosaic. The luminescent colors sparkled — watermelon and cherry reds, nectarine yellow, apricot orange, kiwi green, plum purple, fig black, and banana white. The total effect was incandescent enough to rival the rose window in Notre Dame cathedral. As she lay in bed waiting for daybreak, Lilah made mental notes of all the fruits she would need.

When morning finally came, Lilah secured a date with Alan and promised him the erotic experience of the century. Then, like a shark smelling blood, she readied herself for a food orgy. She began by circling every market in town, stalking only the most perfect fruit. When she returned home hours later, she had a glorious assortment. She washed the fruit, then cut and arranged it on a large tray so that groups of reds, oranges, yellows, greens, and purples converged in a gigantic sunburst. Lilah found the exposed parts of the tray distracting, so she camouflaged them with torn pieces of angel cake. The result was supernatural: her sunburst glittered amid clouds!

Excitedly, Lilah began to experiment with the fondue sauce. She stirred chocolate bars into hot cream over a double boiler until they melted. Then she dipped her finger into the velvet sauce and tasted. It was good but not yet sublime. She added a touch of rum and tasted again. The sauce was better but still wanting something. After several more sips she decided it needed just a dash of instant coffee powder. She sprinkled in a little, tasted, and added a bit more.

Just as the sauce reached perfection and Lilah felt as though she were perched on the threshold of nirvana, the phone rang. It was Alan saying he was with an important client and — "terribly sorry" — couldn't make it. He'd come some other time.

Lilah stood holding the receiver for several moments after Alan hung up. Disappointment flooded her. Reluctantly, she hung up the phone and took the pot of chocolate from the stove. She licked the spoon. Her sauce was exactly right. She stirred patterns in it and grew mesmerized by the soft folds that kept caving in upon themselves. Fantasies of all the games she had wanted to invent with Alan melted into the dark reality of the chocolate. She sipped a spoonful of the sauce. It slipped down her throat, coating her unhappiness with its soothing warmth. She swallowed another spoonful.

Then, very deliberately, she took the biggest strawberry from the center of the sunburst and dipped it into the fondue. The chocolate was still very warm, and some of it slipped off the cool berry and dribbled down her arm. Lilah watched the rest congeal and adhere to the strawberry before she popped it into her mouth. She dipped some pineapple, and with the chocolate coating, it became something new and wonderful. The raspberries reminded her of the bonbons her grandmother always kept—the ones with the runny centers that she liked to puncture. Chocolate-dipped grapes burst deliciously, and she ate one after another, savoring each juicy explosion. The watermelon balls added crunch, a zesty contrast to the softness of the warm chocolate. The dipped banana slices, in comparison, seemed almost pedestrian, but the more Lilah ate, the more she knew she could grow to love them too. Kiwis in chocolate did not quite live up to their visual brilliance, but the mandarin orange segments proved to be a real surprise, and she ate them all. Steadily, Lilah gorged her way through the nectarines, plums, and figs. Strangely, the more she ate, the less full she felt. The weight of her disappointment had mysteriously lifted, leaving her energized and alert. Her voracious appetite amazed her, and she eagerly devoured all the berries and finally the cake, piece by piece.

By now Lilah's dress was splattered with chocolate. She licked the larger spills, careful not to waste a precious drop. Then, very slowly, she lowered both hands into the remaining fondue, raised them up, and watched the chocolate glaze ooze. She sucked each finger, dipped them in again, and delicately pressed a pattern of perfect handprints upon the table top.

As she stepped back to admire her work, Lilah heard Jed shuffling down the back porch steps. Through the window, she watched him find his way around the debris of a summer vegetable garden as he went toward the shed that housed his kiln. Lilah sighed. She hadn't realized how much the garden had suffered. The fragile lettuces had long ago withered to nothing, leaving the vines to take over. String bean stalks now wrestled with yellowed tomato vines. A wilted pepper plant stood apart, barely able to support its abundance of shriveled peppers. Most pathetic of all was an overgrown eggplant. Its leafless branches still bore large, scorched eggplants that sagged like unwanted breasts.

Indian summer was almost over, and the long shadows reminded her that Jed would soon be returning to the house wanting dinner. She suddenly knew it was time to move on. She licked a congealed drop of chocolate from her wrist and went to the bedroom to pack her bags.

Lilah's Chocolate Fondue

Nothing satisfies a chocolate craving more sensuously than chocolate fondue, and no time is better for this extravagance than mid-summer when fresh fruit is in its prime. I always find that shopping for this occasion is every bit as ecstatic as the cooking and eating. The sight of row upon row of ripe blushing peaches and apricots and juicy plums is a feast for the eyes. When no one is looking, I reach out and gently fondle the fruit. I like the flesh to feel firm with just a hint of resistance, and I secretly thrill to the touch of peach down or the unblemished smoothness of a ripe plum, plump and perfect as a baby's thigh. Revel in the abundance of the season, and bring home whatever tempts you that day: nectarines, peaches, apricots, plums, strawberries, raspberries, grapes, watermelon, cherries, figs, pineapple, pears, bananas, apples, or kiwis . . . the more different kinds the better.

Wash and peel the fruit and cut the larger ones into bite-sized pieces. Arrange them in a fanciful design on a large platter or tray. For change of texture you might want to include cut-up sponge cake or angel food cake.

When you can resist the urge for chocolate no longer, set the top of a double boiler over hot (but not boiling) water and combine twenty-four ounces of semi-sweet chocolate with one and a half cups of whipping cream. (You may want to substitute milk chocolate, but I am a semi-sweet lover.) Stir until the chocolate melts and blends with the cream into a velvety smoothness. Dip your fingers in and taste often. Depending upon your desire, add four to six tablespoons of rum or Cointreau or brandy and a trace of instant coffee powder (if you want a hint of mocha).

This amount serves twelve chocolate lovers or one binger.

A Gothic Tale

The old house creaked and groaned. A chill wind sent the branches of the leafless maple tree scratching along the windows of the second-story rooms. Every once in a while there was a rushing sound as the wind pushed piles of leaves off the sidewalk, swirling around the carefully tended lawn of the large house. For a moment the sun came out, and a bright light enveloped the elegant Victorian mansion, and then, slowly, thick clouds moved over it and cast the house into a somber gloom.

The front door opened, and a man walked out, wrapping his thick overcoat securely around him as he descended the stairs. He turned and looked at the house for a moment, then walked up the street, soon disappearing from view. A moment later, another man appeared, coming from the opposite direction. He, too, was wearing a heavy overcoat. A small black leather bag was clutched in his hand. He glanced around nervously, then quickly ascended the stairs to the front door and gave a quick tug at the brass knocker. The door opened, and he quickly disappeared inside the house.

They clung to each other in the hallway for a moment. Then, with their arms around each other's waist, they climbed up the long curving staircase of the elegant house.

"You're sure he's gone for the afternoon?" asked the man, his dark, handsome face smiling at her through the gloom of the hallway. She was tall and thin; her long black hair flowed over the red velvet robe as she hurried him into her bedroom.

"Oh yes," she breathed. "Isn't it wonderful?"

He quickly undressed and threw himself on the bed, pulling her down beside him. They lay there for a moment, silently listening to the wind and the creaking of shutters against the large windows. Then, suddenly, they looked at each other and laughed and embraced for a long time. His body lay on top of hers, and her arms stroked slowly up and down his back. She loved his body. It was so tall and slender. The texture of his skin was fine and smooth. His chest was covered with a heavy down of black hair. She liked to caress it with her palm. In some places it was so thick she could wind it around her fingers. Sometimes she gave a little tug with her thin sharp fingers, and he shouted at her in mock protest. Teasing and caressing each other, the minutes sped by.

"Do you like my nightgown?" she whispered.

He looked at her, admiring the pale transparent skin of her face as it set off her large brown eyes.

"Miss Innocent," he teased. For the first time he noticed the nightgown she wore under her heavy robe.

"Oh, I see, playing sick and waiting for the kindly family doctor!" He burst out laughing. "Oh, I do have wonderful medicine. But what is this you are wearing, a curtain?" He frowned wickedly. With a quick movement he pulled off her robe and pulled the thin material of her gown over her head, throwing it carelessly on the floor.

The yellow gauze of the nightgown collapsed in a soft heap beside the bed, lifting and falling gently with the drafts of cold air that streamed through the big bedroom window. It drifted lightly along the side of the bed, a neglected bit of yellow stuff.

He squeezed her hard. "We don't need clothes. God, your body is so soft and warm . . ." He stopped in mid-sentence. There was a sudden ominous creak on the stairs. They both held their breaths, not daring to make a sound, straining their ears, holding the very blood in their veins still so they could hear better.

Cautiously, he rolled off the bed and crept to the door. He tiptoed to the landing and looked down the stairs. No one there. With a laugh of relief, he threw himself back on the bed.

"Whew, I could get killed!"

He laughed, and she smiled knowingly. It was the danger they loved, the tight merciless danger of being found, making love when it was forbidden. It stirred their senses and made every moment important and intense. They dallied and caressed, their bodies fitting together so perfectly, so gracefully, it seemed they had been made for each other, and not for all the other meaningless people in their lives.

Their lovemaking was passionate and prolonged. They clung together so tightly, a ray of sunlight could not have come between them.

The yellow wisp of gauze danced on the floor, the lonely sunbeam cast out of its place.

Every sound in the old house was magnified, bigger than life, like the family Bible that sat ponderously on the bureau. Relaxing at last against the big pillows covered with immaculate white-starched covers, they stared solemnly at the ceiling. An impish smile flitted across her face, and she suddenly got up from the bed and walked to the bureau. She picked up the heavy Bible, hugging it to her. Laughing delightedly, she fixed her gleaming brown eyes on him, her long hair streaming over her soft shoulders. The doorway outlined her slender body with the fragile breasts crushed against the heavy book.

The yellow gauze stopped dancing and hunched up in sudden apprehension.

"Yes, judge and jury, I swear it is true," she intoned in mock seriousness. "We dared to do it. We broke the command. . . ."

The yellow gauze crept behind the bed. A gust of wind rattled the windowpanes fiercely and the startled lover half-rose from his icy pillow, a smile frozen on his handsome face, a smile of eternity.

"Yes, ladies and gentlemen, this is the room, the very room, where the heinous murder was committed." The guide pointed to the pictures hanging on the wall.

"This little lady's husband came home and found her with her lover. Enraged, he shot them both with a pistol he always kept downstairs in case of intruders. It was the crime of the century! They found her lying on the floor, right there where you can see the dark bloodstains. She was clutching an old family Bible to her breast. He must have tried to force her to confess or something. And that other picture, that smiling, dark, handsome man, he was the family doctor, a trusted friend. He was her lover. They found him lying on the bed, one shot through the heart. They say he had a smile on his face."

And the wind blows around the corner, and her lover lies there with his slender body, smiling, smiling as the blood washes his life away, and the thin wisp of yellow gauze dances lightly like a sunbeam and the thick black hair veils the luminous body as it sinks to the floor.

"Yes, judge and jury, I swear it is true. We dared."

Grooming Fishwife

Grooming fish, in some species called "damsel fish," enter the mouths of larger fish, even predatory ones, to rid them of parasites and debris. Some of these "fishy" relationships are intimate and permanent; others are looser. Whether both benefit from the relationship has not been conclusively established. The damsel who takes up housekeeping in the mouth of a predatory fish is generally assured of a safe lair and immunity from harm, although mishaps do occur.

Deep in his deepest yawn
I have lived and moved and had my
Being
Like grooming fish, lodged in his mouth,
I have picked the debris of countless breakfasts
From his teeth
Sometimes, admittedly, posing as a
Maid
In my starched uniform
To gain entry
Startling him only when, berserk, I
Strip off my clothes
Commit mayhem,
And run, screaming,
Down the red-carpeted runway of his tongue
With cameras flashing
And women snarling
"She never really *cared* for him, you know."

V.   BACK IN MY LIFE

O*ne distinct pleasure generally denied the very young woman is the experience of having a former lover reenter her life. Each recurrence carries with it the headiness of previous encounters. Like sexual experience, whether in the moment or over the years, the ecstasy of the present clearly owes its richness to ecstasies past.*

The first experience of meeting the eyes of one who knew you intimately in another time, another place, is a piercing exchange in which you both stand, terribly naked, for an elongated second before speech comes.

You swallow hard and say: "Is it you?"

Then the rituals begin.

"It's been a long time . . ."

"Tell me about yourself now . . ."

"What ever happened to . . ."

If there is any magic left, you arrange to meet again. You prepare yourself for this meeting with elaborate care. The dizziness you felt when years were compressed into seconds is now exactly reversed: you see yourself in slow motion, and your self-preoccupation is total. You find yourself protective of your memories, perhaps unwilling to damage their crystalline containers with the invasive present. You dress, hiding this a bit, accenting that, remembering a color you shared like a favorite song. You sprinkle your appearance with something old, something new, all the while watching new memories, like embryos, expand and elaborate their delicate features.

When you meet him now, the exchanged look has lost its nakedness. You are both planted firmly in your present and separate selves that challenge each other to hold out against the quicksand of nostalgia. You wait for him to push you to the edge of the swirling eddy. He circles cautiously and waits for you. You talk, and— sooner or later— in a sudden remembered incident, you reach out at the same moment, and it begins.

Il Mio Tesoro

I was standing with other students half my age, waiting for the class to break so that we could pile in. We heard the familiar rustling noises inside as books closed and papers were jammed into bookbags and briefcases. Above the rustle, there came loud shouts of the professor trying to give last-minute instructions to a class eager to move on — to the next class, to a café, to a waiting friend. The door burst open, and the students all around me began pushing their way into the room before those inside could get out. I hung back, waiting for a more civilized moment to enter, when he appeared — like me, distinguished from the others by his age. Except for a little more pronounced stoop to his shoulders and a few gray hairs in his sideburns, Giorgio had not changed that much in the twenty years since I had last seen him. He still had the kind of face that in repose was so doleful you almost wanted to laugh. It was a large face, with solemn eyes that stared out at you and a nose that looked as though its maker had intended to come back and finish shaping it but forgot.

I said "Giorgio" and he said "Beth" in the same instant and with the same tentative intonation. By now, the other students were coming between us in their scramble to get inside. We moved away from the door and, in quick, overlapping sentences, said all of the dumb things you say when you haven't seen some-one in twenty years and can't quite recall the relationship. When I saw that a student was about to close the classroom door, I pulled away from him, nodding in assent to his invitation to have dinner that night. "Yes, here's my address. Fine . . . see you at seven."

As I showered and dressed that evening, I was still frustrated by how little I could remember of Beth at nineteen and Giorgio at twenty-one. The fragmented memories that drifted in and out of my mind kept getting stuck on the silliness between me and my girlfriend as we vied for his attention at a campus dance.

"I think he's interested in you," she had said.

"Don't be silly, it's you he's been staring at all night."

"I think he's just shy."

"Look at those eyes!"

"What nationality do you think he is?"

I stopped to stare at myself in the mirror, straining to see my face as he would see it, as he *had* seen it earlier that day. Of course I had changed—for the better, I thought. I tried again to conjure up more details of our relationship. When I shut my eyes, I saw him sitting in an old, falling-apart stuffed armchair in my little $32-a-month apartment looking with interest at a drawing I had done. Had we ever kissed? I squeezed my eyes tightly together as though it would help bring him back more clearly. Blank. Nothing.

On the way to the restaurant he had selected, we managed to fill the space with more trivia, interrupting each other in our nervousness and laughing like new lovers. When the waiter left us to look at the menu, Giorgio reached across the table, took my hand in his, and gazed passionately into my eyes.

"How wonderful it is to see you," he said in a husky but low whisper. In his Italian accent, the "wonderful" became "wonnnn-derrrrful." I found myself confused and embarrassed. It was obvious that he remembered far more about me, about us, than I did. He asked what I was doing now, and I covered my distress by launching into unnecessary detail about the present.

It was clear throughout what turned out to be a long, lingering, romantic dinner that he assumed we shared the same memories. I finally relaxed and treated him as though he were a new man in my life (he might as well have been). If something about the past came up inadvertently, I avoided making direct responses, letting my smile cover my uneasiness.

My distress returned when we got back to my house. It was simpler to invite him in than to stand outside searching like an adolescent for the right parting words. I left him on the couch and escaped to the kitchen for brandy and glasses. I was aware, with mixed feelings, of playing the older woman whose furnishings were a far cry from the hand-me-down armchairs and stacked orange-crate bookcases we all had in those days. I placed the snifters on the coffee table and sat a cool distance from him on the couch. Without looking at his glass or reaching for it, he again grasped my hand in his and said "Darrrling." I took a deep breath and ventured a remark.

"You know," I laughed — lightly, I hoped — "I don't seem to remember a lot from those days."

He didn't answer but looked down at my hands, both now clasped in his, and raised them slowly to his lips, tenderly kissing one and then the other. When he finally looked up at me, he was smiling broadly.

"Of all the memories I hold of you," he said, "the one I think about most these many years is going to the little store in the morning to find you a cantaloupe. Do you remember how much you liked the cantaloupe?"

I felt the blood rushing to my face and knew that he would interpret my blushing as a response to shared memories, when, in reality, it was my shock at the implication of what he had said. What is wrong with me? How could I have forgotten so much? I agonized, making a mental note to see a therapist as soon as possible.

As my mind raced in circles, he pulled me to him and, the next thing I knew, his mouth was on mine — full, soft, and sweet beyond description. I melted against him and found myself becoming Ingrid Bergman whose lover's cinematic kiss in some long-ago movie opened door upon door upon door in seemingly endless progression. (Whatever the film, I remember being young enough to have said to myself: "So that's the way it is!") And now, the 39-year-old woman wanted to feel Giorgio's body hard against her while, at the same moment, the adolescent girl wanted to go on kissing him with the virginal passion that has no further expectation. As for him, he seemed equally content to stay with long, passionate kisses, as though there were no place a kiss need go.

I savored the sense of timelessness I was experiencing and, as the kiss went on, I marveled that his mouth alone could bring me to such a state of excitement. As we stirred between kisses, his lips and cheeks brushing lightly against mine, I caught a glimpse of his face. It wore a delicately pained expression that excited me as much as if he had touched me with his big, warm, gentle hand.

He finally did pull away and, with a 21-year-old's playfulness dancing in his deep, melancholic eyes, said: "Do you still have that lumpy bed?" (adding before I could respond) "You must know how much I would love to find you a cantaloupe in the morning."

The observer in me was taken aback at my boldness as I took his hand in mine and, without hesitation, led him to my bed-room. We flung ourselves on top of the covers and I beckoned him to let me have his mouth again. Only now did he move his kisses from my face to my neck to the vulnerable spot between my breasts, and back to my waiting mouth — all with the same unhurried and tender care, as if, indeed, there were "world enough and time."

Our lovemaking accelerated, yes, but it did so in liquid slow motion, our silence broken occasionally by whispered gasps, barely audible groanings, and muted cries, until, at long last, an enormous peace filled the room. Too languid, too peaceful, to worry any more about how he would react to my obvious repression of our shared past, I asked sleepily whether we had ever "done this" before. Giorgio raised himself on one elbow and looked down at my face, tracing his finger along my cheek and across my lips.

"Tesoro," he whispered. "Surely you remember?" He smiled down at me. " You always said I was too fast."

With the word *tesoro,* the locked-up or forbidden memories suddenly avalanched into consciousness. "Tesoro," I cried.

"That's what you used to call me . . . 'Il Mio Tesoro.' I remember, Giorgio, I remember."

Giorgio reached for me and we held each other close, laughing like two errant children caught in the warp net of time, unwilling to come home.

Obbligato

It is November. I have come back to England after nearly twenty years of living, an expatriate, in a city of seaweed and mother-of-pearl. Since July I have been back. This gaunt city of London is a felled giant, gray and sprawling, and as crypt-cold as it has always been in my memories. I remember now the city's cold wet tongue licking my legs as I hurried to meet (on Waterloo Bridge with free tickets for a concert in Festival Hall) the man who was then too shy to be my lover.

At that time he despaired of me, finding my seagreen eyelashes and my promiscuity (with its underlying sorrow) bewildering, but now that he is my lover he is full of hope. He has taken me in hand. He is a tall, neat, narrow man, and he wears the same clothes he wore when I first knew him, almost twenty years ago. Then he was a music student, poor and pale. Now he is a famous musician. He is still pale. He lives in a tall, neat, narrow house on the edge of Hampstead Heath, and I spend a lot of time gazing at the poplars that border his garden.

I reflect how unlyrical is our love affair. Within this garden there are many apple trees. Last summer we lay in an uneasy embrace under these trees while apples dropped all around us with dull explosions, like hand grenades. I was tense with the mortal terror of a direct hit, so our reunion (the first in nearly twenty years) across the spiny desert of our respective histories was fraught with suspicion. The falling apples did not worry him at all: it seems he spent all his free time there on fine days, composing harmonies under a barrage of vegetable fire. Of course, I was deeply moved by this fine oblivion to death or maiming. But I grew increasingly alarmed at the precision and timing of the missiles.

We went indoors as the sun sagged behind the poplars, and in the familiar deadening chill of an English house at day's end, we huddled together in a large leather chair. My remembered glamour, he told me afterward, was in contrast to my bright red nose, corpse-white hands, blue cheeks, and to the socks, sweater, dressing gown, and blanket, which I had borrowed to keep from freezing and through which he tore access to my shivering skin. Had he undressed me fully, I would have died of exposure. He took me home, intact, astonished, and more than a little grateful.

Now, in the bleak mid-winter, I spend more and more time indoors, in his house on the edge of the heath, watching the lovely, lilting formalities of his garden change under the veils of frost. His body bursts into flowers and ashes each time we collide in the straits of his narrow bachelor bed; mine retorts like a firearm to his shadow across the light, to his shape on the hanging air. It is so cold. Central heating accepted and installed, English houses are still marrow-cold.

In his house, in the entrance hall, his two great harps loom like cathedrals. Silent, fabulous, phantasmagoric, they are the guardians of his enshrined heart. One harp wears an overcoat and galoshes. They have a pact. He can fall on it without warning, spin it around, heft it to his shoulder like a stunned Sabine and stride away, slamming into his car and driving off at dawn to have his way with it in a recording studio somewhere. The other stands with naked feet in its own spilled cornucopia of strings, scrolls, and languid, drooping curves. It is arch, provocative, and as blatantly, conditionally available as a high-class courtesan.

I am in love with it, of course. I am besotted by its promises. I feel it alive. I flirt with it when he's not present: whispers, glances, smiles, all the minute sensual signals of the body's language. I wish it would notice me. Once I dared a caress: I touched it, lightly, a lover's touch; I almost screamed with the pressure of excitement. I ran my fingers along the thrilling strings and received the clear, low, singing response like a hand on the base of my spine.

But he heard. Oh, no! He came thundering down the stairs. "Strength, darling!" he shouted. "You must *not* be afraid to attack!" And he flung the lovely creature across his shoulder like a fireman making a rescue from a seventh story. I fled to the opposite wall and shrank against it, watching the ritualized ravishment with blood beating in my throat, my skin raw, as the crystalline bubbles of sound filled the room, piling up on the ice-bound silence of the implacable winter dusk.

Oh, he is magical, magical. He is a Pan figure painted on the lid of a crumbling sarcophagus, a mythological projection from the vapors of my own heavy-lidded dreams, grappling a sacrificial swan. I know I should pour libations, proffer appeasements, flowers, incense. I feel myself sliding down the wall as a captive creature, possessed at last, completes its ecstasy and is brought to shuddering stillness. I cannot move. My breath binds my feet to the floor and my back to the wall. I wonder if I am dying. I stare at him, at the priestly reticence of his body taut in the containment of mastery. He is a fossil, he is ancient, an extinct sea-form stretching back in time. The flow of his body is all benign.

When the very seconds are textured (as at times just prior to lovemaking or now, like this), I stare at him, at the sweet, fragile facts that never change: skin like powder polishing his brow, his cheekbones; curls clustering on the tenderness of his nape; the frailty, the endurance of the shoulders and chest in contradiction to the sinewed arms; the muscular, competent, jealously guarded hands. There is too much magic. Too much time has passed. Too many mysteries, enormous, shrouded, are hovering with pterodactyl wings across the oyster light of my deductions. *Who is he?*

He finishes the piece: one tiny gesture — chill as a truth — of his palm upon the vibrating membrane of sound, and the harp falls silent, the room returns, and with it my lover to me. Oh, my magician. I move across to him, sitting at the harp, and as he gently rights it, I slide my hands over his shoulders, under his jacket, and across his chest. I bury my nose in the fabric of his skin below his jaw. I inhale him like fine powder. I enfold him like a snake. He turns his head, surrendering the alabaster mask of his face to my fingers, which press everywhere because I am making memories. Where is my awe of him? In this moment I love him. I dissolve in a storm of fire and roses, lost indeed to clarity and vision, for there are eagles screaming from all my hidden ledges, and tigers are prowling the surfaces of my skin. The fabric of time has acquired a nap like velvet for us to loll upon: languid, orgulous lovers with age-old pretensions to an ultimate power.

Bernadette's Warthog Pie

This recipe, sifted through the Mediterranean strata of my consciousness, derives from a blameless, pastoral preparation known to the English as "Shepherd's Pie," lauded for its economy of purchase and preparation. In its original form, using mutton, it conjures up rather dismal images of survival: lonely crofts, worn women in shawls stooping over smoking peat fires, acres of heather, and flocks and flocks of eminently shockable sheep.

Well. The odalisque palate (and mine was ever such) stirs restlessly on its satin couch, yawns, touches its lips with its napkin, and, excusing itself, falls asleep. Not because mutton is used. No, indeed. For me, mutton is a fertile, racy ingredient. The very sound of the word propels my imagination toward all manner of exotic, pearls-in-the-navel culinary extravagances — couscous, aubergine, choux farcis, petits pois à la menthe.

Yet Americans, alas, respond to the mention of mutton with the same dread as they do to the idea of socialized medicine. It is not clear what nameless pox will fall upon our house if I bring mutton past its portals. I have therefore adapted the recipe to the use of ground lamb, easily found in the meat section of the supermarket or ground to your request by that sweet man with the laugh crinkles around his eyes at the corner butcher shop. For two people, a pound of ground lamb is quite sufficient.

*Next, purchase one of those exquisite curly cabbages called savoy. They're very round and crisp and of a particularly subtle shade of green. The other cabbages, those pale, tight, smooth spheres, **smiling** their virginal Mona Lisa smiles, will not do at all. You never feel that you've violated a savoy: it gives itself joyfully and without regret.*

Now choose the potatoes. Inhibit, if you can, your desire for those small white globes whose skins roll back at the touch of a thumb;

quickly cooked with mint, they are rhapsodic, yielding, and yet resistant on the tongue, but they are unnecessary here. Keep them for another lamb occasion (and Rose the leg woman has one): a succulent three-inch chop, perhaps, jeweled with mint jelly; or a leg of lamb roasted to the palest pink, brushed with tarragon, stuffed with apricots, preceded on the same menu by a sardonic sorrel soup.

The potatoes I prefer for Warthog Pie are the forthright, Idaho kind with rough, clean skins and shapes that exactly fit your hand. Take about four of these, peel them, cut them into slices, and set them to cook covered in a saucepan of water, to which you have added a few grains of sea salt.

Put the ground lamb into a seasoned iron skillet with salt, pepper, and about five cloves of finely crushed garlic. Make sure the meat does not clump into balls; it must be granular and well separated when cooked. Lower the heat under the skillet, and turn your attention to the herbs you will use for seasoning.

I use only fresh herbs, ones I grow myself. If you have an herb garden as I do, now is the time for a pause in the fresh air and the redolence of these aromatic shrubs and leaves. To enter an herb garden is to embrace a trance state, and it is very much a part of the experience of cooking. Take time, then, to select and pick the herbs you will need: rosemary, mint, and lemon balm. Roll them in your hands, and inhale the aromas of the sprigs on your palm. Close your eyes, breathe, relax.

When you are refreshed, return to the kitchen. The lamb is cooked and is bubbling gently in its juices. Skim most of the fat from the liquid, and add one ounce of brandy. Increase the heat slightly. When the agitation in the skillet becomes intense, add four ounces of white wine. Cook gently. Crush the herbs with a pestle and mortar so that the herbs give up their oils and mingle with one another. Add them to the lamb and stir.

Inspect the potatoes. If they yield to the merest stroke, remove them from the stove, drain them, and return them to their saucepan, adding salted butter and a touch of coarsely ground pepper. Pound the potatoes to a velvety smoothness; then add a spurt of cream. Gently tease them with a fork, easing away any rigidities that may have formed, transforming the whole into a supple, yielding mass. Cover the *pan, and set aside. Do the same with the lamb.*

Turn your attention to the savoy cabbage. Remove the stem with a sharp knife, and ease each fragrant leaf apart so that it resembles a great green rose. Place it in a colander, and bathe it in a shower of warm water, making sure the base of each leaf is drenched. Shake the excess water from the leaves, and set about shredding them finely, perhaps using one of those curved, two-handled blades that lend themselves so readily to a rhythmic, rocking motion. Use the entire vegetable: the strong thrust of the leafy slivers will subside dramatically when cooked. Cook the cabbage uncovered in about two inches of boiling salted water for about a minute and a half. At all costs, the color of the leaves must be retained; there can be no limp and pallid results. Drain the savoy, and retain the liquid in which it has cooked.

Slowly add the liquid to the cooked lamb, stirring gently and avoiding any premature outpouring of fluid. If the sauce becomes too diluted, thicken slightly with a teaspoon of potato starch mixed to a thin cream with cold water. However, you may want to taste for seasoning if you do this, and adjust accordingly. I would just mention at this point that variety is the very essence of success in this field. Be adventurous and experimental. A slavish obedience to instructions could result in an insipid and disappointing experience.

All is ready for the climax, the union of all these detailed preparations. Select an attractive, shallow dish that responds favorably to heat. Warm it slightly. Spread the cooked ground lamb on the bottom of the dish, then the cabbage in a joyful green layer. Surprise it with a quick squeeze of lemon, and now the coverlet: the creamy billows of mashed potato slightly rumpled, a little disheveled by the fork you use to spread it. Soothe with little dabs of butter over the surface. Then broil briefly until the peaks and troughs are touched with gold.

And now, take off your apron. Step back, inhale deeply. The air around the stove shimmers and becomes translucent. Is this a mirage? What are these silken tents, these veils, these sounds of finger cymbals? Go to your divan, stretch out upon it, and deliver yourself to the expectation of bliss.

The Hot Tub

"Nothing," said the hostess, "nothing ever happens in a hot tub." She had said this reassuringly to Christina as she showed off her new house and not incidentally her new marriage. Christina not only mistrusted Gwen's assurances but wondered why she was the sole remnant of the old crowd to be invited for the house- and husband-warming. Enthusiastically, Gwen had scooped her up from the crowd to pass her around like an hors d'œuvre: "This is Christina, my oldest friend." Christina realized that the word "old" did not have a particularly valuable connotation with Gwen. Typically, she had not even bothered with her old furniture. Presumably, it had stayed with her old husband or her old job. This time she had not even taken the children with her into another brand-new life. That's how spontaneous Gwen could be. "You've got to keep moving," she used to tell Christina, "or you'll be stuck in a hole so deep that you can't get out." Although she blamed Gwen for all the devastation she left behind, Christina admired her courage to blast off into the unknown.

Christina guessed she had been invited merely to witness this new venture, to learn a lesson from the hostess, who now sat down on a large orange pillow, floating on a white carpet, between white designer tables and flower containers, alabaster sculptures and art deco mirrors. The orange pillow set off Gwen's black designer dress; open to the navel, it exposed her tiny breasts from a seductive angle. Neil, the new husband, made drinks and worked the blender, often kissing his bride on the shoulder.

Christina felt like an antique with her twenty-year marriage, her secure job in the library, her inherited Victorian furniture, and three practically grown daughters, who still lived at home with all their pets.

Would she have accepted Gwen's invitation if David and the girls had not gone off on their annual backpacking trip? She knew that David sided with Gwen's first husband and refused to have anything to do with "that woman." But Christina remained loyal to their lukewarm friendship for old time's sake when she too had been reckless, high-spirited, and nonconformist. Not that she regretted her own choice of settling down, but she couldn't refuse a chance to glimpse Gwen in her newest element.

Finishing her martini, Christina wandered aimlessly toward the swimming pool where several guests splashed noisily. They wore no clothes, which didn't matter because the lights had been turned off. Only candles in glass containers beckoned softly. The martini made it easier to give in to a strange sense of rebellion and curiosity. Christina opened her blouse first, then her bra, a little startled by the breeze that touched her skin ever so slightly. Then she quickly dropped her skirt and panties and plunged into the pool's anonymous darkness.

"I thought it was heated!" she screamed. Her voice drowned in shrieks and gurgles from the others, who all seemed to feel that safety was in noise and numbers. I don't have a bad figure, Christina thought. Actually I look better without clothes, which is more than Sue or even Gwen can say. They overdo the tennis and the fasting, which gives them that old leather-over-bones look. Christina swam vigorously to give herself a sporty, purposeful air, but the cold was getting to her, as was a large body with a long beard—not her type at all. He seemed to invite sudden collisions by cutting into her lane. When he tried to catch her by the ankle, she decided to take refuge in the hot tub.

It slurped in darkness, filled with bodies. "One more, make room for one more," they cried gaily, compressing themselves so that she could slide in between assorted legs. A glass of wine found its way into her hand. Somebody began to massage her left calf deftly. The conversation turned from the election to a pub on Picadilly Circus that everybody loved without remembering its name.

"I remember when it was so full that you couldn't talk, you had to shout into each other's ears, and there was no place to put down your glass," shouted Bob, a political science professor. To demonstrate, he reached behind Christina's back and around her front. More willing hands came across her neck and under her arms, as well as under her thighs. A hand massaging her calf moved up to her thigh and fumbled a bit, trying to move higher. Christina was too busy interlacing her hands with arms and legs to be able to interfere with that hand, even when it no longer rested quietly but felt its way deeper, accompanied by the thrust of a Jacuzzi jet. Closing her eyes, she barely listened to the cocktail-party voices, concentrating on her wish that the hand on her thigh would continue to fondle her crotch. It was so easy to enjoy the play of an isolated hand extended from an unknown body. Then she felt a second hand around her waist, and a third began to make delightful rounds between her breasts and her stomach.

It seemed only courteous to pass along such favors to some-body else within comfortable reach. To her surprise, she found a woman. The sensation of touching a breast surprised Christina. It was different from her own — longer, softer. "So that's what a man feels — maybe the one who now touches mine," she thought in a rather detached way. Her own breasts were definitely in the hands of a man. The woman gave no sign of encouragement to Christina. Maybe she preferred to ignore what was happening to her. Maybe she too savored it all in utter concentration.

After her initial exploration, Christina found it impossible to pay further attention to her passive neighbor. There was some-thing disturbingly familiar about that playful hand under her buttocks. Keeping her eyes closed, she felt for the arm that belonged with it. But before she could get much closer, the hand took hold of her own and guided it to a penis, which quickly hardened in her politely accommodating fist. "Hi there, how are you?" said a very familiar voice. Her heart skipped a beat. She pulled back her hand as if she had touched fire. Only one person in the world said, "Hi there, how are you?" that way — Stephen.

"It's you," she answered tonelessly, refusing to open her eyes.

"You didn't know, did you?" he asked triumphantly.

"I guess I did, but I didn't want to," she sighed remembering their last partings. Through all these years the memory of her pleasure with him was as sharp as the pain that lingered after each encounter, so that once and for all, she had decided to stay away from him. The price was too high.

"We must stop meeting this way," he chuckled.

"I thought we had," she replied dryly.

His hand came back to her. She did not push him away. He gently flipped his fingernail against her pubis. He remembered. There was no man who knew so well what turned her on. Sometimes his expertise had annoyed her because, like all experts, he took great pride in his work. Sometimes this was exactly what she wanted. She would fling herself on the bed anticipating what he would do, high, before he even pulled her panties off. There were so many variations to every meeting, to every game they played. Sometimes they only had a few moments in the car; sometimes they stayed together for a day. Sometimes they saw each other surrounded by people; then every word was meant for the other. They had a wide scale of special innuendos that nobody else could understand. The knowledge that he was never hers, except for these brief moments, created a special passion. The memory brought tears to her eyes. They mixed with the steam of the hot tub. "Passion," she thought, "I had so much passion."

All this time the other bodies purred around them flirting, splashing, climbing in and out. Gwen shouted from the far end of the garden that dinner was being served. One after another they heaved themselves out of the water. Automatically Christina got up to follow the dripping contingent to the house.

"Stay," Stephen held her foot anchored to the bottom of the tub.

"I can't," she protested, "I must go."

"We've never done it in a hot tub," he insisted.

"We didn't have hot tubs then," she couldn't help laughing, although the tears still kept coming.

"Well, then, we owe it to ourselves to give this a try. It's a first for me. We don't have them in the East, at least not where I hang out."

"And where is that? The last I heard from you you were in London. You sent me a postcard of the queen."

"We didn't hit it off. I have a nice place in New York now, a condo near the Cloisters; why don't you come with me?"

"How long do I have to pack?"

" 'Til tomorrow. I'm leaving on the eleven o'clock flight."

They were alone in the water. To have him back, to have him one more time, one last time. She sank back into the warm water. He scooped her up in his arms.

"I mean it," he whispered into her ear, "I want you, I want you all the time. There is nobody as crazy as you. You are just about the craziest woman I know. Remember that time when we couldn't wait for a motel, when we parked right behind the library like kids?"

"Shh." She covered his mouth with her hand and licked his earlobe. His face had not changed, though his beard was now gray. If he shaved it off, he would look no different from when they had first met, more than twenty years ago.

"The first time you said that you were also going to New York, to Columbia, remember? They offered you a fellowship. You told me to pack my things and be ready the next morning."

"You weren't."

"How could I be? I hardly knew you. Besides, you didn't mean it. But I came close to taking you up on it, simply to call your bluff. The idea turned me on: bride runs off with best man. I just loved it."

"Did you love me?"

"Of course not. I was in love with David. Having two men was not in style then."

"Neither were hot tubs."

Her head floated on top of Stephen's chest. Cradling her buttocks, he moved her around in circles like the hand of a clock. Time went back, the years disappeared, then it stood still. They had caught up with each other.

"Your breasts are the same—so round and firm. I've never forgotten the feel of them. I can lie in the dark and hold them in my empty hands."

"Kiss them, suck them," she begged. Then she turned over and let him kiss her buttocks and the small of her back. The water made their movements languid, unhurried, soft. Christina's frenzied shivers melted in and out of dreamy stillness. All remembrance of pain evaporated in the resurgence of their intimacy. They kissed their old kiss, their lips brushing softly against each other. Then the tips of their tongues teased each other while their bodies pressed together and their hands touched those secret places that they had discovered long ago. Whether he was with her or not, he belonged to her life. What would it have been without him?

Later, they sat arm in arm in their bubbling kettle, looking like missionaries boiling for cannibals. At least, that's what Gwen said when she found them and brought them back to reality with a tray of chicken teriyaki.

Relics

Rummaging through my childhood room
I retrieve your letters
which have been lying in state these twenty-five years
in a bottom drawer, my private archives.

Wizened rubber bands break open in shock,
and stacks of blue airmail envelopes collapse,
scattering their patriotic shrouds
bordered in red, white, and blue.

Torn envelopes, bent and brittle as dead moth wings,
guard the contents respectfully,
but flag-covered coffins and six-cent stamps
don't stop grave robbers.

The pages are lined, yellowed vellum,
starched and pressed into neat, indelible folds,
inscribed with calligraphy pen
that breaks the rules
and vomits inkblots and soul-felt confessions —
your heart always showing between the lines.

Some letters typed on onion skin
feel like braille:
the force of your periods and exclamations punctured
the thin membrane, leaving
tiny holes.

I would gladly have traded these scriptures
for your touch,
but the continental distance
and your sentence to boarding school,
without bond or bail,
forced this evidence.

We went on to love and marry others,
have children, lose touch,
but your airmailed words lift me up
as much as they ever did,
and I float knowing that
we cared.

VI. GAMES WE PLAYED

WARMING UP

In the early days as we struggled to embrace the slippery Muse, Sabina dreamed up writing games to get us started. This playful technique unlocked our sensual imaginations. One of our first games required each of us to fill in a story about a random encounter between a man and a woman. Jenna pioneered with a vignette about a woman at a hotel who inadvertently opened the wrong door and confronted a total stranger. Her pen froze at that point. Nell burst into the room and undressed the stranger like a big wonderful doll. Bernadette was even more daring. She called a cab and whisked him off into the night. Months later, "releasing the lock of the heavy door," Jenna was at last able to face her stranger in the security of her own room in "The Prisoner."

The Room

Dripping rain, with her briefcase in one hand, purse over her shoulder, a sack of books in her arm, she opened the door to her hotel room, stumbled inside, and kicked the door shut with her foot. To her surprise a strange man looked up from the over-stuffed chair, his eyebrows in his handsome face arched in surprise too. She blushed and turned to go, realizing she must be in the wrong room. Again to her surprise, the man rose and gestured to relieve her of her packages. She relinquished them gladly and stood there blinking.

He took her coat off, shook it, and hung it up to dry. Then, without hesitation or awkwardness, he walked over to where she stood, bent his head, and pressed his mouth to the steamy place between her breasts.

Instantly she shivered and felt all sorts of unnamable sensations. For surely this could not be happening to her; it must be happening to someone else. She would never let such a thing happen — being in a room with a perfect stranger. But there was this undeniable head of hair just under her nose.

The smell of her own perfume released by her body heat was intoxicating and made her realize that she had never really smelled it before. The sweetness in her nostrils made her forget her usual self. Was she actually allowing the unallowable?

She disentangled herself, went into the bathroom, and leaned against the door for a minute, savoring how she felt — glowing, charged, and single-minded. She decided to give herself some breathing space to get used to her new self. She would postpone her pleasure with a luxurious bath. She filled the tub, threw off her clothes, and stepped in. While she lay there, she heard the muffled sound of his voice on the telephone.

She washed and dried and wrapped herself in his terrycloth bathrobe. She smelled his fragrance on the robe as she tied the belt, and her head began to reel slightly. She took a deep breath and opened the bathroom door. He sat holding a glass. When he saw her, he leaned toward the table, filled another, and handed it to her. She took it, brushing his hand lightly, and sat down across from him. They exchanged no words. Her fantasies filled her mind. She wished she knew his fantasies.

She was more aware of her body than ever before. She felt her nipples straining against the terrycloth as her breathing became heavier and more in her chest than in her belly. She could not control the tensing and relaxing in her groin.

Her attention was diverted by a knock at the door, which brought dinner on a rolling table, complete with candlelight and wine. She ate lustily, exchanging a few long glances, but mostly attacking her food voraciously.

Before dessert, he stood up, came around to her and pulled the robe down over her shoulders. She stood up unself-consciously, and the robe fell to the floor. He took her into his arms and gently pressed his body against hers for a long, long time. Headiness overwhelmed her — she, totally naked, he, fully dressed.

The candles burned down. The room was perfectly dark. The prospect of playing a new role excited her. Very slowly she released herself from his arms and unbuttoned his shirt. When she had removed all of his clothes, she led him to the bed and pressed him down. Lightly, she stroked every part of his face and then down his body, finding his state of full erection incredibly exciting.

In turn, he stroked her body with his lips and tongue. His tongue and breath in her ear shut out all other sounds. Her pleasure at some moments became acute pain. Her head rolled from side to side; her legs drew up and fell apart. He brought her to the brink of orgasm with his tongue, and then entered her roughly with the first near-violent gesture of the night. They both came instantly, moaning and aching with pleasure.

Stillness for almost an eternity—maybe even sleep. She stood, as light was beginning to enter the room. Once again she bathed, then dressed and quietly left the room with her coat, her brief-case, and her books. Her first workshop was to begin in two hours—time to become herself again.

Night Riders

Although he had given the cab driver the address in English, and then again in French—as though both languages had equal subservience to the fluid dominance of his own—she realized that she had no idea where they were going. The taxi was going very fast; the rain whipped against the black cab windows, splintering the lights of the ancient city into neon arrows. She felt immense liberation and joy, a sense of power, that surpassed the fear that whitened her clenched fingers and fluttered in her stomach. Her face felt stiff, and her eyes were stretched wide. The cab was evidently driving near the city's docks. She could smell the sharp, female odor of the ebbtide and could hear the fog horns blaring into the night. Sea images swirled in her mind: barnacles silent and exposed upon the pilings and algae floating like wet hair in the phosphorescent, sucking water.

She loosened the collar of her sheepskin coat and turned to look at him, at his familiar, unknown bulk beside her. Again she felt the surge beneath her skin. Entranced and as yielding as wet wood, her being flowed toward him as relentlessly as the flickering water in the river's mouth. She felt herself a mass of contradictions, a witch woman, as ancient as the moon but also as young, as silken, as miraculous as a crocus through snow.

She made a quick, involuntary turn in his direction. She felt wonderful. She wanted to laugh and clap her hands and bounce up and down on the worn leather seat of the taxi. She wanted to creep inside his heavy coat with its close-curled astrakhan collar and burrow like some hedgerow creature next to his skin. She shivered, and a small cat sound escaped. She felt the thrill of the unknown, of adventure, coupled with the splendor of expectation that all was possible. She felt she held her life in her hands like an old and precious coin at the same time that a high, thin voice in her head sang of danger, of risks too serious to contemplate. She felt herself inside her skin and behind her eyes and beneath the tight tethered net of her hair. She wanted the taxi ride in the wild wet night to go on forever.

It did not, of course. Very shortly they stopped before a large, dark building almost invisible through the driving rain. Vaguely, she discerned steps and pillars, an air of genteel decay. He paid the driver, and they alighted. Then they were hurrying (heads bent, his hand lightly guiding her elbow, her feet in their absurd heels clicking in the stabbing rain) around the side of the house. She was aware of bushes, a small shed perhaps for tools, cobblestones beneath her feet. Then a light in a window, and they came to a halt before a low, wide door.

He fumbled for a key (his first gesture of uncertainty in their acquaintance), swung open the door, and urged her inside. She stepped across the threshold, shaking out her hair and blinking raindrops from her eyes. They were in what was obviously a studio, separated from the main house. A fire burned low and red in a large hearth, its light revealing rafters, a skylight, a spacious couch. Easels, stacked canvasses, the pungent smell of turpentine, draperies—all these filled her with happiness—were discernible through the red shadows in the room. She felt chalk crumble beneath her foot as she drew off her gloves and turned to him with a smile of pure radiance.

With quick, urgent movements, he unbuttoned his coat and let it fall. Then he eased her coat from her shoulders, tossed it aside, and deliberately, with the tenderness of enormous and conscious strength, took her in his arms. She responded at once, a total capitulation: his bulk and the contradiction of his gentleness as he brought his mouth down to hers filled her with such liquid desire that she felt her skin would peel back and reveal her bones. His hands moved about her body with competence and power as the kiss continued. Her spine melted and curved into his, and her hands on his face grew urgent, frantic, so that he put her away from him, into the curve of one arm, to undo the buttons of her dress.

As her skin bared to his touch, it seemed charged and alive, and she quivered and jerked in his arms, making her small cat sounds, as the big blunt fingers spanned her breasts and caressed her throat. He urged her gently toward the couch and pressed her back. Her hands reached out to him as he stood above her pulling off his clothes. He knelt over her, pulling off her remaining undergarments, and she was amazed, spellbound by his grace and deftness, his swiftness in disposing of the final flimsy barriers. With each article he removed, she became sleeker, more fluid, as if her flesh were turning to molten gold. She could see its patina in the flickering light of the fire. Her legs, as she flexed and stretched them, raising her hips and arching her back to facilitate his efforts, had the lithe lines of a dancer's, the insteps arched and gleaming.

She was suddenly aware of her own allure: the sheen of her body, the pale arc of her throat receiving his mouth, the lovely, languid motions of her limbs, her breasts bursting like blossoms, her mouth a bruising flower, her head turning on the cushions with the aching restlessness of bound passion. She touched her skin and felt its fine-grained, flowing softness. She touched her lips and breasts and the flesh inside her thighs and marveled at the texture of her body. And as her hands went from her body to his, it seemed to her that she could not be certain where the one began and the other left off. In a way she had never known, she felt herself magnified through his hands. She thought: I am beautiful, I am desirable. Then she raised her arms over her head and arched her back and opened her body. He covered her then; he entered her and, as she caught her breath on a cry, slowly and rhythmically began the deep thrusting that brought her soul springing through the top of her head like a fish from a wave. She watched herself spin away from her body into the blackness beyond the velvet light of the studio room, bright and thin, a fine silver wire glimmering, unraveling, into the lonely, filigreed, fog-horned night.

The Prisoner

She lay across the bed and leaned on one arm. The heat outside was intolerable. In her shorts and halter top with the air-conditioning blowing on her, she felt relaxed and dreamy. She undid her sandal straps, letting her shoes fall carelessly to the floor, and then, slowly, she reached for the twenty-five-cent paperback novel she had just bought at the university store. She had heard of the author but had never read his stuff. She opened the book and read idly, her mind wandering a bit. It was so cool here. She had looked at the workmen in the courtyard as she entered the building — big strong men with sweat glistening on their faces. They worked slowly and methodically, and she had admired how masculine they looked despite their monotonous work. She smiled at the memory.

The characters in the book were two young men talking about going to college to beat the draft. One said: "I can't feel guilty about beating the draft. I can't help those who can't, and I don't want to commit suicide. Anyway, John Kennedy said life was unfair." Yes, she thought lazily, so . . .

She was startled by a sudden rapping at the door. Kurt wasn't due from class until five. It was only three thirty. She moved off the bed slowly. Maybe he'd left early. She pushed the center of the door knob, releasing the lock on the heavy door. Almost immediately it flew open and a large male figure pushed past her, pulling the door shut behind him and locking it. She was too startled to speak. She had the impression of a big, good-looking man who was worried. In an urgent voice he said: "Give me something to drink."

She blinked but felt strangely unafraid. Moving away from him, she said: "I don't have any beer, but I can give you some juice." He nodded, looking quickly around. There was no one else there. He seemed reassured. She wasn't screaming. He drank the juice she offered and then held out his glass for more. It was a small gesture like a child's. It took away her fear and made her feel in charge, like a mother with a thirsty child.

She shrugged and smiled, gesturing to the worn couch.

"Well, sit down."

He didn't look like a rapist or a strangler, just unexpected company. She sat on the chair facing the couch and smiled at him. Hmmm, yes, good-looking and masculine. His head was good, his features irregular but pleasing. She conjectured, laughing Irish eyes, good strong workingman's arms. He wore jeans and a cotton shirt, all light blue like a uniform. She began to understand.

"You escaped from the work farm," she said matter-of-factly. He nodded his head in assent. He seemed tired and glad to sit for a moment in a cool, friendly room. She thought, He's nice, intelligent, hard-working, and his father was a drunk. Aloud she said: "Got a plan to get out of here?"

He was surprised at her coolness.

"How come you ain't screaming?"

She shrugged. She answered sarcastically: "I think all the criminals are running around on the outside."

He looked surprised again.

"You're damn right about that!" He looked at her more carefully. Thin and blonde and lazy-looking, with her hair falling all over her face. Tanned arms and legs. Her halter top hung loosely as she sat. It escaped him.

"Man, you sure got knockers!"

She felt pleased. No one had noticed that for a long time. She looked at him speculatively. Hank wouldn't be home for another hour at least.

"You haven't seen a woman for a long time?"

He snorted. "Two years I been locked up in that hell hole. Oh, I seen women. Bible-toting bitches. They come to see you with their boobs all held up by wires and wave them at you, and if you look a little and believe a little, they might put in a good word for you so you can get paroled. Bitches!" He snorted again in frustration. He looked at her openly. "But I never seen a soft yellow one like you."

She got up, lit a cigarette, and offered him one. He sucked in gratefully and leaned back against the chair.

"And legs, believe me, you got legs."

"These Bible women," she asked, "did they have legs?"

"Oh, sure," he puffed again. "They had legs"—a short pause—"and cement crotches!"

They both burst out laughing at his unexpected poetry. He shook his head and smiled.

"Your crotch ain't cement. I shore bet it ain't cement."

They savored the thought. It was so quiet. The muffled sounds of cars outside, the humming of the air-conditioner. They felt isolated and alone in their own little world of understanding and acceptance. He could only stay one hour, then he would have to run. His destiny was set. He would always be running. Hers was set too. She would always be alone, waiting. Her beautiful body would always be taken for granted and never really seen or felt or tasted.

She stood up and sauntered about the room while he gazed appreciatively. Cement crotch? She giggled and he laughed too.

"I used to think about girls like you, all blonde and away from me. No one I could ever touch, with big white breasts and little nipples hard . . ." He stopped talking. She had undone the clasp of her halter and thrown it off. She came near to him and held her breasts in her cupped hands.

"Like this?" she teased softly.

He reached out instinctively and stroked the firm, white skin, and then, suddenly, she was all wrapped up in him. They were a gasping tangle of arms and legs and skin and hair and breaths moving back and forth like their overturned bodies.

They were together a long time. Their destinies seemed suspended. They had been given an hour's reprieve, and their hands and mouths stroked, felt, searched. It was as though they were tasting nectar fed to them from outside time and space and rooms.

She stroked his hairy chest for the last time and got up. They dressed silently. He looked out the window. No one there; he had to run again. She looked at her wristwatch. Almost five. She would have to wait again.

They moved to the door, their arms clasped around each other's waists. He kissed her once.

"You got a name?" he asked softly.

"Yeah, I got a name."

And then the heavy door had opened, and he disappeared as quickly as he had come. She went to the window and watched him run across the courtyard. He stopped once and waved — his mouth moved and she could make out the word.

"Angel," he said.

THROUGH A MAN'S EYES

Ready for a further stretch, we dared each other to flex some unused muscles and to write from a man's point of view. Sabina teased Rose for always setting the stage and backing away from the climax. In the guise of a man Rose felt free to go "all the way" and as a gift to Sabina wrote Fever. Sabina, too, put her hero flat on his back and gave him what he's always wanted.

Fever

Z-a-a-a-a-a-p! I'm hit. I'm a broken man. A stab of sunlight pierces my retinas. Z-a-a-a-a-a-p again! The venetian blinds are raised all at once. I recoil like an assaulted sea anemone. This awakening is too violent. Wincing, I see an ocean of mauve. I pull the covers more tightly about my invertebrate body, seeking safety in camouflage. Cool hands touch me on the back of my neck and on my forehead. Cool hands, so smooth and gentle. Not the attack I had feared.

"Oh, my! You're hot! Awfully hot! Wait!"

She rushes to the bathroom and returns. A damp, cool wash-cloth, faintly scented with carnation soap, lands on my face.

"Open."

A cold thermometer is placed in my mouth. A cool hand lifts my head while another shakes out my damp pillow. I open my eyes just in time to see her loose breasts framed by the gaping V-neck of her T-shirt. They flex each time she tugs at the pillow. She straightens the crumpled top sheet and sits on the bed beside me to wait.

She is heavier than she looks. The mattress sags, and I roll toward her. I settle against her large thigh. In its denim casing it is as firm and warm as a sausage. The double-stitched seams and brass studs can't subdue it. She is brushing back the hair from my forehead in a motherly way. I am seven years old again. Her forearm is plump and succulent. The skin glows with a rosy sheen like a plum. What a juicy morsel! Oh, food—how can I be thinking of food after a night wracked by dry retching, chills, and spasms? I shudder. I'm glad she doesn't talk, glad she keeps stroking my head, glad to be inert beside her generous thigh. The silence and her closeness hide our strangeness.

She takes the thermometer from my mouth. "It's 103. I'll get some aspirin. Think you can keep it down?"

I nod helplessly. She returns with two aspirin and a glass of water. I manage to swallow them, and she smiles approvingly.

"You'll feel better."

I am suddenly disappointed. I will no longer have a reason to be lying here. I will have to be accountable. I will be embarrassed at getting sick. I will apologize for the gross inconvenience. I will brush my teeth, shave, and comb my hair carefully over the thinning spot in back. I will feel guilty for having lascivious thoughts about someone else's wife.

But I am very ill. My fever still rages, and if I move, I may vomit again. I submit to fate, which has kindly placed me between flowered sheets in a sunny room. I lie flat on my back, helpless, a barnacle upon a rock. Blameless, unprotesting, I accept whatever comes to me.

She is standing at a desk now with her back turned. She is arranging flowers in a small vase. The vase has high rounded hips like hers. Pleased, she pauses, sniffs the bouquet, and turns to bring it to me. Her brunette sheen and nutty fragrance envelop me.

Something stirs. Twinges deep in my groin remind me I am not a barnacle. My soft underbelly has no protection. I have no shell to close over my growing erection. The sheets rise to a point. I gaze at a billowing circus tent.

She laughs and whispers "Big Top" and gently grips my penis. It does not go down. Smiling, she rolls back the top sheet, then firmly wrestles my distorted jockey shorts down over my erection. She lifts my hips easily — how strong she is! — and slides my shorts off. Then she leans over, places a warm hand beside each buttock, and begins to kiss my penis. Her shiny brown hair cascades over my belly, and I touch it to be sure it is real. Her tongue is tracing Corinthian scrolls upon my incredible column.

Will it stand intact, or will it crash to earth in great chunks to be worn away by wind and rain? I am in awe of myself, of her; my prowess, her boldness.

She stands up and removes her T-shirt. Her breasts spring free before the shirt clears her head. I eye the menu greedily: ripe melons, translucent plum skin, and fragrance of roasted nuts. I will have them all! She unsnaps her reluctant Levi buckle and rolls down her jeans. The seams have left indentations across her hips and thighs. I run my fingertips over the soft, narrow roadways as she climbs onto the bed and straddles me. Her pubic hair is straight and shiny, and I watch it lower slowly over mine. Bit by bit I see my shaft disappearing from view. I close my eyes and explore her warm, wet, welcoming vault. We are architectural masterpieces! She leans over me and presses her breasts to my burning face. I am being buried alive, how alive! I breathe in my fate, succumb to it, and hope this cure will never end.

In Praise of Panty Hose

He rarely spent the night with a woman any more. But he was stranded with this one until he could get to a gas station. He wondered whether she had slept next to him. He was alone now between green satin sheets. If only he could make a quick exit. What time was it? His watch said seven o'clock. The gas station opened at eight. He felt his face; he needed a shave. He heard water running. She was in the shower. He had to get away before she came back. He was sure they had slept together. At least he remembered that much and that they had talked. No, he had talked and talked and talked. Good God, what a fool he had made of himself. Just because he couldn't get it up. What the hell did he care? He didn't have to make it with her. She wasn't all that special, just a nice girl who patiently listened because she didn't have the guts to tell him to get lost. Christ, he had spilled his guts out — about the promotion he wouldn't get, about Helen suing for more child support. And then he couldn't get it up, or was that before? Could he have tried twice? She had even tried to help him, very graciously, the perfect lady. And then, when he had finally left, his car was out of gas. Out of gas, the perfect irony.

She had watched him from the window. There was nothing he could do but accept her invitation to spend the night — insisting that he take the bed. Well, she too had slept in it; she had fallen asleep before he finished talking. No, he could not face her this morning. She wasn't even his type, maybe that's why — no! Be honest, he told himself, it's not the first time.

"I have to get up early," she had told him before dropping off to sleep. "Just stay in bed until the gas station opens. Don't forget to pull the latch."

When he noticed that the water was no longer running, he panicked. The door opened. Quickly, he pretended to be sleeping. She approached the bed to check on him. Noiselessly, she moved away. He heard her open a drawer. The more carefully she went about, the more nervous he felt. Finally he peeked at her with one eye. She was naked: a perfectly shaped back, narrow waist, and a fine behind. He could see her breasts, too, in the dresser mirror. They were long and pendulous; he liked them round and small. She had taken her clothes off last night, but somehow he had not noticed what she looked like. She looked better in the morning. She looked very good from behind.

Yesterday he had not seen her from that angle. He had taken her home because of her face. It was the only face at the party that was alive. Dull faces, dead conversations, tired jokes, and stale drinks marked that party. Could be that he hadn't been in the mood. He should stop going to parties just to avoid being alone.

She studied her face in the mirror, penciling her eyes. So that's how they started, with the eyes. He hadn't even noticed that she wore makeup. What had he noticed? A serious face, not pretty, certainly not striking, but intelligent. The face of an efficient secretary or nurse, a face that blended unobtrusively into the work atmosphere, one that could be trusted. He would have hired such a face for any number of demanding jobs. But he would not have made a pass at her.

Oblivious of him, she painted her face with slow and deliberate care. What kind of work did she say she did? He couldn't remember; maybe he hadn't asked. Different instruments went with different processes, it seemed. Delicately she lifted something with tweezers and guided it to her eyes — lashes. She glued them on one by one. It took her forever while the clock ticked away on the mantel.

He suddenly became impatient with her for taking that much time with herself, for being so absorbed, so removed from him. She was still not finished. Now she sat down sideways from him. Her hands passed through a pair of panty hose. When she pulled up her leg, he felt an unmistakable jolt in his groin. Desire was stirring in him, making him swell.

She had long and muscular legs; she danced. She had told him about her dancing, but she was not a professional dancer. The panty hose melted over her foot and ankle. When it got as far as her knee, she lifted her other foot and repeated the same procedure. Then she stood up. Bending over slightly, she painstakingly pulled and stretched the sheer fabric over her thighs and finally her buttocks. She turned around to examine her work in the full-length mirror by the door. He could see her pubic hair through the hose. She wore nothing else underneath. By now he had a real hard-on. Something bothered her; the seam was a little crooked. She pulled the panty hose down over the buttocks, spreading her legs slightly to keep her balance. This drove him wild. She did not rest until the seam fit perfectly over the crack — a neat demarcation line finally traced her cleavage separating one cheek from the other. But there was more to come. Bending down again — the cheeks stood well chiseled within confines — she tied the straps of her high-heeled sandals to her ankles. Her light brown hair tumbled over her swaying breasts.

Sweat poured from his pores into the cool green sheets. High-heeled and tight-hosed, she stalked back to the dresser to fetch her bra — a flesh-colored lacy bit of nothing that fastened in front. The effect had to be checked and rechecked before it was covered with a matching slip. This had a slit all the way to her crotch. What followed made him suppress a laugh. Her punctilious art work eventually disappeared under a sober brown skirt and a sporty white blouse. She was ready to go to work — the perfect machine, all tuned up for a day at the office. Why did she go through all the trouble? What was waiting for her at her destination? Who would see that perfectly straight seam under her skirt?

At the door she hesitated. Surely she could add nothing further to her disguise? She could. A belt had to be pulled around her waist, a dab of perfume still waited for her earlobe, and one more stroke with the brush pulled her curls down over her forehead. Then she smiled at herself—pleased, comfortable, ready to face her perfect day.

He couldn't stand it any longer—he wouldn't let her go to that perfectly groomed desk. There was nothing he could do except catapult himself out of bed in her direction. He didn't care that he startled her. Before she could resist, he ripped off her blouse, zipped down her skirt, and stripped the bra from her shoulders together with her slip until she wore nothing but her panty hose. Then he carried her over to the bed and dropped her on top of the green satin—a mermaid in a green pool, her tail shimmering under silky scales.

"I've got to go," she laughed.

But he could not let her go to work. He must conquer her, possess her, devour her. He must set her free. He struggled valiantly with her panty hose. But each time he managed to pull them half way down her beautiful ass, she slipped away from him.

Two hours later, he said dreamily: "I'll get some gas now and drive you to work."

"Oh, that's all right," she smiled. "Today's my day off."

RSVP TO HENRY MILLER

B*ecause Henry Miller epitomized the male point of view, we decided to read aloud from* Tropic of Cancer. *Half the ladies fell soundly asleep. Sabina and Jenna chose to respond in kind.*

Solo Virtuoso

Ruth dropped the book on the ground and settled back in her softly padded chair. After the morning fog, the sun felt hot. Leisurely, she peeled off her jeans and pushed her T-shirt up over her bra without taking it off. She enjoyed soaking in the sun like that, sensing with pleasure the difference between her exposed and unexposed parts.

The telephone rang. She let it ring—a newly acquired skill. Earlier in her life she would never have had the nerve to hold out against ten repeated demands for attention.

Peace today, peace for the whole day. Nothing could reach her unless she desired it. On one side of the garden, brambles and a mixture of native and exotic shrubs walled off the neighbors, and on the other, a majestic stand of redwoods. The landlady had shown her the patio first, probably to justify the exorbitant rent. "Look at those trees—redwoods from the original estate! It used to be a private summer retreat before it was subdivided."

Ruth sipped her wine, Stag's Leap 1979. Drinking good wine by herself was part of her Sunday ritual. Then she loosened her bra and pushed her panties down to her knees. Lying in disarray excited her. It made her feel wanton, wicked. It was so simple to please herself. Today she would take her time—no rushing, no impatient staccato stroking, just a gentle tugging at her pubic curls, a soft tracing of her clit. The sun licked her nipples, her belly, then greedily penetrated her thighs, urging her to open herself wide.

"Are you pleased with me, sun? Do you like what you see?"

Ruth took pride in her healthy, well-functioning body with its ample breasts and strong hips, the same pride as others took in their cars. She took good care of it too: her skin was taut, her muscles tight from regular exercise and running.

Reaching for her flask, she barely lifted her head, leaving her legs loosely spread to keep her excitement simmering. Then she wiggled her toes, rotated her ankles, and tightened her buttocks, breathing fully with her stomach, yoga style. She let her hands rest on top of her face, loving the smell of herself from "down there." Slowly she removed the remaining pieces of clothing and turned her backside toward the sun. The blaze caressed her shoulders and the whole length of her spine. It kissed her buttocks, entreating her to surrender more of herself. Crouching on her knees she allowed it to penetrate her from behind as her mound arched toward her hands, wanting to be stroked and teased. Subtle variations turned into a strong rhythmic rocking of her body to the beat of her sliding fingers. In . . . in . . . in . . .

Climax crept up on her in tingling waves, each announcing the next one before subsiding. Finally, her whole being contracted into a ball of fire. She was giving birth to her own pleasure. Exhausted she sank back into blissful relaxation.

Resting between sleep and heightened awareness, she suddenly sensed that she was no longer alone. Perhaps it was the slight breeze that sent a frisson up her spine. Sitting up, she discovered a figure in one of the redwood trees. It was a man.

Agile and muscular, he climbed down the tree trunk as though he had done it many times before. She covered her breasts. Too late — he jumped the ten feet onto the patio. Only now did she notice that he was wearing a uniform. What war? What country? Fear paralyzed her voice, but her mind was racing through a number of possible defenses: I'll kick him in the groin, she decided.

He remained firmly planted right where he had landed.

"Whore," he spat out, "I know what you want. You want my cock right between your legs. You want me to grab you down there, take you like a man, a real man. You want a man to grab your bushy twat. You crave it, don't you? My prick in your cunt?"

When he moved closer, out of breath and perspiring, Ruth sensed something helpless about him, some trace of defeat, of battles lost. She noticed that two buttons hung loose from his jacket and that his shirt was rumpled. His obscenities, like his uniform, no longer convincingly displayed power. She began to see him as more pathetic than dangerous, but she stayed on guard. What kind of charade was he putting on? Impulsively, she offered him her glass. He drank thirstily.

"Slut, don't think I don't know what's going on . . . lying there with your pussy in the air, begging for it. I guess you know your business. Believe me, I do a good job too." Hastily he unzipped his trousers. "Here, feel my dick. I bet you don't get that every day? I bet you haven't had a good fuck for a long time, not with a real man. What do you say to that, eh?"

Ruth recovered her voice. It sounded cool.

"A real man, is that what you are?"

He lunged forward. Hovering over her, he grunted: "Take it, cunt."

"I don't want it."

"Cock-teasing won't work with me, lady."

To her surprise he smelled pleasantly of pipe tobacco. The aroma was somehow familiar.

"Please, leave me alone. I'm not in the mood for company."

"You're a whore all the way through. You'll only do it for money, fucking bitch. Who do you think you are?" Grabbing her shoulders, he threatened to throw himself upon her. It helped her to know that the chair would surely collapse from the additional weight.

"All right, all right," she told him firmly, "but you must do exactly what I say." Startled by the authority in her voice, he let go of her. "I am not afraid of you," she continued, "and I am not a whore." Obviously there was no point in telling him that she was president of the League of Women Voters. "I'm going to tell you what I want."

For the first time, he looked straight into her eyes, puzzled, intrigued, uncertain what to do next.

"It better be good." He lowered his glance appreciatively to her breasts.

"No, don't touch me there. Pull up your pants. Kneel down beside me."

He moved obediently, as if programmed to take orders. She smelled the tobacco again in his thick greyish-brown hair. She sat up straight, opened her thighs, and pulled his face close.

"Kiss me very, very gently."

He obeyed.

"Now lick my cunt—savor it, explore it with the tip of your tongue. Good, that's it. Continue exactly like that. Deeper now, taste me, feel me. Yes, that's it." As his tongue went to work, her body twitched and throbbed in immediate response. Pressing his head tightly against her wet crotch and feeling her moisture on his face, she came quickly with a violent shudder. Spent, she kissed the top of his head and released him.

"That was very nice. You really do know your job," she complimented him.

"Okay, my turn now," he grinned expectantly, touching his fly.

"You may leave now," she said, her tone imperious as before.

"Hey, wait a minute—you're going to go down on *me* first, cunt."

"I'm sorry, I don't have the time. I have to get dressed. But you have possibilities. We must meet again sometime." He looked dumbfounded, but he obeyed, as she had expected he would.

Watching him retreat like a good soldier, Ruth savored the frenzy and the power, but she also felt a little ashamed of cheating him at his own game. Perhaps I should call him back? she thought but quickly decided not to. She had had enough.

The sound of a car in the driveway startled her back to reality. Doors shut with a bang. Voices called her name. Before she had a chance to cover her nakedness, her grandsons were already entering the garden.

"Grandma, grandma," they yelled, "why didn't you answer the phone?"

"I called all afternoon to remind you that I'm bringing the boys," said her daughter reproachfully as she came out to the patio. "By the way, you shouldn't let them see you in the nude any more. They're too old for that now. What on earth have you been doing all day?"

"Nothing, dear. I guess I fell asleep reading Henry Miller."

"That old fart? Don't tell me you get off on that macho porn? That kind of garbage should be banned," scoffed her daughter as she set down the stuffed animals and blankets the boys required for their sleep-over.

"But it *was* banned," smiled Ruth mischievously, picking up the book. "I smuggled it in from Paris as a student. I was scared to death customs would find it in my underwear."

But her daughter did not hear. She was already halfway out the door.

Animal Lust

"You really are a madonna, Frances. I'm so glad you're not like all those other girls. They're disgusting. I mean, the things they do! They're like animals."

Hank wrinkled his nose in dismay and dropped down beside me on the high school lawn. I was lying face down on the cool grass, and I was glad my long blonde hair hung over my face so he couldn't see the sudden pink flush that crept up my neck. He had been telling me all kinds of lurid and exciting stories about a party he had attended, a terrible party where the girls and boys had disappeared into rooms and behind couches. I was secretly impressed and dying to hear more.

"Oh, yes, terrible, terrible," I lied. "What else did they do?"

Well, he put his hand inside her blouse. It was soft and warm, and he even . . ." Hank's voice sank lower, and his whisper was a little hoarse. "He rubbed her nipple, and it got big and hard."

I wanted to pull down my sweater and let my hand fall along the line of my own breast. I wondered what it would feel like to have some boy open my blouse and caress my breast with the breeze flowing over my naked flesh. What would happen to my nipple?

"Now this will really get you, Frances," Hank went on. "After he did that, he ran his hand under her skirt and felt her crotch. And she let him! Can you imagine?"

I could imagine, and the palms of my hands began to feel very damp. I lowered my head even more and let Hank's words slide over me.

"The thing I really like about you, Frances, is that you don't have animal lust."

Years later, after we were married and Hank had become a busy and successful business executive, the story-telling continued. After dinner every evening, Hank told me stories as we lingered over coffee.

"Boy, Frances, this one's too much. See, his mistress works the telephones, and his wife is the secretary right now because the other one had to leave. So his mistress brings in this sexy black nightgown, and his wife holds it up and admires it, and he's standing there looking cross-eyed. And now his wife and mistress are becoming friends, and he doesn't know what to do about it. Now isn't that something?"

Hank would whistle, and I would hang on to every word, trying to fill in the details in my mind. Where would they go? To a motel? I would try to imagine the mistress in the sexy black nightgown with her long hair trailing down her voluptuous back. Would she lie on the bed waiting for him to tear the cloth from her big Italian breasts? Or would she be the passionate one and tear the clothes off him? Then I would think of them moaning and moving all over the bed, and I would lower my head so my hair fell over my face and Hank wouldn't see the flush on my cheeks. Hank always ended his stories in the same way.

"I'm so glad you're not like that, Frances. You're so cool and restrained and pure. Yes, you really are my madonna."

And then one day, the stories ended abruptly. I stood by the hospital bed and wondered about the kidneys that failed. Pale and weak, Hank reached out for my hand and gave me a final squeeze.

"Frances, be very careful. Men won't understand you. They won't know you're a madonna and don't have animal lust." His nose wrinkled one final time, and then he was gone, and I was sitting at the dinner table again, but this time alone with no one to tell me exciting stories to end my day.

I avoided men completely, although many tried to woo me.

"A gorgeous thing like you can't just wither away," one scolded me. "You're young. Don't let life pass you by."

Finally, I bundled my grief away. It was just a little bundle really. Hank had always been my friend, but he had never touched me deeply. I had never felt we were really lovers—not really. I knew there must be more. I knew there was a man somewhere, a man who had animal lust, who was sexy and daring and outrageous and fun and wonderful. Over the years I had painted him, and I knew exactly what he looked like but not where to find him.

One day as I wandered aimlessly through a department store, I saw a lovely sheer blouse on the stand. It was draped over a slender mannequin that was nude. I admired the way the soft cloth clung to her breasts. On impulse, I took the blouse and went into the dressing room and tried it on. I didn't have the nerve to wear it over my bare skin, but even on top of my slip and bra it clung lusciously and gleamed golden in the harsh light of the dressing room. I admired myself dreamily in the mirror, then bought the blouse and wore it out of the store. I felt elated by my sudden purchase and went into a cafeteria for a cup of tea and to think about the wonderful feeling the blouse gave me.

The cafeteria was crowded, so I had to sit at a table with a man, a stranger who was writing furiously on a thick pad of yellow paper. It's funny how things work out, isn't it? As I sipped my tea, I stole glances at him, letting my hair fall around my face in my old way, so he couldn't observe me observing him. I studied him discreetly and wondered about him. What was he writing? I liked his looks–big and rough with lots of character and something else too. I was painting in passion and lust and black negligees and moaning on the bed when suddenly he lifted his head and looked straight at me.

"All of a sudden," he said matter-of-factly, "this has become a beautiful day."

I felt as sheer and sensuous as my golden, silken blouse as he ran his eyes over me and my body, at least what he could see of it above the table top. I could see my knee cap gleaming in its nylon cover. Was it that exposed before, or did my hand casually pull my skirt up a little higher? He leaned over and ran his hand along the fine silk fabric as it lay on my arm.

"You have given me a totally new outlook on this day. I'm a worn-out writer; I need inspiration. How about coming to my apartment and having dinner with me tonight?"

He didn't wait for an answer but handed me his card. In a second he had disappeared into the crowd, carrying his yellow pad. For a second I was dismayed, and then suddenly, there he was again, standing on the other side of the window, smiling broadly and silently mouthing "Yes, yes, yes!" And then he was gone again, crossing the street and turning a corner.

I studied his card. He lived near me. I savored my memory of him, and then, with sudden resolution, I decided. I would go.

That night at six o'clock I telephoned him and said just one word: "Yes." Two hours later I sat across from him at the dinner table. My hair was combed back. It couldn't fall across my face, at least not yet.

My golden, silken blouse lay lovingly on my soft pearly skin with nothing else beneath it. I felt as rich and lustrous as the material that clothed me, as elegant as the blue and white chinaware that lay before me, as warm and inviting as the little flames that rose and fell in the fireplace beyond the table. He was no stranger; I had made his acquaintance over the years, painting in each detail a little at a time, so that now he felt completely familiar to me. We sipped our wine and smiled at each other in the candlelight. It was no surprise to learn that he wrote romantic novels.

Later, as the sheer blouse hung carelessly from a chair and the light from the fireplace warmed our naked bodies, I smiled in secret delight as he stroked my skin and murmured, "The thing I really love about you, Frances, is that you have animal lust."

VII.   THE KENSINGTON
LADIES REVEALED

We are a potpourri of slightly hysterical contradictions: bold, reticent, eager to divulge, hesitant to expose, garrulous, tongue-tied, lighthearted, and deadly serious. All these divergent forces operate at once in each one of us and tend to make our meetings rather raucous affairs. When we do engage in a psychic tug-of-war, everyone wins. Cautious thinkers begin to take chances and find themselves doing unexpected things in the joy of the moment. Impulsive doers who ricochet through life stop to reflect — and regain control. Unwittingly borrowing from each other, we discover new dimensions in ourselves which seep into our stories, weaving our desires and differences into a rich tapestry of collective experience.

Not all of us choose to write. Ann Gordon, Nicola Hamilton, and Judy McBride channel their creativity into ardent listening. Their exuberant comments and continued presence have insured the survival of the group for without their applause and encouragement many of our stories would never have been written.

I have always felt that I am a member of the Kensington Ladies' Erotica Society under false pretenses, waving a flag that isn't mine. I am not a writer. I don't want to write. I loathe writing. I am a sculptor, possibly a painter, and my creative energies naturally flow into visual images.

Three years ago, Sabina, who saw me floundering through the agonies of a very bitter and painful divorce, invited me to join the group. Writer or not, she said, it would be good for me and maybe stimulate me in new directions. I told her that to be reminded of erotica was the last thing I needed at that juncture. It was the one thing I had always felt I would be forever deprived of. But I was curious and lonely, and so I went to a meeting. Soon the group was a major focus in my life.

Everyone was kind and patient, but after three years of constant work by all the "regulars," I sensed some impatience and frustration with my inactivity. After all, they had freely nourished me, bodily and psychically, with their delicious cooking and bared literary souls. It takes skill to cook well. It takes both skill and bravery, particularly bravery for us who were born into the tag end of the American-Victorian-Puritan era, to expose our erotic imaginings and tentative literary skills to outsiders, even friendly ones.

Needless to say, I had exposed nothing. I was the coward, safely ensconced in my cocoon: "I can't write: I am a visual artist." Parenthetically, I also have the irresistible habit of falling into a pleasant snooze or two after dinner, particularly if wine is served. I am a morning person with a very low alcohol tolerance. Naturally, this is embarrassing, and I have become quite adept at covering my weakness: I catch myself awake just before my head bobs, always sit in high-backed chairs after dinner, and generally fake a nonexistent and spurious alertness.

One evening, after very satisfying predinner chatter and delicious, filling, and soporific food and wine, I followed my abominable pattern and dozed through the reading of a sketch by a new member. I retained enough consciousness to be aware that I was missing something unusually well written and that I'd be sorry later. But first things first, and after food comes sleep!

I awoke abruptly when the voice changed, and I heard my name. As I guiltily jerked to attention, Sabina was saying: "Well, Ann, what about you? Why don't you do a sculpture?"

In my half-awake state I panicked as visions of very specific and gross images passed through my mind — more in line with the crudest Japanese erotic woodprints with their enormous exaggerations. My sluggish mind jumped to an innocent lady answer, half the world away from Oriental prints. I hinted that Rodin had pretty well exhausted the subject, and in addition to not wishing to plagiarize his work, it would be the greatest arrogance on my part to compete with his genius. They agreed, but Sabina said: "Why not sculpt just part of a body?" — at which point I truly panicked — "like the hands in the story Elvira just read?"

Faster than greased erotica, the various things that hands could do reeled through my brain, and I could find no reason to object. Though I hadn't the faintest hint as to the story's plot, what the hands actually looked like, or what they had been doing, I covered my assorted confusions and guilt by immediately agreeing, on one condition — which I was certain would save me from any effort. I insisted that the original owner be the model.

As a matter of fact, I cannot sculpt anything without a living model, from whom I get an emotional impact. I prefer a responsive mammal to any of the lower orders, and I much prefer a verbal animal, though I have done elephants, horses, butterflies, dragons, birds, and other pets. I noticed that most of the husbands, lovers, and sons of our various members avoid our meetings like Herpes II. If they must come into the house to eat or retire while we are convening, they try to slip in through the back door and are laboriously inconspicuous as they slither or leap to their destinations.

I was completely flabbergasted the next day when Elvira

phoned to say that she had contacted the subject of "Hands," and he was sufficiently amused and intrigued to agree to pose. Assuming I'd have to endure some conceited, self-satisfied ass whose hands had better be great to make up for the boredom I anticipated, I spent the time prior to his arrival conjecturing every variety of beautiful, graceful male hand in a million exotic, erotic, sinuous poses.

When the owner of the fabulous hands walked in the door, I was speechless. He had a set of the homeliest digits I had ever seen — and homely in a way to which I was peculiarly sensitive. They were an extreme exaggeration of the rather unattractive bone structure of my own hands, plus an unusual fleshiness and a curious suggestion of something arthritic in the horizontal angle of the fingers at the knuckle joint. His first words were that he couldn't resist the temptation to find out how anyone could make his hands beautiful and sensual. Silently I had to agree, and silently I ditched all my preconceived compositions. I told him it would take me a while to decide on a pose, and, in the meantime, let's relax and get acquainted. I've learned how to set a subject at ease and dive into his or her psyche. To do it, I set up a very intense intimacy that is almost — in fact, really is — a mini love affair. When I am through, it abruptly ends.

As "Hands" talked about his work, I noticed that his hands assumed several characteristic and intriguing gestures or postures. In one, he would hold or, rather, cradle his right hand with his left and seem almost to massage or caress the palm of the right with the thumb of the left. At the time I didn't analyze why this caught my eye but simply started to sculpt. I felt I'd discover what the gesture was saying as I worked.

In the meantime we talked and talked and talked. Since we met for more than one session, I would sometimes "import" a friend to amuse him, as I was now determined to prevent *his* boredom from turning him away before I was through. I knew that he was very busy, and I felt he was in some way impatient or restless.

In the end he was pleased with the enormous size of the finished work. My instinct is always to work larger than life, and for me these hands really are larger than life.

I was born in England of Italian parents and spent most of my life engaged in an internal emotional battle between my Mediterranean temperament and my all-too-well-acquired British reserve. Many years ago I traded in the gray London fog for California sunshine, eventually married an American, and now spend most of my time raising two young, energetic children.

I was educated in England at an all-girls Catholic convent school and suffered the inevitable stifling consequences. So when my friend Rose suggested over lunch one day that I join her Erotica writing group, my ears perked up like a dog who's offered a juicy bone.

Right away I sensed a feeling of deep trust among the members even when different factions appeared to emerge within the group. Best of all, I loved to hear the women talk about sexuality and read their work over good potluck dinners. The energy of the group was infectious and I felt encouraged enough to continue with my own nonerotic writing, which I had firmly put on the back burner with the arrival of my first child. My function within the group has evolved into one of encouraging listener, gentle critic, and unflagging supporter.

Seven years ago I attended the first meeting of the Kensington Ladies' Erotica Society out of curiosity and loyalty to my friend, Sabina. Although it was very threatening to me then, the unexpected is often sweetest, and I was relieved that I had found a safe place for exploring fantasies. The other women were real people, not silly stereotypes, and I was struck by their beautiful, simple, and humorous approach to such a universal area, sexual fantasy.

As I reread the stories produced from the erotica group, I wish to take up a banner and cheer for the successes of my sisters, hidden in this book by pseudonyms, but who hid nothing the many times they revealed their own deepest thoughts in conversation and in writing. I myself made many attempts to put into a playful art form my memories and longings. I recounted my own stories to private pages only to bury them in a crumpled ball in the wastebasket. I am certainly thankful that my friends' stories were not similarly wasted.

Growing up in dry southern California in the economic drought of the Depression, I knew every lily pond, birdbath, and fountain in town. There weren't many, and in the bland, dusty, middle-class environment these tiny oases of coolness and mystery were the secret joy of my life.

My public joy was the barefoot life, running with the boys when I could, leading the girls when I couldn't: baseball in the street, basketball in the vacant lot, wrestling matches, tree climbing, and swimming in the surf. I was long on daring, skinny and fast, with big strong hands and feet, a tomboy with glasses and straight brown hair bleached blond every summer. I was plain and awkward, but looking back at my pictures from those days, I see an uncertain grace and sweetness trying to come through.

I repressed that because I didn't want to become "such a sweet lady" as my mother. I knew what marched behind the sweetness, and I knew there were no lily ponds there. Her interest centered on my brother, five years older, and she didn't really notice my lack of imitation until it was too late. I knew she loved me in the abstract, and it baffled and infuriated me. No one wants to be loved in the abstract: if it can't be for the real you of the flesh and the dreams, you don't want to hear about it, or at least you don't want to hear it called love.

At twelve I found my intellect, and it surprised me so much I gave up the barefoot life forever. I'd always read my brother's books — it helped to close the gap between us to know whatever he was learning at the moment. But when I started on his high school physics books, the rivalry vanished, and I fell in love with the celestial order of the universe expressed mathematically.

Things moved fast then. At thirteen I was in love with the school genius. I stalked him intellectually, wreaking adoring acts of will on his unconscious. He succumbed, and we sailed out on that eternal lily pond of the very young in love. There were depths there—the power of sex revealed itself to me in my lover's renunciation of it. We caressed endlessly and deliciously, our senses raw with arousal, but never admitting the possibility of fulfillment. In that direction lay the corruption of lust, and we would not be corrupted. But I saw how one glance of the right kind, one voice inflection could spellbind him for more, all the brilliant mind and brave ambition silenced by the eloquence of the flesh.

I knew very clearly then that I would be a daring woman scientist, swimming strongly through the surf of ignorance into the bleaching sun of truth. There would be a secret garden though, full of sensual beauty, the drip of water on fern, the glint of dragonflies over lily pads, the rustle of bird wings in water basins at evening. A man who adored my very shadow even while he achieved his own work of genius would wait there for me, and there our lives would come together in magical union.

At fifteen I left this love for a conventional high school romance, one from which each of us bore the scars of unfulfillment for many years. It was the beginning of the drought on dreams.

At eighteen, in college, reality began to quench the flash of academic promise. It had been launched with scholarships and prizes. Now it bogged down in competition with young war veterans for the sparse attention of overworked professors. My college boyfriend hated my science. Art and literature called me seductively—they were so much easier and more feminine, and I'd always been good at them.

Now I knew where I really belonged, having fun with boys, painting, writing, skimming like the sorority girl I'd become. But just before my twentieth birthday, word came that that boy I'd never gotten over in high school had married someone else. The inner crash I experienced left me a lost soul. Without letting anyone know I was doing it, even myself, I dropped the few remaining threads of ambition and structure in my life and married someone quick to love who seemed to fill the terrifying void.

Decisions like that have their price in lily pond reveries. The unexpected blessing of a child was the last brief oasis before the desert of divorce, financial problems, and child-raising single-handedly.

In time the true, enduring love arrived, but shimmered miragelike just out of reach until patience was exhausted and longing relinquished, then suddenly was mine. Marriage was tried, agonized through, given up, retried. While love somehow survived, the wells of strength were found to be depleted and the imagination dimmed.

Meanwhile there was always the daily living to be made, always at clerical work it seemed. There was the daily life to be kept in order, guarding the residual sanity and the few tenuous family connections. But the dream of intellectuality, creativity, sensuality, so vivid at fourteen, is still dreamed in the late forties with all conviction gone.

On the edge of my unconscious the golden fish dart under the lily pads, a secret fountain murmurs in a grotto, and ancient stone figures are reflected in a mirror pool. The child of drought knows instinctively of a greener land, but not how to get there.

The Kensington Ladies' Erotica Society had been meeting for more than a year when I first met Sabina. Over lunch, Sabina began to tell me about her latest venture—women's erotica. As she talked, I found myself drifting back to my young Hollywood-dominated years when my ultimate heroine was Rita Hayworth —Rita in slinky satin, her long tousled curls caressing bare shoulders, as Gilda, her husky voice curling around a microphone telling me that whatever Lola wanted, Lola got. I started musing about where these sex symbols, as tough as they were victimized, would be in the liberated eighties. I thought of the composite I had made of myself between then and now: a little Rita (I loved perfume, satin, and polished nails), a little Ida Lupino (I pretended to be tough), a little Doris Day (I married and dutifully had children), a little Katherine Hepburn (I insisted on being my own person), and a little "bookish" (for which Hollywood provided no model). Now divorced for several years and somewhat unnerved about the possibility of love-ever-after, I see myself as a realist—that is, a romantic to the cynic and a cynic to the romantic.

The attraction to accept Sabina's invitation to the next Erotica dinner meeting was irresistible. The first potluck dinner I attended disappointed me. I had not expected the hours of hors d'œuvres and chatter about one woman's salad, another's entrée, and another's dessert. Then, too, I saw the other women as more in Marilyn Monroe's generation than in Rita's and mine, and the racy stories I had expected to hear turned out to be handkerchief-dropping romance and Victorian-era fantasy. So I thought. Furthermore, aside from the group's rejection of pornographic images of women and Sabina's insistence that our heroines not be shown as victims, I did not find the feminist consciousness I had assumed would be there. (I confess that in some ways that was a relief, for I had found it difficult—though not impossible—to justify my Hollywood image-makers to young feminists.)

In that critical state of mind, I dashed off my first story about a rotten lover. My intent was to be explicit, to come from real experience instead of fantasy, and to present characters with some years behind them. When it came time to read my story to the group, I was suddenly assailed with a mixture of shyness and apprehension. I gave it to Sabina to present to the group, and stayed at home, chewing my long, lacquered nails. From her report, few (if any) of the women found it erotic; "too clinical," "too close to victimization," they had said, although it evidently stirred up a lot of down-and-dirty talk.

I almost left at that point, but writing that story (which for obvious reasons is not included here) had whetted my appetite and, despite the prickly reaction it had received, according to Sabina they had talked about it with animation. I then embarked on "Hands." I wanted to capture, in a torrent of words, the power of a man's lovemaking hands. Again (in my cowardly-lion fashion) I slipped the story into Sabina's hands and stayed at home. And, again, there was a reaction—this time more positive, enough so that "Hands" became the stimulus for other "body language" stories.

Perhaps it was the excitement that came from seeing myself as a catalyst that shifted my view. At any rate, I was now hooked. My hypercritical regard for the other women gradually crumbled, and although I remained hell-bent on our coming out with a written product (at a time when eating still seemed to be the major preoccupation), I relaxed my position about what the group was *supposed* to be and do.

Not surprisingly, I guess, it is only now that I can see the degree to which the "free spirit" I thought I was has been slave to old forms and images—every bit as much as my more conventional writing mates. And only now do I feel ready to take on the challenge of writing erotica that can stand as "woman-owned"—distinct from Hollywood and pulp magazine prescriptions of how it "should be" for our gender.

I met Sabina one New Year's Day and found her one of the liveliest and most energetic women I had ever met. She said she'd been thinking about starting a group to look at what turns women on and calling it the "Kensington Ladies' Erotica Society." I said I'd love to join. Three months later Sabina called and told me that our first meeting would be at her house. I have strong memories of that meeting. A wonderful feeling for me was that I didn't know anyone really well, and so my sense of safety was from feeling both a trust and also a distance — a separateness. I didn't know where it would go from there; I just thought it would be fun and interesting. Then we started to focus on writing. I would never have written anything if I hadn't been given assignments to write. I felt really nervous at first. If I could write it and then burn it, that would be fine, but the thought of aunts and uncles and grandfathers reading my erotic stories — that was just awful.

When I wrote my first erotic story, I was surprised to discover how *empowered* I felt. In that story the woman undresses the man. I liked writing about fantasies with strangers, but I also like writing about real experiences with my husband of twenty years, as in "Tantric Sex." Our body language stories were inspired by Elvira's "Hands," and mine was pure fun to do.

For a time I was impatient with the group, feeling that we were all too inhibited — not enough *fucking,* for god's sake! I found that down-and-dirty was most erotic to me, but it isn't easy to write or to sustain good erotica. I learned that there can also be eroticism in atmosphere and even in humorous situations.

Most of all, I've loved the sharing of stories, food, wine, and laughter. I've learned a lot about myself in this joyful process.

Ever since I was a child — an only child — I have been spinning out fantasies and telling stories to my friends. At the age of forty I suddenly found myself in a mood that recalled in a way the time when I was ten years old. Tied down by commitments to family and work, by daily routines, and by my strong sense of responsibility, I once again wanted to escape to my own fairyland where everything was possible, where anything could happen. So I sat down and said: "If all your wishes could come true, what would you wish?" That I picked erotica as my fairyland seemed appropriate because in mid-life I was curious again about the mysteries of sex, about my own body and other bodies, and, as in the whispering times of my youth, I still rebelled against authority. I no longer wanted to follow the prescriptions for so-called sexual fulfillment. I even doubted whether there was such a phenomenon as an erotic turn-on.

When the Kensington Ladies rallied around me, I felt again like part of a gang. Comparing my vision with theirs made them sharper, more daring, more exciting. By writing stories, my fantasies took on real dimensions, and I began to look on real life more as fantasy. The sight of a long-lost lover still gave me the most exquisite sexual thrill, yet I had no desire to be with him again. I now preferred the dream of what I wanted him to be. Besides, writing a story about him was a lot safer than an actual meeting would have been.

At first I was afraid that my escape from reality might jeopardize my down-to-earth life and love. As it turned out, no dangerous chasm existed between my imaginings and my real experiences. Rather, a meandering stream of consciousness carried my stories back into my life like water into the ocean. Behind the exotic mask of a leopard, for example, I discovered the familiar face of my husband of twenty-five years.

The moment I saw EROTICA! emblazoned in bold letters on Nell's kitchen calendar, I was hooked. What was my friend up to? I had to know! Nell invited me to the next meeting, and after eagerly accepting, I rushed home to write EROTICA! on my own calendar.

It is now nearly six years later, and I still pepper my calendar each month with EROTICA! The word stares back at me from a schedule overflowing with the usual events that are as unerotic as anything can be, but seeing EROTICA! reminds me to stop and notice, to revive and savor the sensuality that gets trampled in the haste of everyday life.

I write erotica to celebrate the ordinary. Being near-sighted, I happen to notice things closest to me and find great potential for lust and excitement in whatever finally comes into focus. Often a ludicrous discrepancy exists between reality and my perception of it, but this results less from myopia than from my expectations that so often eclipse actual events. The interplay between fantasy and reality colors my life as much as my stories.

After so much time with the Kensington Ladies I notice that my more respectable friends and relatives are growing restless. They had expected me to outgrow this fling with erotica or, at least, to hide it in the closet where it belongs and to get on with more important pursuits. To spare them further discomfort and embarrassment, I have adopted a pseudonym whose origin I enjoy so much that I must tell it.

Long ago, in a tender moment, when I and my husband-to-be were still very new to each other, I whispered to him that his ears smelled like roast almonds.

Like a man accused, he spun around and cried out: "ROSE SOLOMON?"

"Who's *she*?" I demanded — equally alarmed.

Ever since, Rose Solomon has represented that terrible "other woman," and it seems only right that she should speak in these pages for this other me.

I am the product of an uneasy alliance between the Welsh and the French. I was born in England and educated in France, Senegal (in what was then French West Africa), and England, so by the age of four I could speak three languages. Unfortunately, I never learned the alphabet in any of them, and to this day I consult dictionaries only when no one else is around. Despite this drawback, I have been writing since the age of nine. I love words and tend to get a little out of control when writing them down on paper, as Rose and Elvira know to their editorial chagrin. (I don't care too much for rules either, except for the one about split infinitives, which I now learn to my surprise no longer matters in America.)

I joined the Kensington Ladies' Erotica Society at its second meeting. I was thrilled to join a writing group because there is always so much yeast in the atmosphere when more than one person is engaged creatively at the same time, and I was drawn by the context. EROTICA. Sabina had crystallized the vague discontent, the fretful, petulant, cloudy subthought that I had dragged around by the foot like a doll in the dust ever since I started reading modern literature in my mid-teens — the feeling that *something is wrong here* when I read virile red-blooded prose. When I first met the Kensington Ladies, I was writing a series of prose-poetry pieces that dealt with my relationships to God, men, and my mother, and the phrase "God and His Brothers" kept creeping in. I have a great deal of respect for the unconscious: I assume that these gentlemen were my silencers and my judges.

So I joined Sabina and Nell and Judy and Jenna that evening in Judy's airy house high in the Kensington hills. I remember a fire and soft couches and a breathtaking view of the bay. I also remember a feeling of shyness, which we all shared at that stage, as we struggled to find our voices. What was it we wanted to say exactly? What was at stake if we said it? Was it acceptable to write autobiographically? Would the outcome be reward or punishment? God and His Brothers were out there in the sparkling dark, shadowboxing.

We shrieked a lot, I remember. We laughed a lot, too. Somebody wept. (Was it me?) Judy served a marvelous thick soup. There was a feeling both of release and of tension: some break was going to be made, some Bastille stormed. Visions of slightly tipsy pioneer women, sunbonnets askew, holding off bears and astonished Indians with a kitchen chair, wove jerkily about my consciousness like an old silent movie. What was erotica, anyway?

By the end of the evening I knew what we were about: we were claiming joint ownership of the human condition, refuting the male monopoly of sexual fantasy. It was an exhilarating, terrifying, and liberating experience. But I still find when I am patiently explaining to a strident man the difference between pornography — insidiously maiming all it touches — and erotica, which is joyful, pervasive, and utterly life-affirming, that if I turn my head a fraction over my shoulder, I can see God and His Brothers wagging admonishing fingers.

I was nurtured in the lazy heat of a San Joaquin Valley vineyard. My erotic roots grow deep in California soil — sun, water, oak trees, and the dusty gold of rolling hills. Being primitive and part of nature are my earliest and most delightful memories. In rural life, time can hold quite still. I have frozen images that carry over into my writing: the triumph my six-year-old girlfriend and I felt as our photo was snapped, our toes clutching the sand of an irrigation ditch, cold water lapping at our ankles, and a blazing summer sun browning our bare midriffs. Being early liberated ladies, we had persuaded our mothers to buy us boy's swimming trunks, and we felt the world envied us standing there stripped to the waist, glorying in our symbolic freedom. It's only natural that I should want to continue this fun.

The erotica group was formed to explore women's true feelings as opposed to men's notions of how we felt. Our writing expressed ideas and feelings each member considered to have erotic appeal. To my chagrin I found that it was difficult, even in such congenial surroundings, to avoid the constant lament: "Well, *I* don't think that's erotic!" Obviously, there are great individual differences. In the end I decided to be myself and write about my feelings, so my stories and poems are very personal and I felt very erotic when I wrote them.

VIII.   A PROPOSAL

For you, dear Reader...

If the idea of an erotica society appeals to you, why not form one of your own? All you have to do is whisper "erotica" at parties, at work, and even at home, and kindred spirits will reveal themselves. Once you have aroused the curiosity of enough pleasure seekers, set a date and inscribe the word erotica on your kitchen calendar. The magic of this word is powerful. The mixed reactions of friends and family will be the first test of your resolve to follow through. Invite your fledgling group to your house and ask each one to bring something enticing to eat or drink. Good food and wine create the safe ambiance that allows you to take the first step into the erotic unknown.

There is a huge gap between wishing and doing so don't despair if only half of your seemingly enthusiastic supporters actually appear on the chosen day. If those who do come fall silent or chatter nervously about everything but erotica, it is up to you, the hostess, to bolster them. Allow for enough small talk to get acquainted but don't get diverted. Assure the faint-hearted that nothing personal need be divulged and that whatever they reveal can be accepted as wild fabrication.

During dinner, read a story aloud from Ladies' Own Erotica. This tactic will ease your guests into the topic of the evening. Ask your listeners whether they found the story a turn-on. If not, together you can play with it to make it more erotic. Treat it like a stew. What will make it tastier—more spice? more thickening? more meat? Before you realize it, you will be making up your own tales, and your Erotica Society will be launched.

At your monthly Erotica meeting, leave the good housekeeper, mother, and job-holder behind and come as the playful child. The erotic spring is buried deep inside us beneath the rubble of childhood taboos, cultural stereotyping, and lifelong inhibitions.

When you feel the urge to write, concentrate on the erotic mood you want to create. Don't rush it. Give in to chaos for a while and free your self-indulgent spirit.

Having unlocked Pandora's box, let the others have a peek. Whoever is most daring among you can be the first to read aloud. You may prefer, as we did, to hear your story read by someone else. Hearing your words is a fascinating experience, especially in the voice of a good reader. It is important to listen with empathy, to show enthusiasm, and to be lavish with your encouragement. Don't worry at this point about syntax or style. Nothing is more damaging to the erotic spirit than a lesson in English composition. Not everyone will want to write, and that is fine. Lively and responsive listening is vital. After all, you are doing this for fun.

To strengthen your conspiracy of self-indulgence, go on an erotic retreat together, even if only for a day. The farther away you are from the distractions of home, the closer you come to your erotic self. If we have learned anything from our long journey together, it is that the most erotic story of all is the one waiting to be told.

Bon voyage!

The Kensington Ladies

Look Homeward Erotica

More Mischief by the Kensington Ladies' Erotica Society

ILLUSTRATED BY PAT ADLER

We dedicate these pages
to *our* angels—at home, in neighborhood bookstores,
and in the glitzy outer reaches of the media.

CONTENTS

EROTICA MELANCHOLIA

PERIOD PIECES

ERODYSSEY

Dear Erotic Reader,

How good it is to be in your hands again! We have longed for you to find us and take us home. Let's curl up together in your favorite place—a velvet sofa beside a fire? a bed with goose-down pillows? a sheltered beach? Your letters have stirred us deeply, and now at last you're here! What can we do for you—perhaps something hot to drink, such as Minnehaha Soup, or something fresh and sweet, like Ooo La La! Berry Mousse? Or would you rather get straight to it?

The first time we met, between the lines of Ladies' Own Erotica, *we romped on foreign shores and ate forbidden fruit. Do you remember? We played with popes and truck drivers, professors and construction workers, gardeners and naughty grannies. This time we just want to stay home with you. We quiver when you turn our pages gently, when your hands cradle our spine, when your eyes roam over us uninhibited. Each time you smile, each time your breathing quickens, you bring our words to life. Let's stay up all night the way we used to—and then, a Breakfast Orgy! Whom shall we invite? Lovers old and new? Husbands? Wives? Even mothers can come! Who knows what will happen? We are older but no wiser.*

Love and kisses,

The Kensington Ladies

PREFACE

Unlike our first book, a love child born of unchecked desire, this one was a *planned* baby. To conceive it, we ran away to an "erotic retreat" that lasted three days. We danced in the waves of our collective lust at a wonderful white stretch of northern California beach. Every evening the sun set like a red enamel casserole on the rim of a copper sea. The first night we stood for a long time in the dunes searching the horizon for Halley's comet. Halley never showed, but instead a great horny owl swooped silently over our heads and perched nearby in the branches of a huge black pine. He watched us for hours, hooting ardently and inspiring us to lascivious acts of creation. All the next day we wrote, and the following night amid shrieks of raucous laughter we played "Masturbate Theater" with each Lady leaping in and improvising her own character on the spot.

Our erotic retreat spawned many of the stories in this book, and as we went back home to bring them "to term," we felt much more passionate, more robust, than before. We were reminded again that an erotic story doesn't end at the typewriter—once it is read and known by others, it takes on a life of its own. Whether fantasy feeds our erotic muse or whether she feeds our fantasies doesn't matter as long as the portions are ample and we all get seconds. As magically as our potluck feasts materialize whenever we converge, so did a banquet of stories gradually take form. In this book we look at the whole spectrum of our erotic life—the sassy and the sad, the bitter and the sweet. The table is set. Please come in and help yourselves.

LATE BLOOMERS

LATE BLOOMERS

We have finally learned to say yes when we used to say no, and no when we used to say yes. Yes, we are "late bloomers." We come in many varieties, and we have bloomed in different seasons. Some of us were late in claiming our sexuality, some were late in talking about it, and others were late in acting on it. Once we found our voices, it took nine years of dallying over sumptuous potluck feasts before we felt audacious enough to publish what we had written—yet when we were asked to show our faces, we wore masks.

Looking back at our loves and lives, we have learned that nostalgia becomes even sweeter with age, for what it loses in high drama, it gains in laughter. "Whose flesh is this?" remarked one Lady recently, as she sped along with her convertible top down, noticing the skin on her upper arm flapping gaily in the breeze like a piece of pink tissue. Still, we like being older women telling tales of erotica laced with mischief. The stories that follow are a mixed bunch of the conventional, the absurd, and the romantic, tied together with a strand of the out-and-out sexy.

Macho Woman

Macho Woman
that's who I am
I'm big and strong
and I need a man.

Be he alive
or be he dead
I'll grind his bones
in my macho bed.

I'll tweak his nipples
play his game
snap my leather and
make him tame.

Lurid, torrid
hot am I
I'm Macho Woman
where's my guy?

My Lioness

Alice was not a woman who had lived her life in the fast lane. In some ways, she made you think of a century past . . . a "bygone era." Certainly that was the way she had appeared to Dirk, who had first set eyes on her in the restaurant where he worked. Alice came in every Wednesday at 8 o'clock. He noticed her particularly because of her hair.

Dirk, a man of fifty, had been in the United States only a year and, if he had found someone to confide in, would have confessed that he missed a certain quality in American women. Although he would have been vague about what that quality was, make no mistake—it was Alice's hair that had stirred up old nostalgias, recalling for him a yearning he thought he had long since buried. When Dirk's wife had been killed in an accident, Dirk had been devastated. Picking up and moving to the United States from Wiesbaden was a remedy his friends had offered, knowing that such a trip had once been in his mind, and that if ever he needed to get away, it was now. As head waiter in an internationally famous restaurant, Dirk spoke several languages fluently . . . with a discernible accent, yes, but fluently. And so language posed no barrier to his relocation. In fact, his adjustment had been quick and smooth.

That first Wednesday, he had watched her walk in and glance around, a bit anxiously, quite clearly looking for someone to seat her and thus relieve her of this awkward standing about. When no one did, she glanced at the different tables and selected one by the window, whose panes were almost—but not quite—smothered in various species of ferns. The table she had selected was in his station. He stopped to watch her a moment before he went over to her. He loved her nervousness, the color in her face because of it, and, most especially, her hair.

Her hair was what poets have described for centuries as "golden." But not only was it golden, it was thickly waved, pulled back from her face, and caught in back with long crinkly hairpins, the kind that have been sold in five-and-ten-cent stores for decades. It was unruly hair . . . naughty hair which, men sensed and women knew, had refused to be tamed from her girlhood, when, anyway, such hair as hers was not the fashion. Had Alice only known how it excited him to see the curly wisps of hair which, escaping her carefully constructed bun, now clung to the pale skin below the curve of her ears, and the slightly longer wisps that trailed down the nape of her neck where small beads of perspiration often tickled her at inopportune moments, such as now, for example, when a waiter stared at her from across the room.

He watched her searching for ways to cover up her anxiety, which she did first by reaching to the back of her hair and pulling out a few hairpins and replacing them in what appeared to be exactly the same spot, and then by glancing out the window, affecting the look of someone who was waiting to be joined. But she would not be joined these Wednesday evenings, as Dirk soon discovered. As he watched her face framed in the window and half obscured by the plants, he fought back the desire to go to her—to sit down across from that apprehensive face, take it in his strong hands, and insinuate his thick fingers into her hair until every pin gave up its position and dropped to the ground in joyful surrender. He knew that to possess Alice's hair was to possess Alice, and he knew also that he *would* possess this unlikely woman. The power of it—not just his emotion for her but his certainty that she would be, was already, his—was not born of arrogance but came naturally from a man of his time and place who had lived and loved for half a century.

With the recognition that their lives and bodies would inevitably be entwined like the red rose and the briar, Dirk was able to stride over to her table. A slight stiffness in his legs and gait reminded him of the toll on his body that the years of waiting on tables had taken. If he longed to be younger and more vigorous, however, it was only in the small hours of the morning when, awakened by an insomniac mockingbird outside his window, he would permit himself the self-indulgence of reflecting on his life in a kind of philosophical melancholy that saddened and satisfied him at the same time.

As he approached her table, he kept his eyes on her every step of the way. He wanted to absorb every detail of this living portrait and, especially, to be fully there at the precise moment when she would look up at him. And so it was: He stood at her elbow and she looked fully into his face, which he quickly averted. Letting his pencil lightly touch the surface of the menu she was holding, he said: "May I suggest the médaillons de boeuf? They are excellent tonight."

More than simply being attended to, Alice found something comforting in his gesture. It permitted her to fix her eyes on the menu and to feel a human presence, if conveyed only by the hot-iron smell emanating from the sleeve of his freshly starched white shirt. Rather than accept his suggestion immediately, she deliberately murmured something about having wanted fish, but, "Well . . . yes," she said, looking up at his impassive face, "the médaillons de boeuf is appealing." Dirk smiled discreetly as he scribbled her order on his pad. How startled Alice would have been to know that this suave German waiter walked away with an urgent stirring in his groin, as he reflected on the delight her seduction would be.

Each Wednesday, she would come in and look about tentatively—always glancing around quickly to see whether the table she had occupied the first time was available. After two times when it had not been, and Dirk from across the room had seen her acute dismay, he had gone to some pains to be sure that when she came in, that table would be free—even if it meant lying to a customer that it was reserved. His reward was the quiet relief he saw in her face on subsequent evenings as she walked quickly to the table they both now regarded as hers.

Occasionally she would sit on the opposite side of the table. The first time she had done so, Dirk found himself taken aback, for it was as if another woman—who looked very much like her, to be sure—had taken Alice's place. He studied this new profile until he felt at ease with both sides of her face—indeed until he knew every nuance of its contour, color, and expression. He loved that she had distinct sidedness to her face, seeing it as reflective of two distinct sides to her person—the light and the shadow, the candid and the mysterious, the innocent and the passionate. It was the same quality that had initially excited him about her hair—at once sophisticated with its elaborately twisted knots and yet childlike with its curly golden swirls pleading to be let loose. Dirk felt his decision to seduce her as something about which he had little choice. It would be so, and that was that.

The day finally came when Dirk was certain he had gained her confidence sufficiently that she would not reject his advance. He had changed into street clothes and was approaching her table. Alice had finished her meal and was rummaging through her purse to find her wallet. She was lost in her own thoughts. It had become clear to her that his attentiveness these past weeks went beyond that of a good waiter to a faithful customer, and while his behavior was always appropriate, Alice knew in her heart that he was taken with her. "Taken with her" was about all she could bear to think, although in the privacy of her dreams he "took her" in far more direct and physical terms. So when she saw him standing by her table, her surprise was not that he was there but that he was not in his familiar uniform. Without his crisp white shirt and black trousers, his presence felt disarmingly personal. There seemed to be no distance at all between them. Alice was suddenly aware that for her Dirk existed only in this restaurant and only for that period of time she was seated at her table. No matter that he appeared in her dreams and startled her body with unspeakable intimacies; those nocturnal visits were entirely under the control of her vivid imagination and took place in the illuminated world of fantasy, not in the less predictable world that was her reality.

Dirk had known that his appearance in ordinary dress would be as disconcerting as the expression on her face revealed it to be, and he waited for her to regain her poise. Carefully controlling his voice and standing at a comfortable distance from the table, he finally spoke.

"I am off duty now, as you can see" (he smiled to reassure her), "and I wonder if you would let me join you for an after-dinner walk."

Her smile reassured him that he had not frightened her too badly. "Well, yes . . . that would be very nice," she responded. She looked as though she were going to say more, but no words followed. Dirk signaled silently to another waiter to pick up her check. Then, touching her lightly on the elbow, he steered her gently and swiftly to the door. Once outside, he turned to her and asked "Which way?" She didn't answer immediately. Finally, she pointed and said "That direction looks inviting; there's a café a few blocks from here." "Then may I?" he said, and at the same moment he linked his arm in hers and began walking.

Something in his firm grip, easy smile, and confident stride made Alice feel protected. She liked the roughness of his tweed jacket and the faint smell of pipe tobacco that forced its way out of the herringbone. For Alice, it was that texture and that odor that gave a man his maleness. As they walked along, she learned that he was from Wiesbaden, that his wife had died, that he now lived in a studio apartment a mile or so from the restaurant, that he walked to work and back every day, and that he had always wanted to be in the theater. He learned that she had worked for years as a laboratory assistant, had never married, and took a flute lesson every Wednesday evening. By the time they reached the café, they had the look of old friends.

Dirk was pleased with her, and pleased with himself. He felt in tune with her rhythms, aware of just how far he could press himself on her and when it was prudent to withdraw. Once seated at the café, he let his eyes meander lovingly over her hair whenever she looked away, imagining the joy in store when he would break his way into its golden mass and take possession of its thickness with his hands and with his mouth, and inhale the scent of her. He imagined her great tumble of hair, once freed from its prison of pins, trailing down his body from lips to breastbone to navel to genitals, where it would come to rest, covering him in a soft mound as she burrowed her face between his legs and he burrowed his hands into its labyrinthine depths. Strangely, the thought brought him close to tears and he looked quickly away.

By the end of their first evening together, Alice felt comfortable enough with Dirk to let him walk her home. He left her at her door with the promise to prepare a sumptuous picnic for them on her next free weekend. She was clearly pleased. They shook hands, and, as is permitted new lovers, held on for a provocative second longer than was strictly necessary. Had the god of love been watching, he would have smiled down on each of them, Alice for the high color in her cheeks as she moved around her apartment restlessly, finally taking out her flute and playing a sprightly Elizabethan madrigal, and Dirk for walking so swiftly home, totally forgetting the stiffness in his leg that had always served so faithfully to remind him of what his life was about.

The high color remained in Alice's cheeks all week long. The head of the laboratory noticed it and said nothing; her co-workers asked whether she had been in the sun. The fact was that her dream life during the several intervening days had been as tempestuous as that of a heroine in a gothic novel, which might have explained the blush Alice had carried with her to work each day. As for Dirk, each night he spent his time off scribbling out new menus and revising his shopping list for their picnic. Perhaps he should bake something . . . perhaps make a soup . . . or would she prefer . . . ? Even though Alice had told him she would not be at the restaurant the next week and that their "tryst" would have to wait, he had not prepared himself for the affront he felt in seeing strangers at her table the following Wednesday. He found himself behaving in a stiff, almost rude, manner and was not surprised at the insulting tips each party left for him.

When their weekend came, both Alice and Dirk—despite the cool composure they showed to others—were in a state of agitated longing that, in another century, another place, would have occasioned an outpouring of poetry from their anguished hearts. On the day of the picnic, Alice changed her outfit five times . . . finally opting for a cotton batiste shift, a light sweater, and sandals. Her skin was the kind that took poorly to the sun, and she had long ago accepted with resignation its year-round paleness. She was ready a full hour before Dirk arrived.

When the doorbell rang, Alice was at her music stand playing a melancholy étude from Chopin. She opened the door to him, and his first words were, "You must bring your flute with you. I insist."

Alice laughed. "Yes, I suppose I could," she answered. "But I promise you I won't play if there are too many people around." "But of course," Dirk replied. "You will play only for me. That is as it should be."

Dirk had piled picnic basket, blankets, wine, and extra clothing in the back seat of his car; now he added her flute case. Alice did not ask where they were going. He loved her simple trust and her willingness to be taken care of. Once out of the city, Dirk drove fast but carefully, talking more animatedly than he had in years. It was an hour and a half before they got to his selected place—a tiny island in a man-made lake near an old winery. She was openly delighted, and he was pleased that she had never been there before. He wanted it to be his secret and her surprise. He had "rented" it, she discovered. The winery allowed no more than ten people on the island at a time, and he had pretended they were ten so that no strangers would be able to join them.

Dirk donned an apron and forbade her to do anything. "I am your servant," he announced with mock flourish, and proceeded to spread out a white tablecloth and explain each dish as he unpacked it from the basket. As he worked and talked, Alice looked out across the lake at the vineyards in the distance where a lone man on horseback was riding alongside the fields. In their near vision, swans were gliding with lazy determination through the waters of the lake, making sudden abrupt turns as though controlled by a child's remote device on shore. That she was enchanted was clear from the expression on her face.

They talked all the way through the banquet Dirk had set out, and they drank up all the wine. Exhausted from eating, talking, laughing, they finally fell asleep on the grass. It was Dirk who awakened first. He sat up slowly and looked at her, soundly sleeping on her stomach, her head turned to the side. The pins that held her bun in place had loosened, and strands of ebullient hair were beginning to escape in great number. Dare he? he thought, even as he began gently pulling the hairpins from her wiry curls, which, one by one, sprang free.

When he had removed as many as he could find, he sat back to gaze at her: The portrait he had created in his mind so many times since that first night had come to life before him.

"My lioness," he said softly. She opened her eyes and rolled over on her back to face him. Before she could say anything, he enmeshed his fingers in her hair, which haloed her face like a giant sunflower, and lifted her mouth to his—pausing when his lips were a breath away and remaining there, lightly brushing his mouth on hers, and then tenderly returning her head to the pungent grass beneath them. Their eyes fastened hard on each other, and neither spoke. She reached out and traced his brow, nose, jaw, and mouth with her fingers. Then she stopped abruptly and said: "I want to play for you now."

She stood up and got her flute while Dirk moved to prop himself up against a tree. She returned and stood a few feet from him. Planting her legs firmly apart in a stance that was clearly designed to assure her balance, Alice raised the flute to her mouth, wet her lips, and rolled them together as if she were blotting lipstick. Only then did she purse her lower lip against the mouth of her instrument and, with a sharp intake of breath, begin to play. Suddenly, her whole body was alive—her foot beating out time as her head bobbed rhythmically from side to side, her arms leaning into the sound as if they were wings attached to the sleek silver bird she held in her hands, and her belly heaving visibly as she blew such life into the instrument that Dirk felt the ground shudder beneath them. When she finished, he clapped and shouted, "Brava! Brava!" She threw her head back and laughed wildly. Watching her, Dirk found it hard to believe this was the same woman, his "golden madonna."

"I never realized how *physical* an instrument the flute is to play," Dirk said. "Oh yes," Alice answered quickly. "When I give lessons, I always make my students take off their blouses, sometimes more, so I can be sure they are breathing from the belly. The flute is not a timid instrument. It wants all of you, and you must give all of yourself to it."

Dirk's response to this revelation showed quite clearly in his face and in that savagely unpredictable place between his legs as well.

"And how do I know that *you* are . . . how did you say it? . . . giving all of yourself to it? Must I merely trust that it is so?" Dirk had permitted an old forgotten mischief to come into his voice. He looked at her from his vantage point a few feet away. She was still standing, feet apart, her light dress caught in a breeze that sucked the fabric between her thighs. She was wiping the mouthpiece of the flute and smiling.

"Well, at home, I usually practice in front of a mirror with no clothes on so that I am sure of my breathing."

"Ahhhh," Dirk answered. "You must let me play your music teacher. Now show me, sweet Alice, that you are breathing properly."

Alice could not restrain a laugh. She laid the flute down in its case. Then she reached for the hem of her dress in both hands and, in one deft motion, pulled it up and over her head and hung it on a tree branch that was reaching out at precisely the right height. She hesitated a second and then put her arms behind her and unhooked her bra, dropping it into the cover of her flute case. When she leaned over to retrieve her flute, he felt his breath stop as her thick hair fell like a heavy curtain over her full breasts and then slowly rose to unveil them as she straightened up. Once again, she placed her mouth a hair's breadth from the mouth of the instrument and hovered there, as if waiting for the conductor's signal. As he feasted his eyes on her, he did not know which thrilled him more—her breasts or her marvelous belly, which was not steely flat like the magazine ads of bathing beauties, but swelled round and full over her bikini panties. Indeed, as she began to play, it came to life, pushing out as she blew a deep musical breath into the mouthpiece and suddenly retracting as she sucked her breath in to reach for a high note. Once again, her entire body was alive even though her feet remained firmly positioned on the ground.

Dirk was dazzled, transported, and beside, beyond, and above himself with longing. He kept his eyes fixed resolutely on her, even though he feared he would die of it. Occasionally, she would catch his eye, but he couldn't fathom its message because the flute obscured and distorted her expression. (He had always felt it was not the eyes but the mouth that was the tattletale of the soul.) At some point—he was sure of it—she had nodded to him in a gesture that said, "Take off your clothes, too." Without waiting to be certain, he leaped to his feet and stripped himself of clothing as she came closer and circled around him like a nymphean Pan, playing faster and faster. Abruptly, she stopped playing and held the flute lightly between them. He could see a pink flush spreading across her upper body and neck and into her cheeks as he moved in closer. He took the flute from her and placed it gently in its velvet-lined box. He turned to see her slip quickly out of her panties, stretch out on her back on the grass, extend her arms to each side, and open her legs. Had she stiffened her body at that moment and allowed herself to be raised to a standing position (a game of trust perhaps only children dare play), she would have been in perfect flute-playing posture.

Dirk was enraptured with the sight of her. Alice's thick wiry hair was splayed in an arc around her face, and the sunlight sparked through it like a welder's torch. Without taking his eyes from her face, he slowly lowered his body down onto hers until his mouth was a whisper away from her mouth. She was looking up at him with an expression he had never before seen on any woman.

"Come, my lion," she said, "come play me."

Music Lover

Adele was certain that it was change of life, not lust, that prompted her renewed curiosity in men. Not since her teens and twenties had she been getting so off-track. Lately she often caught herself in the most uncharacteristic behavior—gawking at the butcher's muscled forearms instead of his handsome display of prime rib roasts, complimenting the bank teller on his new moustache rather than filling out her deposit slip, and stalling at the drive-in car wash whenever her favorite attendant, Mario with the tight bottom, came into view.

By now all the employees knew her by name—"Good afternoon, Miss Adele. Hot wax today?"—and Mario always bestowed special attention on her. He liked aloof women of every age and found Adele's haughty elegance and feigned indifference especially alluring. He smiled flirtatiously, revealing a gold tooth that inexplicably delighted her, and wooed her with free bonuses—shining her hubcaps or polishing her chrome with extra care. He even promised to simonize her car on his next day off. Suddenly life teemed with an array of men to whom Adele had never felt particular attraction before, and she felt as though she was in the driver's seat.

Adele saw to it that the rest of her life ran as smoothly as her car. She did not miss the tumult of her youth. Two violently possessive love affairs had eventually suffocated on their own intensity and left her feeling lost to herself. Over the intervening years she had learned to live and love in apparent moderation while secretly mastering the art of sublimation. She worked as an accountant at home in a small, immaculate study that had dormer windows overlooking a quiet residential street. Though she preferred living alone, she sometimes thought it would be nice to have a husband who could fix things, who would be "on call" any hour of the day or night—someone like Maureen's husband, Gus.

Gus was truly a master of physical know-how. Whenever he ran out of repairs at home, he would ask Adele if she needed help. At first Adele, too inhibited by the imagined boundaries of her friendship with Maureen, could ask for nothing more than a quick unstopping of a toilet or the unjamming of a window. Over the years as her friendship with Maureen deepened and began to include more and more household tips, Maureen herself volunteered Gus's services. One day while he was installing track lighting in her kitchen, Adele learned that his real forte was wiring.

"Could you install stereo speakers for me in here?" she asked. "I'd love to listen to music while I cook."

"Sure, I can install them anywhere you want," laughed Gus, and before the month was over, he had installed them in her kitchen, her study, her bedroom, and even her bathroom. Adele wished the task had taken him longer. She missed the cheerful sounds he made as he worked. She had grown used to the John Philip Sousa marches he whistled between his teeth, and she found herself humming them to herself at absent-minded moments. She missed the way he talked to himself when a job absorbed him: "Here we go—just one more twist—'at-a-girl. Aha! Got it!"

To thank him, Adele prepared his and Maureen's tax returns for free. Gus was so grateful that he suggested all sorts of new projects for Adele which she never would have thought to propose. He grew especially animated when he described an alarm system he thought she should have, especially as a woman living alone. It would be a perfected version of the one he had installed for himself and Maureen, and it would make her feel a lot safer. Adele didn't have the heart to tell him she felt quite secure without one, and she accepted his offer more for the promise of his continued presence than for the finished system.

Physically Adele did not find Gus attractive. He was big and burly with the shape of an overgrown toddler—a shape which tempted her more to tuck in his shirttails than to pull its paunch against the concave curve of her own slim figure. What hair he had was crew cut, a style left over from army days and one that certainly did not cry out to be caressed. What disturbed Adele and what she had to conceal from Maureen was the way her flesh rose into goose bumps whenever Gus's presence passed by unexpectedly. Like a giant gerbil, amazing in its pliability, Gus could manage to squeeze between walls and navigate the dark crawl spaces that composed the attic and basement. The swish-swish of his torso inching along the other side of a wall or the grunts of exertion emanating from the floorboards beneath her feet caused Adele's heart to leap. She frequently had to recalculate long columns of numbers and to recheck her work late at night long after Gus had gone home.

Adele's conscience required that she remain busy at her desk whenever Gus did his wiring, but she welcomed his frequent interruptions. His muffled voice would call out from some cramped interior, and she would abruptly abandon her calculations mid-column to go find him. This often required her to tap her way along the walls to pinpoint his exact location, and they would converse through light switches and cracks in the sheetrock. Ostensibly he would need a tin snips or a screwdriver or a different size wire, but mostly he wanted conversation and companionship.

Adele enjoyed these casual exchanges. Talking to someone so close and yet unseen filled her with a sense of ease and intimacy that re-created the flirtation of telephone courtships. She talked freely, recklessly, and laughed more than his jokes deserved. Leaning against the wall, she thought she could detect the heat emanating from Gus's girth. While his hands engaged in intricate circuitry, his words insinuated their way into her flesh. The cavity between her slim waist and still discernible pelvic bones began to feel turgid and engorged. The heaviness usually lasted for several hours and precipitated troubling secretions. Unwilling to admit that her best friend's husband's presence had awakened her love juices, she ascribed them to the havoc of impending menopause.

At times like these Adele needed to abandon everything for a while. Occasionally she would take a brisk walk, but more likely she would drive to the Stop 'n Glo car wash and let the roaring machines cleanse her mind as well as her car. Without leaving the driver's seat, she allowed herself to surrender safely to the sensuality of the moment. Being towed into the spooky, dark tunnel so close to the rolling brushes and mysterious, dangling objects and feeling the hot breath of the dryers blasting from all sides filled her with a piercing thrill. She would lean against the steering wheel and let the vibrations resonate through her entire body. Afterward, a limp calm would settle over her, and Adele could return home clear-headed, ready to resume her accounting and her life.

One Saturday morning early in April as Adele worked in her study to complete tax returns, the doorbell rang. It was Gus bringing an extension ladder so that he could install sirens under the eaves in front and in back. Adele went downstairs to let him in.

"Myyyy! Don't you look nice!" he said. He loved the way Adele's outfits always matched, the way her pageboy was never mussed, the way she always wore accessories. Maureen had observed that Adele was one of those rare women who could wear scarves, and she was right. Gus had seen how a scarf could remain elegantly draped about Adele's neck and shoulders all day without wrinkling. There was a regal, feline quality about her that he couldn't put into words: something detached and composed. She was an exquisite ornament he wanted to protect.

While Gus was hammering out in back, the doorbell rang again. Adele opened the front door to find Victor, her musician neighbor from across the street, waiting on her doorstep. Being very tall, he had the habit of stooping close when he spoke, and his long chin hovered at eye level. Adele could tell from his supplicating posture that, as usual, he was going to ask a favor, and as he clasped his boney hands beneath his chin he looked very much to her like a praying mantis about to pounce.

"Dear Adele, please excuse me for disturbing you like this, but my phone is out of order, and I have got to reach my accompanist. Would you let me call on yours?"

Victor's long hands gestured emphatically. His expressive awkwardness had endeared him to her and made his frequent intrusions amusing.

"Of course, Victor. Come in. I haven't seen you in a while."

"I know," he laughed. "I guess nothing's gone wrong lately."

Adele showed him to the wall phone in her kitchen. Outside the window just above the sink Gus's feet perched on a high rung of the ladder.

Victor made an inquiring gesture.

"My friend's husband, Gus," she explained. She was suddenly struck by the way the shape of the room seemed to expand and contract in order to accommodate it inhabitants. When stocky Gus stood in her kitchen, it felt narrow and high-ceilinged, but now with tall, wiry Victor, it felt low and squat.

Victor dialed his number, then hung up.

"It's busy. May I try again later?"

"Sure," said Adele and followed him to the front door feeling as though all the ceilings had dropped six inches. With much resistance, she returned to her paperwork. If the pressure of a deadline weren't so close upon her, it would have been a perfect time for a car wash.

Around lunchtime Adele took a break. She put on the teakettle, then flipped on the stereo and played whatever was still on the turntable—the second side of a string quintet. Just then the doorbell rang again. She opened the door to find Victor who was craning his long neck forward and peering beyond her toward the living room. As though invited in by the music, he moved closer and gasped, "Aha! Schubert's Quintet in C Major! The scherzo! To think that I came looking for a phone and found a scherzo! And my favorite one at that!" He began to conduct a few bars of the movement, then lunged toward her in a burst of enthusiasm. "Oh, Adele, you have inspired me to play this piece! My chamber music friends meet on Sunday evenings, and next week we'll sight-read the Schubert at my house in your honor. Will you come? Oh, please! You will? How wonderful!" he exclaimed backing down the front steps. "Oh, thank you, thank you."

"Wait," called Adele after him. "Don't you want to use the phone?"

"Oh, yes! Dear Adele!" and he scrambled back to make his call.

Although Adele had had a symphony season ticket for fifteen years, she had never heard chamber music performed privately. In anticipation of Victor's special concert she made an extra trip to the dry cleaner's to pick up her favorite dress, a pastel floral silk. On the way home she almost bought a pair of opaque white pantyhose, but decided the look would be too girlish. Then, a half block later, she turned around and went back to buy them anyway. By the time the chosen Sunday dawned, Adele was ready to celebrate. All her tax returns had been mailed, and Gus had only to add some finishing touches to the alarm system.

Uncertain whether or not Gus was going to return that evening to retrieve his tools or to putter some more, Adele left a key for him under the doormat along with a note saying she was visiting a neighbor and had saved some carrot cake for him in the refrigerator. To further garner Gus's approval, she was careful to activate the alarm system before she closed the front door.

Once outside she could distinctly hear the instruments already tuning up in Victor's living room. She hurried across the street and up the front steps. The door was slightly ajar, and as Adele slipped inside suddenly everything went dead silent as though all the others had run away to play hide-and-seek and she were "it." Adele paused at the foot of a stairwell, uncertain what to do next, and then a chorus of stringed instruments burst into song overhead. She followed the sound to its source and stopped spellbound at the entrance to the living room. The whole upstairs throbbed with music. Adele marveled at the waves of sound cascading palpably around her. Despite Gus's efforts, the acoustics in her house were nothing like this! The piece, a Mozart quintet unknown to Adele, was a merry chase between two violins, two violas, and a cello. The room crackled with so much intense energy that Adele felt as though she were a spectator at a tennis match; one false move on her part would foil the whole thing. She waited, breathlessly still. The players, totally caught up in their piece, sat on folding chairs in a semicircle to her left. In the center of the room and to her right was a lone armchair set out in her honor, but Adele did not dare move toward it.

"Vivace! Vivace!" Victor suddenly called out rapping his bow on his music stand. In a flash the musicians broke into an excited babble: "Presto, presto!" "Fortissimo!" "Ma non troppo!" Unnoticed, Adele took her seat, and the musicians played the passage again, this time to their satisfaction. As the allegro gave way to the minuetto and finally to the adagio, Adele began to absorb the sights as well as the sounds. She could hardly believe her eyes! She had never seen performing musicians "undressed," without concert garb. The cellist, a portly woman who gamely straddled her instrument, was encased in a knit dress stretched to capacity at mid-thigh. One man playing a viola wore an aloha shirt, gray flannel slacks, and thongs, while the other looked like a stockbroker in a three-piece business suit. The woman violinist beside Victor could have been the leader of an Audubon bird-watching expedition in her sensible brown walking shoes and safari skirt. But for Adele the biggest shock of all was seeing Victor in a white undershirt, plaid shorts, and black socks with black concert shoes. Once she wrenched her gaze past those flimsy socks that clung to mid-calf, she could not take her eyes off thin Victor's shapely, well-muscled legs. They could have belonged to a cyclist or a sprinter, not to such a gangly, gray-haired man. It was as though Victor were a thirty-year-old from the waist down and a fifty-year-old from the neck up. Just as Adele was speculating about his midsection, the piece came to an end, and the musicians broke into animated conversation. Victor rushed over to her, wiping sweat from his face with the cloth he used to cradle the violin against his chin. "I'm so glad you're here. We saved the Schubert especially for you. We'll play it next. Wait 'til you hear the adagio! Come, meet my friends."

Adele could not grasp a single name, so distracted was she by Victor's hot hand upon her waist as he introduced her to each person. She could feel its heat and energy sear the folds of silk and shoot like lightning bolts down her hips and legs.

"Can I get you some wine or Calistoga?" offered Victor, gesturing toward the bottles set out on a card table near the piano. The damp spot where his hand had been turned cold. Adele felt her temperature plummet, then just as quickly soar again when his fingers brushed her ear lobe, and he whispered, "I like these earrings—aquamarine like your eyes!"

The musicians were rearranging their positions for the Shubert quintet, and Victor got out his cello. For this piece everyone except the other cellist was going to play a different instrument. Adele felt awed by their versatility. In perfect unison they embarked upon the slowly swelling allegro, leaving Adele alone in her big armchair to envy their special bond. Their rapport, so intimate and intense, had the very quality Adele once sought in love. Freely given, it strengthened and completed those it touched. She wondered how Victor, who appeared so clumsy in other contexts, could be so well coordinated here? His performance now was every bit as physical as an athlete's—alert, precise, totally absorbed. A healthy show of sweat glistened upon his face. His loving touch made the cello sing, and the melody made Adele stir in her armchair with a sensation of lush over-ripeness. Her all too predictable organs were already responding. She leaned forward to better conceal her pleasure.

The second movement, the adagio, had begun, and the growing tension between the violin and cello parts revived her heartache. The plaintiveness in their voices could only be described as human. Something about their dialogue, at times discordant and grieving, at other times sighing and loving, felt as piercing as the most intimate conversations Adele had ever had. Tears welled up in her eyes as voices of long-ago lovers cried out: "Be mine—only mine!" "You want more than I can give." "Wait! Don't go." No sooner did the cello and violin find peace, than new waves of tension destroyed their brief reconciliation and held her hostage for the rest of the quintet.

Adele's eyes fastened on Victor's long remarkable fingers. They danced their way up and down the cello's neck as quickly and nimbly as spiders' legs. They could hold a chord with a strength that made them tremble, and the cello groaned. Adele's heart pounded. At times Victor's fingers brushed the strings so lightly they gasped, and when they paused and gyrated on a single note, the vibrations matched Adele's own shocks of pleasure. His other hand held the bow, and when it slid across the strings, responsive ripples shot through Adele's belly, too. And when occasionally that hand plucked a pizzicato, Adele's perineum tightened in a knot of ecstasy. She had to cross her legs and press one hand to her lips to keep from crying out.

Silence lingered after the last chord died. Adele and the musicians were limp with triumph and emotion. Victor rested his head upon his cello and dangled his long arms to the floor—clearly a man spent.

Adele's tears had dried, leaving smudges of mascara high on her cheeks. Her dress had wilted and clung damply. Slowly people began to stretch and move about.

"Is something going on at your house, Adele?" she heard Victor asking. He was looking out the window.

She rose, going toward him. "No. Why?" And then she saw her house, ablaze with lights flashing off and on at crazy intervals in every room, both upstairs and down. The musicians crowded round, and someone joked, "Hey, Vic, that's what we need—*son et lumière!*"

"Should we call the police?" asked another.

"No, no," said Adele. "I think it's Gus. He had said something about installing a backup for my burglar alarm."

"You'd better let me walk you home," offered Victor, "just to be sure everything's all right."

He bounded ahead of her down the stairs and opened the front door.

"Wait! Do you have a coat? The fog's come in. Here, you'd better wear mine," and before Adele could protest, he'd whipped an old windbreaker out of the hall closet. He wrapped the jacket around her shoulders, her arms still dangling at her sides, and drew her close by pulling the collar toward his chest. He smiled tenderly at her mascara smudges and said, "My, you really are a music lover!"

"No, it was your playing," she confessed in a soft voice.

Then suddenly his mouth was upon hers in a virtuoso kiss that seemed a fitting coda to the piece he had just finished. Adele could feel her legs begin to buckle as she melted to his touch, but Victor clasped her with surprising strength and pressed her hard against his rigid, trembling body until chord after chord of passion has passed between them. Then, when Adele's shuddering subsided, Victor carefully released his grip, making sure she had regained her balance. He kissed her tear-streaked cheeks and whispered, "There's so much I never knew about you." And without another word, he shepherded her out the door and toward her house. They crossed the street hand in hand. Above the wailing sirens of the burglar alarm gone mad, Adele heard an imaginary choir break into the Hallelujah Chorus.

Who Is Sylvia? What Is She?

It is a clear, refreshing English day. I leave the circus of the small, out-of-London airport to board the commuter plane that will take me to Glasgow.

Excitement and anticipation overcome the fatigue of my twelve-hour, arduous trans-Atlantic flight. The voice of my daughter, her call so frantic and unexpected, is still in my ear. "Come quick, Mom, I need you. My pianist sprained his finger. You're the only person who can play my repertoire." And my startled protest, "But, I can't do that! You know I haven't been anywhere by myself since . . ." She accepts no excuses. "You can do it, Mom. And remember what you always tell me. Don't talk to any strange men."

With that final teasing warning, I have accepted the challenge. I now find myself a cautious American carrying a packet of Barclay's Bank English money, walking down the aisle of a plane bound for Scotland.

I check the number of my boarding pass again. Fourteen-B. When I find the seat, I am dismayed. It is in the middle of three seats; a pimply-faced youth already sits by the window. He looks gloomy, and I have a quick fight with my conscience.

The aisle seat is still empty. Perhaps its owner will not show. Deciding to take a chance, I slip my carry-on bag and coat under the seat and settle in, relieved by the space between me and my unpromising plane companion.

A lovely blonde stewardess waits by the door. As departure time nears, I become hopeful that no one will come to claim the seat I have chosen as my own.

The passengers settle down, seatbelts are fastened, things look good. Suddenly, there is a flurry of last-minute arrivals who run through the door as the hostess begins her ritual of locking us into her silvery, compact cocoon of flight. A man, very broad and out of breath, hurries toward me. He is carrying a briefcase in one hand and his boarding pass in the other. He stops to study his ticket with a puzzled frown. "Fourteen-A? I'm very sorry, lassie, but I believe you're in my seat?"

"Oh, yes, I know," I reply, "but would you mind trading seats? I'm feeling so tired. I need more air."

He is not delighted, but he is a gentleman. "Och, well, of course not." He squeezes past me to take the middle seat. Stowing his briefcase under the seat, he slips awkwardly out of his heavy coat and stuffs that under too, and then, carefully, he eases himself into the small space I have allowed him.

No words are spoken. Facing the aisle, I am grateful for the precious oasis of space and air I have deceptively gained for myself. The plane takes off smoothly. The charming waitress-of-the-sky begins her smiling, benign voyage up and down the aisle. The more I enjoy my freedom and the spacious view through the far window, the more I become conscious of my struggling companion.

I don't want to turn toward him, but I begin to feel the overlap of his body. He is so tightly wedged in, the sides of him seem to bulge over onto the seats on either side. I can feel his warmth. His heavy arm touches mine, it has nowhere else to go.

I begin to feel guilty. What a rotten trick, I think. Can I be noble? I turn at last.

"You're so big," I blurt out. "Would you like to change seats?" I see a stalwart chest with a face to match.

"Och, no," he says.

His answer gives me such relief, I begin chattering uncontrollably. I have obeyed my daughter and hardly spoken a word to anyone for almost a day. My worries and anxieties flow out of me.

"Oh, the trip over from America was so long. I've hardly ever gone anywhere by myself. Do I tip the stewardess? Can I drink the water?"

He looks surprised and then amused, but he is still polite. He doesn't laugh. "Now, now, I'm sure everything will be all right." His voice is strong, vibrant; his Scotch accent carries charm and calm.

The stewardess is standing beside me. The man looks at her. "A wee drop of brandy, if ye don't mind," he orders. The sullen youth continues to stare out of the window.

"A glass of sherry," I request, and am pleasantly surprised to have the woman hand us a tray of delicious-looking, crusty pastries. My new seatmate reaches into his pocket. "D'ye mind if I smoke?"

"No, no," I assure him, "I smoke too." Actually, I am delighted with his presence. A real he-man, I think. Just my kind of guy. I hand him my packet of English money. "Would you mind paying for me? I don't know the money yet."

He seems pleased at my trust. Carefully picking out a few coins, he hands them to the hostess and then returns the packet to me. He sits quietly, holding his drink and cigarette like a commuter who is used to his routine.

I am facing the aisle again, thinking hard. I feel a strong need for more of his reassurance. Would it be too pushy to continue the conversation? It is a short flight. We will land in Glasgow soon. I begin to feel a little panic that I will leave this man and never see him again. I feel attached to his warmth and his sturdy frame. I like his heartiness, his plain, clean features, his heavy thighs bulging under thick, English wool. I savor the smell of his cigarette. The smoke curls gently around us like an intimate embrace.

I turn. "I'm Sylvia Morris from the United States. I'm on my way to Aberdeen to meet my daughter. Do you live in London?"

He is sober and polite. "Ian Ross here," he replies. "I don't live in London, but I do go there quite often. I'm a Scot, you see. I live in Glencairn."

I tell him about my daughter's emergency, her sudden need for an accompanist, the concerts we will give in Aberdeen and in London at the Royal Albert Hall. His interest picks up.

"Och, aye," he says with enthusiasm. "I like music, and I'm returning to London soon. I could go to your concert. When is it?"

"August fourteenth," I answer, "or maybe it's the fifteenth. Actually, I'm not sure." I am disgusted with myself for not knowing the exact date.

He nods his head and thinks a little. "How long can ye stay in Glasgow? I should like to show ye the sights."

Too quickly, I answer, "I can't stay at all. I have to catch the four-thirty flight to Aberdeen."

"Too bad, too bad," he sighs and again lapses into silence. Taking a copy of the *London Times* out of his briefcase, he begins to read. I press on. "Is Aberdeen a big city?"

"Och, no," he laughs. "It's where the country folk go to do their weekend shopping." He goes back to reading, and I am bitterly disappointed that he doesn't ask for my Aberdeen address.

I wonder about him and his sketchy history. He goes to London often. Maybe he is a businessman or a salesman. Maybe he is a member of Parliament! Glencairn sounds quaint and wonderful. I picture a charming country house with flowers and trees. There is a pretty, petite, red-haired wife and two rambunctious children, a happy, frisky dog . . .

He is turning a page of the newspaper. His hand is strong with short, squared-off fingertips, well-cared-for nails. I begin to imagine that hand on the dog. It is rubbing the silky fur, smoothing along its back, slipping carefully down over the long, moist nose. I am jealous of the dog.

Ian moves his cramped limbs, and I feel the rough tweed of his trousers brush my leg. I look down. The plane has banked a little and changed direction. A golden glow of sunlight suddenly fills the cabin. I stare at my legs. The short skirt of my suit has pulled up, and my kneecaps are luminous in their nylon sheath; a galaxy of sunbeams is dancing on my small, round knees. I admire them in surprise. How well shaped they are! The newspaper rustles, and I know that he, too, is staring hard at my glistening knees. Their seductive promise hangs between us like a fragile spider's web. I see his leg move ever so gently toward mine, his arm presses more tightly against the soft fabric of my wool jacket. I sense a sudden yearning in him, a strange kind of loneliness that I share.

I have always wondered who I am, what I am. Now I know. I am Sylvia of the Knees. The Knees that beckon and promise, entice and beg. Oh, yes, I am Sylvia and the Knees are me. The sherry lies sweet in my mouth.

Ian leans forward to tuck his newspaper under the seat. I see the back of his head—thick, brown hair close on sturdy neck. The hand moves under the seat and then, ever so slowly, I feel the tiniest pressure of his fingers on my ankle, moving up against the curve of the calf. The enticement of my knee lures his electric fingers, his firm hand. I know my promise is inextricably bound to his. The smell of fresh heather and sweet violets engulfs me. I have a vision of open moors where the ghosts are, mysterious as our undiscovered passion. I sense the comfort of ancient gravestones merrily askew on sinking earth. The curved fingers are an enduring stone bridge spanning the torrent of a rushing dee. I watch in fascination as the hand seeks its fulfillment.

The plane is losing altitude and beginning its short descent to Glasgow. There is a wrenching moment of suddenly reduced speed, and then a hard bump as the plane's tires touch the smooth ribbon of the landing field. I realize we both are holding our breath. I give a little sigh as the noisy jostle of passengers intrudes on our reverie.

Without looking at my companion, I get up, gather my belongings, and walk in a daze down the aisle. I stumble, and a man's hand shoots out from somewhere to steady me. "There now, lass, careful," a kindly voice murmurs.

Descending the stairs to the ground, I stand in the midst of a busy crowd of passengers greeting people, talking to each other. I see Ian walking slowly away. The late-afternoon sun silhouettes his square frame, and I am surprised at how short he is. I look so hard, he feels my gaze and turns completely around. He sees me and raises one hand in a farewell wave. I wave back. He turns and trudges steadily away from me.

Sadly, I check in at the reservation desk. A young, jolly man says, "Oh, I'm so sorry, the Aberdeen plane has engine trouble. It will be delayed until tomorrow morning at eight o'clock. Here, I'll give you a hotel chit for the night."

"Never mind, och, never mind," I laugh, and run down the long hallway of the terminal. My coat is dragging on the tiled floor; I can hardly hang on to my swinging bag. Turning a corner, I see Ian about to enter a taxi.

"Wait!" I cry. "I can stay. My plane doesn't leave until tomorrow morning at eight o'clock."

Ian doesn't say a word. He takes my coat, folds it neatly, and tucks it into a corner of the back seat of the cab. Then he hands my carry-on case to the driver. Climbing into the rear of the taxi, we nestle cozily together. Ian leans forward to order the driver, "Move on now, we've got a lot to do before morning."

I relax against the rich plush of the soft seat and think, I must call my daughter. I must tell her I spoke to a strange man.

His hand rests lightly on my knee.

Autumn Harvest

Ellie was aware that she came from a long line of late bloomers, but she felt that to blossom at fifty was carrying family tradition to absurd lengths. Here she was, by caveat of divorce, suddenly bereft of money, status, glamorous house, and, for what it was worth, a lifetime male companion.

She was having a glorious time.

For starters, she had recently developed a noticeable bosom. After a half century of size 30AA she had blossomed into a generous 34C. It was accompanied by a bit of a tummy, but no one seemed to mind. Ellie discovered that she attracted men. What a paradox, considering her male-scarce teenage years. And what fun! She felt like a kitten in a catnip patch.

She must have been pretty in her youth, but nobody had bothered to notify her. At that time the curse of excessive shyness had kept men at a distance; but with the divorce, almost without Ellie's noticing it, she had shed shyness along with her insignificant figure. She had no one's taste to please but her own. Her tiny new home was cozy and warm, and she had cultivated a small and luxuriant secret garden. She slid almost by accident into a thoroughly enjoyable editing job to augment her writing income, and she found that it wasn't necessary to attend the Metropolitan Opera or ski at Mont Blanc in order to have fun.

Hesitantly Ellie resumed the social dancing which she had abandoned when she married. It offered delightful avenues for meeting men while waltzing or relearning the tango. She rediscovered sailing, a joy of her "first" adolescence. Her new existence was as exciting, unexpected, and sometimes scary as those early teenage years—and much more satisfying, thanks to the demise of her shyness. To complete the change, her four children had been raised. They were no longer an issue.

There were other differences. Take sex. She'd had no sexual experiences outside her twenty-year marriage. During that time she had come to view the penis as a perpetual motion machine that would automatically snap to attention whenever the coast, so to speak, were clear—and it had her in a room, safe from outside interference. She had the feeling that its owner, her husband, could force it to lie down only by a major feat of will but that any time his attention wandered it was ready to jump into action and take off. She understood this to be the nature of the beast, no tribute to her attractiveness. She felt that he had been an inventive and acrobatic operator, but his machine was often alarming. Refusing to acknowledge her distraction or fatigue, it seemed eternally to have expected the same spirited and spontaneous response from its object, Ellie, as its owner contributed from his side. As she couldn't always live up to its expectation, she cursed the liberated day that female orgasm was discovered and subsequently sainted.

Paul was a revelation. They had met crewing a friend's small boat. It was a balmy day, with a leisurely breeze that encouraged dalliance. They surprised themselves with parallel tastes. Both city animals, they loved to dance, listen to country music, and read. While she gobbled every printed thing that came her way, he was more selective. Paul was an artist and she a frustrated art collector. His visual command excited Ellie, and he warmed to her enthusiasm. Ellie was a professional writer, and he admired her craft. Unknowingly they had even lived a few blocks from each other during their children's grade school days.

This mingling of skills and interests was so vastly different from those last loneliest years with her husband, when all they had truly shared was their children. Many a time she could not remember why they had originally coupled at all. In retrospect their "common interests" seemed quite ephemeral, perhaps nothing more profound than their families' expectations or the desire for children: maybe simply the beast with two backs taking its mindless due. From the beginning her husband had strongly resented the time and energy she had guiltily hoarded for writing, as if it in some way diminished her commitment and care for him.

Shortly after meeting Paul, she vividly dreamed of being a teenage girl who awakened one night to find a long procession of asparagus marching to her bed, over her, and away. One stalk was not rigidly perpendicular like the rest, but somewhat U-shaped. Mildly startled, she said to herself, "I didn't realize they ever came that way." She woke up bemused.

She and Paul began to meet for coffee. They met to dance. They lunched at work, attended movies. Sometimes they sailed or biked. She always protected herself with safe, nonintimate surroundings.

In the beginning Ellie would not believe that any man could care for her womanliness and still be pleased and proud of her creativity. She had forgotten how to trust, and she was sure that his interest in her profession, sincere and knowledgeable though it sounded, was some order of hypocrisy. She found it easier to believe his physical attraction to her than his intelligent praise. It was too foreign to her expectations. He would often coax her to show him a recent story. Once, in exasperation at her coyness, he asked what she thought he intended to do, rape the paper? But little by little his persistent interest and encouragement soothed her fears. She slowly loosened her grip and invited him into her word-colored universe. The day she finally permitted her cowardly psyche to completely trust his wonder at her skill, she undammed such a rush of grateful, giddy, unbelieving emotion that her reserve was abandoned as easily as a child discards a pair of outgrown shoes.

Ellie called him that evening and awkwardly invited the surprised and delighted Paul to dinner—at which celebration she dropped her hesitation, her compunctions, and her panties. This sudden about-face unnerved him briefly. She grabbed his hand and playfully dragged him to the bed. Then perversely wrapping herself in a blanket, she made him chase her. He lunged at the cover. They rolled and tumbled onto the floor, while the dog and cat retreated to the kitchen in stunned and disapproving silence. She played; she came; she roared. He joined with enthusiasm both wild and tender. After their passionate race had run its course, they curled into each other's arms, laughing, limp, and satisfied.

She fell hopelessly, helplessly, into passion, sex, infatuation. The world's great, sudden brilliance blinded her, and Paul became the center of her light. She could no longer see him clearly. She could not think. She did not care. She was gloriously, crazily in love.

When at last they rose to eat and play again, she found her dream's odd truth. Paul's rod was not an automatic vending machine that popped off every time one touched or looked at it. With all its owner's best intentions and desires, it occasionally beat a limp retreat and went to sleep. Embarrassed, Paul confessed it had begun this torment with the dual advent of divorce and middle age.

Ellie was first startled, but then she felt a glow of rich consuming tenderness and warmth. Serenely she set about to use her every art, tried and untried, to ease Paul's too-light load. She stroked his back. She teased his loins. She held his flaccid penis in her hand and petted, tongued, caressed, and teased. Together they explored her gentle, fiery art, her coaching touch. She poured out feel, desire, and sensu-ease. And when he rose up hard, she knew, at last, exploding glory. To give and give, feeling no sense of expectation, no demands, was bliss. Paul's need became her need, her pleasure indistinguishable from his, his bursting triumph now her own. What once had been an order came uncalled.

Sometimes they loved—and simply loved in closeness. Sometimes their sexual passions arched the Pleiades. It mattered not at all. He gave. She gave. With almost casual grace they walked into that well-read book of sex—by way of love.

DEAR CROSSING

Three Who Share Everything

Cynara, the artichoke, loves Allium, the onion, who loves Gallus, the chicken, who loves both of them. When conditions are right, each gives all they have to the others and creates an ultimate sharing, which can be delicious.

The place of assignation can be your kitchen, oddly enough, in two sauté pans. Gallus makes the opening move—just his thighs, please—eight or ten as fresh as possible, washed, dried, and sautéed golden in butter with a touch of olive oil and a dusting of poultry spices and white pepper. Set them aside on a platter.

Now Allium enters, as small and round as you can find, and as numerous as you care to peel. (If you weep too much, the joy to come is compromised.) Sauté Allium in the butter and juices left by Gallus until the inherent sugar begins to caramelize. Place Allium to wait with Gallus on the platter.

Finally Cynara bares her heart (most easily that which comes frozen in packages, which you have thawed and dried when first contemplating this three-way union. However, if you should have several fresh artichokes at hand, cooked and cooled, their hearts can be used instead, to add that much more richness to the final consummation.) Sauté these hearts in the same pan juices after pouring off any oil which seems excessive, and slowly squeeze fresh lemon juice over each piece. As the hearts approach a darkening intent, remove them too, to join their eager consorts on the platter.

Now lower the flame, and blend the golden brown sauces in each pan with some chicken stock, stirring and reducing them to a finer essence. Place the three ingredients back into the pan together.

Breathe over them a blessing in the form of a few bay leaves, and cover them to simmer over very low heat for a half hour or so, while

The fragrances color the air with their famous and suggestive personalities. The platter stays warm in the oven, and you rest.

For the final act, arrange the three participants in sensuous disarray on a platter, and give the juices a final stirring reduction while adding a few spoonfuls of white wine.

Pour the sauce over Cynara, Allium, and Gallus, and prepare to share the subtlety of rich flavors intimately exchanged.

HOMEBAWDIES

HOMEBAWDIES

It is probably less surprising to you than it was to us to find that a healthy number of our stories fell into the category of safe-at-home sex. In the past we may have come across as Ladies who stand dreamily at our kitchen sinks, gazing with glazed eyes into the distance, waiting for the call of the wild. At least we have made a big to-do about our rich fantasy life, our love of the exotic stranger, and our longings for forbidden fruit. But that was a book ago, and here we are, if not the conventional homebodies, quite ready to be bawdy at home, for home is more than unmade beds, wandering dust balls, and meals waiting to be prepared. Home is that ambivalent place we long to be when we're away and the one we try to run away from when we're there. In the stories that follow we pry into our home lives, peek behind closed doors, and look for clues that might tell how we have managed to become aroused at all.

Breakfast Orgy

Let me love you with breakfast, not words. My plump oranges ache to burst their shiny skins. Their sweet juices will fill your glass to the brim. The aroma of bacon gently sizzling in a frying pan wafts into the bedroom to wake you more seductively than my softest touch. The roasted scent of freshly brewing coffee adds urgency. I know by now your senses are unfolding—first smell, then sound, then sight—until finally the need to taste and touch will rout you from warm sheets and lure you to my lair waiting to bait you with fresh flowers and today's paper beside your place.

You hear the ringing of my wire whisk striking the sides of a copper bowl. Suspense! Are you wondering whether it will be blueberry pancakes or popovers? scrambled eggs or french toast? buttermilk waffles or a chive omelette? Ah—the infinite variety of breakfast! My love knows no bounds. My cumulus egg whites foam into stiff peaks; my creamy yellows ooze and swoon. How gently I fold them. What height they will attain in the privacy of my hot oven I alone can guess. With a sudden hiss my steaming milk comes to a boil. I rescue it from the open flame just as it explodes in a froth of passion, coinciding exactly with the winking red light of the coffee maker signaling that all is ready. Right on cue the toaster joins the act: With a sudden jerk its crisped contents jump to attention. Butter, jam, and honey, cream and sugar—stand by! Breakfast is coming!

The Fix-It Man

We went downstairs into the semidarkness. "I tried to do it myself, but I was scared. I didn't know where it was exactly," I apologized.

He nodded matter-of-factly and stretched out on his back. I stood above him. With his feet almost touching mine, our bodies together formed the shape of an L. I saw his exposed neck muscles—he wore no undershirt—they looked both strong and vulnerable, his chin raised as if he expected to shave. All too quickly he turned, propping himself up with his elbow—too high: There was no way he could see properly from that angle. It had to be lower. So he turned sideways, beaming the flash into the dark hole. His face followed the same direction, peering in, and then he leaned back as his right hand—his left clutched the light—probed the smallish cavity. It was not wide enough for his fist, so he only used three fingers. "I can feel it now," he smiled happily. "Each is different, you know." Then he put the light on the floor and changed into a crouching position.

He lit a match. Steadying himself by embracing the water heater, he pushed the flame toward the gas jet. For a second I wanted to trade places with my shiny new water heater. Then he would crouch in front of me, and with one arm around my rear, he would search for my delicately hidden pilot light. But quickly he bounced to his feet. The work was done. He adjusted the dial to "economy."

The Morning After

My childhood was devotional, ordered by the Calendar of Saints. The names of the Feasts and Vigils glitter with gold leaf on the dim parchment chronicles of my pious past. But time and a thousand heresies have drastically altered my relationship to the Director of the Universe. Many of the names and dates, the feast days and the Holy Days of Obligation, have vanished from my memory.

But there is a day which arches like a slender bridge between my magical child self and my more skeptical adult habits. For St. Valentine, I have changed the rules of vigil-keeping. The celebration happens on the eve, when instead of keeping watch before the sacred day, I rejoice. The feast day itself is spent in restoring order, and this I do with the same ardent dedication that I demonstrated as an enraptured schoolgirl.

I awake early, for St. Valentine's dawn is particularly mysterious and full of portent. I look at the window, at the long glass distorted with streaming rain, gleaming with opalescent light from the blindfolded sun. Acutely aware of the sleeping form beside me, I slide out of bed like a seal off a rock. I pour myself onto the floor, letting the covers settle gently back into the vacant depression in the bed. On hands and knees, hardly breathing, I locate my nightgown and robe lying on the carpet in startled attitudes, their hands flung out. I put them on now, remembering how I donned them the night before. I remember the rich, quiet evening of firelight and Vivaldi that we planned and reveled in, with old port and shelled walnuts after dinner. I remember how I dropped those garments on the floor and moved toward the bed and our transports together.

Now, as I get to my feet and walk toward the door, I look over at the bed, at the dear head barely visible above the edge of the quilt, at the shape barely recognizable as human beneath the covers. On the floor beside the bed is a tray with a bottle of Grand Marnier and two iridescent glasses; one lies on its side. In the eye of each glass there glints a coin of crystallized liqueur, intense as a pigment scraped from Rembrandt's palette. The patterns of the Persian carpet are sinuous and jewel-colored, like snakes. In them I begin to discern a scatter of abandoned objects: reading glasses, a watch, a sock, a silver quarter. The trail of artifacts leads to the closet. By the door is a pillow, flung to the floor. A robe across the chair is sleepy and watchful, its belt looped over an arm. On the bureau, more scatter: a crumpled handkerchief, a wallet, an address book, a comb, a tube of white peppermints. I am enchanted by the sight of a second sock draped on the lampshade, which it met in its passionate flight.

Still taking inventory of our celebration, I crane my neck to see where the open page of Auden's poems has come to rest. I glimpse: "Lay your sleeping head, my love / Human on my faithless arm. . . ." The page lifts in the current of my careful movement, wavers, turns and shows me: "Open your eyes, my dearest dallier. . . ."

Softly I stoop and pick up the tray. I right the toppled liqueur glass and silently pad down the carpeted hall. We left the light on in the bathroom, I notice. Switching it off, I see a toothbrush, not mine, lying face down in the sink. On the vanity my cleansing cream in its squat pink jar sits smug and broody in a nest of cotton balls. The toothpaste is unstoppered; the electric shaver leans its elbows on the edge of its velvet case and winks at me. At the top of the stairs, the dog is sleeping like a trollop. All four feet in the air, she rests her spine against the wall; her belly, with its delicate pink skin showing through the hair, displays the set of matching studs that no blind voracious puppies will ever suckle, for she is spayed and unmaternal. She slits open a somnolent Nefertiti eye and sees me. Her comment on my appearance is gutteral, laconic. I murmur a morning greeting. She goes back to sleep.

Now I am at the foot of the stairs, making my way toward the kitchen. At this time of year in California the rains have not yet spent themselves, but the amazing blossoms, fragile and defiant, are beginning to show on the bleak branches of the plum trees. There is one outside the kitchen window. Each summer, as the pale fruit ripens to scarlet, the birds loot it noisily and become mightily drunk. Now it is glittering with a million tiny mirrors of moisture. Beyond it, the other trees, the live oaks, the redwoods, the Japanese maples and the lemon eucalyptus, recede into the rainy morning mist like travelers waving good-bye.

I look around the kitchen. In the sink, the little red-enameled saucepan in which we made hot chocolate last night is soaking, flanked by the two ceramic mugs we bought last Christmas at a potters fair. The effect is of an unusual still life, red, brown, and robin's-egg blue, shapes of leaping curves. There is a powdering of chocolate on the kitchen counter. A tea towel, printed with botanical designs, is lying on the floor beside the stove. I pick it up, shake it and hang it on its hook beside the refrigerator. Then I fill the kettle and put it on the burner. I can feel my need for morning tea growing urgent. I return an oven mitt to its drawer. Then I fetch from the cupboard the little speckled teapot that has shared my life and fortunes for twenty years and lift down the eggshell cup and saucer given to me by my children after a visit to an aunt in England before they entered their teens. I am wantonly sentimental about these objects: that teapot, that lurid cup and saucer, all gold and crimson and curlicued, "A Present from Lynmouth" inscribed on its side in florid script. To save them, I would battle my way back into the burning house. One day they will break, and I shall bless them and let them go. But right now they start my day, and I fill the cup with smoky Darjeeling from the snub-nosed urchin of a teapot and carry them into the sitting room.

Here is where the attar of the prior evening's luxury is most pungent, most volatile. As I walk into the room and survey it, setting my tea things down on the low table by the sofa, I can feel the memories of my vigil congealing on my skin like spilled wax from a candle. Thin and opaque, they are sealing themselves into the fabric of my flesh. In front of the fireplace, where a dim ember still gleams among the white ashes, the big flokati rug is rumpled and askew. On the coffee table, the roses that arrived in the dusk of the previous afternoon have burgeoned overnight from prim Victorian buds to wildly decadent art deco floribunda. They are lolling and sprawling in their vase, their leaves in disarray; they are spilling their petals indecorously upon the table surface and breathing their perfume raunchily into my face as I bend over them. I love their overblown barmaid dishevelment, their saucy, raucous availability. I kneel down, straightening the rug, and scoop some fallen petals from the floor, crushing them together and inhaling winey distillation. I notice that the record player is still on— something else we neglected to turn off. There are records strewn about the floor: "The Velvet Gentleman," "Songs of the Auvergne," a Wyndam Hill album, "Don Giovanni," with an unbelievable picture of the great lover. He is all in costume for his wooing, a great plumed satin hat upon his head. We laughed at it a lot, last night.

I walk over to the sofa and stretch out, pouring myself another cup of tea. I tuck the little mohair blanket around my feet and take the teacup in both hands, loving the way it fits plumply into my palms. I let its warmth creep along my arms and down my spine. St. Valentine's day has dawned wet and wild. I shall spend it tidying up—preserving last night's vigil-keeping between the pressed parchment sheets of my own illustrated Book of Hours.

Constant Interruptus

(Writing erotica at home, especially on a weekend, is a test of sexual prowess, for it requires the same intensity of focus as an actual sex act. Since I am often easily distracted during lovemaking at home, writing erotica in broad daylight without any locks on the doors helps to increase my staying power. It also may explain why so many of my stories are short.)

Our attraction ionized the air as palpably as lightning about to strike.

First son: Hey, Mom! Today's the day I'm gonna get a parrot! Can you give me a ride?

The passion that danced in the wings of my daydreams was about to take centerstage. Caught by

Daughter: Why doesn't the dishwasher go on?

his unswerving gaze, I watched him dodge the other passengers as he hurtled after me to the back of the car. I was afraid our urgency would set off emergency alarms, and I nervously scanned the faces of the rush-hour commuters,

Husband: I need the 1984 tax returns right away.

who continued to stare impassively ahead, resigned to their fates and oblivious to ours.

The train pulled away from the station with a lurch, so overloaded was it with the weight of our desire. Trembling with mounting speed, it lumbered toward the dark shaft

Daughter: There's no water pressure.

of the tunnel.

Every seat was taken, but we found room enough to stand together at the rear of the car. Trenchcoated veterans surrounded us, hemming us in behind a wall of khaki. Secure in our pocket of privacy, I tore open

DOORBELL

Workman: Pardon me, ma'am, but there seems to be a leak in the water main. Do you have a wrench?

my coat, and we pressed even closer. I could feel his exhalations coming in humid puffs in my hair just as the hot breath of a passing train blasted the window to my back. With one deft movement he lifted my sweater and unclasped

TELEPHONE

Friend: Oh, I'm so glad you're there. I really need to talk. Martin has just moved out.

my bra. His kisses began to rain down upon

Second son: I need some wrapping paper. Where is it?

my bare breasts

Second son: Which closet?

"Oh, God. Oh, God," I moaned,

Second son: Where did you say?

as he gently traced

Second son: Now where's the present?

each areola

Husband: Did you want to leave those potatoes burning?

with his tongue. The liquid proof of my desire

Daughter: May I wear your black pants tonight?

dissolved all sense of time and place, deafened us to the song of steel rails, and blinded us to the streaking lights that flashed past.

Husband: You forgot to list the charitable contributions.

We clung to each other, clenched more tightly than a fist, holding our

DOORBELL

Workman: Ma'am, the valve is rusted so bad I can't get it to turn. You'll have to get someone from the water department out here right away.

breath, until the pressure became unbearable, and we

TELEPHONE

Mother-in-law: Hello, Rose. What are you doing today?

Rose: Oh, nothing much.

HOW ABOUT A LITTLE SEX INSTEAD OF ALL THIS EROTICA?

Just My Type

Once upon a time I had a lover. You know how it is after forty—a little boredom, a little restlessness, a new sense of freedom after the kids leave home. Suddenly there is a lot of space. Throw out the stuffed animals and claim the playroom for yourself: You're worth it. I'd never had an affair—it didn't fit in with my schedule—but I'd always wanted one. Now that I had my own room, a tryst could be arranged.

It was passion at first sight. The moment we were alone together, we lost all sense of shame. Everything was permitted. Nothing was impossible. We were made for each other. He always surprised me with ever more daring ideas, and they turned out to be exactly what I secretly wanted. He had his moods, of course, but as long as I gave him my complete attention, he never let me down. For that reason, I preferred the morning hours.

As soon as my husband left the house, I rushed upstairs to our secret den of iniquity. My fingers needed only to touch his sturdy frame, his beckoning buttons—how well I learned to play each and every one of them—and off he went. Hour after hour we churned away together: lascivious phrases, languid pauses, lecherous poses. I no longer answered the telephone. I forgot to cook supper. But my husband never complained because he had never seen me so stirred up, so eager to go to bed. I had a perfect thing going.

No wonder I began to boast about his rapid returns, his smooth shift and handsome carriage. At first I told only the Ladies, who all wanted to try him out. One day I recklessly invited them over to play with him. What are friends for? Even though we limited our number to ten, things soon got out of hand. They started a stampede—ten passionate Ladies create a lot of dust and heat—and we drew a lot of attention to ourselves. Newspapers and television spread my affair all over the map.

At first I thought: "Great, I don't have to feel guilty about it anymore. I no longer have to hide my secret. I can flaunt it. Everybody approves. Everybody applauds. Wonderful." I stayed in fancy hotels. I gave interviews.

"How did this all get started, Sabina?"

"Well, you know how it is after forty."

"But what does your husband think? Isn't he jealous?"

"Why? Nothing can go wrong. It's easy to control." I shouldn't have said that. The talk show host was offended. Mothers removed their children from the audience. Phones began to ring pro and con.

And worst of all, he began to sulk. When I returned from my glamour trip, he complained that I had cheapened our beautiful affair in front of the media, that I had failed to explain our true relationship, that I had abandoned him to a host of banshees who had invaded our sacred turf. And sure enough, our quiet and intimate playroom was now occupied by all kinds of people whom neither of us recognized. How did *they* get here, I wondered, and, what do they want? They wanted a lot. The young mother from Minneapolis wanted to protect her baby boy from my bad influence. Steely-eyed, she hovered over my chair, refusing to let me sit down. A kindly sex therapist offered suggestions about effective writing for orgasm. More than anything *he* hated the Ladies, who were wearing him out. No matter how hard he tried to please them, they wanted more and more and more: "Remember, we've got a deadline to meet. We're getting paid for having fun—why can't you deliver?"

I agreed with the Ladies and blamed him for losing interest: "Why can't you put out like you used to? Why are you holding out on me now when I need you?"

He claimed that it was my fault, that I had spoiled the game: "I'm not a public performer," he huffed. "I can't do it in front of them. Nothing I do meets with their approval."

I finally managed to clear the room, and we were once more alone together. We tried our best, but he failed to satisfy my needs: "We've said 'tingling breasts' at least six times already, and please stop using 'probing fingers'—I can't stand it any more." Whereupon he ignored my shift and continued sluggishly in lower case only; then he stalled and finally went completely on the blink.

In the nick of time, deus ex machina, that is, my husband, saved me from disgrace by letting me use his equipment. "Leave that old thing and follow me," he winked. Downstairs in his study he introduced me to his magnificent brand-new word processor. It was the latest model and had the floppiest of disks, the kinkiest of programs. He could hardly wait to show me its megabytes.

I had to face it—my dear old Remington was burned out and could no longer keep up with my requirements. Our last time together produced a long overdue letter to my mother: "Dear Mother," read the uneven type—the "p's" were missing—"forgive me for not writing to you sooner, but as you know I had to meet my erotic quota."

WELL, _MY_ MOM WRITES EROTICA.

John

When I was a girl, we used to drive to Minnesota to visit my grand-parents. Horses, I noticed, as we swooped past on our cross-country drive, had great round haunches, and sometimes—I never knew why—long expanding and dark penises. And bulls, with their huge, hanging sacs, held some special secret that was carefully omitted from my education. These first images of naked maleness—placid, gentle, mysterious forms standing dark and still in the earthy summer fields—were to remain with me.

I was forty-three, still hoping to realize that elusive dream of the perfect relationship, when I met John, my long sought-after love. I want to tell about the lavish care he gives to his body. Everything he does is fastidious and clean; he mixes oils and lotions to spread on his skin after every shower; he splashes cologne around his face and neck and down his body; he uses a gel to soften his hair; and he uses a balm to soften his full and expressive lips. There is no getting ready fast for this man—he is dedicated to the care of an almost-perfect, sleek, brown, and gently muscled body.

John is tall and slender. His fingers are a pianist's and a masseur's, and his legs are a basketball player's. Although he has a slightly relaxing stomach, his figure is amazing to me. I love to look at him from the back. His legs are long and very slim, but the muscles of his thighs are full, easing smoothly into his fanny. The sensuous sculpted muscles of his back flow evenly from his broad shoulders to his narrow waist down to the surprising twin spheres of his buttocks. Here these wondrous bulbs seem firm and tight, yet to the touch, they are both smooth and pliable. They are round and full only in the back (not bulging on the sides like mine). And where the full cheeks tuck under toward his thighs, the skin is darker, as if to accentuate those perfect orbs. I cannot keep myself from softly tracing this fascinating area with my fingertips—but almost sadly, for he is wildly ticklish here, and I often overstep the boundaries of his good nature. So we battle, since I am impishly persistent; I wiggle my fingers toward the dark and disappearing place between the great cheeks, and this to John is deeply taboo.

I once dreamed about having a penis. I still remember the sensations of peeing, of touching it, and of just plain admiring it. But it was also an obstacle that inconveniently hampered my movements. What struck me most was how vulnerable I felt. To my great relief, I woke up to find my hidden and practical vagina.

Male anatomy remains a mystery to me. John cannot explain to me what it's like for him to have all that hanging there. His whole penis and scrotum are the real black part of him, those and the big triangle of pubic hair. The rest of him is a softly glowing brown. Here there is no glowing—just dark black—and the texture of his skin changes and varies with his different states of arousal. When I take his scrotum fully in my hand, this dark and heavy sac, I wonder how it is that men act so aggressively when they are really so exposed.

I've never figured out how all this fits between those full thighs. How is it that it doesn't get squished when he sits or crosses his legs? And a final mystery—how did men get pants and women skirts? John pulls on boxer shorts, which force the trio off to one side, then pants, whose structure would seem to imperil the whole cluster with every move. But he goes about a normal day without an obvious hitch.

Sometimes in our lovemaking, he kneels over me with this wondrousness hanging full in my face, and I can see and smell and taste the very forms that haunted my girlhood. I can see, too, the perfect shape of the top of a heart, as his haunches round into a hairy valley. My hands trace over his velvety, muscular back, and I am moved by the richness of shapes and the contrast to my own body and color.

The texture of his hair is different everywhere. Under his arms, it is very dark and soft. On his lower stomach, the black curls loosen and soften as they buffer the thighs from each other and from the heavy sac. On his head, his hair forms the round theme of his beauty. The fullness of his heart is manifested in the curves of his mouth. Are his lips too large? Are mine too small? But fit and blend they do.

Even when I'm doing something else, I think of John. His caring and tenderness are inseparable from his rich physical qualities. Our life together is as boundless now as my youthful dreams, and we are just getting started.

Marriage in the Morning

*Oh, sweetheart! You know I'm not a morning person. I'm asleep, really
I am. Please tell* HIM *to stop nudging.*

He took the slender cord of her nightgown strap and slipped
it off the one bare shoulder that had tantalized him in the first
place. The cord rested quietly on her forearm as he leaned
forward to place a trail of kisses along that delicate, slightly
concave stretch of arm from her shoulder to her elbow, one
of the soft downy areas on her body that, in the right situation, evoked the uncontrollable passion of his late boyhood.

Please . . . I'd give my soul for another hour of sleep.

What do you want me to do with this thing? he implored. *Just look
at him. I mean, isn't he at all appealing? Anyway, it's all your fault.
You do this to him.*

As he spoke, he swung his leg over her side-turned body and
sat in a kneeling position, HIM in his hand as "Exhibit A."

She turned a sleep-creased face toward him, aware that her
nightgown was twisted and that one of her breasts had escaped. It crossed her cobweb-festooned mind that the sight
of her breast would surely incite him further, but she was
pinned beneath his weight, and, if the truth be known, she
was too tired to adjust fabric and flesh even if her body had
been free to do so.

*Listen, Exhibit A has nothing to do with me—not at this ungodly
hour of the morning before the radio alarm has gone off, it doesn't. It's
just one of those nocturnal things that creeps up on your gender in the
early hours—strictly neurophysiological. You're wired that way. I'm not
jealous or anything. Now go to sleep or get up and take a cold shower.*

The speech had taken extraordinary effort. At the end of it, she let her head fall back onto the pillow, hoping that her eyeballs had that sleep-sunken look to remind him of her uncanny ability to rouse herself from stuporous sleep and instantly fall back into it.

You know I wouldn't have a dream about someone else and take it out on you . . . pardon the pun.

Her eyes opened just in time to see his move to her exposed breast.

Help me get this nightgown on straight, she mumbled. *It's beginning to cut into me.*

Whatever it's doing, it's kinda cute.

He leaned down and covered her nipple with his mouth. Still in that state of preconscious lucidity, she caught herself thinking: He's going to give it artificial respiration. She stared mindlessly at the top of his head seeing not his head but, instead, concentric circles diagrammed on a poster of a disembodied breast that was pinned against the sterile white wall of her gynecologist's office.

Honey, this is beginning to feel like bondage. I can't move my arms.

He gently raised her head from the pillow and pulled down the other shoulder strap so that both breasts were now free. He smiled—mischievously, she noted—and moved his mouth to the newly released nipple. As she spoke ("only people under thirty like to do it in the morning with the sun streaming in over their perfect little bodies"), she was aware that the first now sun-dappled nipple—the one he had abandoned for the new kid on the block—was cool, wet, and lonely. Meanwhile, HIM was seriously casting about for the warm haven hiding under the peach-colored rayon nightgown she had bought at a discount lingerie store called Cheap Thrills. As the name appeared on the screen of her mind, a sleepy and somewhat sappy smile spread slowly over her face.

So don't tell me you don't like this. I know that smile.

He swooped his face down to hers and let his lips sink into her lips with that down softness she used to try to describe to him on those occasions when he seemed to have forgotten how to kiss. (Oh you devil, she thought, as she clasped his head in her hands and laced her awakening fingers into his thick, alert hair. You do know how to kiss when you have a mind to.)

A tiny corner of her almost fully awake mind watched as she gave in to the habitual impulse to raise her pelvis up to him in a quick, deft reconnaissance move that caught HIM unaware, still groping with boyish exuberance for the treasure trove he knew was hidden close by. Quickly closing her thighs around his hips, she held HIM quivering, as she savored every trembling sensation and urgent-but-stayed impulse to move.

His mouth and tongue once again were on her breasts, now darting from one to the other in rapid succession. She arched her back as he pressed her breasts together (to shorten the journey from one to the other? She made a mental note to ask him later.) His kisses moved to her neck and ear and back to her breasts in slow, even, deliciously unhurried progression. Her breath came in short, dry gasps. She closed her eyes tightly against the sunlight that was now full upon them, and when she opened her legs, HIM, delirious, quickly found his way home.

The room began to shake. From somewhere she heard the sound of fabric ripping at the seams. HIM seemed to be everywhere. She hung on, feeling beads of sweat on her body and on his body. He pulled her head and torso up from the pillow and, holding her tightly, rocked back and forth making guttural sounds of pleasure through clenched teeth—sounds that signal exertion to a man, violence to a child, and ecstasy to a woman. In the second that their bodies seemed to fuse and explode as one, the now pinpoint area of her brain that hovered between the wildness of life and the peace of death pushed her eyes open. They alighted on her big toenail. It needs cutting, she thought. At that instant, the radio alarm clicked on and the room abruptly stopped spinning.

"The Boy Scouts of America are in great need of your support, this year more than ever before . . ."

She turned her face from the glare of the sun and the sounds of Boy Scouts marching and stroked the back of his head absentmindedly.

Face it darling. I'm just not cut out for morning sex.

DONNA'S BODY SHOP

REBUILT HUSBANDS

ALL MAKES
NEW PARTS
SPARES

NOTHING DOWN
FREE ESTIMATES
WHILE-U-WAIT

Anniversary Waltz I

The evening is warm—one of those when the air is soft like a tender hug, and I feel my body surrender to it. We chatter and giggle as my old friend walks me to my car. Another playful erotica meeting has ended. I enjoy belonging to a permissive sisterhood that encourages me to think as outrageously as I dare.

Tonight is my friend's anniversary. I remember the envy I felt at the party she and her husband threw for their twenty-fifth. Tonight, their twenty-eighth, she spent with us. As the last of us are leaving, I call out, "Happy Anniversary!"

"Oh, that," she responded flatly with a laugh.

"Well, go and make something of it," I coaxed, and immediately I began to imagine what the evening could become.

"Ah, too much to do," she laughed.

Now my heart follows her back to her house to a husband deserted on his anniversary—for erotica! I should have traded places with her—let her drive away in my car to my empty house while I enter hers. For twenty years, I have fantasized about her husband. I have been turned on by this strong and steady man. Tonight, we could celebrate his anniversary, and I could be her . . .

The hall down to their bedroom is long. It is guarded by photos of his life with his family, overseen by the stern watchful eyes of parents and grandparents. It is dark, and no light shines from under the door. I suppose he's sulking himself to sleep. I slowly creep past the door, peering in at the dark shadow on one side of the double bed. I sigh. Wonderful.

I move into the bathroom, plug the old-fashioned bathtub, and pour in a generous stream of pink and perfumed bubble bath. Dreamily, I peel away my clothes; they fall in a pile to be reckoned with later. Now, in the foamy water, I imagine his familiar body. He has always been slim and very energetic. I usually see him in his startling white tennis shorts. My eyes feast on his darkly tanned legs and imagine them under satin sheets.

Creeping into the dark room toward his sleeping form, I wonder how he'll respond. I don't know this man's touch. My skin is throbbing in the stillness; I feel blood rushing to my cheeks and my breath quicken with anticipation. I lift one edge of the covers and slowly slide into the warmth, fitting myself against his back. My knees and thighs press against those wonderful legs that have haunted me. I trail my fingers down his arm, and his heavy breathing changes slightly as he responds to the gentle touching. He mumbles. I whisper "shshsh," as I keep tracing my fingers up over his shoulder to his neck and face. The perfect man, this. In real life he is always congenial and reserved. I want to see him out of control and reach beyond restraint to trigger raw responses.

My breasts glow round and warm. My stomach pulls tight, contracting into the center of me. I am in tune with every move, every response from him, and he is waking to my caresses. Softly groaning, he turns around, and I explore his face with my fingertips, seeking the subtle muscular responses. I tease the fluttering eyes, the soft answering muscles around his mouth. He is innocent and trusting, and I am a burning woman here to celebrate his anniversary. I taunt the beast in him. I am every female with power over every male since time began. And when our bodies can say no more, we melt entwined into a snuggling sleep.

And that's what would have happened . . . if I had traded places with my friend.

Anniversary Waltz II

When I drove up to Emma's house, I found a party in full swing. "How embarrassing," I thought, "they're all waiting for Emma. Perhaps I should go back, but that would spoil her fun as well as my husband's."

I crept through the back door trying to sneak unnoticed through the kitchen, when a vaguely familiar figure scurried by me with a tray full of champagne glasses. Then somebody grabbed me from behind and pushed me forward, shouting "Here she is! Attention everybody, she came in through the back!"

The living room was packed with familiar faces. A cheer went up: "Happy Anniversary! Happy Anniversary!" There was not a woman in sight—only men! Some I had met over the years at Emma's parties, but others belonged to totally different chapters of my life. My confusion turned to shock when Robert Redford waved gallantly from the center of the crowd.

He lifted his glass and delivered a toast congratulating me on my twenty-seven year tenure as a faithful wife. He then explained that he was master of ceremonies for the orgy that had been prepared for me—an orgy with all my admirers—some of them lifelong, some secret, and some who had come simply because they had heard about me. Quite a few had traveled from afar to make amends for bad behavior in the past, eager to clean up their record and prove that they had changed their ways.

"Please," I lifted my hand as if I were instructing a class, "I am sorry, but this cannot be. At my age I no longer wish to sit in judgment of the past. I doubt very much that those who did not do me justice then would be able to satisfy me now. Anyway," I toasted the crowd, "let's remember the good times."

I was quite amazed to hear myself speak out that way. Obviously

Emma's spirit had entered my body as well as my marital bed. But an orgy? On the other hand, what could go wrong with Robert Redford there? So I climbed on top of the dining room table and said, "Gentlemen, there is nothing I'd like more than to have you take my clothes off. Hold it, don't rush . . . slowly . . . piece by piece . . . to the sound of bongo drums."

Robert Redford stood by my side, watching closely as each man lined up for his turn. Suddenly I realized I wasn't wearing matching underwear—no merry widow underneath my summer skirt, no lace, only a white nylon bra and a pair of blue cotton panties. Too late to stop. Number one, a balding but abundantly bearded man with whom I had flirted in the sixties, laid claim to my left sandal while our new neighbor, an earnest but smooth-muscled jogger, loosened the straps on my right, adding a quick foot massage for good measure. Philip, who once upon a time wreaked havoc in my life, sighed wistfully as he fingered my Ralph Lauren blouse, pushing each tiny button through its tight little hole. He tried to slip his hands around my back to open my bra, but somebody was already working on it while two of my husband's colleagues were pulling down my sleeves in unison as if performing a nightclub act. Then Donald, our insurance broker, as slim and athletic as ever, brushed Philip aside to grab my skirt. Animal lust had attracted me to him, and animal lust had scared me away. But here he was lifting my skirt over my knees. "Not so fast," I laughed, for this was my favorite part, and I intended to make the most of it. Obediently he dropped the hemline and started again. Inch by inch he pushed the billowing fabric higher with tantalizing concentration. Shuddering with delight, I stretched out on my back so that he could reach my panties.

"Can I take your skirt off now?" he asked.

"No, do the panties first," I begged. Greedily he put his hands under my buttocks, but Redford intervened, insisting that others who had been waiting patiently should have their turn.

"No, I want Donald," I argued. "I too have been waiting patiently. And more bongo drums, please." Donald's hands slipped inside my panties, stretching the elastic around my waist and crotch where his fingers playfully picked up the beat of the drums.

"Take it off, take it off," I gasped.

"Take it all off," echoed the men.

"Are you ready?" inquired Redford. I nodded. Two Chinese students from my class softly cradled my back as Donald drew the blue cotton briefs down over my legs where they dangled capriciously on my right ankle. Several hands reached out to catch the trophy. Magnanimously, I exposed my naked body to the gaze of my admirers who cheered and chanted my name or burst into loud exclamations of praise. At the same time, they, too, stripped off their ties and shirts and pants until I was surrounded by hairy chests, tanned shoulders, white bellies, and buns of all shapes and sizes, not to mention a phalanx of male members in various states of arousal.

True to his image, only Redford kept his clothes on. From time to time he allowed one man to touch my knees or another to glide his fingers around my nipples. One ardent soul began to suck my toes, while a very distinguished-looking fellow (where had I seen him before?) licked the inside of my upper thigh with a passionate tongue.

"No, I'm not partial to ear nibbling," I warned another. "It tickles." But somebody was doing a great job rubbing his beard over my belly. A divinity student put his finger worshipfully into my font, murmuring, "Why didn't I think of this before?" By now I could no longer control the urge to arch my spine and rock my pelvis to the bongo rhythm.

"Don't move," ordered Robert Redford. He held up his hands like the conductor of an orchestra, directing the entire male chorus to join hands and form a human hammock under my body. Their rocking motion gradually built up to a more frenzied pace and carried me straight into his arms.

The bongo drums stopped and a Rachmaninoff piano concerto wafted across the room as Redford took me to Emma's gigantic pillow pile in front of the fireplace. The chorus stepped back, knowing that this was his scene. He looked at me with his roguish, Robert Redford grin . . . It was a long, movie-star kiss, instantly recorded and replayed on the large video screen in the corner. It had been so long since I had been kissed with such artistic momentum. Could I keep the tape? The replay ended on a burst of applause. Suddenly I was very tired. I asked for my clothes, which had to be retrieved from every corner of the room. No, I wouldn't let them keep my bra or my panties. Redford offered to take me home, but I told him I had Emma's car.

I found Emma wide awake next to my husband. "How was it?" she beamed.

"Great, but you shouldn't have gone to so such trouble."

"Oh, well, you've got to do something to mark an anniversary."

"I did. By the way, Redford is still at your house."

"Oh, I forget all about him." She dashed into the bathroom to fetch her clothes and left the house without bothering to put them on.

I climbed back into my own bed with relief and put my arms around the man I had met when I was young, younger than our daughter is now. His body fitted next to mine like a twin. His skin smelled of freshly baked bread. Our nest was still warm from our first passion. "Happy Anniversary," I whispered.

The Dis-tresses of Claire

Hair is like money. It becomes terribly important only when you don't have any.

As Claire brushed her hair that April morning to find auburn curls dangling from the brush she had lain on the counter, she felt a dizzying sense of fear and shock. The fire two weeks ago in her living room had been a real disaster. In one hour she had lost twenty years of lovely furniture and valuable possessions. But in the moment of realizing her hair was falling out, she felt fifty years of herself falling away, never to be retrieved. Her whole identity and relationship with herself was clinging to the bristles of her hairbrush.

She stared in the mirror and felt such pain and horror that she could barely keep from screaming aloud. Carefully, she twined her fingers around a curl above her ear and pulled. The strand left her head soundlessly, and there she held it in her hand, totally disengaged, never again to be a part of her. Her ultimate adornment was leaving without even a good-bye, no nostalgic cry, not the slightest effort to hang in there and stay with her forever.

Her hair had always been her Bird of Paradise, a treasure she had always taken for granted. Now that it seemed to be falling away from her, its plumage plummeting to earth, like the bird, she felt she must shed celestial tears.

Picking up her bedroom phone, she called her doctor. He listened to her distraught voice calmly. "Don't worry, Claire, this is probably just a delayed reaction to the fire. Being all alone there with Ward off on his lecture tour was a very scary experience. Sometimes people lose their hair from shock, and it almost always grows back. If I were you, I'd get a good wig and no one will ever notice. You always handle things so well."

Claire hung up the phone. It was true she was a calm, capable person. At fifty, she looked good and felt chipper. She had hardly any wrinkles, her gray eyes almost always had a twinkle in them, and lots of walking and bicycling kept her legs in great shape.

When Ward returned from his latest tour, he would be surprised to see everything in almost perfect order again. Workmen were already busily repairing the damage. Claire always managed everything perfectly when he was gone on his long trips.

But right now, Claire was reeling. This was beyond her managerial talent. This was a part of HER she was losing, and no workman could quickly replant her hair roots to stop this awful process. She made another telephone call to Mary, her hairdresser, who assured her she could order a wig so lifelike no one would ever know. Only then did Claire dare to look at the hairbrush again. Her dog and confidant, Malibu, sat at her feet.

"Come on, Malibu," she whispered, "I'm going to find a beautiful container and save all these curls."

She rummaged in the bedroom closet and found an old treasure box lined in satin. She set the open box on her dresser, carefully removed the silky, auburn curls from the brush and gently placed them inside. The satin lining was white; her gleaming, red locks glowed against the fabric.

"I'll call this my Dorian Gray box," she announced. "Every day I'll save my hair, and as I get older and balder, I'll know the youthful me, the real me, is inside."

Mary soon delivered her wig, and Claire was pleased it looked so natural. Nobody seemed to notice that it was a hairpiece. At home she wore a scarf tightly wrapped around her head and tried to avoid looking in the mirror. She decided not to tell anyone, not even Beth, her closest and best friend. No, she would just keep this between her and Malibu.

Each morning as she did her careful brushing and another curl collapsed onto her brush, she would lovingly place it in the treasure box. Each time she would recall some wonderful memory.

One day as she brushed out the vary last shining threads of her original self, she recalled the sultry, warm evening of her high school senior prom. Ward had brought a pungent, glorious white gardenia to pin in her hair. She had a ghostly image of the pale, waxy exotic bloom pressed against her heavy, red curls. It made her heart ache to think about it. Her fingers traced the sensuous flower in retrospect. Later in the day, she went to the florist to buy one large, white gardenia. Taking it home, she inhaled its heavy scent with nostalgia.

She showed it to Malibu. "See how beautiful it must have been?

That gardenia against my russet hair? Really a knockout!" She got out her satin shrine and carefully placed the flower in it, and then, sighing, hid the box away.

Ward came home that night from his lecture tour. After telling him all the events of the last two weeks, Claire decided to tell him the really *bad* news.

"My hair has fallen out. Dr. Stuart says it's shock from the fire." She patted her head. "This is just a wig. It looks pretty natural doesn't it? The doctor says my hair will probably grow back. And not to worry about it."

Ward felt real surprise. Her wig did fool him, and as usual, she was coping, but he could sense misery in her voice. He thought quickly about how to reassure her.

Smiling wickedly, he growled, "I'm sure it will grow back soon. Just so you don't lose your pubic hair. Now that would be a real disaster! My wife has the best pubes in the country."

Claire laughed at his nonsense. Thank heavens for Ward's sense of humor. She felt a little better, but when he left again a few days later, she lapsed back into the morning reminiscence time with Malibu.

Picking up each precious curl tenderly, she sensuously stroked it, pressing its silky texture against her fingertips. Each strand was an electric connection to some long-ago time. Slowly, Malibu got filled in on the whole history of Claire's magic hair. He gazed at her with loving, liquid eyes and watched with great patience as his gentle mistress picked through the contents of her box, telling him little stories and then hiding the satin-lined secret in the back of the closet behind her bathrobe.

The first time it happened was accidental and unexpected. Claire had driven her car to the repair shop and taken the bus home, as the mechanic had wanted to keep the car overnight. The bus was almost empty. She sat in the back seat alone, holding her head erect and proud, congratulating herself that the wig fit so nicely, she could go out on a windy day and not worry it would fly off. As she sat thinking about her wig and her lost hair, she slowly focused on the head in front of her.

A young woman was reading a book with intense concentration. Claire was very taken with the woman's beautiful, golden-blonde hair. Long, wispy tendrils flowed down over the seat behind her, drifting languorously past Claire's admiring look.

She stared at it in surprise, thinking she would like to stroke that fine texture and press those smooth strands against her fingers. Before she really thought about what she was doing, her hand had opened her purse and crept inside to fasten around a tiny, gold embroidery scissors she always carried. The scissors almost magically opened, snipping off one long, slender piece. It fell silently into the yawning mouth of Claire's open purse.

Time to get off. Nervously, Claire hurried down the aisle of the bus, clutching her bag. The woman continued to read her book, unaware that one of her golden tresses was now lying in Claire's purse, traveling down the aisle, out the door and soon would be . . . yes, soon would be dropped with trembling fingers into the Dorian Gray box.

Malibu barked.

"Oh, I know, I know, it's a different color. It's not really mine, but isn't it beautiful? See how the colors blend?"

Fragments of dried gardenia, the smell was musty now, clung to the red and blonde curls. Claire thought it was a lovely sight. She sniffed dreamily, inhaling the heavy scent. Then, closing the box, she carefully hid it in her closet.

Slowly, other colors began to appear. Claire could hardly wait for the mornings when she could touch the pieces of flower and hair glowing so seductively against the white satin cloth. Once Malibu whined his disapproval, but she hushed him. "It's okay, nobody knows. I'm always so very, very careful."

Claire began turning down luncheon invitations with her friends. When Ward came home again, she tried to listen to him, but he felt her distraction. Even though Claire had everything organized and working, she always seemed to have her mind on something else. He couldn't imagine what the problem was. Occasionally Malibu whined around him. What was he trying to say?

One evening when her friend Beth was having dessert with them, she said, "Claire, I know you're wearing a wig. Why? Your hair always looks so great, you don't need a wig."

Claire was surprised. She had better tell Beth. "My hair fell out because of the shock I received from the fire. Gee, I thought I had fooled everyone. But, never mind, it's growing back." She joked, "Soon I'll be my old hairy self."

Ward was glad Claire could talk about her loss so casually. He had tried not to mention it or say anything about the tight scarf she wound around her head when she was home. But there was something different, something he couldn't put his finger on—just a look in her eyes. He looked at Malibu. His eyes were a little different too. Ward felt a twinge of discomfort.

When Ward left on his next lecture tour, Claire said good-bye happily. He had interrupted her morning sessions, and it was hard for her to keep her mind on what he was saying. Now, she could go back to her box—she felt drawn to it more and more. She loved looking at all those colors, and her fingers ached to stroke the increasing number of locks and curls and strands. The odor of the dry gardenia triggered quivering molecules of lost memories and feelings. Fondling and pressing the sensuous tendrils, she would recall the delicate fuzz on her baby's head, so soft she could hardly believe it, or the thrill of running her fingers through Ward's hair on their very first date.

The little embroidery scissors continued magically to snip away. She never forgot to put them in her purse when she went out. She took only little bits; no one ever realized that a tiny piece of them was nestling cozily in the Dorian Gray box.

Every Thursday afternoon, Claire liked to take time off from being the perfect manager to attend the afternoon matinee at the neighborhood theater. Losing herself in some frothy fantasy, she would feel refreshed and young when she came out. Ward left on Wednesday, so Claire looked forward to the Thursday movie and didn't invite Beth. She just wanted to be alone these days. Her long mornings with Malibu grew more and more entrancing, and today, going to the film alone gave her more free time to think about things. To think about her memories and her gleaming storehouse of hair. Short red ringlets were beginning to cover her head again; the doctor had been right. It was just a temporary loss, but the sight of her intercoursed locks in the secret box filled her thoughts. She was mesmerized by the seductive glistenings she smoothed and stroked every morning. Her very natural hairpiece still sat on her head.

Sitting in the back row of the darkened theater, Claire began to stare in startled fascination at the thick, enticing black curls on the head in front of her. What a marvelous head of hair! The kinky rolls were really staunch, so big and tight. A lightning bolt of pleasure surged through her whole body.

Her hand crept into her purse and the little, gold embroidery scissors began a stealthy climb toward one big, black curl. Carefully, so carefully, Claire wound a strand around her silent finger. The scissors opened its hungry mouth.

At just that moment, the owner of this fine head of hair dropped his popcorn container. With an oath, he leaned forward to pick up the scattered bits. To her utter horror, Claire was left holding his gorgeous hair in her hand, while his head descended toward the floor.

"Oh, my God!" she gasped. She had pulled off the poor man's wig.

She heard another oath from him as he grabbed for his empty head. The gold scissors clattered to the floor. Claire was up and away in an instant. Running out of the theater, she got into her car and drove home at breakneck speed. Her heart was pounding.

Unlocking the front door, she ran into the bedroom with Malibu at her heels, barking in a puzzled way: It was the afternoon; they did the memory trip in the morning.

Claire opened her satin treasure box, looked at it, and then closed the lid tightly. She carried the Dorian Gray box with all its memories and seductions into her kitchen, stuffed it into the garbage bag under her sink, and then sat down at the dining room table. She slowly let out a long, deep sigh of relief.

When Ward returned that evening, just in time for dinner, Claire was busily putting food on the table. "Hey," he whistled. "Your hair is back."

"Yes," Claire answered easily, "a little short, but you know, it's the latest style. I think they call it punk. Actually, I like it. I feel very free."

Ward nodded, pleased at her fresh appearance. Eating with quick zest, Claire excused herself. "I have to run off to my meeting. . . ." She gave him a quick kiss and ran out the door.

Ward watched her drive away. How exuberant she seemed, like her old self. He promised to clean up, so he rinsed the dishes and put them in the dishwasher. When he opened the garbage bag to throw away the paper napkins, he noticed the treasure box in the bottom of the bag. Puzzled, he took it out and examined the contents carefully.

The locks of red hair he recognized as Claire's, but there were many assorted curls and strands of various hues and textures as well: blonde, brown, black, and even a few slips of gray. Tiny bits of dried gardenia held the soft, lustrous mass together like an artist's collage. Ward gazed in amazement, then, shaking his head, he carefully replaced the box back in the garbage bag.

Malibu was watching him with apprehension. He patted the dog on the head reassuringly. "I'm going to cancel my next lecture tour," he said. "I think I need to spend more time at home with you and Claire. Yeah, we'll have fun."

He eyed Malibu critically. "You know, that hair over your eyes is getting too long. I think you need a little trim. Hmmm, I wonder where Claire keeps her little gold embroidery scissors?"

NO MAN'S LAND

NO MAN'S LAND

In this section, we let our erotic imaginations and memories wander into the delivery room, the beauty salon, and other places where menfolk fear to tread. One by one, we strip ourselves of the layered veils that separate the sexes, that hide us and protect us at the same time. With the mysterious and childlike laughter that emanates from a harem community of women, we expose the sensuality that trembles through our separate life—a life that gives birth, nurses babies, celebrates beauty, and pleasures its own body in quiet perfumed moments.

CAFE CLITORISSE
SPECIALITÉS:
Crudités
Salade Virginoisse
Fellatio Sauté
Moelles d'Amour

IS THE FELLATIO FRESH TODAY?

When the Bough Breaks

He might be dying, she thought. She felt that her misery would crack the bowl of the sky, which whirled in a blue glaze above the line of shadowy green that was the pine forest along the ridge. The wail that bubbled in her throat seemed to come from her very womb, and her dread, precise, acute, inconsolable, pierced the tossing air of the gold-rimmed afternoon.

"He might be dying," she said, aloud this time. She leaned her head against the wooden frame of the open window and watched the wind catch her voice and whirl it away like a scrap of paper bearing dreadful news. The message flew through the garden, across the lawn, into the overblown rose bushes that bordered the kitchen garden, through the lavender and rosemary and sage of the herb patch. She watched it leap and sink into the shadowed pool, startling the quiet carp that hid among the water lily stems and listened motionless to the liquid verdigris of the leaden, pan-piping fountain.

Abruptly she turned away from the window and looked into the room. It was empty. She stared at the walls, at the pristine white of the woodwork, at the rug, so recently and joyously chosen. This was his room. He had not yet moved in, and now he might never. She wrapped her arms across her chest, feeling the strange separate thudding of her heart, the involuntariness of her own continuing life. With each sob her ribs rose and fell behind the flesh that mounded into the breasts she cupped in each hand under the thin wool of her dark red robe. All day she had been resting, drinking glass after glass of water, commanding her body to responsiveness. She had held him in her arms, lying there on the big bed as wide as a meadow, her violet-veined breasts bare, feeling his skin against hers, his mouth around the delicate nipple, as she stroked the line of his cheek, marveling at the wide black fan of his eyelashes against his cheek. She had murmured his name, telling him he was her darling, her angel, her constant, her redeemer. She told him other things about himself that she thought he might not know—they were so new together—that he was witty, urbane, chic, well read, suave. In response to one of his comments she quoted St. Paul, "Love does not behave itself unseemly," and when he remarked that he loved her voice, she sang Shakespearean songs to him, "With a hey, ho, the wind and the rain." And for a while he had listened, profound appreciation widening his amazing ink-blue eyes.

But it had all changed. Disappointment, frustration, and finally fury had darkened his face and swelled the alarming veins of his temples. He had struck at her, branding a red welt on the flower petal flesh of her breast. And she, feeling the now familiar, dull dread dropping from her heart to her belly, had finally capitulated. The action must be taken. It was against her most sacred principles, but disaster must be avoided. Seeing again the monument of her commitment and the grandeur, the oceanic panorama of her love, which was so recent, so new and so astonishing, remembering the months of uncertainty and the explosion of joy that attended their first glimpse of each other, she comprehended, suddenly, in all its cold horror, the jagged, irreparable rent that would appear in the fabric of her world if he left it, forever gone, gone, gone. *And it would happen, she knew it now, if something were not done soon.*

She straightened and strode across the room, out to the landing. Staring down the shallow stairs to the hall, she saw, in a splash of sunlight, the shriveled, white blossoms of the roses and lily-of-the-valley in their bowl on the hall table. Her husband had brought the bouquet to the hospital the morning after the birth of their first child. They had worked hard together through the long night of her labor, and her husband's face as he tiptoed in with the flowers was drawn and gray with fatigue. He had sat beside her on the high hospital bed, resting with her against the pillows, thoughtfully observing the sleeping baby in the bassinet beside her.

That night her milk had come in. That night, her neck muscles sore from the effort of bearing down chin to chest, she had awakened at the hour when the nuns, in the convent where she had been raised, prayed for strength against the midnight evil: the evil that stalked in the shadows and devoured unwary souls. She had awakened into a maelstrom of chills and sweat, her brain bursting, her entire body the site of some insane, unscheduled firework display. It was as if the orderly, electrical impulses of her system had fallen into the hands of madmen, lunatics running berserk through her veins with fiery wheels and screaming, flaring rockets. Gasping and determined not to die, she had struggled to full consciousness, watching the twitching tail of a long-abandoned prayer vanishing back into the crepuscular recesses of her mind.

She must have rung her bell because suddenly the dim light by her bed illuminated the kindly, round face of the night nurse, swinging solicitously above her like a gibbous moon. "I'll sponge you off, honey—just lie back and relax, it's only your milk." Her milk? Only her milk? This full-scale assault, these tanks, guns and storm troopers, these landing craft and flamethrowers—could all this be *only her milk*?

Then, from down the corridor, she heard the devastating drawn-out wail, held through the limit of suffocation into certain death, of the newborn awakened by hunger or nightmare in the still watches of the night. And immediately, like a sky full of shooting stars, she felt the milk burst almost audibly from both breasts and course down her body, in spate, savage in its primitive need to find the fretful infant and soothe the ravenous new viscera now shrieking for food. She looked down, amazed, at her thin, cotton hospital gown and saw the colorless, spreading stain that she knew, from this moment on, represented the capitulation of her body to the occupation of her hormones. And when she stripped off the gown to replace it with the fresh one brought by the nurse (waving aside, for the moment, the offer of the nursing bra with all its complications of padding and fenestration), the sight of her breasts had filled her with astonishment and awe: two firm, full cones, transparent, lit from within, it seemed: the veins drawn with a dark lavender felt-tipped pen, the nipples painted with deep rose-gold.

"Oh, beautiful!" she had murmured. "Beautiful, beautiful!" And then the baby was brought to her, and the ancient knowledge welled up in her, and she knew exactly what to do, settling the moist, furious bundle in the hollow of her arm, guiding the nipple into the wet sucking circle of his mouth, holding him up to burp as he wheezed and chirped and fastened his gums single-mindedly into the flesh of her shoulder.

They had fallen asleep together, a soggy, effluvious pair, redolent of milk and curds and perfumed soap, pungent, odorous, content. And the next day, her husband had come to fetch her, and they had brought their firstborn back to this house. They had all lain together on the big, white bed like a meadow, and her milk flowed and flowed. The baby attached himself to her breast like a succubus, sometimes sleepy and slow, sometimes wild in his need, but always connected, always attached, so that soon she stopped wearing clothes and simply went native, in a sarong, a primitive being in a primitive season, both breasts available at any time.

All that ended two days ago, when suddenly, for no apparent reason, the wonderful, wild obedience of her body to the random warnings of need (an owl in the night, a siren at noon, a high operatic note from the radio) rebelled, refused, and went silent. Her milk no longer flowed, and the baby sucked first with passion, then with disappointment, crumpling the corners of his gummy mouth, then with a fury that terrified her.

She walked across the landing and threw open the door to her bedroom. She crossed to her dressing table, with its long, triple mirrors and disordered, scattered objects. Untying the sash of her robe, she let the garment slide to the floor and stood naked in front of the glass. Then she laid her hands on her stomach, palms down, and slowly slid them down her body until they rested above the dark triangle. Inside, here, was where it all happened: the ordered, silent marshaling of forces for the monthly menstrual display, the mystery of conception, the orgasmic storm, and, finally, at menopause, the folding back of the wide, fecund wings. She thought of herself as a child, thought of her mother, touching her forehead, her temples and her eyes. Leaning into the mirror, she lifted her breasts, delicate and small, as they had always been, and heard her husband's remembered voice saying the word she dreaded hearing.

"Formula." As she began to shake and weep, he said, "This can't go on. He's not thriving, and you look like a ghost. I'll drive into town and buy some bottles and some formula."

"Rubber!" she sobbed bitterly. "The first perversion! Why not leather and chains?" And she blew her nose as if sounding the Last Trump. She wept more and more, resting and drinking glass after glass of water, then milk, then orange juice, and then even beer, which she loathed. She tried to nurse the baby, and when no milk came, she began to fear that her son, her firstborn, her treasure, must be dying. He might never move into his room with the pussycat wallpaper, the bright, white paint, and the charming, hand-loomed rug. He might never see the old, pale carp among the reeds and lilies in the tiled cistern or hear the water falling merrily from the panpipes into the green pool. He might never see the high, blue, scudding sky and the clouds piled like unspun wool above the pine trees on the ridge.

Tears flooded her face again, and she pulled her red robe back on, standing in front of her mirrored dressing table and wondering why love made one so afraid of death, of loss. She thought about her breasts and their betrayal. She thought about her body and the dictatorship of her hormones. And finally she thought of her little son with his deep-sea diver's eyes and the way he moved his head, like a salamander under leaf mold. And she remembered how her husband's step on the stair as he was leaving had been uncharacteristically heavy, his retreating back oddly slumped. It occurred to her that all his professional expertise was useless right now, would not salvage what she felt was lost, and that he knew this and was full of dread.

Suddenly she was swept by a strange vehemence. She wanted to talk to her son, explain to him that it was *her* need to nurse him, *her* need to marshal the hormonal forces and return triumphant. Hadn't they had long, silent conversations, the two of them, during the nine long months of waiting when he was hidden from her and sent his messages by telegraph along the pathways of her nerves, her veins? There was nothing they could not talk about. She lifted her head and shook her hair from her face. She tied the belt of her robe around her returning waist and bent to look at her baby. He was sleeping crossly between two pillows on the bed. His week-old fists were flung up on either side of his head, his eyes were sealed shut with a shiny, black rim. For a moment he looked so much like a sea creature, the denizen of some temporary tidepool, that she wondered if he had gills; he seemed to be in the process of emerging from the ocean to the land, flippered, stranded in time, as if nature were still unsure whether to toss him onto the shore and make him human or let the sea reclaim him on the next wave.

Slowly she untied her sash and slipped off her robe, lying down beside him and easing one of the pillows out of the way. Immediately, the baby began a snuffling series of movements in her direction, scenting her, preparing his mouth for the first suction attachment. She lay back, one arm behind her head, the other encircling the squirming infant. Closing her eyes, she reminded herself that a million years of evolution had gone into designing the system that had inexplicably betrayed them both, reminded herself that her devotion to life was stronger than her fear of death.

The long, lavender shadows of the summer afternoon began to stretch langorously across the walls of her bedroom, bringing a cool breath to the febrile air. She began to understand that it was within her power to solve the mystery of her body's sudden instability. Then she felt his nuzzling nearness and she opened her eyes. Lightly she touched the damp fuzz covering the barely completed head and guided the questioning mouth toward her nipple. He caught and held. Sweet warmth began to creep up her back, across her shoulders, her throat, her breast and belly; she felt the tight weight, the aching engorgement, the prickling release, and she gave a little moan and turned over on her side, enveloping him in the warmth of her milky body. She inhaled her own sweet and rancid odors as the milk began to trickle from the unengaged breast and the tiny, fierce fists struck and kneaded the flesh around the other nipple, hastening the flow into the famished, new mouth.

She sighed, touching his wondrous, jewel skin, gazing into his luminous, great eyes. She talked to him quietly, fluently, stating her case, listening attentively to his succulent responses. Drowsily they shifted position, nestling deeper into the billows of the bed, their eyes drooping, jerking open, falling shut. Then, sated, they fell asleep.

When her husband returned from town with his purchases, he found them there, lying in a patch of oyster light that haloed their hair. He looked down at them for a long time, curled around each other, their connection complex, convoluted, like a design of ancient fishes. They made him think about time, about the geological patience involved in the etching of fragile, durable fossil forms into the living rock, and his turbulent breathing steadied and grew even. Then he turned and quietly left the room, taking the drugstore package with him. As he ran lightly down the stairs, he whistled softly a song from his own childhood.

Ergasm

She suddenly seemed to fill me to the point of bursting. I was a water-filled balloon, a kite swept high by the wind, a scream about to shatter the glass in all the crystal palaces of the world. Then the voice of the doctor abruptly rose in pitch and decibels where it teetered as if on a high wire: "That's it, that's it . . . take a deeeeep breath now and push . . . here she comes, she's coming . . ."

Part of me hovered overhead watching my concentrated effort to expel this baby. As I inhaled deeply, obediently, the ever-present observer in me couldn't help but notice the excitement of the nurse standing by my side at the delivery table. Even the doctor standing at my feet between my raised, sheet-wrapped legs, alert, attentive, waiting, made no effort to contain his exuberance. It seemed almost as much their birth as mine, let alone that never-to-be-forgotten (or remembered?) experience that belonged to my infant daughter.

The tiny being inside me seemed quite content to let me drive her out of the pear-shaped, rosy-walled, aqueous home that had been hers for nine months—to drive her out with that awesome power some women tap into only in this particular moment. She didn't struggle, but neither was she passive. We were in perfect synchrony—horse and rider, lover and beloved, mother-to-be and daughter-to-be—both of us absolutely ready for the moment when, all at once, the warm, gelatinous home that had been hers alone for so long would collapse.

I filled my lungs with air, exhaled, and pushed as hard as I could until eight pounds and nine ounces slid softly, heavily, trustingly into the doctor's waiting hands as my last wild cry filled the room and hers began.

CBS Childbirth

Walter Cronkite presided at the birth of my second child. Twentieth-century timing and technology coincided on the evening of October 28, 1971, to bring CBS to my rescue. The labor room at Good Samaritan Hospital was very crowded that day. My obstetrician and his partners were making a valiant effort to distract my physician husband from the hospital's antediluvian policy barring fathers from the delivery room. With much backslapping and conviviality my obstetricians regaled him with horror stories of their training years. Several of my husband's colleagues, hearing that I'd been admitted, dropped by and joined the party, eager to share their tales of internship and heroic deliveries. They boisterously congratulated themselves on the miracle of their success and assured my husband that he, too, was undoubtedly made of the same tough stuff.

Inconvenienced and unnoticed, the labor room nurses attended to me with quiet agility, working around the jolly doctors, who pressed in around my husband with their backs to me. Stripped and prepped, I felt as though my name and personality had been neatly removed and sent off in the brown paper bag with my clothes and other belongings. I longed to lie undisturbed on the narrow gurney, but the nurses had to carry out orders and attach me to an IV that administered the pitressin drip to induce my overdue baby. No sooner had they hooked me up than an urgent admission required them to leave at once.

"Here—I'll turn on the TV," offered one nurse apologetically before she dashed away.

I lay flat on my back on a gurney that felt as narrow as a balance beam. One false move and I knew I'd be on the floor. I glanced apprehensively toward my husband to see if he could catch me if I fell, but the merry men crowded round obstructing him from view. My carefully draped legs, spread hip-width, were bent at the knees to give my feet stability. From my vantage point, the overhead television, which tilted considerably toward me, appeared to be wedged between my legs. The electronic static subsided, and a familiar face appeared.

"Good evening. This is Walter Cronkite bringing you the CBS Evening News." Ah, Walter! I knew you wouldn't fail me!

Walter's mustache bristled kindly as he smiled down at me with his characteristic twinkle. Just then my belly hardened in its first contraction.

"Whoa!" I gasped, startled by its intensity. What had been a great mound only moments before now changed into a mountain peak above which Walter's brightly lit face hovered like a full moon.

"Breathe," he reminded me. "Open your mouth and breathe deeply. In, way in—then out, s-l-o-w-l-y. That's right. Good girl."

As the contraction subsided, Walter announced that the Atomic Energy Commission had been authorized by President Nixon to test a five-megaton nuclear warhead on the island of Amchitka in the Aleutian Chain.

"That's nothing, Walter," I called back as a second contraction began. "I'm unleashing a seven-megaton baby right here in a heavily populated urban center!"

"Woweee!" chimed in another voice. It was Roger Mudd. "Prop your head up with that pillow," he said. "There, that's better. Are you more comfortable?"

"I'm okay," I reassured him. "Don't worry."

Roger's eyes narrowed into small crescents of concern and remained locked on mine as he began to report on the anti-American demonstration that took place at the United Nations following the General Assembly's vote to expel Nationalist China 76 to 35. The contraction seized me, but Roger's unwavering gaze guided me through.

I was beginning to wonder if I'd make it to the first commercial break, when Walter reappeared.

"Fine! Fine! You're doing well," he chuckled. "Why look! You're already at three, maybe even four, centimeters. Just keep your eyes up here."

"Oh, help! Here comes another one!" I gasped.

"Keep breathing—I'll be right back," he called as the first commercial break interrupted. Perspiration broke out on my forehead, and a faint nausea threatened. The string of commercials unwound one right after another with a frequency that matched my contractions. I was beginning to fear I'd go under.

"Concentrate!" called Walter, who had returned. "Pant. Try short, shallow breaths. Yes, better. Now it's time to hear from our friend, Charles Kuralt, who's on the road today in Phoenix, Arizona. Hello, Charles."

"Hello, Walter. This is Charles Kuralt reporting from Good Samaritan Hospital in Phoenix, Arizona, where Mrs. Rose Solomon, a housewife, is about to give birth:

"Mrs. Solomon or Rose? Which shall I call you?"

"Rose is fine."

"Rose, is this a natural childbirth?"

"Well, I'm not sure. I'm confused. You see, the television is on, and I'm being induced, so I guess that's not very natural, is it?"

"True enough, but are you receiving any pain medication?"

"No, not yet. Uhh, I don't think so . . ."

"Rose, I'd like to ask you just one more question. A new federal study revealed today shows that half the United States population favors liberalization of abortion laws. How do you feel about this?"

"Gee, Charles, you're hitting below the belt asking me at a time like this, but, yes, I do think every woman should be free to choose. Ooops, excuse me—I'm afraid this isn't a good time . . ."

"Oh, Rose, I understand perfectly. Here, let me get you some ice chips."

As he dashed out of the room, wave upon wave of contractions engulfed me, only this time with unprecedented violence. There was no time at all to recover between them. I thought I was seeing delusions of MacDonald's burgers and Coca-Cola and tampons and toilet bowl cleanser until I realized that the second commercial break had ended. My contractions mysteriously subsided, and Walter reappeared.

"You're almost there! Hooray!" chortled Walter. "Can you hang on just a little bit longer?"

"Yes, I think so," I whispered hoarsely. Involuntary tremors began spreading outward from my gut. I drew my legs up with my hands in an effort to still the shaking.

"I think there's time for me to scrub in. Don't push until I say to, okay?"

"Okay," I gasped, clutching my knees toward my armpits.

Walter vanished from view, and in his place Dan Rather, Marvin Kalb, and Eric Sevareid crowded round. So many in attendance! I held my breath to keep from pushing.

"She's crowning! She's crowning!" shouted Dan Rather.

"STAND BACK! WHAT'S GOING ON HERE? WHAT IN HELL DO YOU THINK YOU'RE DOING? GET OUT OF

MY WAY!" snapped Walter. I had never heard him use that tone on the air. I raised my head to get a better look.

"Ahhhhh," he purred, "you *are* ready. Now you are *really* ready! Let go of your breath, and inhale deeply, very deeply. Then exhale gradually and begin to push, but with control, contrrrrollllll," he growled, for emphasis.

As I released my breath, a strange stillness filled the room. Now it appeared that Walter and the correspondents clustered behind him were holding their breath. For once the mighty pulse of broadcasting skipped a beat. The next move was mine. I sucked in all the air my lungs could hold, emptying the room of every molecule of oxygen. My swollen abdomen eclipsed the screen as I clenched my teeth and began to push. I bore down with all my might. Nothing, nothing could stop me now—neither commercial breaks nor late news briefs nor emergency bulletins. Every cell in my body shuddered and rejoiced as the great mass within me began to slide the barest fraction of an inch. One push, then another, and as if by the force of my exertion my husband popped loose from the tight cabal of doctors and rushed to my side.

"Your face—it's all red! Here, let me wipe it," he offered, frantically flailing around for a towel. "How are you doing?"

Except for a grunt, I was pressing down too hard to answer.

"Wait! OH LOOK!" he called to the other doctors. "SHE'S HAVING A BABY!"

And that's the way it was, Thursday, October 28, 1971.

Deborah

I am a sculptor.

I can recall with absolute vividness my initial step into the universe of clay and the wonder of creation: To a shy four-year-old the first day of nursery school is terrifying, with its monster crowd of purposeful strange faces. A sympathetic teacher takes me gently by the hand and coaxes me into the art corner where I am drawn to brightly colored paint jars and the crock of clay. I have never seen the stuff before. My previous explorations into possibilities of mud and dirt have been frowned upon by the adult world.

It is love at first touch, magic. As I knead and mold, a robin's nest with four eggs evolves, then a glorious purple kangaroo with all her important essentials—pouch, tummy, and head—no arms, no legs, no tail. I can still see the lumpy, bumpy, almost formless creation, meaningless to anyone else, but to me reality—the touch of the hand of god. And god's hand was mine.

Fifty years later, after animal statues and human portrait busts, modeling the human figure has entered my work as a late blooming and gradual awakening—like the first taste of color, a bit shy in the beginning, for fear perhaps of being blinded, but now it is a dazzling light.

For two years I have been thinking about hiring a truly fat model. I have sculpted dozens of the youthful, the slender, the muscular, the curvaceous—and one marvelous, venerable Chinese ancient. A truism of sculpture has always been the marvel of rendering a full, fat figure. It has taken me time to track down a really large professional model: not just full-bodied, but *large*. At last I have found her.

Deborah arrives.
She is huge.

She is monumental.

She is overwhelming.

In the beginning I am repelled by this figure in front of me, so remote, so far removed from current canons of grace. How does one begin? Where is the beauty in this form? Where, in fact, are the lines and structure under all this mass, its contours exaggerated and distended by gravity and bulk, a body with no restraints, no bounds? It is volumes beyond the women of Rubens's art, whose fleshy nymphs seem so much pink and formless meat.

I hide my confusion, and after a brief and awestruck hesitation, the model and I play with various poses. There are problems created by massive weight which a slight person wouldn't guess. Gravity topples an otherwise ordinary position, and even strong muscles sometimes can't hold limbs and torso in their place. Masses of flesh must find some available and accommodating space to occupy. The very weight of an arm or leg can cause too much pressure on the vulnerable body.

Her shoulders are narrow, her breasts enormous and pendulously curved over the flesh of a belly that folds onto her thighs. Her full hips are almost narrow in relation to the voluminous balloonings above them.

Deborah finally sinks and reclines into a favorite nineteenth-century pose. This settling figure is neither Ingres's "Odalisque" nor Goya's "Maja." They are but ripples in the sands. This is a behemoth, a mountain range: body glorifying in body, shouting its excesses, indifferent to human opinion and uninterested in fashion. Such volumes! Generosity incarnate! Voluptuous is too tame for such an arrogant celebration of undulating form.

As a sculptor I see no angles. My eye follows as line flows into line, surfaces turn and convolute upon each other, transmogrify and change direction with the perfect tension of an ocean wave. Gravity stretches and curves flesh into sinuous asymmetry, as a pear or egg seems more sensuous than perfect sphere. The two-dimensional evaporates. Every line and plane pulls my eye around and over and under and through.

I feel the wet, malleable elasticity, the texture and give of the clay welcoming my fingers' pressures as I begin to mold. It is a material alive, responsive, and visceral. I would, if it were possible, reproduce in the finished terra-cotta the look, the sheen, the feel of this moist and living clay. My fingers are my tools. Through them I touch and reach my mind, my emotions, my senses. My work's vitality springs from these hands. The palm and heel pound rough shapes into life.

The fingers form and then define, create surfaces and textures, smooth or rough.

Beginning to model Deborah's huge torso, I segment the clay into rolls and unformed chunks, struggling to give it shape. My eye, hypnotized, informs my hand. Fingers turn and caress the folds and open arches. The line of the hip starts midback, forms a mounding helical plane, which my palm slowly circles—following hip, thigh, and knee and emerging again in the heavy-hanging arc of calf.

I flow breast curve onto folded belly fullness, gently bulge the clay into effulgent arcs. Hips round over buttocks and thighs. The bones, mere guidelines, are hidden from sight except at Deborah's precisely tapered wrists and ankles, her small and beautiful hands and feet. While working for purely sensuous lines, I carefully build each gliding surface, each peach curve, round grape, nautilus shell volute. I form a living arc where shoulder and arm join. An inexorable internal seismograph registers every inharmonious lump and dip and draws my fingers. Hillock and valley give way to firm, exacting pressure. Fingers lovingly stroke round forms—neck and arm, shoulder and hip, face and breasts—a hundred hundred times. They see what eyes can only sense. Slowly they move, refining every surface. Curves enlarge, close in, expand, contract and meet. My touch flows on.

Days pass. Deborah has long since left, and still I am lost in her. Shortly before a Sunday dawn the figure is finished. It will feel foreign in a while—simply another completed piece of work, good or bad. But tonight, though I have touched her damp clay for the last time, she is still, briefly, a part of me.

She is done, but I'm too tired to leave. I cannot bring myself to crawl into bed. Lightly resting my hand on the statue, I am suffused with urgent sexuality and release; in my artistic exhaustion I do not know where it comes from. It is not physical attraction; I do not lust after a piece of inert clay. Nor has my own figure, fat, skinny or pregnant, ever approached this one. But, staring, I recognize my own internal sexual mirror. Her opulent body has not my look. By psychic extension alone is this flesh mine: exaggerated, gravid, fecund— open, at ease, and generous: flesh upon floating flesh, quiescent and expectant, expanding, flowering, engulfing softness rich to receive and bubble into flame. The instant before the fire consumes, the phoenix is reborn.

Woman, I know you.

Homunculus, Homuncula

It was only nine-thirty in the evening when I flopped into bed, deliciously tired and grateful that nothing was preventing me from turning in early.

"How about a new game tonight?"

"Oh, I'm not up to any games tonight. I'm exhausted."

"Well, the game I have in mind is just perfect for tired women over forty."

I turned over onto my side. "Oh?" I responded, sleepily.

"You'll love it, really. All you have to do is lie there, very still, and let me do it all. Even better, pretend you've never had sex before. If you *do* get turned on, don't do anything about it—just lie still."

"Well, if it's all the same to you, then, I'll just drift off to sleep."

I yawned, stretched, and closed my eyes.

Almost immediately, a hand began to wander lightly across my face, over my lips, and down my neck. Fingers then entwined themselves lightly in my hair and paused to gently massage my scalp. The soothing touch on one area of my scalp made the nearby areas beg for the same, just as with a backrub the warm pressure on each vertebra whispers to the next in line, "Do me, do me, do me." The hand in some uncanny way knew what I wanted, and, as I lazily turned (trying not to appear responsive), it continued to massage my head before moving on down the nape of my neck and across my one exposed shoulder. (Somehow, when I wasn't looking, it had pulled down the strap of my nightgown.)

I was now still, feigning absolute lethargy, so that the hand could "have its way with me" without accusing me of complicity. I was aware that my breathing had slowed and that I was enjoying the feeling of being weighted down with fatigue and, at the same time, released like a marionette whose strings were being gently cut, one by one, to free it from the day's performance. Now luxuriating in the sensation of sinking, sinking, sinking down into ecstatic oblivion, I easily surrendered to the knowing hand as it strayed toward my breast, the nipple (mischievously disobeying the rules of the game) beginning to push against the soft cotton batiste of my nightgown.

The hand made no effort to pull the gown away from my body; instead, it tenderly covered my breast with its palm and let it remain there until I felt its soft heat through the flimsy fabric. I began to feel familiar stirrings and, again pretending that I was simply shifting my position to sleep more comfortably, I rolled to my back and let my legs drop open. If the hand knew, it didn't let on. For my part, I allowed my breathing to slow and deepen; inwardly I smiled at my adolescent pretenses to be much closer to Mr. Sandman than in fact I was, and, if I had dared to laugh, would have at my adult pretenses that I preferred sleep to sex.

There was no sudden leap to the now hot and moist region between my legs. No. The hand simply moved across to my other breast and began to trace a figure 8 between the two. Before I realized it, I had curled my shoulders inward in a habitual gesture that served to push my breasts more closely together and heighten the delicious sensations that were gathering force.

The hand stopped abruptly. "Don't move!" the voice reminded me with gruff tenderness. I was taken aback to realize how easily I had been aroused in spite of my protestations. Was this the time to think about my unbalanced checkbook, I thought, the way men distracted themselves to prolong foreplay for the woman? Why had I made this foolish promise? Well I *had*, I reminded myself, and once again, I let my body relax into what I hoped would pass for "innocent stupor." The hand was not going to make it easy for me. Fingers began to slowly crawl down my belly with soft, purposeful steps until they reached my groin, when five fingers suddenly became ten that buzzed in and around my flesh as bees to an open flower.

I wanted to lift my body up to greet these boisterous honey-seekers and shout out, "Yes, yes, let's play! Do hide-and-seek!" but I remembered the admonition and forced my body to remain still and let these wicked, friendly intruders dart in and out as if I were not there. Squeezing my eyes shut like a child, I tried to recapture what it was like before my body knew its "wheres" and "hows"—that girlish time when the present ruled simply because I had no memory for the future. In rapid and repeated succession, a hand sped back to my breasts and down again to frolic between my (motionless) legs. My breathing was coming harder and faster now, and I was beginning to seriously wonder why I had agreed to this silly game.

"Oh, please!" I cried out finally, and didn't wait for an answer. I arched my back and twisted and moaned. My head thrashed from side to side, I cried out, and, finally, my body crumpled and I lay still, very still.

After a few minutes, I pulled my nightgown back down over my knees and returned to my favorite side position to sleep. "I guess it's not so bad to be alone, after all—at least I have that little person in my head to keep me company." In a few seconds, I was fast asleep.

My Gorilla

"Honey, you're a million miles away. What are you up to *this* time?"

"Oh, I'm lost in the gorilla fantasy I adore so much."

He smiles and says, "Tell it to me one more time."

It's a beautiful day and I'm at the zoo, just ambling along from cage to cage. The animals are so wonderfully uninhibited, grooming and sniffing each other, and mating openly. I pass a male tortoise whose leg is in a splint. The zookeeper tells me it happened when he fell off his lover.

Still chuckling over this mental image, I wander past the birds, the big cats, and the monkeys. My pleasure is enhanced by knowing what awaits me at the end of this path.

Here I am, finally, in gorilla territory. I always save the gorillas for last. As I come dangerously close to Simba's cage, my mouth goes dry and my pulse accelerates. He's waiting for me as always. Grasping the bars slightly above his head, he rivets his small black eyes directly on me and begins rhythmically swaying from side to side. People nearby remark on the intensity of his gaze and the power of his grip. The bars now visibly move as he sways. Somebody throws a peanut at him. I shudder at the humiliation and move even closer—close enough to see his wet nostrils flare and to hear and feel his hot breath. Every nerve is alert to the smell of danger. I am woman; I am animal.

In one powerful stroke he pulls at the bars with all his brute strength until they begin to part. As he strains his mighty back, I enter through the opening he's made for me. People are watching, transfixed.

"Simba, I've been waiting—aching for you," I say to him as he lifts me in his strong arms and holds me high above his head. Vocalizing his passion with a prolonged guttural cry, he turns in all directions, then lowers me onto a bed of leaves. I move quickly out of my clothes. My skin is white and glistening; his fingers are black and dry. I am amazed at how nimble they are. He touches me everywhere, probing hungrily at my mouth, my ears, my armpits, my breasts, and finally parting my labia to gently taste my juices with his rough tongue. He intends to have me soon, I know, but not before smelling and licking me everywhere. His flat nose, usually moist, is dry now and moves roughly on my flesh. His nostrils pull on my gentler parts, suctioning, then releasing audibly. Just as his giant, hairy body engulfs mine in a lightning swift motion, animal passion overwhelms me. His great hard animal cock slams into my sweet flower pussy—over and over and faster and faster. I am doing it and I am watching it. I am the taken and I am the taker. I am the fucker and I am the voyeur. I hear my own scream of primal ecstasy. I thrash and grind my body against his. Our orgasms shatter the afternoon. Afterward, we lie there grunting and panting and sweating. Simba knows that I am fulfilled. He rises and beats his chest, calling out in wild pleasure. He reaches under my body and once again lifts me to the sky. I practically faint with dizziness as he spins me over his head. When he lowers me to the ground for the last time, I whisper to him, "I'll be back, Simba. I love you."

I leave through the bars Simba had opened for me. The crowd, which has been watching us in speechless silence, parts to let me pass. I smile and nod. I am Simba's chosen one.

I look up at my husband and smile shyly. "You're too much," he says.

Norman's Conquest

I was brought up to believe that hair was a dangerous substance which should be handled only by trusted experts. My mother, a veteran knitter and crocheter, never even touched a hair on her head except to comb it gingerly into place between weekly "do's." Her adherence to professional hairdo's was accompanied by a creed of hair don'ts:

1. Don't let it get messy.
2. Don't wash it too often.
3. Don't let it dry by itself.
4. Don't let it grow into your eyes.
5. Don't let it grow.

Ever since an experiment at a very early age with my own scissors incurred Mother's wrath, I gave up having any say at all about my hair. I obediently went to her haircutter at six-week intervals to maintain peace in the family as well as the blunt Dutch cut that everyone at the beauty parlor decreed was adorable on me. I came to assume this regimen was as essential to my future well-being as orthodontia, sensible oxford shoes, and eyeglasses.

Then, quite unexpectedly, about the time breast buds appeared, my hair changed. What formerly had been straight, silky, and cooperative now grew thick, bushy, and wild. I began to wash and brush it more often, hoping to tame it, but that only encouraged its willful growth. I watched in fascination as the rebellion, which I was too repressed to permit consciously, broke out on my head. I let my hair grow.

No one had ever told me about the thrill of having hair that moved! A simple shake of the head or a sudden gust of wind was enough to ravish my hair follicles as though they were a trillion Gspots studding my scalp. No wonder my mother never fussed with hers—she never would have knitted another sock!

Luckily I grew up in the sixties when it was permissible to flaunt this erogenous zone. Lovers came and went, but my free-flowing hair remained. For me it was instinct incarnate, proclaiming my sensuality with all of the unsubtlety of the defiant sixties. Though more subdued hair styles signaled my coming of age in the sensible seventies, I never ceased to equate long hair with passion. After I married, I regarded my collection of barrettes and combs with the same affection I had for my diaphragm and vibrator—revered hallmarks of adult sexuality.

It wasn't until the birth of my first child that an inexplicable urge to cut my hair overwhelmed me. At first I was too ashamed to admit what I considered to be an unnatural impulse, and I feared it meant I was unfit to be a mother at all. Reluctantly I confided in my neighbor, Sylvia, a mother of three, who insisted on taking me to her stylist, Norman.

Norman turned out to be a slight, unadorned, reassuringly gay man in his early forties. He listened without judgment while Sylvia condensed my plight into a reasonable request for a shampoo, cut, and blow dry. He understood all about life's silent crises that precipitate drastic new hair styles and color changes. Norman smiled at me in a warm and unappraising way and showed me to his station.

"Before I shampoo you, let me just brush your hair and see how it grows," he said as I sat down. He placed a towel around my neck and draped me with a plastic cape. I secretly thanked Sylvia for taking me to an unassuming salon where it wasn't necessary to disrobe. With no further warning, Norman's deft fingers undid the great rosewood clasp that pinned my hair into a French twist. It sprang free with a silent explosion of relief. Norman's hands groped through the undergrowth and came to rest on my scalp. As he began to massage it, my groin leaped toward my throat, and I gripped the sides of the chair. No man's hands had ever before explored this wilderness. Occasionally my husband's hands had strayed there and gotten lost; they would panic and hastily retreat to seek their way more confidently along more accessible terrain.

Norman's hands seemed to know the way, and with gentle pressure they moved up from the base of my skull and around my ears to come to grips with the upper scalp, which he awakened with quick finger presses. This time my groin somersaulted in excitement. Norman could as well have plunged both hands inside my bra and fondled my breasts.

"What wonderful healthy hair you have!" he marveled. "You'll be surprised how much darker it will look when it's first cut." He feathered his fingers through the wavy clumps all the way to the split ends, freeing the strands and playfully arranging them in a massive halo. Suddenly he paused and asked, "Are you sure you want to do this?"

"Oh, yes! Yes!" I insisted. ("Yes, yes, I want you to go on touching my hair forever—keep on—don't stop—never stop!")

"Okay then, let's shampoo you," he said. I followed him across the room to the row of sinks where other plastic-wrapped women reclined. A few were unattended, and foul-smelling fumes rose from foaming potions on their heads. How helpless and trusting they looked, I thought, as I approached the vacant sink beside them and lay back in my own reclining chair. I closed my eyes and began to have second thoughts: I should have told my husband I was doing this. Why hadn't I? I knew he'd object. He adored my hair. He may have married me only for my hair. The bone-hard trough in the enamel sink on which my neck rested felt cold as a chopping block. I glanced upward expecting to see a guillotine, but Norman hovered overhead in his fresh pinstriped oxford shirt, calmly adjusting the faucets. When the water temperature was just right, he guided the strong jets of water through my hair.

My worst fears began to dissolve. After all, I reasoned, I had nothing to lose by luxuriating in a shampoo. I could always call off the haircut, go home and discuss it with my husband. Except for the matronly overtones, being back in a beauty parlor wasn't so bad. I had never before realized what a sanctuary it was. All that was required of me here was to lie absolutely still. How utterly novel! For the first time in weeks I could relax. My gaze settled on the motionless pairs of feet that belonged to the other reclining ladies, who were probably regulars here. Aloft on the footrests, suspended from the busy tracks of daily life, the feet just lay there turned slightly apart— aloof and catatonic. Were their owners as weary as I? Was the fatigue permanent and incurable?

Norman had turned off the water and was squeezing cool glops of an apricot-scented gel shampoo through my hair. Once again his attentions scattered my fears, and I allowed myself to sink more deeply into passivity. My head and torso, each arm and leg, became as heavy and unmovable as sandbags. Nothing would rouse me from this chair—I had relaxed to the point of paralysis. Norman's amazing hands returned to caress and coax forth a soufflé of bubbles. He worked outward from the roots, starting near my forehead and working downward toward the ears and neck, leaving no follicle neglected. His hands moved in unison beneath the rich lather, improvising rhythmic patterns as they went along: slow figure eights yielded to short back-and-forth strokes, which in turn melted into lazy circles that spiraled outward to the farthest lengths of my hair. Then his hands returned to press and squeeze my scalp in a breathtaking sequence of movements that produced tremors strong enough to curl my toes. How astoundingly unlike the shampoos of my childhood, which had made me feel like a pot being scoured.

After dallying amid the luscious bubbles, Norman's hands slowly began to slide and shape the great mass of lather into one giant cloud. I could no longer contain my pleasure in silence. A groan so low and deep that it rose from the farthest reaches of my surrender escaped my lips. I listened to the sound for several seconds, awed by its otherworldly eeriness: I heard the longing of a wolf's cry, the beauty of a whale's song, the growl of the wind. And then the shocking realization that this cry was coming from some strange new part of me strangled it abruptly and completely midthroat. My eyes flew open, and I could see the fleshy underside of Norman's chin above me. The curve of his lower lip stretched into a wide smile.

"Would you like conditioner?" he asked as he squeezed the last bit of foam from my hair.

"Oh, yes," I whispered. And as the warm jets of water guided by Norman's knowing hands roared and chased away the last of the shampoo, I closed my eyes again and groped my way back to the present. My neck still rested on the enamel curve of the sink. The plastic smock remained untouched. My hands hadn't left the armrests, and my feet lay undisturbed on the footrest. Just for safekeeping I tightened my perineum in a couple of Kegel flexes: yes, everything remained intact, unviolated. The jets of water rained relief on all my follicles. Pleasure circulated with every heartbeat, and, as I lay there with each hair drinking up conditioner, I began to tingle with newfound energy. I noticed a flush appearing on my cheeks after Norman readjusted my chair to its upright position. By now the thought of leaving without the haircut had totally evaporated, and I eagerly anticipated whatever unfamiliar sensations Norman had in store for me. Completely under his spell, I glided back to his station for the styling.

He piled my water-laden hair on top of my head and secured it with clips. The weight and earthiness of my wet hair reminded me of compost after an autumn rain. Just as visions of garden shears and rakes came to mind, I felt the teeth of Norman's comb slicing through the lower portion that was allowed to hang down my back. Then a pause and the moment of truth: the icy scissor blade pressed against the back of my neck and, with a delicious crunch, it bit into clump after clump of wet hair. Each bite sent soggy curls to the floor. Bright pink blotches appeared on my cheeks.

After three or four more snips Norman stopped and asked, "Are you all right?"

"Oh, yes—keep on," I assured him.

"Do you like this length?" Norman gave me a handmirror and spun the chair around so I could see the back of my head in the mirror.

Annoyed by the interruption, I answered, "Sure," before I had really located my reflection in the glass.

Pausing thoughtfully, he asked, "What do you have in mind?"

"What?"

"A particular look or style?"

"Oh, whatever you suggest," I answered, impatient for him to continue.

"Then I would recommend a feathered cut rather than a blunt one."

"Oh, fine, fine," I agreed, frantic for Norman to unclip the next clump of hair. Layer by layer he combed and snipped and felt his way along, seeing with his fingertips, always with care and complete concentration. The soft crunching sound of the scissors mesmerized me. As piece after piece of hair fell to the floor, I began to feel lighter and lighter. If he took off much more I thought I would be able to levitate.

"Your hair has so much body!" Norman exclaimed as the haircut neared completion. "I'd like to towel it dry and shape it with my hands."

"Oh, yes, do," I said, wishing he would work his magic all over my body.

"I'll show you something so simple you can do it yourself," Norman volunteered.

"What? Do it myself?" I repeated. ("Never see you again?")

"Yes. Most women like a style they can manage on their own."

"Oh, no, not me," I insisted. "I'd much rather come back every week and have you do it."

All at once I realized: Mother was right!

Ooh La La!
Berry Mousse, a Recipe

During the years since I turned fifty, I have observed in myself a shedding of a timorous skin. It is most apparent in the culinary sense. I think it might have something to do with my French mother, who ruled her kitchen with hysteria and ambivalence and thrift. I am hoping that my new, bonnets-over-the-windmill attitude toward cooking will invade all my life's directions. I want to sit in the sun of my half-century and blink rapturously at the concept of More Than Enough Is Better Than a Feast. I think this used to be called greed. I am in love with it. In any event, Ooh la la! berry mousse is one of the serendipitous delights that has emerged from my recent dedication to excess.

It began one day with my desire to create something lush and yielding for dessert, something connected in some way with the cheese and fruit I normally serve but not as honest, not as wholesome and direct. I wanted something a little more devious and seductive, something that whispered sweet-melting nothings to the taste buds, caressing the tongue as it sang its siren passage down the throat. Something roguish and mocking to enrapture the palate and leave it longing. Something to leave the pallor of desire upon the countenance after the act of consummation. Cake was out of the question, definitely *hors de combat*.

I am a sporadic and unreliable baker, given to abrupt loss of interest in the mathematical strictness of measurements and prone to embarrassing accident, like gluing myself to the counter when something sticky spills over. No luscious chocolate éclair or wistful madeleine ever beckons *me* onto the kitchen dance floor. No. This had to be something else, some *belle époque* concoction to salute my Madame Récamier cuisine voluptuousness.

Fortunately, I had in my possession prodigious quantities of ooh la la! berries. The ooh la la! berry must be a native Californian fruit. I think the name derives from a French corruption of an Indian word. People in New York and Texas and places like that have never heard of it, at least not those to whom I have extolled its exquisite properties. This is a fruit so perfect as to elicit cosmic applause: dark and pendulous and juicy, it is a cosmopolitan *roué* of a berry, a sort of blackberry *boulevardier* of mysterious provenance with an ancient escutcheon (raspberry couchant, boysenberry rampant) and more than one bar sinister.

I pick the ooh la la! berries myself, each year in July. I drive down toward Half Moon Bay where, off the coast road, there is a farm of the most gratifying abundance, with acres of berrycanes dwindling in neat rows off into the middle distance and an open-throated invitation to hedonists like myself to spend the whole day, the whole week, the whole month, just picking.

Not a mile away, the ocean surf booms upon the beach. The fog lifts suddenly just before noon and the high sun switches on its floodlight, making me glad I brought a shady hat and some iced lemonade. The air is as soft as a velvet curtain, palpable amid the mumbling of bees and the mingled incense of the herbs, vegetables, and flowering plants that are grown for sale. There are animals: two nanny goats, medievally pregnant, observers of the world through heavy-lidded, cynical yellow eyes. The effluvium of their body heat rises like a pungent smoke signal to the restless male tethered a few feet away, making me think of Napoleon's message to Josephine: "*Ne te lave pas, je viens!*" ("Don't wash, baby, I'm on my way!"). Some rabbits pose like a Dürer engraving, with drooping ears and frantic noses. They ignore the many mama cats, each busy with her enchanting, famished, furry brood all in different stages of squirming development. The environment makes me light-headed: such mellow fruitfulness, such exuberant generosity! As I plunder the berrycanes, my fingers quickly turning purple, dusty little grass snakes wriggle across the paths, looking like ropes of tarnished jewels. I gather more fruit than I can possibly use during the remaining months of the year. I buy flowers for the house, for the garden, loading up the back seat of the car with hibiscus, bougainvillea, ivy geraniums, roses, aromatic herbs. A sort of Demeter folly seizes me.

I drive home with wild plans to make jam, re-cover the sitting room sofa, bottle, preserve, can, freeze, feed the world! I sing Carmen's aria about *l'amour* being *enfant de bohème* along with the mezzo on the car radio, conducting the orchestra myself. Everything has connection and the universe is plainly proceeding as it should. I get home, wash all the berries, put them in shallow bowls to stay cool, and I ice them. The flowers I put in buckets of water, the plants in the shade outside. Then I slip into something comfortable and wait for inspiration.

I have found that in order to be receptive to the creative gush when it comes, it is necessary to make certain mental adjustments. Begin by waving away any habitual responses. Resolve to have nothing to do with calculations—teaspoons of this, cupfuls of that. Vagueness and a sense of waiting, of sensing, must take the place of the cold steel of numbers, weights, and measures. Stay connected. Let the inner voices speak, let the eyes in the head envision the end result. Give up. Who cares? If you've turned fifty, you can pretty well do as you like. After all, you live here. And there's always the compost heap, the garbage disposal, or the bucket under the sink to receive your efforts if they don't turn out too well. Let the lurking specter of opprobrium dissolve! In its place, permit a new and unusual relationship to your surroundings: lie down on the kitchen floor. Breathe deeply. Feel the lengthening of your spine on the cool linoleum tiles.

Now fetch some of the ooh la la! berries, still stunned in their chilly prison. Lie down again while the ice around them melts. This will happen more explosively with an artificial application of heat waves, if you are really that eager to arrive at a climax, but I do not recommend this course. It might involve the distraction of hovering over the ooh la la! berries with a hairdryer—quite unsuitable on this dreamy afternoon. Instead, before you lie down, I suggest you pour yourself a cup of delicate, perfumed tea. Sip this as you recline, and let your imagination flirt with the ingredients of your mousse. You will need unflavored gelatin, the powdered kind, hot water (you have it, in the tea kettle), the bottle of cassis you bought for last Sunday's brunch (and forgot to add to the champagne), sugar, lemon yogurt, and heavy, thick cream, the kind that would give your cardiologist the vapors. You will need molds, the prettier the better, and for some reason you will need to rinse these in cold water. I do not know why, but it works.

When you are ready, melt the gelatin in the hot water, flicking it this way and that until it is all dissolved. Let it cool. This affords another opportunity to lie down—perhaps this time on the sofa, while you respond to *"prélude à l'après-midi d'un faune"* or some other sensuous, impressionistic piece of music. Resist the promptings of your intellect. The temptation to think must be inhibited as much as possible. Return to the kitchen and add to the liquid gelatin all the fluid that has gushed from the ooh la la! berries during their thawing. Really, you would not have believed there could be so much. Add sugar, to your taste, and the lemon yogurt, dreamily combining these with the gelatinous juice until a satisfyingly tumid coalescence occurs, colored with streaks of primrose and purple—rather like the evening sky after sunset. Now, with a few deft strokes, slip the pliant and quiescent ooh la la! berries into the glistening mixture. Tease them about as you flood them with cassis, letting the heady bouquet of the liqueur pervade the very depths of their being. Then, in another bowl, whip as much of the cream as you think will distend the mingled sweetness to twice its size. Carefully fold the turgid peaks into the mixture, using a repetitious motion of the hand and wrist. The mousse will now be fragrant and slippery, ready to slide into the molds. Set aside in a cool quiet place to solidify.

When the time is right, perhaps late at night before bed or on a golden, lazy afternoon later in the same day, decide whether you want to share this dessert with a special friend or indulge yourself alone. Either way, you will need to turn out the mousse on a platter spread with shards of crushed fan wafers. Before taking the first liquescent mouthful, prepare your palate with a sip of cold Sauternes, letting it warm briefly under your tongue before swallowing. All motions should be hypnotically slow. Raise your glass to Dionysus and remember, in all things, immoderation!

Masturbate Theater

Our miniseries this week is an adaptation of
A Tale of Two Clitties
A Foreplay in Three Acts with Multiple Climaxes

EPISODE I

Narrator: Phallustaire Cock (impeccably dressed in silken sleepwear reclining on a circular bed amid satin pillows and matching Irish wolfhounds)

Good evening. Tonight we embark upon a thrilling venture. Never before has a work of cliterature been adapted for a miniseries. *A Tale of Two Clitties*, recently awarded the Pubiczer Prize, heralds a new genre in the history of theater. When it opened in Kensington, California, in the spring of 1984, it shocked critics and audiences alike with its daring plethora of characters and its open contempt of narrative line. "We care about characters!" declared one of the authors during an interview on opening night. "Plot is a male invention!"

The action (or should I say inaction?) takes place in southern England in the late fourteenth century. It was a time of rampant superstition and ignorance borne out by the widespread popularity of the yoni cult. As you know, a yoni is the symbol of the female organ of generation and was, in pagan times, an object of veneration. In nature worship all natural orifices were revered as representing the yoni of the mother-earth goddess, and throughout southern England archaeologists have discovered yonic tokens, or talismen, fashioned of stone, wood, and even bronze that date from as early as the fourth century B.C.

Now, at the prompting of the Venerable Bede in 813, the Christian Church, on pain of excommunication, forbade all yoni worship in the British Isles, and from that time on yoni-bearing became clandestine. Anyone owning a yoni immediately buried it, ensuring that it would remain within the family. Thus, the cult grew into an underground movement. Now, you may be thinking that this is all very well, but a terrible thing happened. No sooner were yonis buried than cocks all across the land grew cold. As a result all decent folk took to wearing merkins. . . .

Enter the Cycling Minstrels: What does it mean?????

Return Phallustaire: Hush, you will have to wait for the next episode.

EPISODE 2

Phallustaire Cock: Good evening. Last time we discussed the yoni cult, an underground pagan ritual that attracted a large following from every social class. Gardeners, nuns, innkeepers, lords and ladies alike—all were closet believers because all were equally afflicted. (Only the very powerful and defiant escaped its scourge. It is said that William the Conquerer kept a secret yoni in his possession and that Richard the Lionhearted took one with him to the Crusades.)

I would like to take you now to the village of Much-Humping-on-the-Crotch in southern England where our story takes place. Now, *A Tale of Two Clitties* quite literally is a *play* in the gaming sense of the word. The characters sprang spontaneously from the imaginations of the Kensington playwrights, and their lines were made up on the spot by the players. There was no script; consequently, no performance is ever alike, and the play becomes whatever the players make it, which is always fertile, innovative, unpredictable, and rife with possibilities. You may use their formula or, if you'd rather, invent your own.

Let me introduce you to their cast of characters:

Lady Pudenda Yoni-Twat and Sir Rod Yoni-Twat, Lady and Lord of
   the Manor
Sisters Twatina and Titiana of the Order of the Holy Panties, high
   priestesses of the secret yoni cult
Lady Labia Witworth, wife of the late-departed Major and mother
   of the Honorable Labia Minora
Squire Dickie Ramballs, owner of the Randy Cow Pub

Leif Mold, Sir Yoni-Twat's gardener, who slept with Mistress Climax
and fathered Maggie Titsfull
Maggie Titsfull, serving wench ("Can I serve you now, Sire?") and
illegitimate daughter of Leif Mold
Vageena Snatchworthy, servant
Sheilah Shockingsocket, servant
Lady Lascivia, twin sister of Lady Pudenda who later appears as:
Dame Dementia Praecox, madwoman
Mistress Climax, lady-in-waiting ("She comes too soon!")
Inspector Hoarhound
Blessed Rancho Gonzales Prickstalk, ghost and worker of miracles
Roving Minstrels: cycling chorus
Vicar

Phallustaire Cock: Oh, dear, I see our time is up! Until the next episode. . . .

EPISODE 3

Phallustaire Cock: Good evening, and welcome back to this, our
third episode in *The Tale of Two Clitties.* Before Act I begins I would
just like to say a word about a merkin (also, mirkin). The origin of
this word is unknown, but the *Oxford Dictionary of English* finds
references to it in literature from the fifteenth century on, so I think
it's safe to conjecture that merkins were in use a couple of centuries
earlier. A merkin is described as the female pudendum, or, more specifically, as the counterfeit hair for a woman's privy parts. Clearly,
these became the rage by the seventeenth century. (A want ad in the
Mercurius Fumig in 1660 read: "Last week was lost a merkin in the
Coven-Garden." Coven-Garden, you know, was the scene of highest
fashion.) You can be certain that every self-respecting lady in Much-
Humping-on-the-Crotch took great pride in her merkin. And now, I
think we are ready to begin.

A Tale of Two Clitties

Prologue: (sung by Blessed Rancho Gonzales Prickstalk and Dame
Dementia Praecox)

> Of yonis lost and yonis found
> Cocks cold above the sacred ground,
> Beware the hoar:

Eschew the hound,
And be not by the merkin bound.

Act I, Scene 1
At the Randy Cow Pub, day's end

(Much carousing)

Enter Leif Mold carrying yoni wrapped in a silken scarf. Leif Mold tells Dickie of his mysterious find while digging up the earth for an organic vegetable garden at the Yoni-Twat estate. He furtively unwraps it and reveals a yoni. He gloats, "Every yoni needs a merkin!" Squire Ramballs whispers that he, too, has found some yonis in the church's graveyard.

Maggie: "Can I serve you now, Sire?"
Mistress Climax: "She comes too soon!"
Squire: "Hush! Don't tell the vicar!"

They decide to place an ad in the *London Times*:

MERKINS WANTED.
NO QUESTIONS ASKED.

They call in Inspector Hoarhound.
Maggie: "Can I serve you now, Sire?"

Enter Minstrels (in faux pas harmony): What does it mean?

Act I, Scene 2
Canceled for lack of interest

Act II, Scene 1
Lady Pudenda's drawing room

Lady Lascivia: I know you're hard to penetrate but that does not make you superior to me.

Lady Pudenda: My deah, come to the point.

LL: You didn't suppose the last thing you lost was your virginity, did you?

LP: Then you know! (She swoons.)

Enter Dame Dementia singing, accompanied by Blessed Rancho on the castinets

Across the moors cold winds doth blow
and here in Humping it too is so

that cocks brought forth do feel the snow.
Oh-ho! Oh-ho! Cold wind doth blow!
(And what will Cock Robin do then, poor thing?)

Enter cycling minstrels:

They swooned! They swooned!
Too soon to tell—
One missing merkin's going to hell!

Maggie comes in and in alarm summons Sister Twat and Vageena.
Maggie (to the audience): Which twin has the yoni?
(End of Episode Three: "Until next week . . .")

EPISODE 4

Narrator: Good Evening. Last week we saw . . . (summarizes)
Prologue: Sung as before by Dame Dementia and Blessed Rancho

Act III, Scene 1
In the merkin woods on the Yoni-Twat estate

Leif Mold enters, dragging the swooning twins deep into the woods for rites. Found yoni is wrapped in the silken scarf.

Square Ramballs, Sir Rod, and drinking friends stumble upon the scene on their way home from the pub. Much singing and rabble rousing.

Is this a merkin I see before me?
Out, out damn twat!

The din attracts the inspector.
Inspector Hoarhound: Hold your cocks! Who goes there?

Mass confusion. Swooning sisters awaken. Yoni accidentally falls from scarf. Inspector Hoarhound can't crack the case, but Sister Twatina does: She knows whose it is. Vageena, heroically, rushes forth and rips off her own merkin to cover it. Everyone gathers round to warm the cocks before returning the yonis to their rightful owners for reburial. Sir Rod declares a Humpingfest, and everyone goes at it in wild celebration.

Maggie: "Can I serve you now, Sire?"
Mistress Climax: "She comes too soon!"
Minstrels sing of the cycle, warn that the yoni may be uncovered

but once a year on the Humpingfest or cocks will grow cold again. Ceremony ends with great rejoicing.

Epilogue

Maggie Titsfull: Can I serve you now, Sire?
Narrator: What? Oh, no, I've lost the thread.
Maggie: Dear Sire, it's in the merkin.
Narrator: But that's where we started.

End of another frustrating episode of Masturbate Theater.

No Hands!

She was glad it wasn't her first time going alone for a hot soak—and that she had got there before all the tanned and flawless young couples arrived. She handed the young woman a five-dollar bill and took her fifty cents change and the key to her assigned room. She quickly set off down the corridor, past the room marked "W" and the room marked "M" to the room marked "24."

Once inside, she locked the door behind her and immediately turned up the volume on the radio that was set in the wall next to the shower. In an instant, the room was filled with the sounds of soft rock. She undressed quickly, flinging her clothes on the firm, white-sheeted, foam mattress perched on top of a high-gloss wooden platform, also in its own niche in the opposite wall. Her bra landed in a lopsided heap, one cup puffed to its full D cup as if she were still in it, the other collapsed to the size of a very young girl or a very old woman, of which she was neither.

She moved quickly to the shower and, soap in hand, began lathering her neck absentmindedly before moving its thick sudsy gel under and around each of her ample breasts. Her motions slowed dramatically as her soap-filled hand reached down over her belly and disappeared between her legs, rolling in and out and around until her body began to sway ever so slightly, her head drop back, her eyes close. When she finally stood still, the bar of soap that she returned to its resting place showed the imprint of the fingers and thumb that had gripped it momentarily. Now she stood with her legs apart and rolled her head around in a circle, letting the hot water beat down on her face, her hair, her breasts, and her belly from where it cascaded down her legs.

When she turned the water off, her skin was flushed from head to foot. She felt as if she were wearing an invisible, skin-tight garment, and imagined herself to be some newborn furry creature encased in a membranous sac, squirming to be set free by its mother's rough and loving tongue. Her freedom was a few steps away in the dark and quiet water of the hot tub. In a quick gesture, she turned the volume down on the radio until only a pulsing beat could be heard, but a beat that was enough to evoke the whole song to anyone who knew it. Then she stepped up the two polished wooden stairs to the circular perimeter of the tub. Slowly, she lowered herself onto the bench, which was already immersed in the dark steaming water. From the hot shower, her body radiated enough heat that the 104° temperature of the tub water was only a slight shock to her flesh. Once she felt the reassuring hard plank beneath her, she extended her arms along the circumference of the tub and opened her legs. The liquid heat rushed into her and she gasped audibly, raising herself up momentarily against the sudden invasion of her private world. In a second, the heat was no longer her enemy, and she surrendered to the water without protest.

After closing her eyes for a few minutes to let time and space drift eerily away, she surrendered body and mind to the enveloping heat with a trust born of familiarity and experience. Still holding on to the sides of the tub, her arms fully extended, she stretched out her body so that her feet touched the wall on the opposite side of the tub. Her pubic hair was reddish and long. Strands of it quivered on the water's surface like helpless fragments of a frightened sea creature. As her expansive belly rose and fell almost imperceptibly with her breathing, water filled the concavity of her navel and gently spilled out again. The alternate filling and spilling took on the cadence of the almost soundless musical vibrations, which in some way anchored her to the reality of her surroundings.

She suddenly opened her eyes as if from a vivid dream, and maneuvered her bulk back onto the bench. As if she hadn't seen them before, her eyes now took in the bubblers that were stationed like gleaming chrome-attired sentries along the periphery of the tub. She found the control switch on the wall and turned the timer to 10 minutes. At four locations and in unison, bubbling jets of water burst forth instantly and noisily from the blackness of the water. The sound was as jarring to the stillness of the room as the action of the bubblers "breaking wind" in the sacred water was hilarious. She was still for a moment, unsure of whether to scream at the shock it brought to her psyche or explode in the laughter it brought to her soul.

Smiling, she moved toward the closest bubbler, turned her back to it and, by moving her body up and down along its path, forced the hard, hot stream of water to pound on her vertebrae, one by one. It was as if this mindless fixture were a Japanese massaji-shis, for both hid behind a stern façade that seemed to convey an utter disregard for the delirium of pleasure-pain that it was their gift to produce.

When she could tolerate it no more, she straightened up her body and turned around, thinking—her mind on automatic—that she could simply turn off the bubbler as if it were a faucet. She was startled, then, when the force of the water struck between her legs. She gasped and pulled away. She stared at the mindless churning and whirling of the bubbler stream, water galloping out of its soul in technological delight, and then glanced around the room hesitantly before moving toward it with deliberation.

Once again, the water struck her "head on." This time, she tightened her sphincter muscles against the assault and then pulled herself up ever so slightly out of its demanding reach. That steamy place that had received no gentlemen callers for a very long time now began to awaken. She felt thick, swelling throbs of pleasure as she moved her body forward and back, up and down, around and around in belly dance circles atop the hot pounding jetstream of water. Her hands gripped the edge of the tub. The noise of the bubblers became a roar in her ears as her body worked furiously to hold on to this shameless ecstasy. Her face was contorted. In a sudden spasm she stiffened her legs and pressed them tightly together. With a deep exhalation of air that resembled the roar of a woman giving birth, it was over. She felt weak and limp.

She climbed heavily out of the water, turned off the bubblers, and staggered to the waiting mattress, where she fell asleep instantly. When the voice of the attendant purred over the speaker: "Five minutes, Miss Richardson," she opened her eyes and scrambled to put herself back together. As she unlocked and opened the door to Room 24, she turned around and glanced from shower to bed, to tub, to bubblers. "You were marvelous," she said—"simply marvelous."

The most delicate of smiles graced her face as she walked out through the lobby, now filled with Mr. and Ms. Cardboard Lovely.

Aching for Mr. Dovebar

The first time I saw you stripped, I nearly gagged. You are stockier, thicker than most—clearly too much to consume at one sitting. Your marble hardness stretches your flawless skin to its limit. I hold you by your stick and turn you round and round in my hand. A growing sense of familiarity soothes my fears and inhibitions: I wish you could last forever.

Gluttony, I know, is a sin; I must avoid it. Setting a slow, deliberate pace, my delicate mouthwork coaxes forth your true scent and flavor. My tongue traces rococo curlicues upon your shaft; you appear unmoved. My lips add suction, and you respond. A fissure appears in your taut coating. Suddenly warming too fast, you threaten to run out in creamy rivulets. I pull away and blow cold breaths upon your wetness. To my dismay you are growing soft. I dress you quickly in your wrapper, pop you back into cold storage, and pray that you'll recover.

Keeping you captive makes me feel rich. You are better than money in the bank: You are all the pleasure that money can buy. You were made only to arouse desire, to make a quick buck, to be consumed. Please be good, Mr. Dovebar, and get hard again. Then I will come for you at some illicit hour—maybe in the chill hours of the night when my sleep is shattered for want of you; maybe in the midst of a workday when thoughts of you wreck my concentration; maybe even right now—before dinner—when hunger for you, only you, blots out my need for all other nutrients. And if, after countless tastings and tongue teasings, you show signs of weariness—loss of weight, lackluster coat, fading firmness—then I shall not prolong your agony. When the final hour comes, I will take heroic measures. I will caress you with sure strokes, breathing my heat into your cold heart, finally allowing the consummation you have sought so long: to melt and merge deep within me. Stay hard, Mr. Dovebar, and you will be rewarded.

I Can't Believe I Wrote This!

My old friend, Sally, abundant with unedited statements, recently blurted out: "If you've been with one man, you know what all men are like." Now there's a remark to throw me into reverie. As if vying for recognition, the different men that have been in my life scramble to be remembered.

One of my first loves in high school was close to 250 pounds, and it was not muscle. He was a wonderful, jolly rotunda of a man, and I learned to love the feel of my arms around his ample body. His personality was as big as he was; but alas, I was seventeen and wanting to be mauled, and he was twenty-one and determined to make it to his wedding night . . . a virgin.

Later, I lived with a man of similar proportions, but he was no virgin. He was a twice-a-day man, if he could keep it down to that. His rounded body had its own characteristic movements, especially when making love. Once, when I was driving down a modest residential street, I saw a St. Bernard mating on a shady front lawn. I was so shocked by the similarity of his wonderful, rhythmic movements to my lover's that I nearly drove off the road trying to watch. After that, when we made love, I imagined us, primitive and free, on the green grass, under the billowy trees.

Then, there was a robust, athletic lover: broad shoulders, mighty voice. He was rowdy, gregarious, and outgoing. But, alas, he was a once-a-week lover—always outgoing, never incoming. While I could never miss this man in a crowded room, I certainly did miss him in my uncrowded bed.

Those were my big-bodied men. There were also several wonderful ones closer to my own size, and I must say, for a good tumble, that works out best. With one, I remember how easy it was to roll and wrestle, so equal were our weights; and with another, I recall the full length of his softly muscled body covering mine, from our intertwined toes to his hands in my hair.

Maybe what dear Sally meant is that men are all similar when they have orgasms. Let me see. I had one virgin, so I never knew how he came. I had one insatiable St. Bernard, in whose tutoring hands I learned to let go. His rhythmic orgasm was gentle, and he came after even, deep breathing, with soft moans and a watery mixture of love juices and sweat. We were like one in this soft and safe experience, and I felt adored and cherished.

Then, I had a once-a-week athlete, who, I have to assume, was either not very attracted to me or sexually very inhibited. He came in great puffing bursts, like a locomotive. *Chug, chug* and then, pulling on the brakes with all his power, *schschsch* . . . while he let out all the steam. His body would stiffen, his back arch, and I felt like a foreign object being expelled with his semen.

Now, size of penis doesn't matter, right? In my experience, that is really right. However, I do remember one man who did have a memorable member. He was greatly proud of his "gift to women." He was of medium build, but I must say that his broader than normal, more willing than normal, cocky wonder still stands out for me. He came in spasmic jerks, not rhythms, and silently, lost in his own world.

The richest of lovers, for me, responded with moaning songs and sounds that are incomparable. These were natural give-and-take lovers, men who would laugh or sigh or cry in lovemaking with equal spontaneity. I remember these encounters for their emotion and impulse, not for the mechanics used. Sometimes we cheered each other on, sometimes we were shy, but, mostly, we celebrated the silliness and wonder of it.

I guess I don't agree with Sally.

EROTICA MELANCHOLIA

EROTICA MELANCHOLIA

*M*uch as we love to play and be frivolous, we must admit, dear reader, to a darker side. 'Til now we have kept our sorrows and regrets a secret, but as Ladies "of a certain age," we occasionally revel in the wild mood swings and hot flashes that lend more full-bodied flavor to our "aged, choice" erotica. We find we have less tolerance for the undiluted sweetness of romantic fantasy. The craving of youth to sugarcoat the moment forever has yielded to more sophisticated tastes—thank God! We have come to acquire a taste for the bitter and the fleeting, those pungent spices that now make our pleasures so poignant and intense.

Pleasure Promises

Pleasure promises, promises . . .
Through furled bud and new green leaf,
Through banked brook and sun-warmed stone,
Through star-rise in violet skies,
Pleasure promises, but pleasure lies.

Through feast set forth with savored care,
Through flame-refracted wine and fragrant rose,
Through silvered bowl on mirrored wood,
Pleasure makes its pledge to lips and eyes.
Pleasure promises, but pleasure lies.

But let a long-sought glance cross yours,
Carrying the look of love, intent
Like sun through lens, to burn;
Let knowledge leap the circuits held apart
By frozen doubt, and overload the heart:

To shock delicious shudder from the flesh,
That felt dawns past, and now new dawns to come;
And let the fused energy ignite
All senses promised-to in vain.
Then pleasure promises, and does not lie again.

Property Settlement

The day my husband moved out, I helped him pack. We worked straight through from morning to afternoon without stopping for lunch. I pretended I was embarking on a trip only this time without the anxiety of flying anywhere or of arranging for the house and dog. My "tripidation," as Carl called it, always annoyed him, but now for a change I found myself happily immersed in the hustle. "This is fun!" I laughed. "Why didn't we discover this years ago? I like the pack-ing—I just don't like leaving."

We did the downstairs rooms first, stacking Carl's things in neat piles in the front hall. The activity invigorated all of us, even arthritic, flea-bitten Boris, who hobbled after us from one room to the other, gamely wagging his bald tail. As the piles in the hall grew taller, he finally collapsed among them and began to pant anxiously.

"Oh, dear. He thinks he's going to be abandoned."

"He is."

"Carl, how can you say that?"

"Don't be absurd. He's always been your shadow. You really didn't expect me to take him, did you?"

"No, but I thought you might want him to visit."

"Visit? And barf all over my new carpets?"

I patted Boris to reassure him and lamented, "Departures depress him so. Remember how he stopped eating whenever the boys went away?"

"Yea, it made him vomit less. Maybe now you won't have to get up so often in the night." Boris rolled a baleful eye at me, and for the first time I wondered if he had deliberately sabotaged us. Boris never threw up in the daytime, only after midnight when Carl turned off our headboard reading lamp. Stunned by the abrupt darkness, Carl and I would lie side by side on our backs in bed as though we'd just been flattened by a truck.

The wallop of each tightly scheduled day compounded by a second wind of activity that swept us off to symphony or opera, board meetings or fundraisers, movies or dinner parties always left me numb. Our social life glittered with achievers trying to keep up with Carl, a self-styled entrepreneur, whose schemes and maneuvers defined the cutting edge. Lately he had just started the first graduate program in entrepreneurship, which already threatened to blossom into another business franchise like his many others.

The effect of so many successes was narcotic, I felt, for as the whirlwind years rushed by, Carl's need to outdo himself grew exponentially. Even recreation became the stuff of legend, requiring fifty-mile bike rides every weekend augmented by ten-mile-a-day runs on weekdays in order to prepare for seasonal marathons, year-round tennis tournaments, the summer relay swim across Lake Tahoe, and the winter Nastar ski competitions. Now that he was fifty-two, fewer and fewer of his old friends could keep up, and Carl reigned supreme in his age group.

My moment of satisfaction came each night when Carl turned out the light. Lying in bed beside him I felt, "Here at last we are compatible!" Our attraction from the first had been intense and physical, and over the years we had never tired of gloating over our unorthodox conquest. We had met at his brother's wedding where I was maid of honor. It was a huge, ceremonial affair with legions of ushers and bridesmaids, flower girls and a ring-bearer. During the long rehearsal I scrutinized the groom's notoriously "unobtainable" brother, Carl, whom I had never met before. Apocryphal tales of his years in the Peace Corps and of his recent Himalayan trek had prepared me for his good looks and athleticism but not for the force of his charisma. His energy chased away the musty air in the cathedral where over and over again we practiced the wedding march. Every cell in my body strained to learn more about Carl, who played his fraternal role with elegant resignation. No gesture escaped me. I saw repressed energy in the way he clenched his jaw and clasped his hands behind his back. I wondered what underlay his restlessness. Did he feel as trapped by the ponderous protocol as I did? Did he yearn, like me, for transformations to happen naturally rather than ceremonially?

A few provocative glances on my part quickly caught his eye, and our visual exchange soon escalated into attraction. All through the prenuptial dinner that followed I pretended to ignore the gleam in

Carl's eye that shone on me. It wasn't until the next day at the wedding reception in the rented mansion that I allowed myself to melt into Carl's arms. One dance led to another and another until it seemed perfectly right for us to float away from the festivities entirely. Without missing a beat we waltzed up the majestic staircase to the empty bedrooms where we twirled after the fleeting strains of music that filtered from room to room. As the bride and groom in the hall below force-fed wedding cake to each other for the photographer's benefit, I shed my absurd bridesmaid's dress of avocado tulle. "God! You look so much better without that!" Carl had gasped, scooping me up in his arms and laying me upon a bed piled high with coats—sable, mink, beaver, seal, fox, and raccoon. There amidst expired wildlife, Carl wrested a rubber from his wallet and impressed me with both his preparedness and his prowess.

It was years before our infatuation with that moment faded. Our daring breach of etiquette felt far more compelling than dating our way to romance, and we considered our shortcut to passion the blessing that bound us. For Carl it became the lifelong measure of performance—a goal difficult to match and impossible to maintain. For me it remained a supreme merging, so delirious that it bordered on hallucination. To keep that climax alive required frequent and conscious intervention in the form of fantasy. Over the years, despite my efforts to recapture its perfect timing and my unequaled surrender, it became harder and harder for me to duplicate. The slow build-up with its accompanying small talk that I had been so eager to spurn that fateful day, I missed in retrospect. A current of my own, a mere trickle of subthought at first, began to swell and gather momentum, carrying me toward some unknown destination. I found myself hoarding daytime hours alone like a miser, supplying for myself all the shades of subtlety that Carl could not. Through the alchemy of my imagination I would transform our life of haste and motion into one of golden serenity. Listening to my favorite records over and over again, I drifted through mindless household chores inventing intimate dialogues that seldom took place. To secure this healing time, I took up painting. Carl had always encouraged my "creative outlet," as he called it, for it kept me happily at home while the boys were growing up and whenever he was away on frequent business trips.

Now with both sons away at college and a social life that kept us spinning almost every night, I still relished the long, uninterrupted hours alone in my studio by day. Carl had no patience for introspection. When I wanted to talk about creative processes, he would manage to steer the conversation toward goals—the finished painting, my next show, the catalog, the opening. He loved the display, not the analysis. He lived for action not rumination. While the backwater I wallowed in offered me a sense of renewal and salvation, for Carl it was a swamp of feminine self-indulgence where he did not want to be.

I tried to explain that I welcomed him there, that in fact I loved him more in my inner experience when we were apart than I was able to in the midst of our so-called shared ones. He would always protest that that wasn't him but just my own projection: *He* existed in the here and now. We would argue futilely. I claimed it was my way of loving him. "Nonsense. It's your illusions you love, not me," he'd counter, and I would find myself derailed by his words, mystified that a conversation I wanted to have about the nature of loving should have become a declaration of nonlove. Carl began to hurl phrases like "nothing in common" or "growing apart," and I would sit there mute, watching in fascination as the words took on a direction of their own and carried us to this logical point of separation. The less I was able to respond to Carl verbally, the more passion I had for paint-ing. How unsportsmanlike I felt at times to have swum out of the rapids into a gentle pool for private reflection. When Carl would ask what was wrong, I would evade him with another question, "What do you mean?" and let the conversation falter. The bedrock of our connection had never had anything to do with words.

It was always in the dark, in our firm, familiar bed, that we had and have everything in common. In the ten thousand or more nights we have slept together, I have replayed the drama of our first passion. Each night when Carl turned out the light, my soul came forth, a nocturnal thing. Swaddled in silence and soothed by the dark, it waited for the mind to click off so that it could tend to its repairs: roll the eyes back in the hammock of their sockets, relax the neck muscles, start the healing dreams, and release the tongue for love. As sweet instinct began to rise, we'd drift toward drowsy contact—my mouth seeking his, his gentle hand cupping my breast, his warm thigh slip-ping between mine. We'd lie like this waiting to come to another kind of life—a life of dreamsleep or a life of sensation, moans, and sighs.

It was always at this fragile moment as we were emerging from our precoital drowse that Boris would begin to retch—usually right out-side our bedroom door on the white hall rug, or, for more special effect, he would steal into our bathroom where the acoustics were much louder before beginning the deep, rhythmic heaving. Even after I learned to suppress the impulse to leap out of bed to whisk Boris downstairs and outside, even when I no longer cared about the ever-widening bile stains that now stretched like a welcome mat outside our door, the moment of communion was shattered. Carl would turn away abruptly, pulling a pillow over his head, sealing me out, and I would lie awake a long time thinking about my separate solitude.

Deciding what Carl should take and what should stay was surprisingly easy and amicable. I would no more have laid claim to the word processor or the tapedeck or the VCR than he would have to my beloved Volvo or Electrolux. As we sorted through a stockpile of lesser appliances—steam irons, cameras, clock radios, toaster ovens, Cuisinart, popcorn popper, crockpot—it was clear we had come to the end of a long line of wishes that one by one had all been granted. The hunger for newer and better things is what kept marriages together, my friend Maude maintained. When she and her husband had satisfied their house needs, they moved on to ten-speed bikes and automobiles, progressing over the years up the rungs of the consumer ladder from Hondas and VWs to Porsches and Mercedeses. At that point their appetite for all objects suddenly ceased, and their marriage went to hell in a cyclone of property settlements and custody battles. As I surveyed our glut from great occasions past, I realized that Maude was right: We had run out of objects to yearn for. Sears and Consumer Distributor catalogs no longer aroused our passions, but I vowed that our settlement would be more civilized than theirs—no scenes, no scars.

I anticipated a new asceticism: blank walls devoid of Carl's chrome-framed print collection, blank calendars with no one else's events to prepare for, blank countertops, pristine shelves, and a bathroom basin devoid of soggy toothbrushes and paraphernalia. Perhaps after Boris died, I would sell the house and live in a whitewashed, skylit loft alone with my canvases and paints.

Working together now in the living room, I dusted off Carl's old yearbooks. They brought to mind the photo albums that lined two shelves in our upstairs study. Until the boys had gone off to college we had kept meticulous records, filling one leather-bound volume each year, duly recording all birthdays, holidays, and vacations. Carl, always too busy behind the camera to have been fully present, couldn't enjoy the occasions until the film had been processed and the pictures labeled and placed in their plastic sheaths. Of all our possessions only the albums refused to fall into "his" or "hers" categories. I tried to anticipate our negotiations. I could say, "Well, what about the photo albums? Shall we divide them by year—you take even and I keep odd?" But the fear that Carl might say, "No, you keep them. I don't want to be reminded of all that," silenced me.

"Oh, don't forget your can of Off!" I reminded him, remembering how I would gag in bed beside him on mosquito-infested summer nights. The can of Off on his bedside table had long been our joke. "What does it say about this marriage?" we'd tease complacently.

"Right! That's a necessity," he laughed looking over from the bookshelf he had cleared.

"You'll need it to ward off divorcees and widows. Have they started swarming yet?"

"Only one or two."

"Do I know them?"

"Aah, aah—that's off limits. Are you jealous?"

"I don't know. I'm mostly numb. I don't know what I feel. Do you?"

"Well, disappointed, I'd say. I thought you'd be angry or at least hurt, but here you are helping me, damn it. In fact, I've never seen you more cheerful, as though you're glad to see me go."

I looked up from the yearbooks and said nothing, no quick retort coming to my rescue. I watched Carl unhook the stereo system. His eyes avoided mine, but I could see the tension around his mouth. My habitual response would have been to utter a denial gently mocking the situation, but there was a kernel of truth in his words that made me pause.

"I guess I feel relief that the months of terrible stalemate have ended. I'm enjoying doing something with you even if it's this. In fact I suddenly realize there are so many things I'll miss."

"Like the can of Off?"

"Yes. And the way the house smells so freshly of your shaving cream and after-shave long after you've left for work. I'll miss the scent of shoe polish. I'll even miss your shoes."

"My shoes? You always hated tripping over them."

"I know—you never put them away, but now that seems endearing. Sometimes I'd find them days later peeking out from under the dust ruffle of the easy chair so that it resembled Aunt Elsie sitting there with her feet splayed. Other times they'd be sticking out from under the bed at such bizarre angles that it seemed someone was still in them doing unspeakable things."

"And will you think of me like that—'endearingly'?"

It occurred to me that our talk always orbited around him as though he were the sun and I some wayward planet threatening to break from my correct path in his solar system.

"Do I make you feel like 'an old shoe'? I wish you could take that as a compliment. I love old shoes. Mulling over all your things leads me back to you. Maybe amid all this slag I'll unearth my feelings again—about you and me."

"Look, let's not stand here ruminating. Let's do the bedroom."

"The best for last," I countered wondering if my remarks were too trivial to warrant discussion. I followed Carl upstairs. Boris, too exhausted to accompany us, heaved himself with a loud sigh of resignation against a duffle bag crammed with camp gear.

In our bedroom the late afternoon sun filtered in through the slats in the levelors and cast striped patterns across the rumpled pillows and quilt piled upon the unmade bed. Carl set to work in his closet, flinging shirt after shirt onto the bed for me to fold. I was glad to have something useful to do.

"Who will do this for you now, I wonder?"

"I don't know. No one does that better than you."

"Ha!" I did up the top button, then buttoned every other one, before turning it over and folding the shirt into vertical thirds. Then one final horizontal fold into half.

"I had a dream last night," I announced.

"You and your dreams."

"Want to hear it?"

"Sure. Was it about me?"

"About us. We were spending the night in a cabin perched high on the coastal cliffs overhanging the ocean, sort of like the ones at Big Sur where we used to rent. Remember?"

"Uh-huh."

"It was daybreak, and we were lying in bed listening to the surf crashing. It was unusually loud, and I suddenly realized that the sound wasn't coming from the breakers that should have been 500 feet below but from huge surging tidal waves that were sweeping in all around our cabin. I looked out the window and to my horror saw the churning water at eye level rushing past and filling coastal valleys, then receding and returning with a force even greater than before—huge swells that I knew would carry us, cabin and all, far out to sea. The water began to ooze in under the door. I watched it get deeper and begin to eddy and swirl under our bed, closer and closer to the chair where your clothes were heaped. We watched helplessly as the water licked all around the room like a curious tongue with its foamy edge, coming closer but never quite touching your clothes or your pair of shoes that lay beside the chair. Then very silently the water receded: Everything had remained safe and untouched."

Carl had stopped what he was doing and stood framed in the closet doorway, one hand pensively rubbing his chin.

"Did you like that ending?" he mused.

"I loved it."

"Well, too bad," he said as he turned his back and continued stuffing his suits into a garment bag. "I've come to claim what is *mine*," he growled. "You'll have to live with reality."

"But the dream helped. I'm sure it was a survival dream. Here are your shirts."

"Thanks. Put them here."

"I wonder if I'll dream after you've gone?"

"What do you mean? You've never had a shortage before. In fact you seem to dream more whenever I'm on a trip."

"But that's different. I dream because you're coming back. It's routine and comfort that make me dream."

I began to strip the bed.

"Well, think of all the new material you'll have. You can go to bed at 9:30 just the way you always want to."

"But don't you see? Sleeping won't be the same. I'll really miss that."

"Of course you'll sleep."

"But not those deep, comatose dreamsleeps I have with you. I can't imagine ever sleeping with anyone else."

"Whoa! Is this a pledge of eternal fidelity?"

"No, it's a fact. I don't mean sex. I mean sleep. It would take years to feel that kind of comfort with someone new."

I had taken the down comforter from its casing and had set it on the rocker. I had pulled the pillows free of their cases and had tossed them aside. Now I carefully peeled off the fitted bottom sheet and the tattered mattress pad. A vast denuded plain stretched before me. It had taken all of twenty-six years to conquer and tame its satin expanse. Night after night our weary, turning bodies had carved gentle valleys and hillocks in the mattress's sediment.

"Oh, dear, just look at all those nice stains!"

Carl had stopped emptying his dresser drawers and stood beside me. My eyes filled with stinging tears. In them swam the shimmering reminders of shared dramas: the spot where Carl had been sick the very first night we had slept on our gigantic king, the place where Jeff had fallen and cut his head, the smear where my water had broken more than eighteen years ago. The salt water of my memories and dreams welled up and broke loose, washing away in an instant the fragile dam of fantasy and denial that I had so painstakingly built. Great squalls of tears splashed down my cheeks and nose. Carl handed me a crumpled pillow case to stem the flood, and I became aware of his hand gently patting my back.

"Don't cry. Please don't cry," he pleaded. "You keep the bed. It's all yours. And the eiderdown, too. Whatever you want. Just don't cry now."

He let me bury my head in the folds of his freshly laundered collar. My tears dissolved the starch—another threatened familiarity that sent me into fresh paroxysms of weeping. Tears flowed faster than either his shirt or the pillowcase could absorb them.

"Oh shit. Why now? Why now?" Carl kept repeating as he put his arms around me. My sobs carried me over the brink, and I completely succumbed to the deluge. It rushed to the very roots of my being. Old resentments, hurts, and angers were tossed aside like so much debris, in a flashflood, and bone-dry passion swelled to realize its thirst.

We lingered in a cautious embrace at the foot of the bed—two cactuses, spiney and enduring, each harboring secret flowers that sometimes burst into rare and dazzling bloom. Carl's breath whistled past my ear, and the hand that had been patting my back now gripped my waist. His other hand clutched my hair and between spasmodic gasps for air I became aware that the shuddering was not mine alone.

"Oh, for God's sake, stop crying," he suddenly blurted out. "Keep your memories. Keep the fucking bed and put it in your fantasy world. Where was all this sentiment before?"

His words harpooned me. I backed away and tried to push him from me, but Carl gripped my shoulders.

"Look at me!" he demanded. "Where have you been? Why won't you answer me? You just disappear. Don't do this to me!"

The sight of Carl's contorted face made me freeze. As the truth in his words seeped through to me, I heard myself saying, "Oh God, you're right!"

"Don't appease me. Don't agree. Why won't you fight?"

"Because I'd have to fight on your terms, and you'd walk out feeling justified. I want the satisfaction of knowing that at least I behaved well. I refuse to fight—especially at a time like this."

Carl's hands flew from my shoulders and gestured wildly.

"What do you mean 'at a time like this'? What better time?"

"I refuse to have that kind of scene!" I declared haughtily. My words burst from the pursed lips of none other than the Queen

Mother, her bosom heaving in indignation, her feathered hat askew. Quite involuntarily I began to laugh. Carl struggled to keep his composure. The magnitude of the situation required something more eloquent, but the more he struggled to find the words, the harder my laughter came. I collapsed on the bed. A smile escaped his lips, tightened into a smirk, and then Carl was beside me exploding with full-throttle belly laughter.

"Well, that's just great. You get me all worked up, and now I'm just supposed to zip my bags and tilt my hat and say, 'Thanks a lot, ma'am, it's been real nice. Guess I'd better run along now . . .'"

I could not catch my breath to answer.

"What kind of 'scene' does Her Highness have in mind?" Carl went on, mimicking me. His performance sent me into fresh gales of hilarity, and it was several moments before I could gasp, "Something memorable . . . something healing."

I opened my arms to him, and we hugged long enough for our laughter to subside. Then Carl began to kiss me with a delicious vengeance, and I returned each one—an eye for an eye, a tooth for a tooth, a kiss for a kiss. Every hair, alert as vestigial antennae, struggled to decipher the surge of emotions. For a moment there seemed to be no clear distinctions left at all: right/wrong, always/never, then/now, his/mine—all were jumbled. The mental chaos felt like youth, and I was once again groping alone in the dark guided only by terror and desire. Simultaneously we stopped kissing and regarded each other warily. As dusk closed in around us, our shadowed forms loomed larger than reality. The protective shield of familiarity had been stripped away, and we felt strange and new to each other again. I knew no sight or sound would distract us from this ultimate duel.

Very deliberately we each undressed, all the while watching the other. Button by button we removed our shirts, slid off our wristwatches, undid our belt buckles and waist buttons, and in unison stepped out of our pants—mirror images of one another. We kicked off our shoes and let them land wherever they wanted. Our white underwear seemed to glow in the dim light. As I parted with this last vestige of our civilized life together, a shiver of fear shot up my spine.

Naked at last and unrestricted by sheets and blankets and old patterns, we began to stalk and wrestle each other upon the stark bed. Our moves and countermoves had a silent grace and balance, one moment yielding and compliant, the next bold and aggressive. Our caresses tread a fine line between pleasure and pain. With a strength and agility that seemed to know no bounds, we found ourselves writing new pages for the Kama Sutra. First one would dominate, then the other. With kisses alone I reduced Carl to helpless moans. Then, as though rallying for his life, he struggled to his knees and took me from behind, until I dissolved in excruciating ecstasy. Unwilling for our contest to end just yet, Carl turned me over and revived me with tongue-bursts of pleasure. Then lifting me to my feet as he got to his, we entered the final round, face to face—a contest of equals: strength matched by perseverance and bulk tempered by agility. I gripped his torso with my legs, and he held me aloft for a heroic finale that blunted my mind to the peril of falling off the bed. When that thought finally occurred to me, the duel was over. It had ended in a draw. We sank to the mattress in a heap.

"I hadn't thought it would be like this, did you?" I whispered.

"No, never," moaned Carl, his head nuzzling my breast, our legs entwined. As Carl lapsed into sleep, I felt my mind already beginning to tread water. It had come through the rapids alive, and its current, freed at last from torpid backwater, was seeking a new course. I opened my eyes and saw the closet, black as a mouth, gaping at its emptiness. Downstairs Boris whined and scratched at the front door wanting to be let out.

The Body Has Its Reasons
About Which Reason Knows Nothing
(Grâce à Blaise Pascal)

I knew how it ended. Mary, Queen of Scots (Vanessa Redgrave), would get the ax and Elizabeth, Queen of England (Glenda Jackson), would wail in protest that it was she, once again, who had to do all the dirty work and why, why, why, had Mary continued to act provocatively when she, Elizabeth, had behaved with such restraint toward her even in the face of Mary's repeated duplicities?

I leaned back against the armchair I was using as a backrest, pulled up the poofy comforter to my shoulders, asked if he were comfortable on my makeshift couch of cushions on the living room floor, and immediately turned my eyes back to the TV screen that gave the room its only illumination. The question stirred him to put his arm across my chest, nuzzle his head against my ear, and mumble something provocative into my hair. I answered with some comment about Vanessa Redgrave: "She's really made to play these historical dramas, don't you think? Glenda Jackson can play any number of characters, but Vanes. . . ."

He turned my face to his and pecked at my mouth and cheeks. I could feel the irritation settling into my jaw and an acrid odor entering my nostrils without permission.

"Don't you feel at all sexy?" he said in a plaintive voice.

"No," I answered.

"Not even a little?" he protested, moving his hand to my breast.

"No," I sighed.

I was squirming. I stared at Vanessa's face as the outlawed Protestant lords, accompanied by Mary's weak and jealous husband, broke into her "apartment," as they called it, to kill Rizzio—her favorite, her confidant, and purportedly her lover. (I hoped the stiffness of my body would dissuade him from any further exploration of me.) Rizzio was not taking it well . . . he was whimpering at Mary to save him. Was that what he had really been like, I wondered? Couldn't (shouldn't) her lover have taken it with less of the insipid cowardice we had seen in Mary's husband?

"Tell me about it. In the ten years we've been together, you've always been such a sexy woman. What's going on? What are you feeling right now?"

Damn. He was going to pursue it. I suppressed the part of me that admired him for not backing off. Unlike other men I had known, he would not simply move away from me on some pretext of not liking TV anyway. He stayed and asked the uncomfortable questions. On the other hand, I was once again annoyed at his poor sense of timing, his disinterest in good television drama, his easy assumption that a hand on the breast demanded an RSVP—and, yes, the damnable questions that took the place of action. "Just do it right or don't do it," I sometimes wanted to say but never did.

Still staring blankly at the screen watching Vanessa's Mary go into mock labor so that she could escape the bloody scene her husband had placed her in, I observed my mind darting back and forth frantically looking for its own out. What could I tell him? That I hadn't been feeling sexy for quite awhile? That it upset me and I didn't want to think about it? That my body felt end-of-the-day hot and sticky? That I still felt sickly from the flu I had just gone through? That there was an odor around his face that I couldn't define but that turned me off? That I had an incipient headache I hadn't wanted to acknowledge even to myself? I said nothing.

Mary was with her lady servant in a small chamber. It was clear now that she had *not* gone into labor but was using it to buy time—to come up with a plan now to save her own life. Her husband, suddenly distracted from his vengeance of moments before by the unexpected onset of her labor, stood outside like the good husband, ready to pace, perhaps to swagger as new, proud parent, and, more important, to reclaim Mary as his. She peered at him from the door, which she had opened a crack. Her only hope, she confided to her maid, was to fall upon him and persuade him that his own life was endangered by the very lords he had set upon Rizzio (knowing that it was she who had been his target more than poor Rizzio). Sending her serving lady for horses, she rushed out and threw herself at his feet, her skirts crumpling on the cold stone floor, and confessed her ruse: James the Sixth of Scotland was still living in her womb and not yet ready to be born. Lord Darnley was easily persuaded that fleeing with her to save both their lives was a sound decision.

My husband was not to be so easily put off. His hand fondled my breast again. It felt delicious, I was able to admit to myself, but not so delicious that my spider webs of resistance were in any danger of billowing away. It gave me a certain satisfaction that I could admit to an isolated sensation of lust and not permit it to "carry me away" if the situation wasn't to my liking. For one thing, I knew I had grown up some when I didn't feel compelled to act on every feeling and sensation. "Wild abandon" was much more exciting when I *chose* to be wild rather than when I propelled myself into being abandoned.

But sometimes he would say: "Now, doesn't that feel good? Come on, admit it." But I could not, knowing that the admission would say to him: "Yes, it's wonderful . . . more, more, more," when it was slightly short of being wonderful and I had no energy to transform it to more. I also resented that he would ask. If it were as stimulating to me as he wanted it to be, his answer would be in the response of my body, not in my carefully chosen silence.

In our lovemaking, I had felt for a long time that it was I who had to conjure up the siren, the temptress, the wild one in myself—a persona to take him by surprise and startle him into doing something different with these bodies he thought we had fully explored. At the moment, all I was willing to acknowledge was that Mary and Elizabeth were more compelling than Peter and I, and that if I responded at all to Peter's hand on my breast, we would lapse into over-too-soon rote sex, and I would go to bed resentful of having missed the conclusion to *Mary, Queen of Scots*. That I had seen it before did not seem to be an issue.

As Mary, Lord Darnley, and their entourage fled, my mind struggled with a tangle of thoughts and emotions. Why couldn't it be simple? Poor man . . . he was turned on; he saw no reason why Mary, Queen of Scots, should command my attention over his eager, warm, exploring hand; I had bundled us up on the floor like young lovers; and we hadn't had sex in days. So what was my problem? Taking his point of view shifted my feelings from aggravation and confusion to sadness and confusion.

It seemed that hardly any time had gone by when James the Sixth found himself ready to enter sixteenth-century Scotland after all. If Vanessa's Mary had looked only five or six months pregnant, the lusty offscreen cry of the new king of Scotland (and later of England) could be attributed to the fact that tall women like Vanessa and I did not show their pregnancies as easily as women of lesser height if not stature. For the moment, all seemed well. Mary, with her babe cradled in the arms of his nursemaid, rode majestically through the crowds. While Elizabeth "troubled deaf heaven" with her cries of envy for an heir to the throne of England (a heavenly plea we somehow didn't believe), Scotland was clearly relieved to have been delivered of a boychild who would one day rule. For while Mary's tempestuous life doubtless added spice to the gossiping of the sixteenth-century's peasant class, a woman, after all, is ruled by her hormones and not to be trusted. Everyone knows that.

"The fact is," I finally offered into the waiting silence, "I feel as if my hormones have gone on strike. Worse yet, I have a foreboding that they may never jangle through my bloodstream again. I am having trouble facing it, Peter: My days of 'turning on' are over. I think I am what is commonly referred to as 'menopausal.'"

Peter laughed loudly. "You, menopausal! Ha! That may be true in terms of chronology, but menopause is never going to get *you* down. Trust me," he chortled like some department store Santa Claus.

Again, I couldn't help feel a flush of relief that he had such boundless good cheer about my aging process, and that it apparently had no effect whatsoever on his desire for me. But mixed in with that not insignificant satisfaction was the indisputable fact that I preferred to watch a celluloid representation of Mary, Queen of Scots, struggling with other issues in times long past to having right-now sex with my husband. Next to that recognition was my incredulity at Peter's way of dealing with my painful revelations. It happened every time, but I was never ready for it. I would finally express (or he would finally wrench from me) some miserable, curled-up-in-a-ball plea for empathy and soothing, and he would either find it hilarious, or jab at it as he would a murky pool of black water to see how deep it went, or pick it up and throw it against the wall to see whether it would bounce. My first reaction was usually to be stunned and hurt, maybe with a little how-dare-he? anger thrown in. But if by some miracle I managed to stay afloat and grab hold of the life preserver he held teasingly in front of me, he would grip my hand in his with the strength of all the lords of land and sea and pull me to shore. He would then listen silently to my melodramatic protestations, all the time waiting for the moment that invariably enveloped us when I was ready to laugh with him at the nonsense of it all.

Elizabeth stood stiffly to announce to England the birth of James the Sixth of Scotland and to deplore the despicable murder of his father, Lord Darnley. In the next scene (or had Peter distracted me again?) Mary fell into the arms of Lord Bosworth, to whom she had quickly turned at the death of her cowardly husband, and we watched as they groped for each other's mouths and murmured passionate vows into tear-stained faces. Peter took firm hold of my face and forced his mouth on mine, kissing me hard and long while his hand roamed my breast and pulled roughly at my clothes. The shift in his demeanor was dramatic. No longer was he pleading and nibbling tentatively at whatever bit of flesh he found exposed and available, he demanded my presence. He wanted me. Some force roared up in my body and kissed him back with an urgency that came from another self, another place, another time.

I watched that self in my mind's eye as she struggled, with him, to divest herself of clothes—yanking and tugging, heedless of delicate buttons and sheer fabric, heedless of awkward postures and flailing limbs, heedless of headache and sticky flesh. As the thundering sound of horses' hooves were speeding Mary and Bosworth to safety, we had overcome the last of the buttons and hooks and straps. I pressed the milk-white flesh of my small, sensitive breasts hard upon him, feeling my nipples ensnare themselves in the soft and wiry hairs of his chest. I felt willingly bruised by him—by his hands, by his mouth, by his compelling grip. I was riding with a sense of desperate need that only the tiniest flicker of my thinking self scorned as born of dime-store novels or the early Hollywood movies on which I had been raised. After all, I quickly assuaged it, it *was* good old Peter who was ravishing me and not some brutal intruder. With that, the wants of my body claimed unequivocal surrender from the shoulds of my mind.

When it was over, we didn't say a word. Peter fell asleep instantly, and I reached over to turn off the TV set. Again pulling the comforter around my shoulders, I lay next to him on the floor, which suddenly reminded me of its hardness, and listened to the sound of his stolidly contented breathing. I soon found myself drifting back into that familiar and predictable century inhabited by the long-time married. How good it was to know that the old body still worked, I thought, and then fell into my own deep, smiling sleep.

Nightingale

She left him sleeping on the daybed, the white sheet luminous against his bronze skin, his breathing soundless, light and regular. A brief search disclosed a small bathroom along the corridor from the salon, and there, amid thick, fluffy towels and Limoges pots of expensive face cream, she erased the marks of yesterday's stale makeup and showered the scent of his body from her skin. Now, her face cleansed to a camellia pallor, she dressed again in her black chiffon blouse and skirt, swept her damp hair behind her ears, and, picking up her little embroidered evening purse, let herself quietly out the front door. As she sauntered down the shallow, stone steps, the early morning sun winked at her high-heeled gold sandals, directing shards of light into the thyme-grown crevices and scattering the spare, brown lizards already basking in the promise of the day's heat. She walked easily down the curving driveway, breathing in the sharp, familiar scent of the Provençal dust and reflecting idly that the smell had not changed since she was a child in the region, playing with her dolls in the court-yard of her grandfather's villa.

The prospect of returning to her hotel, of taking her breakfast of coffee and warm, ripe fruit on the balcony adorned with vines, pleased her. She wanted to be sure that she dressed for her mood today: a sundress, a gold bangle, a wide, white hat; she loved the way she felt. She felt light and clear, as though a long, debilitating illness had been miraculously cured. She wanted to spend the day sifting the events of the previous night, to be still and quiet and solitary in the dappled shade, among familiar objects, safe from interruption.

As she walked down the driveway toward her car, she took in the landscape which surrounded Daniel's house. Seen now in the early daylight the colors—rose and lavender and moss—were all muted, as though layered with dust. Sunlight spilled like sparkling wine over the terraced olive groves on the hillside and on the cluttered rooftops of the dazed, hung over, seaside town.

She turned to look at the house, at its exuberant structure and clear, empty windows, the line of cypresses marching, somber and purposeful, downhill on one side. She thought about the accumulation of events that had led her here, having embarked for France at a time in her life when her need for light on her inner landscape was at its most intense. She knew that she needed time to reexamine both the gentle pastels of her married life and the bruise colors of her girlhood, so she had gone first to Paris and stayed with her sister. Together they sauntered the boulevards and quartiers of the city, visiting friends in the Hotel de Ville neighborhood (where she eyed the garrulous, cheerful, battered prostitutes with a look of serene complicity). Then she had driven to Montpellier to visit her expatriate son—a passionate time, concentrated and ambivalent, but she had done well, keeping her eyes and ears open and her mouth shut. Ten days ago, chic, svelte, and very much concerned for her white skin in the brass glare of the southern sun, she arrived in Ste. Maxime.

She quite literally ran into Daniel, after not having seen him for thirty years, since they were lovers in London. It was at a gallery opening for a suddenly productive friend—a mutual friend, as it turned out, for as she crossed the threshold into the smoke-filled room, she heard: "Elizabeth." And there he was.

"Daniel?" A memory of times past streaked across her mind. Certain that she had seen him on a crowded street in New York or Rome or San Francisco, she had raced after him, parcels flying, umbrella a lethal menace, only to realize her mistake.

Now he stood before her, simian, swarthy, humorous, slightly acerbic, as if he had never left: tie loosened at his throat, collar button undone, cuffs as white as aspirin folded back in dazzling wings upon the black hair of his forearms.

"You haven't changed at all—how is it that you haven't changed?"

It was as if time had retreated to the shade and waited, patient and smiling, for her to travel here. As she stood before him, feeling her skin expand and shrink, feeling the cool pallor of her face subdue the unequivocal sweeping heat that bellowed up from her buried life, it seemed to her that if she half-closed her eyes or looked up suddenly, the room would dissolve. She would enter a past world where days dawned and died according to his presence in them. She moved toward him, her movement as viscous as spilled syrup.

"Oh, my sweet. It's wonderful to see you again. You haven't changed." His voice snapped shut the chasm of the years like a beaded, jet purse. "I've changed at lot . . . How are you, my sweet? How is your life?"

They began to recite their capsuled chronologies, their conversation giddy and green, leaping over each other's sentences like grasshoppers, watching each other's body, each other's face and the shadows that chased across them. "Do you remember. . . ?" And once he said, "When we were together in London. . . ," and she felt her heart crack like an egg, like a hundred-year-old egg. She knew him to be a respected director of films. He spoke lengthily of his work, laconically of his personal life. Referring to his wife's death, he caught sight of Elizabeth's face, soft with sadness for his loss, and changed the subject abruptly.

"Come and see my house," he said. "I'd like to spend some time with you. Come and see me—tomorrow. I'm busy with the festival, but there is someone I'd like you to meet. Come tomorrow, late evening. I'll be back around eleven. Twelve. I have so much to tell you." And as he talked, she studied him as though she were designing him, working him stitch by stitch upon a taut, unfinished circle of cloth. She put her hand against his cheek.

"What luck," she murmured. She smiled, watching him bend to kiss her withdrawing fingers. Time had remembered them. A tryst had been arranged.

"I'll be there," she had said.

In the daylight everything looks so ordinary, thought Elizabeth. Perhaps "ordinary" was not the right word, because her feelings about this area had been formed before she could speak and were rooted in the dark soil of her infancy. Safe, then. She looked at the low wall she had lain on last night, waiting for him to return from town, and remembered her feeling of apprehension as the retained warmth of the sun-baked stone eased along her spine. She remembered last night: a transfigured night, restless and driven, dry as a parched mouth. The leaves of the olive trees flew in the wind like tiny, silver sails and the languid sea caressed the blond beaches and licked with equal murmurous insistence the hulls of the insomniac vessels fidgeting in its arms: the dories and the impudent sloops in the harbor, the haughty, high-necked yachts restively at anchor off the shore.

She had not felt safe, last night, as she waited for him in the crepuscular garden among the cypress trees, waited for the tryst. She had come out here to escape a vague feeling of uneasiness. The flight of shallow steps she had climbed were flooded with star jasmine. The night scent of the flowers hung on the air like torn banners as the door swung open and she met the calm, inquiring gaze of the housekeeper. Daniel had said someone would be there to let her in, so though she expected a housekeeper, she was not prepared for this vision of chic authority. Elizabeth took in the silver jewelry, the purple dress lightly agitated by the night's warm breath, the poise of the woman who stood before her. Surely, she thought, this could not be the housekeeper. This must be a relative, a retired or distressed movie actress, a friend in need of the solace and protection of a home, a job, a niche, but too proud to accept, simply, shelter.

Services returned for services rendered? *Why am I concerned about this?* she thought, and knew that it had something to do with the fluid elegance of this woman: the small, tanned hands with nails lacquered in pearl, the iron-colored hair pulled off the face like a dancer's; the smooth, lined skin bronzed by many leisurely hours at the beach and beautifully touched with coral at the lips and cheeks. Elizabeth, the expectant guest, stood on the step outside the entrance to Daniel's villa, her hand still raised from pulling the bell. She knew that her arrival had been watched from a dark window as she walked from her car.

"I think I'm a little early," she said, "but Monsieur is expecting me—Elizabeth Hurst."

"Monsieur 'as not yet come 'ome from the festival, Madame." The voice deep and rich, a cello's voice, must surely in the past have pealed from the stage of La Scala or Covent Garden. "'E told me to expect you. I am Marie-Hélène. *Entrez, je vous en prie.* 'E will not be long." And she turned and led the way across the cool tile of the entrance hall.

Elizabeth saw that she was lame. Her gait dipped gracefully to one side as she moved ahead, and it was plain that her left foot was damaged, misshapen and useless in its sheer black stocking and expensive, reptile shoe. The leg was many inches shorter than the right, which took her weight and propelled her forward. It was a dancer's foot, well muscled and with prominent veins, a high, pointed instep and a slender, sharp-boned ankle. She moved rapidly through a low arch into the salon and, with a faint smile and inclination of her head, withdrew.

The room was made of glass. Great windows stretched across two walls. She felt that she was at the center of a prism—there was glass everywhere: coffee tables laden with crystal, decanters, ashtrays, candlesticks. Looking up, she caught sight of her own worried face in a huge mirror over the fireplace. On a low table, beside a chair covered in satin brocade, was a bowl of crystalline fruit. Her nervous excitement became vertiginous; her ears sang.

"I can't move," she said to herself, half aloud. "I'm afraid to move." She found she was standing absolutely still, frozen on the white carpet in the center of the room. The air seemed full of tiny, tinkling voices, icicle voices that warned of shipwreck and evil stars.

She took a deep breath and moved deliberately to a chair. Had Daniel always surrounded himself with the potential for breakage? She tried to remember details about his taste, but all that came to mind, apart from the shirt-sleeves, white as Jordan almonds, was a slim, shagreen cigarette case she had once given him for his birthday. The memory made her smile, endearing her anew to the passionate girl who had squandered a month's salary upon her need to give him something sublime, ubiquitous, something of herself.

She sat down, carefully holding her body away from the transparent pyramid at her elbow, letting her gaze travel slowly around the room. A displacement of air behind her made her turn her head. A tiny, clicking sound, on the tiles in the entrance hall, announced the arrival of a little, white dog weaving a sightless path toward her. She saw at once that it was blind, its opaque eyes like brown bowls of milk fixed on some radiant inner vision. She let her hand fall toward its muzzle, murmuring reassurance, permitting the cold nose to ascertain her benevolence. She stroked the velvety old ears, teasing the curly hair into corkscrews and thought: *A blind dog in a glass room.* . . . and she bent over, touched by its undemanding trust.

As she straightened, she saw on the table something that she had not noticed earlier. It was a photograph in a double frame. She leaned forward, frowning intently at the two images: Daniel's so dark, so intense, the young man's so fair, so insouciant and Nordic—wet, blond hair falling across his brow; face alive with laughter; and arms crossed on his bare, muscled chest; wonderful teeth—an image of radiance, of power and of light. A beautiful child. She leaned closer, her heart filling, thinking of her own son and his lean, gallic face, dark, like Daniel's, although Daniel was not his father. Had the tragic marriage been to a long-limbed Viking beauty, now gone to her long home? She felt a surge of sadness and used it as her impetus to rise and leave the room.

"*Je vais me promener un peu au jardin,*" she explained to Marie-Hélène, who materialized gracefully at her side as she reached the front door. "I will wait for Monsieur outside." And she ran down the fragrant stone steps into the shadows of the cypress trees.

Even feeling unsafe, thought Elizabeth, looking down at the stones in a finger of early sunlight, had not prevented her anticipation of their coming embrace. Lying on the low wall in the moonlight of Daniel's house, she had begun to perceive the slow pulsing of desire low in her belly. She remembered looking up at the sky and feeling its weight on her like a velvet covering—like his smooth, strong body covering hers of old—and then sighing, purring in response to her imagination. She had slowly raised one arm toward the sky. The black silk of her sleeve fell to her armpit. It had the same texture and temperature as her skin, the same perfume. She had moved her hand in circles against the sky, feeling the rhapsodic air against her palm as though it were his cheek, through her fingers as though it were his hair. Filling her eyes with the sky, she began to sing, the song fluttering like a moth from the shadows of past time:

Il y a longtemps que je t'aime
Jamais je ne t'oublierai . . .

She stopped singing and sat up, hearing the unmistakable whine of a car climbing the country road. Rounding the bend, the brilliant arc of the headlights bent briefly on the garden and the house. The low, white car pulled through the gates, the gravel grating and scattering under the decelerating tires. The beam of light flashed eerily around the curve in the driveway lighting the steps, and the car growled to a halt in front of the house.

She heard voices, laughter; saw the front door open and light from the house pour down the steps, pooling its radiance with the headlights' glare. Daniel's voice called out a name: "Marie-Hélène!" and the housekeeper's responded, deep and tremulous like an owl's. Car doors slammed. Then, without warning, the light from the front door was partially blacked out and Daniel stood in the doorway, his arms stretched out, cruciform, his palms pressed against the frame. His face was lifted to the sky, showing the sharp, foreshortened triangle of his jaw. He was clearly in conflict.

Hardly breathing, wearing the night like a domino clasped to her throat, Elizabeth emerged from the shadows and stood at the foot of the steps. There they were, she and Daniel, facing each other on the night of their tryst. Then a disturbance behind him jerked his head to the side, and she saw the blond boy from the photograph standing in the entrance hall. He had his arm around Marie-Hélène, who was radiant in his embrace; she was standing on tiptoe to kiss him, a pearl-tipped hand against his cheek, her deep voice pealing with laughter.

"*Mais non, Bruno!*" she was crying. "You must be mad!"

He pulled her close to him, she rocked precariously, and their laughter reached a higher pitch of hilarity. Daniel looked at them and quickly back at Elizabeth. He flung out a hand toward her, and they all turned and looked down at her standing at the foot of the steps, wan and silent in her silken black clothes. Then Bruno deliberately took Daniel by the shoulders, turned him to the light, and kissed him on the mouth. The embrace was long and passionate, the two bodies merged in patterns of light and dark. Elizabeth watched, mute as a shadow.

Later, after a conversation with Daniel on the steps, they joined the others. Bruno's presence filled the glass room as he talked about his meeting and his life with Daniel. Elizabeth watched his lithe, hard body, the gold-white hairs on his legs and arms, the planes of his sunburned, Nordic face; occasionally he met her gaze and crinkled his eyes in a somnolent, easy smile. Marie-Hélène left briefly and returned with food on a serving cart. They sat together on the rug, the four of them, and ate cold chicken, dolmas, cheese and grapes; Marie-Hélène fed them, slicing bread and spearing olives, passing pungent red salt and tightly-curled anchovies. Then Bruno fell asleep on the daybed, his arms flung over his head. Daniel sat in an old familiar pose, his legs stretched out and crossed at the ankle, his black tie undone and hanging loose. Close to Elizabeth's leg, the little blind dog curled up warm and throbbing, wheezing softly in his sleep. The clock on the mantle chimed three.

Marie-Hélène stood up and said: "*Voyons*, Elizabeth, stay with us tonight. It's much too late to return to town." And Elizabeth found that she did not want to leave. Something in the room held her motionless again; she felt unfinished. She looked at Daniel's face with its inward-seeing eyes like shuttered windows and said: "Well, Daniel?"

He roused himself at once, solicitous for her well-being.

"My sweet, of course you must stay. I'm exhausted too. We can all meet for breakfast. Oh yes, do stay with us tonight."

He stood up, reaching out his hands and pulling her to her feet. They stood facing each other, old lovers with no one to blame, and embraced silently, wearily, leaning on each other in mutual support.

"Good night, Daniel," said Elizabeth.

"I'm so glad you came," he said. "Good night, my sweet."

She watched him walk through the arch and disappear down the passage. She heard his voice and Marie-Hélène's response from somewhere deep in the house. She felt empty and light. Walking to the open window, she leaned against the sill, listening to the soughing of the odorous, dark wind, the click and whirr of the crickets, the bittersweet sounds of the southern night. Then she turned back into the room and walked over to the daybed where Bruno lay asleep. She leaned over him and smoothed a strand of hair off his brow. She let her hand linger on his face, drawing the backs of her fingers down his cheek. Stubble rasped her skin, hindering the smooth passage of her flesh on his. His lips were slightly parted. With an insect touch she traced the curve of his mouth. His eyelashes rested on his cheekbones like threads, his eyelids were as smooth and heavy as satin. He reminded Elizabeth of the skeins of burnished silk and mohair in her work basket at home: a tangle of textures, relaxed, physical, tactile, a reward for the hands and for the eyes. The daybed held him so tenderly, so lovingly, it seemed, permitting the weight of his long, loose limbs to sink down into its cushions with such sweetness. His white tennis shorts were almost fluorescent against his tanned thighs and very brief. In the curve of the cuffs Elizabeth could see the shadowed swelling of his genitals and the mossy tracing of his pubic hair. Elizabeth felt her heart begin to race and began to be aware of the heat in her hands. She wanted to undress him, to reveal all his beautiful body, to be naked, herself, with him. She wanted him to swim to consciousness in the circle of her arms, to hold him with her legs and caress him with her secret skin. She leaned further over him and gently ran her tongue along the bridge of his nose, down his cheek and around his jaw. He stirred and smiled, and still sleeping, found her mouth with his. They held together and then Elizabeth gently disengaged her lips and straightened up to remove her blouse.

"*Tiens, ma cocotte.*" Marie-Hélène stood beside her holding an armful of satin. "I 'ave brought you a *robe de chambre. Laisse-moi faire.*" And she gently turned Elizabeth around, unbuttoning the black chiffon overblouse and easing the soft stuff apart, over Elizabeth's shoulders, revealing the black lace brassiere that supported her breasts with a front, center clasp. Marie-Hélène's hands competently undid the hook, and Elizabeth felt their warm corrugation linger on her skin as Marie-Hélène caressingly drew off the undergarment. Then she slid Elizabeth's skirt down over her hips, taking with it the half-slip and matching panties, her hands smoothing their way down Elizabeth's thighs and knees and calves to her ankles. Elizabeth stepped out of her clothes, one hand resting lightly on Marie-Hélène's shining gray crown, and eased off her shoes. Marie-Hélène stood up again and placed the peignoir around Elizabeth's shoulders. "*Amusez-vous bien,*" she said. "*Bonne nuit.*"

She sped silently away, dipping deeply into her useless hip, a vision of broken grace. Elizabeth slipped her arms into the glossy folds of the robe, submitting with a shudder of delight to the lubricous sensation of the satin on her back. The robe hung open in front. She turned toward the open window, and a cool gust of air from the garden rippled over her throat, her breasts, and her belly, billowing the supple material away from her legs. Inexplicably, she was no longer afraid of the room, no longer feared calamity in its splintered light. Now, the multifaceted prism of the room beckoned to her, reflected her, offered her a thousand refracted images. She felt delighted, erotic, and strong; she whirled around, floating the voluptuous weight of the robe away from her body, reveling in her feeling of release, of stability. She swept the peignoir from her shoulders and watched it cascade to the floor, where it lay as relaxed and refulgent as the blond body on the divan.

Then, naked and supple as a seal, she sank down beside him and stretched her length along his, pulling him into her arms and murmuring his name, nudging him to wakefulness with her tongue and her thighs, pulling at his clothes until he awoke and helped her. He was bold and tender, audacious and sweet. His hands and mouth moved about her body like honey and quicksilver, seeking her out and delivering her to herself. She rolled beneath him and reared above him, fluid and powerful. Sometimes she lifted him in her arms, unaware of his weight, just wanting to see his marvelous, muscular torso outlined against the sky. She could not discern which of her senses he delighted most. Gluttonous, avid in her appetite for him, she wanted to stuff her senses to bursting, to surfeit herself on him.

When, sated at last, they came to rest, Bruno fell asleep at once, his mouth on her breast moist and slack, his phosphorescent hair lank and slightly oily from their exertions. Elizabeth lay wakeful for a time, her cheek leaning on the top of his head, both arms locked around him. She watched the dawn steal across the sky and listened to the first tentative notes of the birds. She felt complete, free of dread, and unfamiliar to herself. Then she, too, fell asleep. When she awoke a few hours later, someone had crept into the glass room and had gently tucked a cotton blanket around them.

Elizabeth roused herself from her reverie in the sun, aware that her mind was flashing like a hummingbird around the events of the night, veering away from some, hovering thirstily over others, dipping deep into the drenched and swollen membrane of the most recent. She had left him sleeping there and would now return to the quiet side street in the town where her hotel stood regally adorned with vines and balconies.

Last night, as she waited febrile and spellbound in the garden for her tryst with Daniel, it had seemed that nothing short of an act of God could counter the tension emanating from the house. Energy had crackled on the scented night air like sparks on a live wire. But perhaps, mused Elizabeth, tucking a fluttering strand of hair behind her ear, that's the way God acts.

Suddenly she wanted to walk in the dry grass and the Midi dust barefoot. She bent and removed her gold sandals, then continued down the driveway to her car. She slid into the driver's seat, took her ignition keys from her evening bag and her sunglasses from the glovebox. Glancing into the rear-view mirror, she saw that without makeup the diary lines of her face recited her life story relentlessly to the dancing morning light. She noticed that she did not care and that this marked a first in her fifty-three years. Engaging the clutch, she shifted easily into first gear and, turning the car, retraced the road she had taken last night from town. As she drove she sang to her mirrored reflection:

Il y a longtemps que je t'aime
Jamais je ne t'oublierai.

Holding Pattern

They had met at a train station, waiting for a train which never came. That was a dozen years ago, but passenger trains were already an anachronism, often sidetracked short of their destination, and their passengers put on buses, to arrive a day later at a bus depot, not the train station. Freight trains had the right-of-way because passenger trains lost money. So the passengers merely endured, as did those who waited for them.

This had happened to Laura and the man who turned out to be Ravi, an East Indian forever far from home, as they waited in the cavernous hall of Union Station. It was a proud architectural monument to the age of rails, but its state of desertion made it clear that its time had passed, and that Laura and Ravi were among a breed of holders on who would eventually vanish. The mosaic floors rang out with every footstep, and the decorated roof beams sent back echoes of every sound. For this reason, the man and the woman, having found each other alone in the vast space, found it natural to sit next to each other on one of the voluptuously carved benches and to speak so quietly that they were almost whispering.

Their conversation was not about themselves, although before it was over they had found that they both lived in similar beach towns, of which there were many stretching south from the huge city down along the curve of the coast. Their towns had once been fishing villages and holiday enclaves, but now had expanded into the surrounding farmlands with the relentless migration into that area. This was one of the things they talked about briefly. But Laura realized later that Ravi had directed their talk toward ideas, and although it was a random and desultory dialogue, as they alternately glanced at the huge clock, out to the track, and back to each other, the quality of his which intrigued her was that he was interested without being personal. He never asked who she waited for, so she did not ask him either. Looking back, Laura came to see this as a symbol of their willingness to respect each other's lives.

When they heard that their wait was not to be rewarded and wandered out toward their cars, she found she knew nothing about the man himself, but quite a lot about his thinking, and he about hers, because he had elicited her opinions sincerely and listened carefully as she spoke, and she liked that. So when he asked for her notebook and wrote his telephone number in it, she did not feel a sense of invasion, and when he suggested meeting at a restaurant on the water a week hence, she accepted without feeling pursued.

But he had not come to their meeting, and Laura felt forgotten and strangely disappointed, but somehow not intentionally ignored. Using the telephone number he had written, she boldly called him and asked what had happened. He seemed truly at a loss, and truly apologetic. He was plainly pleased that she had called him. She wondered where his reality lay; of course he could forget about her in a week and forget a date so casually made with a stranger, but why respond now with such sincerity? He insisted that they meet at the same place the following week, and she had no sense of a pattern being set that they would cling to for years.

At their second meeting she was intentionally late to spare herself any anxious wait and to give him the chance to experience the uncertainty she had felt. But he was there, waiting calmly among the fishermen who were most of the patrons of the café. So they drank together and talked ideas, and it was as if two weeks had not intervened and they were continuing from yesterday. But now he directed the ideas toward the subject of men and women, where she felt inadequate to contribute because she had given up ever having a true understanding. When he said the men of his country were the very best with women, she decided to call it an evening and summoned the waiter with her eyes. Laura thought, this is becoming nothing; I know I don't really interest him if he can revert to seductive innuendos of the kind offered to intrigue a casual pickup.

Ravi did not object, and they clasped hands as they said a shivering good-bye out at their cars. Then suddenly he was at her passenger door before she could leave, asking her something. She unlocked the door and he slid in; his arms were around her in the same motion, and he held her so close she could hardly breathe. She thought, this is like adolescence again: sudden embraces in the front seats of cars. But the thought could not finish before his hands had begun seeking the formal barriers of her clothing, and caressing the closely held places.

What surprised her was her own compliance and lethargic acceptance. It seemed to be what she had wanted forever. Still, she was
shaken and made an ineffective move to dissuade his drive. But her
arousal was overwhelming. Their union was quick and melting and
complete, with a sense of something decided long ago. When they
separated, it was understood almost before he stated it in his heavily
accented voice that they would meet here again in a week.

Many weeks and many meetings went by before she knew more
about him. Each time they met for a drink and then moved out to the
darkness of each other's cars. They heard always the bells from distant
sea buoys and the soft thunder of surf, and sometimes even the cries
of seabirds after dark. Often there was fog or mist, and often the
inside of the car fogged up from their heat, because they inevitably
made love.

One night she said to Ravi that she wanted a bed to make love in;
no more car seats on waterfront nights. He was quick to name a small
hotel between her town and his for the next week, and it flashed
through her intuition that this was not a unique situation for him.
This is going to be a fling which will soon end of its own fragility, she
thought, and I will look back and wonder why I was so enthralled.
Nevertheless, she went to meet him the next week.

Laura's first thought of an impersonal and probably drab hotel
room made her pause as she was leaving to meet Ravi. She picked up
a shoulder bag and glanced around her comfortable home as if to ask
it for counsel. There were two candles in glasses, and she put them in
the bag, along with two wine glasses and a crystal saucer, and then
her old and favorite silk robe and a velvet cushion from her reading
chair. On her way out through the garden she stopped and picked the
three gardenias that were blooming on the plant that was her delight.
The blossoms were very small, unlike those in the florist's, but they
were pure white and like wild things in their fragrance.

She found the hotel easily, a half-hour's drive from her house, just
off the highway. Like the train they had waited for, it belonged to
another era, when families came down to the sea for weekends away
from the heavy inland summer. All the time she had been driving, she
felt her body's heat rising, and with it the drugging sensation the
thought of Ravi produced. She tried to review her life in terms of the
men she had loved, and those she had made love with, to understand
why this was different. But her time sense seemed damaged, and she
could not remember the sequence of romantic attachments before
her husband or her lovers after him. Ravi's image came up before her,

the dark body and slender hands and fine dark eyes, and disqualified all analysis or comparison.

When she joined him in the hotel lobby, she felt compelled to offer to share the cost. She had sensed that he had little money and did not want to acknowledge or discuss it, yet had to abide by its strictures. She knew he had a beginning professional job which he had arrived at through years of schooling at night and menial work in the days. She intuited the presence of a family, too, but she did not ask. In time she was sure it would be revealed, maybe when it was over for them. It was part of the sleepwalking not to know. And, because he was younger, she felt she could have a nonquestioning relationship with him.

Their room was simple but clean, and French doors opened onto a weathered balcony from which they could hear and smell the sea, and as the doors stood open, the breeze billowed the curtains as if to make sails of them and send the lovers out to sea. Ravi locked the door of the room, leaning against it as if holding back the world. Laura took his hands in hers and guided him into ephemeral kisses while her heart raced for more. She slipped away from the fever of his look and asked him to wait. Ravi watched her in amazement while she performed the rituals of making a home, which for the first time established a space belonging only to them. She lit the candles in their glasses, and the flames, like the curtains, responded to the fitful rhythm of the breeze. She put water in the crystal saucer and floated her three gardenias in it, and their fragrance was immediately everywhere around them. She set the wine glasses out ceremoniously, then went to the bed, taking off the covers and blankets and arranging the pillows with her own velvet pillow, so that the bed became a divan of snowy linen. She turned off the lights and very slowly undressed, and slipped her old silk robe around her body. Several times Ravi approached her, but she showed him that she meant for him to wait. Then he spoke for the first time, saying, "Laura, we have no wine for your glasses," and they laughed because neither had thought of it. They were pacing their need for each other to a new, much slower tempo. He said, "I must bring something to our new home." He excused himself and left the hotel, while Laura sat by the balcony doors to cool her heat and give herself patience. He returned very soon with a bottle of wine she would not have found acceptable any other time, but it became the sacrament of their union and their nuptial bed.

Now Laura began to undress Ravi, worshipping every part of his body as she freed it from the confinement of fabric, the layers of the world's requirements giving way to the new archeology of the muscles underlying the nerves of the satin skin. Suddenly they could wait no longer, not even long enough to go to the bed. Their new home was christened on the aged pine floors. When they threw themselves on the bed later, they were able to talk together and drowse between reawakenings of their lovemaking. There were new things to try, which their confinement to cars had never allowed, and there was time to contemplate each other, to prolong attack with withdrawal, to tantalize and tease.

Finally they told each other they must dress and leave. As she waited for him to finish washing, she leaned out over the balcony rail to catch the flash of a lighthouse beacon as it swung through a distant arc. Silently he was upon her again, her silk robe was thrown over her shoulders and her bare buttocks delved and searched in yet another penetration which made her cry out in surprise and delight. He put his hand over her mouth before she could disturb the hotel. She bit at his hand and writhed under his force, as new beacons flashed behind her closed eyes. He stopped moving and stayed absolutely still inside her and would not let her move. He made her tell him that she had never felt like this when she had made love before, that it had never been this wild, this beautiful, and on and on until she had conceded his total possession of her sensual self, confirming his dominance of her experience. When they released each other and fell exhausted on the bed, it was Ravi who went to fill the wine glasses with cold water, and when she had drunk some, to bathe her face in it with his fingers, and to bring her towels and to tell her of her uniqueness in his life. She knew there had been no sexual lies told that night and that they would not be quite the same people again in retrospect, ever.

For a time, their meeting place remained the anonymous hotel. Although they came to meet less often, their passion did not diminish, and the prospect of their next meeting was always present on the borders of Laura's mind. Her daily work wearied her, her failed marriage saddened her, and she worried over her daughter whom she loved so much, but who seemed not to accept the world as an adult. When each day's demands were met, the thought of Ravi and their bliss together fell on her spirit like a blessing.

One night, driving to meet Ravi, Laura took the longer route that followed the coast and the beaches. The wide sandy shoreline rolled for many miles and held areas where fires could be made. This night she saw many bonfires on the edge of the blackness the sea creates for itself. She saw brilliant planets near the horizon and a soft moon almost at the zenith, and around the fires, faces illuminated in the companionship of shared warmth, and in celebration of being nearly in the sea's grasp, yet safe from it. When she met Ravi she was full of these visions. She said, "Let's go to the beach ourselves. We will have a fire with food and wine, just as they do, and we will wrap ourselves in blankets like Indians." Then they laughed, because he was already an Indian, but a different kind. They agreed to meet at a beach further down the coast for their next rendezvous.

For that evening she cooked some simple food and brought two blankets. He brought wine and firewood. They tramped through the uneven sand, which with the coming of darkness was already cold, until they found a fire ring away from the others. They put down their blankets and coaxed a fire into being, struggling to keep it thriving in the chill salt wind, and arranging the food so it would warm by the flames. Ravi poured the wine, which Laura had come to understand was prohibited by the teachings of his religion, but which he enjoyed, nevertheless, and they sat on the blankets hugging each other for warmth until the fire grew. Over their heads from time to time there passed huge lighted airliners, circling in the holding pattern for the distant airport. As they exchanged what star lore they had between them, and watched the moon rise to coat the surf with a frost of spectral white, they began to see phosphorescence glowing in the curl of each wave as it crested and shot tongues of water in to suck at the sand and leave it glittering. They felt the sand shift and mold itself to their bodies, and then the need for each other overode all other sensations. They made fierce love, clothes and all, and clung together afterward, feeling too close in the darkness to let each other go. She thought, this may be the most romantic evening of my entire life, and it's with a man I don't really know, except that I know his body so well.

But it was that night, driving back, that Ravi disclosed that he had a wife, greatly admired but not specifically loved, and a continent away with no immediate plan to come nearer. Laura asked when they had married, and heard that it had been at twenty, and that his wife was of a higher caste than he, and required much more than he could offer her in their home country. Then Laura had to ask if he would bring her here when he had enough money, and knew his answer would be yes before he gave it.

The following morning Laura woke before dawn, knowing there was something difficult she had to think about. Then it rushed in upon her that her lover was a married man, marking time until he could be reunited with his wife. All that day, going through the motions of her work, she felt the previous night's sensations settled around her body with the softness of an eiderdown quilt, and at the same time knew with grating certainty that she must break with Ravi now.

When they met next, she was ready to tell him, but instead found herself saying, "When your wife comes to join you, I will still be your friend, but no more than a friend." Ravi was indignant in his opposition: there was no change here that should affect them, because after all he had always been married, and now they had been lovers so long it took precedence over formal alliances. Laura was shaken by this reasoning.

Ravi told her for the first time what his home in India had been like, and how, although he had risen so far, he still missed it. Laura asked him then about his wife, and he showed her a photograph. Laura had imagined a woman in a sari, with gold bracelets and long braided hair. Instead she saw a woman much lighter than Ravi: attractive, serious, pragmatic, and dressed in chic contemporary clothing. In that glimpse, Laura saw how everything in his life had been a struggle to take him to his wife's level, and to justify her choice of him.

Laura asked Ravi why he had been attracted to her at their first meeting in the train station, and what had kept him still seeing her after such a long time. "Love," he said simply. "You are in love with me, and I admire your thinking, and you are the best person for me to make love to, ever." Then a realization came to her which made her flushed and weak. Love had never been mentioned between them until now, but she did love Ravi, quite a lot, even though she could not imagine a life with him. She wondered if love affairs could be more permanent than formal commitments, sometimes; if there could be a commitment in no commitment.

That night she drove out along the shore and stopped where she could see fires on the beach as there had been the night she was there with Ravi. She suddenly felt with a sureness she had never felt before that she and Ravi would end, not just at some vague time in the future, but at any time, maybe even now, tonight. She felt the loss of him as she had never felt it the times she had tried to break with him. She felt the deprival of never again seeing in the dim light his silken, dark skin against her own pale skin, and never again finding the temporal bliss of their rich lovemaking. But she pulled her sinking spirit back. It hasn't happened yet, she thought.

What they were together had always eluded Laura, but now she saw herself and Ravi as two people clinging to opposite sides of a raft in the dark sea, with different perceptions of the sea and of the salvation that might come. Maybe it would not, and one or both of them would drop away into the deep, glad of the release. The salvation may come, as it had until now, in small increments at occasional times, with no enlightenment given and no immunity granted; just the love of the senses for one more moment.

For this, she thought, there should be no prospect of mourning. Each hour should be free to thrive while it lived, and to rejoice in when it had gone. And so she went on home, content, and ready for the next day to arrive, as she was certain it would.

Danny

Dear Danny:

It has been years and years since we shared the same street, walked on top of five-foot-high packed snow on no-school winter days, and, after a fresh snowfall, jumped into its cold white "eiderdown" from the roof of the old shed.

I remember how much you hated school, and I remember the cowlick that used to embarrass you, especially when it showed up on the eighth-grade graduation picture we took of you and Aggie and Hilary down at the Charles River. The wind was blowing, and Aggie's hair was all over the place, Hilary's skirt had blown up a little bit, just enough to expose her knees, and the hair you had carefully brushed over your cowlick to hide it had escaped and there it was, sticking straight up, proclaiming that you were not yet a man, despite the important parchment cylinder you held in your hand. That cowlick exposed your youth as surely as a voice that cracked or cheeks that remained smooth to the touch like a girl's. No one was smiling in that picture, I remember. I guess none of you liked being blown around by the wind on a special day like that when fixing hair and getting dressed up in white was a big occasion, one presided over by the parents. To me, three years your junior, you all seemed so grown up. I felt that I would never make it to eighth-grade graduation, and certainly never have *my* picture taken with a boy.

Actually, I never had any schoolgirl designs on you then. You were "okay," but kids who didn't like school—boys *or* girls (but it seemed mostly to be boys)—made me feel uncomfortable . . . self-conscious, even ashamed, that I looked forward to school, especially to English class. And besides that, you had that little boy smell about you—an acrid odor that seemed like part sourgrass, part mentholated coughdrops, and part milk that was about to turn. I never understood girls who *did* giggle about boys, but I trusted that someday, I, too, would giggle the way they did.

That I would "giggle" about *you* a dozen years later is something I never would have believed, but there you were, sitting on my bed in the rented room that was my home when I was nineteen. (How had we met again? I don't recall.) You had grown to a husky six-footer and had taken to tweed, pipe smoking, and large horn-rimmed glasses not unlike those that Cary Grant wore with such aplomb in the forties. You had brought along a Modern Library edition of poetry . . . Whitman, was it? It was in the army, you said, that you had started reading everything you could lay hands on. And it was the army that had transformed you from a skinny little kid to a large muscled man, thereby making good on what seemed, than and now, like inflated and silly promises on their part to "make a man" of the poor souls who enlisted. I can still envision you in front of me, living testimony to their claims, looking every inch what the giggly girls of today would describe as a "hunk."

I appreciated the look of you, but, even more, that someone of obvious intellectual sensibilities could be packaged like a football player instead of like Ichabod Crane. Best of all was that I discovered a man who loved, as I did, the wonder to be found in books . . . someone to whom I could confess, without fear of being laughed at, how I used to stand in the library and, when no one was looking, bury my nose in an old book . . . any old book . . . simply to inhale its indescribable smell. (I can still close my eyes and conjure up that smell.) Not only did you love poetry and literature, but you had devoured it by yourself and on your own terms, as I had. Maybe our teachers had stimulated our interest in serious reading, but neither of us gave them credit for the passionate attachments we were sure we had formed entirely on our own. You sitting on my bed reading poetry to me was heaven. I wanted no more.

Of course I wanted more. But I was a virgin, and the more I wanted was easily satisfied. On the few dates we had before you left me forever, simply leaning my face against your chest and inhaling the now wondrous smell you had acquired in the intervening years was almost enough. "Almost" because I would have missed it had you not also taken my face in your hands, as you used to, and looked at me with tender love in your eyes just before I closed mine to luxuriate in the sensation of your full soft mouth on my mouth. Surely this was the beginning of the great romance that the elders had promised me in mischievous passing remarks accompanied by a wink ("you just wait . . ."), that Hollywood had hinted at in heart-wrenching good-byes played out at railroad stations, and that was implicit in the titter-ings of my older and wiser schoolmates as they watched the boys walk by.

In my mind, we were at the beginning of it all on that night that turned out to be the last time I ever saw you. It wasn't that we had been together very long or done anything special, and it wasn't that either of us had revealed how we felt about each other. I guess I thought it was enough that I had found *the* one for me—a man who was tender and protective, like the brother I never had; and, at the same time, a man who read poetry to me, held me close, and kissed me with a mixture of sweetness and passion, passion that didn't leave me feeling strangely alone and afraid of its single-minded force but which, for the first time, included me in its fire. And remember how we laughed together as we sifted through our separate and shared memories? You thought that the evaporated milk can my grandfather walked around with was to drink from instead of to spit his tobacco juice into. (When you told us that, my sister and I had laughed until we wet our pants.) And remember the morning you came to church with us and the hymn was "Oh Danny Boy"? We looked at each other and then back to our hymnals, struggling to keep appropriately rev-erent faces.

Oh, what a couple we would be! Simone de Beauvoir and Jean-Paul Sartre. As close in mind as in body. Intellectual and physical. Friends and lovers. Unheard of in the Rita Hayworth culture that had done its lion's share in shaping my values. For you, I would betray Rita in a second. But it was not to be.

You remember. We had come home from a movie and were stand-ing in the doorway to my boardinghouse. You held me against your chest as you always did, while I took in your wonderful male smells and waited for you to take my face in your hands and kiss me long and lovingly. You did take my face in your hands, but the look in your eyes, though as intense as always, was clouded with something un-spoken. I knew the time had not yet come to close my eyes and sink into the delirium of pleasure you would soon give to my young heart and soul. We looked at each other for a long second before you spoke. "I never talked to you about the woman I was involved with just before we met again. I have to tell you now."

The words came out slowly and softly, and, as you spoke, I could feel you leaving me, even though neither of us had moved an inch.

"We were very much in love," you continued, "but she is strongly religious and I'm not. That broke us up."

I remember taking a deep involuntary breath. I felt the prickly hairs of your jacket under my hands that were still wrapped around your neck, and I leaned back against the wall for support—and I guess to put some physical distance between us. I sensed that something was about to happen that would hurt me. The premonition of it blanketed us like a thick and sudden fog. Did you sense that, too?

"So why am I telling you this?" you said, when I didn't respond. Then you looked away again and continued talking as I made a study of your profile as if I had never seen it before.

"I saw her last week. To make a long story short, we want to try to make a go of it."

You stopped talking then and turned to me again. I could see in your face that the memory of *her* face that had possessed you for the last few seconds as you spoke had now faded and that your heart was back with me. It was as if you remembered suddenly that it was I who needed you at this moment and not her. I said nothing. I felt that I would cry if I tried to speak. A million things raced through my mind in those moments . . . the tormenting questions familiar to all who love alone: What could I have been thinking anyway? Why had I exaggerated this simple relationship? Did I really think it had meant to you what it meant to me? I wanted to run from you and into the comforting privacy of my room, but the proper good-byes had to be said, I knew. The cheerful, brave, casual parting that would spare you the pain (or was it simply the annoyance?) of a prolonged good-bye. Then you looked at me with that soft scowl sensitive men wear when inflicting pain and told me what a wonderful girl I was.

"I understand, Danny. It's really been fun." I remember adding a lighthearted "Good luck" before turning to put my key in the lock, hoping that my hand wasn't trembling and that the door would open quickly and smoothly. I went inside and you made no move to stop me. My nostrils suddenly filled with an acrid odor, part sourgrass, part mentholated coughdrops, and part milk that was about to turn.

Still I wonder sometimes . . . do you ever think of me?

All my love,

Elvira

Postcards from the Interior

I

I used to chase iron men in banker's clothing:
fifty deep kneebends and a hundred-yard dash
with heavy hands straight to the finish line.

Now, wound in a cloud of rumpled sheets,
I unfurl. A shaft of morning light slices
the startle of sea air.

The sensual now is meaning enough. Good-bye
father confessor, savior brother,
mind-reading lover,
wherever you are.

Today I flex the flabby muscles of resolve,
vow silent promises, faithful to my orbit
that takes me out of range.

I'll send you postcards from inner places,
telepathic briefings to keep in touch,
tame the wilderness.

Soon I want to take you to the dark side
of the moon.
Will you come?

II

In our beginning
fast (though slow) upon you
I was the starfish,
welded by craving.

Even your violent waves
of indecision
couldn't pry me loose.

My limbs and mouth
(too clingy and needing)
found you irresistible:
a studious concretion,
polished by force of will
into a resilient veneer.

A decade or two of careful suction
wore that away.
Once inside your brave and silent shell
I feasted on sweets
too delicious to share.

How strange then last night
to find myself pinned by your tentacles—
your arms and legs around me,
your mouth a million mouths.
I felt the shell I never knew I had
slowly crack,
and my oyster bed of secrets dissolve.

Catch and Release

"But we've always had lakefront. Every year we make the reservation when we check out. If you'd care to look it up—Alice and Brian Layton for July first."

As the negotiations between the girl behind the desk and the woman dragged into another round, Monica waited with less than good humor for the key to her own suite. The eager, but untried summer clerk was clearly no match for her opponent, who had the unfair advantage of lifelong training in polite obtuseness. Monica recognized the type: tiny old ladies with pink curls and southern accents. They always won the right-of-way: on city streets they blocked traffic with their Oldsmobile tanks; in supermarkets they turned their shopping carts into tactical weapons; in public restrooms across the nation they forged ahead of the line to monopolize the only vacant stalls.

"Your reservation is for tomorrow, Mrs. Layton, I'm sorry. The cottage won't be available until then. We have a vacancy in the back where you could stay until that time. It is very nice, right by the creek."

"Show her our reservation, Brian. No wait, I think it's in my purse."

What intrigued Monica about the couple, and kept her from leaving, was the man's cheerful tolerance toward the woman. Their ritualistic familiarity suggested an old married couple, but his deference to her was different from a husband's tired resignation. Even now, when the woman could not find the confirmation letter in her voluminous purse, and then claimed that he must have it in his wallet, and finally remembered that it was in her nightcase in the car. Even when asked to please go and fetch it, he did not seem annoyed, nor did he treat her with condescending kindness to prove his superiority. Although he did not seem that much younger, probably because of his full gray beard and old-fashioned appearance, Monica guessed that Brian was the woman's son. The mother was tidy and trim in her pea-green knit suit, the son was husky and sloppy as if he no longer looked in the mirror. His red hair stuck out in every direction.

"Does that mean we'll have to pack up and move again tomorrow? Oh Brian, do something," the woman whined. "I don't think I'm up to all this, please. I can't bear to be shuttled from place to place." The voice was tearful, the face a tragic mask.

"Excuse me." Monica beamed her ingratiating sorority-girl smile. "I will only be staying for a day or two. Why don't you take my cottage? It's right on the lake."

"That's very kind of you. Are you sure we're not putting you out?" the mother inquired politely, leaving no doubt that she was accepting the offer as if Monica had vacated her seat in a crowded bus. And again, as required by the rules of etiquette she had taken in with her baby formula, Monica assured the woman that she really didn't need two bedrooms since she was traveling alone. The son thanked her with a bow and an expression of obvious relief before going back to the car to rescue a wildly barking white poodle in a red turtleneck sweater.

Later, lying on top of her bed, surrounded by the knotty-pine walls of the motel room, Monica smoked her last cigarette—she always stopped smoking during holidays—and reflected on her good deed. Compulsive politeness frequently landed her in places she did not care to be. The bathroom in this cabin did not even have a tub, and soaking leisurely in hot bubbles was a cherished vacation ritual. But to be honest, she had to admit that she preferred this cramped little room to the beachfront suite; here she could avoid the sight of sprawling families over the Fourth of July weekend.

Ten years after her divorce, she still could not get over her sense of failure for not having produced the obligatory baby that both sides of the family had expected. It was certainly vulgar to breed like the Kennedys, but to spend years going alternately from fertility clinics to honeymoon resorts without results was pitiful. No wonder her race-car-driver husband had never shifted gears from playboy to family man. Her hard work as an office designer had paid off their debts and won her prizes, but it did not save their marriage.

The cheerful sound of the rushing creek outside the window drowned out her bitter memories and made her think of her next creative project—designing a gigantic atrium inside an insurance building. Why not put a fountain in the center, she thought.

When she finally fell asleep, she dreamed of a three-tiered marble fountain with twenty nude executives splashing around under the cascading mineral water. Some of them climbed all the way to the top, where she, Monica Cassel, was dispensing the sparkling liquid from her huge alabaster breasts. A trickle even escaped from between her thighs, spread majestically over the highest bowl. Only one man dared to drink from this special spigot—Brian, whose terrible haircut stood out among all the other precision-shaped heads. When she awoke at her usually early hour, she clearly remembered the delicious tickle of his beard.

Still smiling, she set out on her morning jog. A well-marked trail led from her motel room down to the river and then for about two miles alongside the fern-covered banks; it climbed over rocks and tree roots to the top of a ravine. Wiping the sweat from her face, she took in the view of the lake that was fed by the rushing river, shimmering dark green under the morning mist.

About twenty feet down the steep embankment she saw him standing high-booted among the gurgling rapids. Glad to know that she was not alone in the Oregon jungle, she waved her arms in greeting, but he seemed unaware of her presence. He looked so much better out here than in the lodge, she thought. Her designer's eye noted that his unkempt reddish hair blended nicely with the prevalent earth tones and that his bulging overalls matched the shape and color of the tree trunks. She ignored the brambles and scrambled downhill to get closer. After all, she felt she knew him intimately from last night's vivid dream.

Either he treasured his solitude among the hidden trout, or he was too absorbed in what he was doing to notice her. He did not look up, even when she sat directly across from him. On first impulse she wanted to retreat from his watery fortress, but she lingered to watch him flick out his line and draw it in, over and over again in a kind of dance solo—his bulk moving gracefully across the wet rocks. Then he waded up to his waist in the water, shooting the line with a powerful backward twist from his hips and turning his shoulders easily into the thrust, his left arm rising to counterbalance the right, which extended the rod. Up over his head the quivering rod arched back, trailing and then spurting out the long S filament. Like a ballet dancer wholly centered in himself, the rhythmic motion coming from deep within, he dropped the line with hair-breadth precision into the pools. Now near, now far—pausing only to focus—he inserted the fly into the secret spots. He climbed onto a boulder to probe the sparkling rivulets underneath and snake his line across a great distance, pulling it back with quick, gliding movements that rippled the still surface of the river's edge. When he brought in a fish, he took firm hold of the body. His hands instantly calmed the frantic creature, which ceased to struggle as if it sensed that it was going to be released from the hook. Carefully he removed the hook and laid the fish back into the water, where it rested, stunned for a second, and then swam away. He treated every catch in this manner.

"Are you taking the same fish over and over again?" she called, only half teasing.

"I'm waiting for the big one," he answered. "I know he's in there. I've seen him, but he's a clever old bastard. He's taken my bait clear off the hook, laughing at me while doing it."

Intrigued, Monica watched for a while and decided for the next several mornings to stalk him from a distance. Playing by the rules she learned from his fishing game, she dropped her usual office tactics. The surface politeness and the buzz words of success were as out of place in this primordial forest as a metal filing cabinet. This was a silent world where creatures signaled their love and hostility through body language.

Of course he knew that she was there, but he was not sure what she was up to. Let her be, this elegant city woman with her silver-blonde hair and bright blue jogging suit. He was not going to get entangled with her. But once, during a sudden downpour, he put his jacket over her shoulders, and she pressed her shivering body close to his.

The next day she brought a six-pack of beer in her sporty freezer bag and invited him to go swimming in the lake. By the time Monica had changed, Brian was already in the water. "Beat you to the other side," Monica dared him as the ice cold water slapped against her chest. She gasped. Her swimming had been confined to the heated pool. For Brian, the lake was obviously his element. With long, racing strokes he quickly overtook her. Struggling to keep up with him, she did not bother to look back until she noticed how far she was from the shore. Then it was too late to turn back.

A growing terror of unknown powers below gripped her ankles. She kicked frantically, but an excruciating pain shot up her left calf— a cramp. The mountains stared down impassively at her. The trees stood darkly in a row far away. The whole lake wanted her to drown. All she had to do was to stop struggling. Drowning was only a matter of giving up, of letting yourself go. Another shot of pain. At that moment her head was lifted from behind, and she felt another body close to hers.

"I've got you now, don't move, don't do anything." Brian's arms locked her into a secure embrace as he towed her in. "We'll make it to the other side; then you can rest."

The ride was over far too soon. She was sorry. It had felt as though she were being carried by a soft, warm whale. He kept his arm around her as she sat shivering on a sun-warmed rock. Only at that moment did she see the scar that ran down his side all the way to his upper thigh. She had first taken it for a tattooed dragon. "Like it?" he grinned, noticing her stare, then added, "It's a souvenir from Korea." Fascinated, she touched the purplish protrusions and felt a quick shock in her groin.

He started to massage her leg. "You do that very well," she said appreciatively.

He lifted her knee to rub the soles of her feet. "We've got to get you warm before you can return to the water. Tell you what, turn over and lie down on your stomach in the sand. It's still warm. Put your head on your arms." Like a lizard, she flattened herself out, eager to soak up the heat from the ground. With the edge of his hands, he pommeled the back of her thighs and continued all the way down to her ankles, then up again over her fanny and dorsal muscles, shoulders, and arms. Then with his hands spread flat he kneaded her upper back, his fingers gripping her skin. A tingling sensation invaded her body, and her flesh responded voluptuously as his fingers and palms repeated the journey. No one had ever lavished so much attention on her.

The urge to pull him down next to her became excruciating, but she did not dare to turn around lest she frighten him away. Her bathing suit grew thick and heavy, a barrier. She wanted to remove it, to feel his hands on her naked buttocks, his dragon on top of her back, lizard style. Although the neutral tone of his voice suggested that he wasn't trying to seduce her, she could see that he was as ready as she. When he had finished the massage, she told him about her fountain dream that first night. In response he pressed his lips up against her thighs. Dizzy with excitement, she swayed back and forth, clinging to his solid shoulders. His beard was as soft as the carpet of fresh mountain grass where they made love. She marveled at his patience, wondering aloud how he could keep his passion under such control.

"An old Indian trick," he said. "I want this to go on forever."

"I'm glad I didn't give up on you," she sighed sleepily.

"I love you," he murmured. "I meant what I said: I want this to go on forever."

Part of her agreed. If only she could root her body into the moist, fragrant soil. Tenderly she traced his scary dragon with the tip of her tongue, knowing that she had to release this gentle, big fish but hoping not to hurt him. "I have to go back tonight. Doris, my boss, is expecting me. I've stayed much longer than planned."

"You mean you've followed me around for a week only to pick me up and drop me? I should have known." His voice was cold.

"Catch and release," she said lightly to conceal her panic. "You are the fisherman. You taught me how to fish."

"But some fish you catch only once in a lifetime," he replied, pulling her back into his arms. Then he talked about lasting love, but his language did not ring true to her slogan-tired ears. It scared Monica to even consider the kind of love he had in mind. Tearing herself away from him, she ran into the water.

"Hey wait, you forgot this," he shouted, waving her bathing suit.

"You put it on me," she laughed.

Lunging after her, he slipped the wet lycra over her buttocks as she twisted and turned in his hands. Then with her legs clasped around his waist she let him pull up the bathing suit over her tightened nipples. Suddenly he backed away, peering past her toward the distant shore. "What time is it?" he asked. Monica followed his gaze and recognized the tiny figure standing watch under a towering redwood.

"We always eat at five," he explained.

"Well then, let's not keep her waiting," cried Monica, heading straight toward the hotel beach. Brian offered to tow her back, but she refused. "I'm fine, believe me. I'm used to the water now."

He seemed relieved but kept his eyes on her. With powerful strokes she surged ahead and this time made it back across without a second thought. They both stepped out of the shallows together. Brian reached for the towel his mother held out for him. Monica smiled as she walked briskly past them.

"Wait," he called after her, "I'll see you later!"

"Sure, let's keep in touch." But they both knew better.

By nine o'clock the next morning Monica was back in her office.

"You look wonderful," said Doris. "How was the fishing? Did you catch anything?"

"Yes, a big one, but I threw him back where he belonged."

Heart Like a Salmon

The salmon is brave of heart, beautiful and admirable. Strong, giving his all to love—a world roamer who always comes home—he is the perfect Valentine symbol. When he does not succeed in his final, fatal love run and, instead, gives his perfect silver body to the fisherman, he is also perfection to eat.

Freshly caught, the salmon cooks gently, easily, quickly to the most delicate sweet tenderness. Baked or steamed, his meat separates easily from the bones, the rosy flesh becoming a pastel coral—a shade so distinct the Western world acknowledges it with the name of the great fish itself. Offer him some small shrimp as companions, the kind the salmon often swam with in his ocean voyaging. The shrimp, shelled and fresh, will be ready with only a rinsing to blend their briny, unique flavor with that of their larger vertebrate friend and to add their pearl-pink color to the hue of the salmon meat.

A small baking dish shaped like a heart would be ridiculously perfect to house them in, but any ramekin-type dish will do. Marry the shrimp and salmon in a roux (melting butter first, adding flour in equal amounts to cook in the butter while stirring, then adding milk a little at a time to expand and thicken). Now add a little white wine, some Parmesan or other mild cheese, and a dusting of your favorite delicate herbs (a crumble of sweet basil, a dash of celery salt, a sprinkle of paprika, the smallest hint of saffron or curry). Tasting, always tasting, think of the sauce as your tribute to the great-hearted salmon. When you are satisfied, pour your sauce over shrimp and fish in the ramekin, and bake at moderate temperature, just long enough for the sauce to bubble lightly and make a slight golden crust.

Pour a chilled Chablis into your most fragile stem glasses, and sit down to savor your salmon—but first drink a toast to the noble fish himself who has contributed to your feast of love.

PERIOD PIECES

PERIOD PIECES

*F*or many of us the attraction of bygone eras lay in their undiluted drama. Like a brew that grows stronger the longer it steeps, the past seasons our present. Now as we waver between restraint and permissiveness, we find ourselves once again lured into the dark and steamy corridors of the past. While none of us would want to live in the Victorian period of sexual repression, we still relish the flavor of forbidden fruit, which produced a whole section in our first book.

Traveling backward in time to relive the passion born of restriction, we probe through diaries and other memorabilia. The stirring exhortation that follows was stumbled upon by Sabina in the course of her research for "The Two Wedding Nights of Euphemia Gray." We offer it here for your edification:

> Those lascivious day-dreams and amorous reveries, in which young people—and especially the idle and the voluptuous, and the sedentary and the nervous—are exceedingly apt to indulge, are often the sources of general debility, effeminacy, disordered functions, premature disease, and even premature death, without the actual exercise of the genital organs! Indeed, this unchastity of thought—this adultery of the mind—is the beginning of immeasurable evil to the human family.

> (J. H. Kellogg, M.D., *Plain Facts for Old and Young* [Burlington, Iowa: I. F. Segner, 1882], p. 177)

Birth Control Fifties' Style

Yes, daughters of today
we did not pick the quickie way.
We kept him waiting
before mating
with endless games
called petting,
never letting
his virile flames
ignite our fire
beyond desire.
In our teens
we were the queens
of ballroom dancing,
one step back, one step advancing.
Tangoing closely with temptation,
we favored piecemeal copulation.

Nice Girls Don't

Today, the aroma of a slightly damp wool sweater jolted me back in time nearly thirty years. The memories of endless hours spent "necking," "making out," or "petting" (as most of us called it then) were so powerful that I could almost feel my chin begin to smart and redden from whisker abrasion. I could smell the night air and his car—a 1953 Mercury. The anticipation mounted as I closed my eyes and felt myself snuggled into the crook of his arm, driving to our special place in the hills overlooking Hollywood.

A lot of attention went into dressing for these dates. A squeaky clean body, fresh breath, and shiny, bouncy hair were prime necessities, of course. But other dress codes were also crucial: a pretty bra and panties, a sweater that was loose at the waist or a blouse easy to unbutton, and a full skirt. No dresses or slacks or anything that wrinkled easily.

The rules were so beautifully clear for me then. There was that point past which I simply wouldn't go, and I always made that clear with many "No, don't"s. My morality was dictated by two combined terrors: one, getting pregnant and, the other, breaking my parents' hearts. Whether my high school boyfriend had resigned himself early on to my principles or whether he always thought "Maybe tonight . . . ," he never pressured me to "prove that I loved him." Our dates consisted of an occasional movie or dinner, but usually we dispensed with these preliminaries in quest of a good parking place on Mulholland Drive, the top of Outpost Drive, or the beach. The pouting, or an argument, usually came first—over what, I can't remember. And then came the consoling and melting into each other's arms, which began what was to be an evening of lovemaking à la 1956. Memories of loving soft lips, tongues, arms, whiskers, sounds, and damp wool sweaters are flooding back now.

His kisses fill my body from head to toe, lighting up little fires inside of me. The kissing lasts at least an hour. Then, slowly, his hands begin their exploration of my body. Around my face and eyes and through my hair he traces the outline of one who is truly beloved. His hands travel down my arms and up again to my neck. I can feel his love for me through his fingertips. Soon my sweater is lifted or my blouse unbuttoned. My breath sucks in as his hand now moves slowly toward my breast and his fingers play just inside the lacy edges of my bra. He reaches around behind me with both hands, fumbling for a long moment with what seems like an endless column of hooks and eyes. I hold my breath to make it easier for him. Finally, my beautiful, cherished, bare breasts are liberated, setting into motion at least another hour of gentle fondling, sweet kissing, and nibbling. I soar, knowing how much I am loved. I bask in the sensations I am just beginning to discover. This isn't foreplay because it isn't *before* anything. This is it, and *it* is pure heaven.

It was when he began to stray below the waist that I started to worry. But, oh, my god, it felt so good. My firm belly firmed up even more as his hand crept downward, slid down my leg, and gently lifted my skirt to explore new parts of me. I would press my thighs together to let him know he was too close to that forbidden place. I had to let him know that I was resisting because "nice girls don't." But I had learned to resist in a way that actually said to him: "Stop it some more." Once having shown him my resistance, I could permit him to keep going, especially knowing that I had the final "no."

As he explored my secret places, we began to tread on dangerous territory. My desire threatened my code as we played "ecstasy on the brink" night after glorious night.

I finally learned what lay on the other side of that abyss. One night we were stretched out on the floor, fully dressed, just kissing and holding each other. He had been comforting me about something, and I remember feeling very sad. With his body pressed tightly to mine, I suddenly felt on fire inside—exploding with sensations I'd never felt before. Yes, it was my first orgasm, and until he told me I didn't realize it. After that night, I openly welcomed his seeking out and finding my clitoris when he explored my body. It was more like "real sex," but my principles, at least, remained intact. Knowing what I know now, I can't imagine how he coped with night after night of what for him must have been excruciating frustration. We loved each other like this on and off for over four years. Then came the sexual revolution of the 1960s and, with it, no more cars parked on Mulholland or Outpost Drive.

As I spread the damp sweater out to dry in a warm place, the musky memory waits for me with the same unbelievable patience of my high school love.

The Lay of the Land: Love Between Gee!Oh!Physicists!

Detecting the
s
t
r
e
a
m
ing potential in her eyes, and
Sensing her lack of
resistivity,
He knew he could get geophysical and carry her
downhole to

BEDROCK.

She found him magnetic and filled with gravity,
and suggested they take a bathymetry together
before he sidescanned her: otherwise, she
wouldn't even show him her
p
r
o
f
i
l
e
let alone her $_{sub}$ bottom, and word would surely
get back to her fathometer.

Ariane, Ariane

I found it one morning in May, quite unexpectedly, while rummaging through a drawer. It was among some girlhood memorabilia easily thirty-five years old—the stuff we keep over time without really choosing to do so. It was just a scrap of blotter. Immediately I made a mental obeisance to the passage of time: In England, we called it blotting-paper, or in inky-fingered schoolgirl panic, merely blotting. It fell out of the pages of the magazine I had edited during my last years at the convent where I was educated. It was old and thin, torn around the edges, defaced with doodles and blots of ancient ink. A fragment of verse had been printed on it, in tiny letters like mouse claws: "No more Latin, no more French, no more sitting on a cold hard bench." I took it between finger and thumb, delicately feeling its fragile, elderly peach-fuzz texture buzzing under my fingertips like a million tiny electrical currents.

My eyes turned inward, searching intently. I heard voices, faint and clear; I smelled the sooty chill, felt on my upper lip, on my hands and cheeks, the prickly damp of an English afternoon in late autumn. I could feel and hear the crackle of brown leaves underfoot on the pavement beneath the skeletal oak trees and see the first lamps lighting up like dim, surprised old eyes in the windows of the solid brick houses. On a quiet, tree-lined street in the residential part of an industrial town south of London, a crocodile of tired girls trailed back to the high iron gates of the school in the darkening mist. Their felt hats sat in various attitudes of ambivalence on hair either braided or cut short, because that was one of the school's most rigid rules: *No girl shall be observed in uniform outside the school gates without her hat.* I saw muddy legs, hockey sticks, wet canvas boots dangling from long laces clutched in reddened fingers. I heard the restrained laughter of girls accustomed to being reminded that no lady behaves herself unseemly, drawing attention to herself and distressing God. I heard the soft, insistent ringing of bicycle bells as the day pupils began their thankful way home.

All the details were there, and I knew they were mere preamble to what I was going to see and hear and smell and feel again: I was being prepared by my courteous mind for the swift stone's drop of a memory from one of my soul's somnolent shelves. Something was going to smash into my consciousness like a brick through a plate-glass window. And it did. I looked down at the rose-gold blotter in my fingers and I saw her again. Ariane. I saw her with the fingers of my adolescent eyes. Ariane . . . I saw the fervid, glowing color of her face, then, the curve of her cheek, the velvet texture of the skin I had never touched yet could feel on my own skin as though it grew from the same cell-bed as my own. Ariane.

Was I in love with her? If I had been, it would not have been surprising. The convent was a tight place packed with passionate hearts. Sexual tripwires were built into the fabric of the cloister walls for all of us—nuns, lay teachers, pastor, pupils. Not even the gardeners were immune, being prisoners of war somehow overlooked by the military repatriation committees. In all weathers, wheeling barrows full of clippings from the playing fields, their biceps bulging and rippling under smooth golden skin, they worked stripped to the waist. But those of my contemporaries who adopted the convention of open "crushes" on teachers and other girls made me uncomfortable. I found them pathetic, embarrassing, repellent, wearing their ripped rubber hearts in plain sight of scorn.

But Ariane . . . Her presence jittered my skin and clabbered my nerves. I saw her through wet red mists. Gratefully, I passed her my careful notes before each exam which she failed to prepare. Hastily, I chose not to mind when she failed to give them back. She was beautiful and brave and strong. I was small, emerging into adolescent slenderness from a childhood of chubby, silent panic, convinced of an eternal curse upon me that summed itself up in the word "absence"— of everything that could be named, but mostly of beauty.

How important beauty was then, how magical and unattainable. It was a gift Ariane possessed in excess, as she did every other attribute for survival. She was tall, substantial, but not voluptuous; she was what the English called "strapping," a dismal word for such a powerful presence. Her face was short and square, almost feral, with high cheekbones, not much nose and a clean line of jaw. Her eyes—I think they were blue—were deep-set and veiled. Her teeth were perfect. My teeth were at that time imprisoned in a silvery, snapping brace that sometimes sprang from my mouth into the startled air when I spoke, like a divine remonstrance. It was impossible for onlookers to keep from laughing after the initial amazed silence. Nobody laughed at Ariane. I think Ariane, herself, actually laughed very little. She commanded respect. Striding off the hockey field, the cricket pitch, the tennis court, her wondrous, luminous skin like flowering moss, her wide, white brow pale from exertion, her round neck gleaming with a vapor of perspiration, she was always triumphant.

I feared and loathed the pointless, ferocious rituals of all competitive games, although I understood that life-everlasting depended upon the successful smacking of balls at, over, or through an obstacle. Hiding my face from the on-rushing crowd as I stood friendless and terrified between the goalposts, running shrieking from the monstrous regiment of lifted lacrosse sticks, I garnered no honor. I feared and loathed the gym mistress, Miss Gwyneth Price, who umpired the games with searing blasts on a silver whistle. With her mad Percheron face and her politician's eyes, she looked as Caligula's horse might have looked after two months as a senator. And her remembered voice fluted in my ear: a fruity Welsh voice, choked with syrup and protest, as if someone had pushed a stewed prune into a clarinet and left it there to deliquesce. "Oh dear, oh dear, oh dear!" I heard her again. I saw her churning toward me on her muscular, brown legs through the mud of the field, her knees like cold poached eggs on rounds of toast below the hem of her gym tunic. "What is this now? Oh dear, dear, dear, dear, dear!" And as I died on the turf of another of my disasters, I had nothing to say, no explanation to offer her. I had just driven the ball through the adversary's net. I was unlovely and unloved; the mud of the field would claim me in the end and Ariane, *Ariane* had seen it all. She was standing to one side, silent, her ochreous face aloof, stern with distaste, as if she had just discovered something putrescent. Through the open-necked shirt she wore for games, I saw a tiny pulse throbbing in the hollow of her collarbone. I could see the round outline of her breasts vibrating through her blouse with the force of her breathing.

Ariane . . . I whispered her name as I turned the scrap of blotter in my fingers. How physical she was, how sure of her body. I longed for contact with her, and I turned on my longing the full force of my turbulent imagination. I imagined us stranded at high tide in a rocky cave in the outer Hebrides as Mendelssohn's overture crashed against the cliff and I calmly found dry matches on a ledge to light the fire that kept us alive. I imagined myself diving like a clean straight blade into boiling surf to drag a half-drowned Ariane, blood streaming from a head wound, up to the surface by the capsized yacht; then swimming with Olympic strength to shore with her sodden body trailing above mine, her flickering life force sustained by the sureness of my arm around her neck. And then visiting her at her home as she recovered: I saw myself, casually but expensively dressed, led by a uniformed maid along baronial passages to the bedroom in the west wing where Ariane lay propped on pillows, wan and quiet, with shining grateful eyes, preparing herself to plead with me for my enduring love.

Visiting her home was an audacious imaginative flight indeed, for Ariane was vastly, mysteriously wealthy. She rarely spoke about her home or her parents, but sometimes a nun, reprimanding her, would speak sorrowfully of "the advantages of someone in your position." The assumption was that she was titled, possibly royal. Her friends at school were the obviously rich girls, the ones who were picked up in chauffeured cars at the convent gates on weekends or at term's end. Their talk was redolent of ease and grace and grandeur, a world where elegant mothers poured tea from heirloom silver in rooms of rosy chintz, long shadows, and slumberous sun. In this world, it seemed to my avid, eaves-dropping understanding, parents loved each other and children were a source of joy.

My father had recently died and my mother, flamboyantly eccentric and buried in past colonial splendor, was quite unable to cope with the penniless harassments of widowhood. Exhausted, I chose my friends from the ranks of the proletarian pupils. I remember them with steadfast love: Stella, a milkman's daughter, who had a face like a Siennese madonna, a marvelous intellect and a sweet, low laugh. Polly, recently arrived in England since the end of the war, her singsong accent proclaiming her upbringing as an army brat in India. And Ernestine, who would mourn aloud if a disaster occurred to her cooking in the domestic science class. Tearing off her white apron and throwing it over her head, she would keen her lamentations with a passion that impressed us all. I always wept for Ernestine's burnt offerings. We were the brainy local girls. If we worked hard and were lucky, we might get to university on a scholarship. If our luck ran out, our brothers would go. Ariane and her aristocratic friends were headed for finishing school in Switzerland.

They all kept horses. I read books about horses, about the care and feeding of horses, about the enormous expenditure of time and money and energy that went into keeping horses, grooming them, showing them, pinning rosettes to them. My closest connection to a horse was through Mr. Hobbs, the greengrocer, who brought his cart to the village on Saturday mornings and sold cabbages, potatoes, leeks, and onions in great earthy handfuls to the ration-book ridden housewives. He drank noisily from the saucer the steaming tea my mother pressed upon him to ensure special service. His horse, to whom I gave secret precious sugar, was of the color I have always thought "dun" to be. A dark, depressed, blinkered beast, it sighed mournfully into its nose bag, sending up great gusts of grain, flicked flies from its calloused knees, and left piles of smoking dung for the victory gardeners to carry genteely away in buckets as night fell. Plainly this was not a horse I could use as a seduction ploy to ingratiate myself into Ariane's circle.

In sewing class at the convent, we were permitted to sit in circles and talk to one another, although not too loudly. I usually arranged to sit almost back-to-back with Ariane, and, acutely aware of the warm drumming telegraph of life from her body so close to mine, I would listen to talk of hunters and jumpers, of bays and sorrels and chestnuts, of mares being serviced and foals being dropped, of tack cleaned and manes braided, stable boys fired (after extensive encouragement) for being "forward," of gymkhanas missed and point-to-points attended. Their language, their lexicon, mesmerized me; I loved to listen.

In the long, dark-paneled room with its vaulted ceiling, the walls were adorned with religious pictures. The sleepy afternoon sunlight would wander from group to group of gossiping girls, occasionally lifting its head to glance approvingly at Our Lady of Lourdes or The Blessed Infant of Prague or the bitter green olive profile of His Holiness, Pope Pius XII. As the feminine air, gamey and soft as an animal's pelt, weighed more and more heavily on my head, my eyelids would droop. The sewing machines whirring and whispering and the muted cadence of the conversations around me hypnotized me and sank me ever deeper into a dreaming lassitude. By turning my head just a fraction, I could see the broad brown field of Ariane's back in its uniform serge, and I would feel a languor creeping up my spine, suffusing my scalp. A sweet green oniony scent of sweat rose from her, like steam. Inhaling it, I could feel my feet flinch and curl around straw stubble on the damp planks of a stable floor, feel my senses rear back in excitement and alarm at the vertical male smells of manure and leather and hot urine. And on my face I could feel the bony ridge of the glowing equine face, the velvet lips nibbling tiny kisses of response on mine as I blew softly into the flaring, mercurial nostrils. And all I wanted in the world was to lie face down on the warm earthy expanse and rock away to a dream world of meadows and daisies and reedy dark ponds . . . a blurred and sun-drenched landscape, misty, aromatic . . . plundered, without warning, by the metal-splintering staccato voice of Miss Reeves, another lay teacher. She taught us sewing.

"Will you *cease* to daydream!" The rapturous air around my ears was shredded by the mechanical twitter. It was as if one of King George's caged clockwork birds had been prodded into demented song. I leaped to consciousness at the sound, leaping again, thirty-five years later, in the privacy of my room, my eyes flying wide in shock and dismay as I recalled the fierce flashing of the twin protuberant agate balls standing sentry on each side of Miss Reeves's long, pink, quivering nose. From the corner of my eye I painfully took in the white column of Ariane's nape, growing longer as she bent her head to giggle with her friends. Then, as I struggled to reenter this reality and apply myself once more to my grim needle, the twitter turned to an attenuated squawk.

"*Look* at the size of these stiches! A great girl like you, making stiches *that* size!" And then the unmistakable sound of my laborious hem being ripped apart caused every head in the room to swivel around . . . the dismantling of half a term's worth of my snail's-pace progress was in full view.

I seemed to be always constructing the same blouse, never progressing beyond the point of dismayed recognition that my efforts were part of a misshapen, unbecoming mistake. Ariane was agile with her needle. She wore an Elizabethan silver thimble. It had been hidden, she said, from a band of looting Roundheads by an ancestral Cavalier. He died defending it, she said, separated from his fanatic Royalist head by a fit of Puritan pique on the part of Cromwell himself. Her thimble bore a minuscule coat of arms. With it she sewed coats and skirts, lined them, turned them. Her fabrics were pepper-and-salt tweeds, muted silks, and slippery supple hopsack. The stuff I struggled with, in what seemed like mortal combat, was, I think, a product of the austerities embraced by the British in the limping aftermath of World War II. The material was horribly named "Moygashel." It was a sort of ersatz linen, limp and recalcitrant, possessed of a parvenu scorn for any kind of stitchery. It was cyclamen pink, pretty enough in the pristine bolt but, once cut and lashed to the vile tissue-paper pattern, depressing and odious. By midterm under my ministrations it would be mercilessly ravaged by blood, sweat, and salt, salt tears.

But the color . . . the color . . . cyclamen . . . I saw the marvelous sunset tint of Ariane's face now with a wash of blue, as though there were some disorder in her vital organs, her heart, perhaps, or her lungs. I remember the web of her hair, rigorously restrained by clips, the long line of her cheekbone carrying the strange violet suffusion toward her ears. And then I remembered the time of year. Of course, late Autumn. The damp chill that lay over the river valley pervaded the corridors and classrooms of the whole school building. Until winter "officially" arrived in December, there was no central heating. Mornings of hoar-frost stenciled the windowpanes, and the nuns wrapped black crocheted shawls around their shoulders and tucked their hands into their mysterious sleeves, "offering up" their discomfort for the Holy Souls in Purgatory. We were urged to do the same, for this was the time of the liturgical year when we made prison visits, so to speak, to the deceased in our lives who were still doing time.

"Help, Lord," we sang lugubriously each morning in choir, "the souls which thou has made / The sou-ouls to thee-ee so dea-ear / In prison for the de-ebt unpaid / Of si-ins commi-itted here." It didn't help. We froze. We were dressed in layers of wool: flannel, Viyella, jersey, and serge. Our legs looked like coffee pots in thick stockings and extra hand-knit anklets. Those of us who suffered from that quintessentially English affliction, chilblains, wore gloves with the fingers cut short so that we could still hold pencils. Several times a day we checked the icy radiators to see whether Mother Superior, in her cozy wisdom, had yet turned on the heat.

Ariane, her vigor and high spirits notwithstanding, seemed to shrink in cold weather. In response, like the invisible prompting that urges a flight of birds to change direction, her flock of friends clustered more tightly around her and fanned the air to keep her warm. I would see her on a dash to class at the center of a rippling, glossy group of bodies, borne along the frigid corridors on the thermal current caused by their dedicated breathing. The bellows of her world blew upon her cold fingers, the passionate fervor of her followers nestled around her chilly shoulders like a cloak. She was so sure she was loved; she believed it to the end.

Even now, so much time and space later, I shivered in the shaded room as the scrap of blotter continued to unleash battalions of ghosts from the wintry, long-ago landscapes of my mind. I heard the unmistakable sound of antique water pipes clanking, gurgling into life. At last, the central heating was turned on, and Sister Raphael, the convent engineer, flitted from classroom to corridor with her spanner, adjusting the radiators. First tepidly, then furiously, for the convent plumbing knew no incremental gradations, the air began to pulsate, and soon we were loosening our uniform neckties, shedding our sweaters and flinging open the windows. The green and white season of Advent was upon us at last. I knew that I should be joyous, and I perplexedly took in the flickering candles, the holly and ivy branches over the doors, the bustle of the big Christmas bazaar, with all its warm scents of nutmeg and ginger and cinnamon and bay, wondering why I felt so alien and detached. Now I remembered the heart-stopping sweetness of young girls' voices embroidering harmonies upon the ancient carols as we practiced for the annual concert in the great assembly hall. The Christmas before Ariane left for Switzerland, from where she never returned, the short-circuit in the light of my world was briefly mended: I was chosen to sing a duet with her. And for the first time in all my ardent days I saw, as I wound the silver thread of the descant around her dark crimson contralto, a look of admiring equality in her deep strange eyes.

"*Deo gratias!*" I sang the words aloud and startled myself. Looking out of the window, I saw the late spring sunset streaking joyously over the hills and trees and houses of my neighborhood. In the distance the bay glimmered like a sheet of hammered steel. I wondered about memories. What are they, really? Does anybody really know? All those electrical impulses and chemical reactions, the crackles and flashes of hidden lightning, tiny H-bomb blasts that devastate and leave in ruin miles and miles of the soul's pathways—all this happening in the brain in total silence amid that strange, slippery tissue, while life sings and danced alongside.

Is there a cellular composition to a memory? Can someone with sufficient skill extract one with forceps from a life history and scrutinize it under a microscope? I wonder if science will ever advance that far. I hope not. For me, memories are times that have been trapped, like bees in amber. They are pieces of the past sleeping in the present, snoring softly behind the closed doors of the mind, curled up in the arms of the soul, their bedfellow. And what thrills me and sends me scurrying down the night roads of my own mind, my hands reaching out to catch the elusive, will o' the wisp illumination, is the moment when the insomniac soul reaches out to nudge, or stroke, or lingeringly kiss a memory into raw, dazed wakefulness.

I turned back to my desk. The room was dark after the golden light of the afternoon, for it had an eastern exposure and flowering bushes pressed up against the windows. The blotter lay on the carpet like a sunset stain. I dropped to my knees and picked it up, smoothing the fuzzy old paper. No wonder, I thought, no wonder I adored her. Ariane. She owned her life in a time and a place that made such an achievement highly unlikely. Her sexuality, potent and intact, had beckoned to me like a gloved hand, and I, an exile in the passionate, political country of early adolescence, had taken heart and responded. I had followed her and walked over this forbidden, ambiguous terrain in her confident shadow. I had survived.

Memory, like prayer and choice, invokes redemption. I picked up the blotter, slipped it back inside the magazine and returned both to the drawer of my desk. I stood up.

"Rest in peace, Ariane," I said softly, "I will love you always. *Deo gratias.*"

Summer Berries

From our summer cabin, high in the Cascade mountains, a dirt path led down a small incline, through wildflowers, fern, and bracken to a rushing torrent, part of the city of Tacoma's water supply.

These mountains were rugged, high, and green, but also endless and remote. There was only one human habitation, other than our own, within a fifteen-mile radius. Nearby a small train station and some decayed, abandoned houses remained where once there had been an elegant hot springs resort. The old hotel had burned down. All that was left of it were some huge, charred timbers and a cave in the steep hillside with hot sulphur water and a natural rock bathtub of sorts. Old gunnysacks were hung over the cave's mouth for privacy and someone had carved crude seats into the stone.

It was World War II. My father felt that in his hidden aerie we three children would be safe from the mysterious enemy. He had buried hundreds of dollars in silver coins. They may be there still.

For three months we were left at the cabin with a hastily procured, disinterested nursemaid, Edith, enough food for an army, and a rattletrap car that wheezily managed the pitted road to the railroad station in case of an emergency. There were no phone or telegraph lines, but the transmountain trains would stop if flagged down.

The little family's only contact with the outside world was the keening whistle of a distant daily train, and our neighbor Milos. I was twelve. For the rest of my life, the sound of a train would instantly replay that summer.

Milos' farmstead was a daunting five mile walk up the road and into the woods from our cabin. An emigrant from Czechoslovakia, he lived a self-contained existence in the wilderness. Like Robinson Crusoe, he was a marvel of inventiveness to my brother, Jake, and me.

He had constructed a wooden waterwheel for electricity and could invent any sort of mechanical gadget. I was enchanted by the wealth of ticking, clicking, whirring homemade artifacts and tools. He raised bees for honey, and goats for milk, meat, and cheese. He grew vegetables and made his own wine from mountain berries. Occasionally, in autumn, he killed a dangerous rogue bear for its fur coat and its large store of useful fat.

Father sometimes invited Milos to the cabin to swap stories and enjoy a beer. He seemed old to me, maybe thirty or forty. I studied this new acquaintance as I listened to his bold tales of adventures with bears and occasional wildmen, of forest fires, and of narrow escapes from avalanche and rockfall. My brain, already full of *Ivanhoe*, *Huckleberry Finn*, and *Treasure Island*, began to picture Milos in my imagination's intimate romantic garb. His triangular face and high cheekbones were those of the brave Trumpeter of Krakow. His muscular short build was obviously perfect in Heidi's rugged mountain world. I decided I liked his faint odor of goat. He called me "Dievca."

Once I noticed him glance at my coltish legs. I knew I was an unrounded stick of a girl, with no lush feminine charms, but his look caused my blood to pound. Although I hadn't enough experience to call it sex, I nursed the pleasure that it gave me. He kindled an unformed, unguessed subterranean cauldron of emotions.

I brooded on "Dievca." Was it Czech for "beloved"? I hoped so. Boredom and the lazy, isolated summer opened an endless panorama of pleasurable daydreams, and a passion for goat cheese.

Returning home from mountain forays with my brother, I managed to stumble onto Milos' farm, even if it meant faking lost directions to hoodwink Jake. The two of us would hide behind bushes or rocks to watch this exotic world. Milos scanned the water-wheel and cared for his goats. He harvested honey, smoking out the bees to get into their hives. Machinery was cleaned, greased and mended. Goat skins and bearskins were stretched and cured. Whenever he disappeared into the wine shed I wondered what strange preparations occurred there. All these small and homely activities I bathed in an aura of high romance and mystery. I was not forbidden to visit the hermit. It hadn't occurred to our guardians that we might go there. But an unspoken taboo, the product of my fervid imagination, held me in check.

When Milos came to visit Father we children were sent out to play. I seldom caught more than a glimpse of him. And then I clothed him in a glory far too dazzling to face. On those rare occasions when I was allowed to remain in the house, I was too suffused with shyness to catch his eye.

Hidden and unnoticed in a sofa corner, I watched him cross his legs. His calves bulging through the canvas trousers, his forearm muscles resting on the dining room table made my father's limbs seem insignificant. Milos caressed his pungent pipe which gave a rich and honeyed woods smell that made my stomach contract with pleasure. I'd never seen arms like his before, covered with short, dark hair. The thick, fuzzy mat fascinated me, and I wondered what it felt like— velvet? fur? I wanted to touch it, to stroke it. I imagined how it would feel against my lips. His adam's apple moved up and down when he talked, and his neck muscles were thick. I wondered if my fingers could reach around them. His features became as familiar to me as my own: his straight forehead, his medium short nose, a little blunt with firmly flared nostrils, his mouth rather large with strong, definite curves. I approved that his ears were small and close to his head, that he was clean-shaven. If he should look in my direction I studied my feet or the sofa cushions.

I liked his odor. His clothes were soiled: beeswax, mulch, machine oil, goat hair, whatever he had been working on. I wanted to finger the slippery gob of beeswax and feel the work-stiffened canvas trousers. When these sensations became more than I could endure, I slipped outdoors.

It was Milos who told us of the hot springs. It must have occasionally been used by whomever had put up the gunnysack curtains, maybe Milos, but we never ran into another living soul. The grotto was warm and steamy and twilit, illuminated only by cracks in the curtain. The crude rock benches were cushioned by feathery algae, which felt like moving satin when my small body sat on them. As I stirred the velvety water, it smelled faintly sulphurous, and its warmth was infinitely soothing to thorn and rock scratches and all the minor abrasions of woodland living. It was as close as we would come to a conventional bath that summer. As I lay back in the hot water, I could dream of delightful confrontations.

For obscure reasons, the others would leave before I was ready. The curtain would slowly draw back, and I, too startled to scream, my heart in my throat, would see a hairy arm and a familiar form gradually outlined in the cave mouth. Momentarily blinded by the dark after the summer sun, he would not notice me until my leg involuntarily moved, and water sent a rippled splash. I would cry out, and he would be overcome with embarrassment. Then a frightened animal sound would escape from me, and he would try to comfort me. Without quite knowing how, we would both be together in the warm, intimate water, me in his arms, he stroking my hair, and gently caressing my face with his fingers. And then . . . well, and then my imagination wobbled. I was vague about what happened "and then," couldn't picture the exact connection between this melting, sticky turbulence in my loins, the irregular pounding of my heart, and the male anatomies of my father and brother. I hung a mental fig leaf over the cave of my mind.

One early August morning, Jake cut himself with an ax. The blood far exceeded the actual damage, but it panicked Edith. She bundled Jake and my little sister into the car. Unable to find me she frantically drove off to civilization. When I came back to the cabin I found nothing but her hurried note tacked to the door. Alone with my daydreams, I drifted into a time of unguarded, untouched freedom. Swinging a peeled willow branch, I skipped and tramped, wandering inevitably toward the focus of my desires. My pace slowed to a dawdle as I neared the house and the goat corral. I heard the spluckasplucka of the waterwheel. A nanny goat baa-ed to her kid. Two young bucks playfully butted barely horned foreheads. A door shut sharply. Should I hide, or should I boldly follow my dreams into Milos' enchanted life? I stood rooted to the spot. He came to the front of the house and shaded his eyes to see what creature was standing in the dappled shade of his dirt track. When he looked at me and smiled, my blood melted to warm honey, and I could not breathe. I saw a radiant god.

He walked toward me, and in a kindly fashion asked what had brought me here. I told him about my brother's accident and said I was alone. He put his calloused hand on my shoulder, and where it touched, my flesh throbbed fire. He asked what exactly had happened. Suddenly I began to cry. He put his arm around me and invited me into the house. There he poured me a cup of warm goat milk. The rich, soothing draught was calming, and I cheerfully munched on a piece of fresh blackberry pie.

I sat on the bearskin covered sofa while he straddled his workbench to mend a leather pack. A feisty bear had ripped it looking for an unearned dinner. He spread the leather out on the work table and forcefully punched holes with an awl, opening passages for the needle and thread. Selecting tough, waxed twine he pushed it through the three-edged needle's eye to repair the damage.

Browned, creased and scarred, his hands were large, the fingers compact and blunt. As I watched him smooth and fold the leather, or firmly force the metal tines, I could feel them on my own neck, on my legs, and then tenderly on my soft and budding nipples. I shivered and jumped.

He filed a blunt hatchet back to life, then pounded a tortured pitchfork into shape and fixed the delicate mechanisms of an ancient cuckoo clock. I admired the way he manipulated his faithful tools and the love he showed the objects that he used.

Finally, his eyes still abstracted in his projects, he said it was time to milk the goats. I trotted after him to the milking shed and stood mesmerized as his experienced fingers followed one another in the rhythmic squeeze that sent jets of milk hissing into a bucket. I felt his grip on the nanny's teats as if it were caressing me. When he asked if I would like to learn, I couldn't look him in the face, but mumbled, "Yes." He enclosed my small hands in his large ones and put them around the teat. Then he slowly closed one finger after the other, and I produced a half-hearted spray. I giggled; the goat chewed a handful of grass with great indifference; and Milos's warm breath prickled the hairs on my back, as he, too, chuckled. When the goats were milked and penned for the day I played with the kids, and tried to make friends with the nannies and even the intimidating billies.

Later, when Milos asked me if I'd care to walk with him to gather berries, I eagerly took his hand. We headed for the river and crossed it on a flimsy, three-rope bridge. From above the turbulent stream seemed threatening and fathoms deep. Milos reassured me. It was absolutely safe if I did exactly as he said. He balanced himself with one hand and used the free one to encourage and steady me. At first I was petrified, but with his coaching proudly gained my confidence.

On the far shore we waded through eye-high fern and underbrush until berry meadows opened out. At first we came upon tart, red huckleberries. As the ground rose, the different varieties became sweeter and smaller. At last we picked the flavorful black blueberries which lay closer to the ground. They were harder to find, but we felt they were worth the extra effort.

As the late sun turned Strawberry Mountain to a giant rose, then flame, we sat upon a sun warmed rock and shared thick homemade bread and berries, drank crystal spring water, then turned wearily back to the river and to Milos's farm.

He wrapped me in a bear skin rug and built a fire. I instantly dropped off to sleep. Did I feel a gentle kiss upon my cheek? It might have been a dream.

I did not wake when Father came to take me home. Next day when I awoke in my own bed, Father asked me kindly what I had done while they were gone. Not knowing quite why I said it, I answered with a sense of vague, confused regret, "Nothing."

The Gladiator

I took off all my clothes and jewelry, wrapped myself in a flannel sheet, and entered the steam-filled room that housed the cement tubs filled with mud. I sat on the edge of the tub, removed my sheet and stretched out on top of the black, steaming, volcanic ash. The attendant scooped and patted the hot mud onto my torso and limbs until I was completely covered and, for all practical purposes, immobilized. I felt the mud clinging tenaciously to my skin. I began to sweat and doze off, my mind reeling back through my life and all the places I had lived. And then I went back into centuries past.

Muted voices in the corridor, greetings and brief conversations in Latin, broke through from time to time. Then four toga-clad hand-maidens tiptoed into the room and lifted me up and laid me on a wood-slatted plank. Each one sprayed the mud gently from my body and rolled me over and sprayed off the rest. Eight hands then briskly dried me off. I was only vaguely aware of the nearby splashing sounds of the baths, the lilting refrain from the lyre, and the breezes wafting through the olive trees.

The handmaidens left and a masseuse entered. She poured a generous amount of warm oil into her cupped hand and slowly began to move her hands along my back. For quite some time my back was the object of her attention as her hands traveled up and down my spine slippery and warm, then reached my neck and scalp. My limp arms were gently lifted one at a time, and stroked down their full length, then lifted and danced about through the air in a graceful, rhythmical ballet. When one arm was carefully replaced by my side, the other was brought into velvety motion. The masseuse never took her hands off me completely—there was constant contact even when she replenished the warm oil. Each finger was lovingly stroked and pulled. And then her attention moved down my body to my legs and my feet.

As she turned me onto my back, I heard the sound of a chariot arriving outside the baths. The horses whinnied as the wheels ground to a halt. I smiled a secret smile, knowing that I had been chosen and was being prepared for the champion of all the gladiators. I heard the clanking and pounding of his leap from the chariot to the ground, followed by the sound of his impatient footsteps pacing outside my door. I smiled again. He would have to wait until my massage was completed.

The masseuse stroked and gently pulled on my hair, then carefully lifted my heavy head and turned it from side to side. She worked out the creases and lines in my forehead and around my eyes and mouth. She moved down around my shoulders and breasts and encircled my waist. As she stroked down one leg and then the other, the four maidens returned and I knew the time was near.

Two maidens knelt on either side of my massage table and began gently circling my breasts—closer and closer to the nipples—licking round and round and finally sucking gently on my nipples. I squirmed in sudden ecstasy and anticipation. One maiden tenderly tipped my chin up and probed my lips and tongue with hers as another slid my legs up on the table.

Just then I felt a burst of heat and dust as the gladiator entered the quiet, darkened room. I kept my eyes closed so as not to break the trance I was in. I knew he was watching as the fourth maiden slipped her oily fingers inside me, moistening and readying my interior chambers. I writhed on the table with all four maidens attending me and the gladiator watching and waiting. Just imagining how arousing the sight was to him thrilled me as much as the sensation of having mouths and hands all over my body.

I opened my eyes now and saw the shimmering flesh of a Roman god watching with his own obvious excitement as he prepared for his pleasure. The maidens, sensing our readiness, slid their hands under my buttocks, lifting my pelvis and allowing my knees to fall open. The gladiator strode forward and loosed a mighty roar of triumph as his rigid phallus pierced me. I shuddered and hurtled over my own brink as soon as he entered me.

I closed my eyes, and when I opened them a moment later, he was gone. I blinked and looked around my lonely, sterile cubicle. There I lay, wrapped in my flannel sheet, not moving for quite some time. Then, as though in a trance, I strayed out the door clutching my "toga" to my oily body. The drone of an airplane and two kids fighting over a can of Pepsi brought me back to the here and now.

The Two Wedding Nights of Euphemia Gray

These are the secret journals of John Ruskin, John Everett Millais, and the woman they married, Effie Gray, as revealed only in the erotic imagination of Sabina Sedgewick. Readers who would like to determine the facts behind my fiction will enjoy an accurate account by Phyllis Rose, in Parallel Lives: Five Victorian Marriages *(New York: Vintage Books, 1984).*

Effie Ruskin's Journal

Scotland, April 1848

For two weeks now I have been John Ruskin's wife. I am afraid there are a great many things I don't know, especially in regard to the physical nature of the relationship between husband and wife.

As the oldest daughter I am of course aware of certain facts connected with my mother's pregnancies, but only as far as the female body is concerned. Very little is known to me about the male participation in human conception. Surely it is different from that of a stallion or a rooster, but in what way? I shall burn these pages as soon as I have finished this train of thought, but I must write this down to unburden myself of doubts and confusion. How I wish that I could write to my dear mother about all this or talk to an older sister. But I have no one. My mother must have had her reasons for keeping silent on this subject.

I admit that I was terrified when John approached my bed that first night. He had given me ample time by myself to get ready for bed, and I was truly tired from the events of the day and the long ride in the carriage; it was past ten o'clock at night when we arrived at the inn. I had dozed off but was too nervous to fall asleep; nonetheless, I kept my eyes closed when I heard him enter. I did not see, therefore, whether John was fully clothed or in his dressing gown. For a long time he stood by the bed looking at me. Then I heard the rustle of paper and guessed that he was about to make a sketch of me. As with his notebook, his sketchbook is always near, and he has tried to draw my face many times without success.

Relieved, I was about to recognize his presence with a welcoming smile when I felt his hand on my chemise, loosening the ribbon which fastened it around my neck and pushing the sleeves far enough down to expose my shoulders. Now I was glad that my eyes were closed, permitting me to turn my head into the pillow to conceal my blushing cheeks. After some hesitation, his hands moved down toward my breasts, resting there upon the ample cambric folds of the gown. Suddenly my heart began to pound, my chest to heave as if I had been running—surely he would notice. He had never made the slightest improper advance to me before. I found the new sensation more pleasant than repugnant. After all, he was my lawful husband and these were his hands—so sweet, so gentle, so fine. They could never hurt me. Echoing my trembling heart, they clutched my breasts, which rose to meet his intimate touch. But then my chemise slipped off further, exposing my upper body to his full view. Modesty now compelled me to reach for the bedcovers, but I did not move. A kind of languid passivity had invaded my limbs, conjured up by what my mother had whispered when she kissed me good-bye: "Let him have his way, Effie."

I acquiesced, therefore, when he proceeded to remove the entire length of my protective garment, exhibiting my most private parts to his probing eyes. Shivering slightly from the cold night air on my naked flesh—or was it from a mixture of curiosity and trepidation over what must follow?—I longed for his embrace. I was about to clasp my arms around his neck when I heard him gasp as if in great pain and felt him draw away. When I opened my eyes to see what had caused him such discomfort, he was hurrying off—still fully clothed—toward the dressing room. There he remained for a long, long time. I am aware that it was my duty to inquire after him, but I shyly refrained from showing my solicitude.

When I awoke the next morning, John was sitting by the window, writing. He came over and kissed me, leaning his head tenderly against my shoulder. Every night during our honeymoon he has shared the same room and the same bed, but his endearments have never gone further. I thought at first that this behavior was perhaps the normal progress of all marital intercourse between God-fearing and self-respecting couples, until my husband explained at length why he had abstained from making me his wife. Although I am still not sure what he intended (and the subject is too delicate to permit me to ask for further elucidation), it is clear to me that more physical contact is required between husband and wife if offspring are to be produced.

Offspring. That is what John wishes to avoid. Over the past two weeks he has talked to me at length about our marriage, and I am beginning to understand that he desires more that I be his traveling companion and note-taker than his wife. It would seem that our affection is to resemble that of a brother and sister until I have reached the age of twenty-five. At nineteen I am too young and delicate to become a mother, and, as he intends to spend a great deal of time traveling abroad with me, a child—or rather a flock of children, if I follow my mother's example—would indeed create a great impediment to his plans. Although I first objected to his reasoning, reminding him that God had intended husband and wife to be fruitful, John convinced me that our spiritual union must grow stronger before we can take on the responsibilities of parenthood. Chastity within marriage is as great a virtue as before marriage, perhaps greater, because it strengthens those ties which are most worthy in human love, says John. Sensuality in marriage, as in art, debases the higher forms of human intercourse. The fact that the Virgin Mary had set an example for all of us of future womanhood should be sufficient proof of God's blessing upon our marital virginity, according to John.

How can I object to such an argument? But why, if this is, indeed, in accordance with God's higher moral order, must I confide in no one about our agreement? On the other hand, I do look forward to a few years of unencumbered travel as well as to an active social life in London, for I have so much to learn about art and literature and history. John has become my private tutor. In return, I shall be able to help him by reading through many texts, which could be useful to him in writing the second volume of *The Stones of Venice*. We are so happy together. He thinks we are a model couple, and I cannot see that we shall ever quarrel together.

It is John's idea that I keep a daily journal, as he does. Then, at the end of every day we shall sit down together and merge our thoughts and impressions into one account of our life together. For it is his desire and mine that no secret must ever come between us. Gradually, as we grow to know each other intimately, we will sense the concerns of the other without having to utter a single word.

John Everett Millais's Journal

London, March 1853

For two days I have thought and dreamed and painted Mrs. Ruskin's face. Now that she is gone, I am far from satisfied with the result. When I asked her to sit for me, I merely wished to find a model for the Scotswoman in my painting, which otherwise had been completed. Being a native of Scotland, she kindly consented, as did her husband, who has taken a great interest in my art. Today was our last session, and I asked her what she thought of the portrait. She appeared much moved by what she saw: the young mother, babe in arm, who is handing a note of release to the jailer bringing freedom to her husband, a Scottish soldier whose head is buried upon her shoulder, his arm extended around her back.

"I thought this was to be a happy scene," said Mrs. Ruskin after a long pause. "If I were the woman in your picture, I should be radiant with happiness."

I replied, "I wanted to render your beauty and your strength when I asked you to sit for me, but as much as I tried, I could not suppress your sorrow." Whereupon she turned abruptly toward the door. I could see that she was again close to tears. "I envy this simple Scotswoman, for she has everything that I shall never have." I remarked lightly that she would soon have a child of her own, but she shook her head as if I had suggested the impossible.

Bewildered, I watched her departure without trying to hold her back. Then I returned once more to the easel and dipped my brush into the glistening ruby on the palette. Over and over I stroked the swelling softness of her lips, defining the corners of her generous mouth. I did not rest until I felt the warmth of her breath upon the temple of the man whose face was nestled against her chin.

Effie Ruskin's Journal

London, March 1853

It is over. These last few days I have been sitting for Millais from immediately after breakfast until dinner time—throughout the afternoon until dark. Two days only, but they changed my life. Pray God it is for the better. The significance of Millais's picture did not really strike me until I saw my face in it today. The young painter has been a protégé of John's—he belongs to the Pre-Raphaelite Brotherhood, which has so impressed him with their artistic truthfulness.

I must confess that I have been exceedingly depressed since our return from Venice eight months ago. The change from the gay society and warm climate of Venice to the cold weather here and the return to the elder Mr. Ruskin's scolding criticism have affected me deeply. But John's behavior toward me and the memory of the scene that provoked it is almost too much to bear. Outwardly I keep up the necessary appearances—I have become an accomplished hostess, having attended a great many entertainments in France and Italy—but deep inside I am torn apart with grief.

When Millais invited me to have a look at the finished portrait, I could not hold back my tears. What he had painted—a mother flanked by her loving husband on one side and her darling child on the other, this simple and common happiness—can never come to pass for me. Nobody, not even my parents and closest friends, knows that I am still a spinster and shall never enjoy the blessings of motherhood. For John has rescinded his promise to consummate our marriage; in his judgment—the most cruel and brutal a husband could ever pass upon a wife—I am unfit for motherhood.

What wrong have I done? Why did he leave me so long after our first year together? He accuses me of petulance toward his mother. Yet, what husband leaves his new wife to travel abroad with his parents for five months? Our friends at home thought I had returned to live permanently with my parents, yet I went merely to recover my strength. The famous Dr. Simpson found nothing wrong with me that a babe of my own would not cure. It is he who suggested that a wife can behave in such a way as to inflame sexual desire in her husband. Thinking that my feigned sleep on our wedding night had stifled John's shy approach, I gathered my courage to follow the doctor's advice (and I shudder to write such words even in my secret journal) that I allow my fingers to travel toward those masculine parts considered sensitive to the female touch. "Most wives would rather reach into an open fire than to acquaint themselves with the male anatomy," the good doctor had said. "But then unlike you, most wives wish to curb the sexual appetite of their husbands in order to avoid another pregnancy." "Must I then act like a harlot?" I had cried dismayed. But he replied that I was merely doing my duty because my husband was neglectful of his.

John's reaction, however, was the opposite of what the doctor had predicted. When he drew close to me in bed one night, I unbuttoned the front of my nightdress; then, since he seemed reluctant to follow this invitation, I reached out toward his private parts, hoping to elicit a favorable response. John recoiled as if in horror. The next day he disclosed that he had been disgusted with my body when he first laid eyes on it on our wedding night. He claimed that it would be sinful for us to enter into a carnal connection, for, if I was not very wicked, so he said, then I was at least insane and quite unfit to bear and bring up children.

How can I ever recover from this blow? How can I ever mention my plight to anybody without confessing my shame? I pray to God every day to help me find a way out of my troubled state. Yet deep inside me I feel that I did no wrong. I refuse to accept a monetary settlement from John, as he has offered if I agree to a legal separation. For then my life would be ruined. I should have to live in seclusion in my parents' home—even worse off than a spinster, for a rejected wife is nothing.

Although I never spoke to him about my sorrow, Millais has painted its traces in my portrait. But he has also endowed my sadness with hope and love. It is his own spirit he has thus revealed through my face, never realizing that his model felt nothing but despair and bitterness. He is so young and handsome and at the threshold of great success; yet he is kind and sincere, humorous and lighthearted. John has taken a strong interest in Millais and speaks about inviting him to come with us this summer to Glenfinlas in the Highlands. I can no longer predict what John's intentions are. I know his parents are pressing him to divorce me. Is he trying to provoke a scandal, using Millais as his evidence? I must be careful. I can no longer go out into society alone.

Effie Ruskin's Journal

Glenfinlas, Scotland, August 1853

Today I cut his hair. Millais has been with us since May. His boyish charms have captured my maternal heart. John lectures him on art, on architecture, and on women. "The true wife is enduringly, incorruptibly good," says John, fixing his glance in my direction. "She is instinctively wise, not for self-development, but for self-denunciation, not that she may set herself above her husband, but that she may never fall from his side." John's hair is wispy, Millais's is thick and bushy. I had to cut a great deal of it, smoothing each curl between my fingers to measure the exact length. He is impatient. To prevent him from moving his head so much, I clasped it in both my hands, and then found I had to stay the impulse to kiss his crown. All the while I kept thinking about his painting, "The Order of Release," wishing that *I* were that woman who bears my features and that *he* were that Scotsman nestling his head against my cheek.

John Ruskin's Journal

Glenfinlas, August 1853

I must warn Millais about Effie. Her corrupting influence has made such an impact on his emotions that he is neglectful of his great artistic talent. Instead of progressing with my portrait, he is absorbed in making sketches of my wife in the most trivial situations. Today he made a sketch of her cutting his hair, and yesterday he drew her sitting by the river with her sewing. I do not think that he means to deceive me. He is too pure a soul and too great a friend. He cannot understand why I leave her alone so much, as if a husband had an obligation to furnish his wife with continuous entertainment. No doubt she has complained to him, and his tender heart has been touched. How can I make him see the truth without playing the role of a jealous husband? All he sees is her unhappiness, without understanding the reason behind her unstable character. Was I not deceived myself five years ago when I married what I believed to be a pure and innocent girl?

I shall never be able to blot out from my mind the painful memory of our wedding night. When I entered our bedchamber, I fully intended to make her my wife. Finding her asleep after our long journey, I did not wish to subject her to further strain and, indeed, was happy to observe her quietly by myself. In her long, white chemise, her hair flowing softly down her shoulders, she appeared to me as the living image of a sixteenth-century Madonna. My eyes—expert at distinguishing harmony and spirituality in man's artistic manifestations—now marveled at God's design in creating the subtle beauty of my bride. Indeed, the sensation of entering her bedchamber freely as her lawful husband was not unlike the exquisite pleasure I experience each time I bring home a new painting.

Compelled by a sudden urge to sketch her virginal form, I had approached her, the lighted candelabrum in my hand augmenting the glow of the fire. I had drawn her features before, but now I wanted to capture her angelic body on the nuptial bed without disturbing her sleep. It was my intention to surprise her with the sketch in the morning. My hands trembled slightly, and I noticed a marked shortness of breath, which I attributed to the rise in altitude from Perth, where the wedding took place, and our current abode in the Scottish Highlands. To expose her pearl-white skin more favorably to the light, I pulled the lace-trimmed sleeves from her shoulders. Then, as if driven by a demonic force of their own, my hands moved further down toward her swelling front even as my mind conjured up a different painting. With her golden tresses cast loose over the pillow and her figure thrown into relief against the green velvet bedcurtains, the resemblance to Titian's Venus was overwhelming.

The thought of sketching the figure nude brought a great rush of blood surging through my veins. Awkwardly, I fingered the voluminous folds of her garment, and, then, almost by accident, I made contact with the warm surface of her skin. Her breasts, two quivering hillocks, slipped beneath my palms. How much larger they seemed than when I had clasped her slender frame in my arms. When tightly laced and covered by yards of fabric and flounces, her feminine shape had never revealed itself in such abundant proportions. But freed from stays, if not yet from the last vestiges of clothing, her breasts weighed heavily in my hands. I should have resisted the impulse to see her naked, but, still compelled by artistic curiosity, I drew her chemise all the way down to her knees. What I discovered is but a hideous mockery of Venus. The unsightly dark nipples hardly mattered to me compared with the ultimate blasphemy her form gave to Titian's masterpiece. Across her lower parts where the artist has excelled in rendering flesh tones in luminous shades of cream, my wife exhibited a disgusting fleece of black hair.

How well I understand now the meaning of Adam's weakness with Eve! As if God wished to punish me for this impudence, my own body began to burn with carnal passion. Like a satyr, I desired only to mount this poor creature. On the verge of committing an act of pagan debauchery, I fled to the dressing room where I tore off my trousers. Horrified, I sponged my hideously extended member with cold water. Only once before had I thus been confronted with depravity when, at a late-night supper among fellow students, pictures of harlots in lewd positions were passed from hand to hand. After having publicly repudiated the evil effects of sensuality and venery, it seemed infinitely worse to succumb to my own base desires. I spent the rest of the night in turmoil over the chasm which had suddenly opened before me. My remorse over having polluted our marriage with lust mingled with my disgust over my wife's repulsive physicality. Had she hoped to keep her disfigurement a secret? Could it be that painters have concealed from us a woman's natural imperfections?

I hoped that in the course of our marriage our love would grow strong enough to overcome my repugnance toward the animal aspects of sexual intercourse. But I was not fully aware of the mental disorder which had afflicted Effie's character even prior to our marriage. I attributed to girlish immaturity her changing moods from exuberant merriment to morbid sadness. But her increasing petulance toward my mother, who should have been her model for successful wifehood, her willful and disrespectful behavior toward my father, and her incessant need for social entertainment soon dashed my expectations of her reform. Although her physical health improved in the indulgent climate of Italy, her moral character deteriorated in the libidinous society of that country to the point of lewdness. Extravagant fashions, late-night dinners and dances, spicy foods, and salacious gossip all attracted her far more than serious study and reflective meditation.

Only a madwoman could have behaved so lasciviously toward her own husband. Instead of shrinking from carnality, she had sunk to the lowest level of a common harlot. Clearly she no longer loved me as a wife—her open disobedience and neglect of my needs contradict the term. For this reason, and owing to her mental imbalance, she is quite unfit for motherhood. In spite of my bitter disappointment, I am willing to go on living with the poor girl, but I shall not stand by to see her bring ruin to young Millais.

John Everett Millais's Journal

Glenfinlas, September 1853

I am sure many allowances should be made for him, but he is certainly mad or has a slate loose. Ruskin is an undeniable giant as an author, and I have much to thank him for, but his inquisitorial practice of noting down everything which could forward an excuse for complaining against his own wife is the most unmanly and ignoble proceeding I have ever heard of. I will not believe that he desires her to fall—I cannot imagine a man of education to be such a devil—neither do I think there was any evil intention in his asking me to accompany him to the Highlands, but I can see that he is more than indifferent to her. To watch daily his brutal want of generosity to her is more than I can bear. Yet how can I leave her?

Ruskin insists on having his portrait painted, but I cannot bring myself to look at his face. Today he talked to me about his strange and lonely boyhood. Although the center of attention for his doting parents, he was not allowed to play with toys. When his aunt presented him with a pair of Punch-and-Judy puppets for his birthday, his mother took them away. Perhaps his upbringing has something to do with his sickening treatment of his wife.

I am doing everything I can to cheer her up—she is making a valiant effort to keep up her spirits. In my dreams I fancy myself as her knight-errant, rescuing her on my white stallion, but we are ruled by Queen Victoria, not King Arthur. All I can accomplish is to carry the picnic hamper for her.

Effie Ruskin's Journal

Glenfinlas, September 1853

I am wicked. Today I watched him swimming. It was an accident, but I did not walk away when I glimpsed his naked figure perched above the churning stream. Spellbound by his manly beauty, I watched him from my hiding place behind the bushes as he dived into the water and climbed up again on the precipitous cliff. Balancing, poising himself on his toes, he plunged down again into the rocky pool. I quite forgot who he was. Without trousers and topcoat, without even a shirt, he looked like a pagan god, so fair, so tall, so strong and vigorous and natural; he resembled no earthly human I have known. For the briefest moment, I envisioned myself by his side—without petticoats, without corset and crinoline—a naked wood nymph gliding next to him toward the mossy bank. I know it was a mortal sin. It has been raining every day as if God intended to remind me that this is Scotland, not ancient Greece. Millais knows my story now. He deeply pities me. I think he loves me, but it is hopeless. I make sure that we are never alone together. Soon we must depart to London, and I shall never see him again.

John Everett Millais's Journal

Glenfinlas, October 1853

She is gone. For months I endured the sweet agony of furtive glances across the room, of accidental touchings during her sketching lessons and when she cut my hair. I am left alone now under the grim, October sky where every house and every hill reminds me of her presence. I can still feel her gentle fingers once more upon my crown, I guide her steps again across a rocky path; I hear her laughter and dry her tears.

To think that she is still a virgin and yet a wife—tied forever to a heartless, unworthy wretch who calls himself my friend and benefactor. Ruskin was so pleased with my design for the gothic window of the local church. He will use it in his lecture, never realizing that the angels I have drawn bear Effie's face: six pairs of angels, each arched toward the other with folded wings, their bodies far apart, their lips joined together in an everlasting kiss.

Effie Ruskin's Journal

Perth, Scotland, July 3, 1855

Today I am to be married to John Everett Millais. Who would have thought it possible that God would finally bring us together as man and wife? My wedding gown of Venetian lace is spread out over my girlhood bed, where for the past year I have spent many a sleepless night praying and worrying about my future. I wish that slipping on my new life as Mrs. Millais were as simple as slipping on this gown and that I could forget that seven years ago I took John Ruskin's name as my own in this very same house. The fact that according to English law I never was John Ruskin's wife does not erase his pernicious influence over my present life. What if history should repeat itself? Did we not love each other when we took our marriage vow? Did he not call me guardian angel, dearest love? Yesterday I broke down and cried when Everett addressed me thus, and he too could not hold back his tears when he learned the cause. "I don't know if I have the ability to blot out the ruin in your first life," he replied.

I have burdened him with my ordeal. He is so young, so good, so impulsive. Although I have many worthy friends who wish me well, there are others who have taken Ruskin's side that I am to blame, that I am insane, or who believe as does Carlyle that a wife has no right to leave her husband for any cause. I can never return to London where my name is connected with scandal. The queen has indicated that she will refuse to receive me as Mrs. Millais, because in her eyes I live in adultery. What will such accusations do to Everett's reputation, to his career? He is visibly nervous about this fateful step. He speaks in such forgiving terms about poor John Ruskin that I believe he may fear secretly that his reaction toward me may be similar. And what if something is really wrong with me, something that a doctor might not detect? For Everett is as ignorant about women as Ruskin. As for myself—I shudder when I must remember my trial and the doctors who testified on my behalf—will I be able to forget those things? I am a virgin, but I am no longer ignorant of what must happen between husband and wife. I cannot say that my greater experience has given me any more confidence. On the contrary, I am thinking of my forthcoming wedding night only with greatest trepidation.

The next evening

This is the last entry in my secret journal. I almost wish that I could keep this last account for my daughter, so that she need not suffer from the fear of the unknown on her passage from maidenhood to womanhood. But who is to tell if she will be as happy in her choice as I was when I joined my fate with her father's. Divine providence has endowed the male sex with that greater, natural force that empowers him to guide our delicate vessel. God grant that she may find as skillful a pilot as her father.

I must confess that all appearances seemed to point to the contrary when my dear new husband collapsed in tears on the seat of our railway compartment. The strain of these past months evidently proved too much for him, and all the way to Glasgow I held his head in my arms and sprinkled his temples with cologne until he smiled his old, boyish smile, remembering as I did how he had painted me. Still we both could not really believe that we had found our release. Ruskin's ghost seemed to have followed us all the way from my old home onto the train and to the doorsteps of our inn. From the solicitous expression on the face of the landlady I gathered that we looked like a most despondent couple, and she quickly sent up tea and a hot-water bottle for the bride, as well as a glass of whiskey for the groom. This made us both laugh, and soon we were dancing together around the room with Everett singing and my cheeks burning every time our eyes met. How well I remembered his hungry eyes in times past when I could respond with nothing but remorse. Now when he finally drew me into his arms to kiss me on the lips for the first time, I clung to him with such ardor that I took him by surprise. For a moment I feared that he might be offended by my wanton behavior, but I soon discovered that he was quite pleased. And he asked me teasingly whether I would like to rest a while by myself. When I shook my head, he kissed me again until my head swooned and my legs were too weak to support me. I begged to sit down, and he led me toward the bed where he began to pull the pins from my artfully coiffed hair until my tresses tumbled down over my shoulders. Then he knelt down in front of me to pull my boots from my trembling feet. With the same unhurried but determined manner he unfastened the silk stockings from my garters and rolled them down over my knees and ankles, which he covered with kisses.

"Do you know how long I have glanced at your ankles wishing I could hold them in my hands and press my lips on your dainty soles like this? You could drive me to distraction when you climbed ahead of me over the rocks of Glenfinlas, and now you have to make amends for all the agony you have caused me."

Although I no longer commanded the power of coherent speech, he guessed my consent, allowing his hands to travel the full length of my legs. When I realized that he meant to undress me further, to give his exploration full rein, I grew anxious that he might come upon some blemish about my person—even then I could not totally forget what had been said about my first wedding night, and even at this late hour the sky was still bright on this midsummer night. Sensing my apprehension, Everett delighted me with his teasing, commenting on the ingenious construction of my undergarments, each designed for a constricting purpose in opposition to the laws of nature. And as soon as he had removed the most complicated pieces—my tightly hooked and buttoned traveling costume and my even more tightly laced corset—he exclaimed that surely there was no greater beauty in the entire world than Mrs. John Everett Millais and what a pity that her body could only be seen at this private exhibition in this humble Scottish bedchamber instead of at the Royal Academy! I was convulsed with laughter. Everett, who reached the same state of nakedness with far greater speed and swiftness, joined me in bed as if nothing could be more natural. I suddenly remembered that I had seen him naked once before, albeit far in the distance and not in what I now saw was a man's exceedingly enamoured state. Although I was a little frightened by this unexpected spectacle, I took great delight in his manly body, feeling quite comforted by his solemn words: "With my body I thee worship. Will you, dearest Effie, take me as your beloved husband?" I can't recall what I replied, for I was almost unconscious with joy that this beautiful man was mine to love and behold. I never took my eyes from him for fear that I might be dreaming.

When I felt his lithe and strong-muscled torso between my legs, I was at first startled by the force of his weight and perhaps a little timorous about his entering my narrow passage. But he did not immediately follow the path of passion—as if he wished to give me leave to get ready, he allowed only his lips to brush lightly over my eyes and cheeks. Then as I returned his endearments, tasting the salty spots left by his tears, his mouth met more insistently with mine, which opened fully to admit his probing tongue. Then he covered my love-parched breasts with long, wet kisses until I floated toward him on a cloud of voluptuous desire that impelled me to guide his manhood where it so eagerly wanted to go.

"I knew there was passion in you, lassie, when I painted your lips," said Everett later, when his arms folded around me in the final wave of his release. Then he slept soundly with his head buried under my cheek while I tried to stay awake, unwilling to relinquish the new taste of complete contentment.

Epilogue

Effie and Everett lived happily ever after for forty-one years and had eight children. One of them wrote the following footnote in a two-volume biography of Sir John Everett Millais.

Miss Gray had been previously married, but that marriage had been annulled in 1854, on grounds sanctioned equally by church and state. Both good taste and feeling seem to require that no detailed reference should be made to the circumstances attending that annulment. But, on behalf of those who loved their mother well, it may surely be said that during the course of the judicial proceedings instituted by her, and throughout the period of the void marriage and the whole of her after-years, not one word could be, or ever was, uttered impugning the correctness and purity of her life.

Millais was knighted by the queen, who in 1896 granted the dying artist his wish and, in the last month of his life, received Lady Millais as his lawful wife.

Minnehaha Soup

As interpreted by Bernadette, who acknowledges her indebtedness to Dell in St. Louis and to Henry Wadsworth Longfellow in his heaven.

In your cupped hand take the granules,
Slim and dark, the wild rice granules,
Culled from a canoe at sunrise
On the shining big sea water
by the braves of Minnesota.

Simmer in two draughts of water
'Til the grains are full and bursting,
And the water all departed;
Set aside, and take an onion,
Pungent, weeping, layered onion,
Yellow as the moon that trembles
All night long, 'til dawn, in yearning;
Now remove the outer blankets
Of the smooth and swelling onion,
Peel it to its very heartland
Where you find its moist interior.

Slice it, dice it, render fragrant
All its stinging, tearful power;
Add to it one nut of butter
Melted down to creamy cascades,
Melted in a copper skillet.
Mushrooms fresh or chopped to pieces

From a preservation basket
Join the onion in the skillet.

Breathe in now the mixed aromas:
Dark and limpid, bubbling juices;
Onion and the swarthy mushrooms
(Like a dream of love, the mushrooms)
Lustful and voluptuous mingling,
Scents of earth and swollen branches
After rain in steep pine forest;
Pliable and clear the onions,
Soft and yielding to the mushrooms;
Pale the pigment, tender, limpid
Vegetables gently simmered
To the point of consummation,
As the south wind softly sighing
Waits upon the joyful flinging
Of the flour into the skillet.

Slowly add the flour in handfuls
White and soft as powdered feathers
Of the snow goose, guide to wanderers;
Stir and knead among the mushrooms,
Nudge and tease among the onions,
Let the butter-chuckling juices
Undulate among the veggies
And the flour, 'til all is concord
And the roux the proof of joining.

Broth from chicken bones you simmered
In a deep and copious kettle,
Add in drops upon the contents
Of your smoking, odorous skillet;
Moisten well the roux of veggies
With the humid, steaming soup stock,
Then transfer, in careful measures,
Glistening roux to panting kettle
Full to brim with broth and bubbles,
Agitate with spoon of willow,
Spoon of birch or spoon of alder,

Agitate and stir the kettle
'Til the union is completed
And the liquid thick and creamy.

Now stir in the wild rice granules
That began this whole endeavor,
Season well with salt and pepper;
Cream is needed, luscious spurting
From its bowl into the kettle,
Stir together all this bounty
'Til the act is consummated
And the wild rice soup is ready.

Now to serve. Before you do so,
Add the flash of lightening water,
Redolent, melodious sherry
Or white wine, like rippling shadows
On the shores of Gitchee Gumee.
Add this sweetness to the kettle.

Onaway! Awake, beloved!
Soup is ready—are you coming?
Hail, the noble wild rice granules!
Hail robust, engorgéd onion!
Hail the mushrooms, seethed in butter!
Hail the flour, the dusky sherry!
Hail the soup! My song is ended.

ERODYSSEY

ERODYSSEY

*O*ur *"erodyssey" started more than ten years ago when founding-mother Sabina first asked herself: "Are women turned on by what they read?" A few curious, bold spirits joined her quest, gathering under the banner of "the Kensington Ladies' Erotica Society." No more than a lighthearted reading and eating group, we could never have guessed how far we would dare to go. Now, ten editions and several promotional tours later, we have crisscrossed the continent from Seattle to Boston, thinly disguised by masks and pseudonyms. We have been swept away in limousines, been welcomed at unfamiliar airports, and heard our assumed names called out "to the white courtesy telephone please!"*

Our momentary fling with fame did not swell our heads, but it did stuff them with questions from talk-show hosts. Were we frustrated writers or just frustrated? Were we cuckolding our husbands in fantasy? What about our children? Were we publicity-hungry housewives or, worse, were we pornographers masquerading as supermoms? At the same time we were constantly pressured to be outrageous and titillating, to fire off quickies on the spot, and, in short, to make the program "hot" without getting the station manager fired. Given that prime time TV each day serves up sex and violence as though it were peanut butter and jelly, we didn't expect our gentle, homespun, bookbound erotica to hold shock value at all. Yet before many shows we were cautioned not to use such words as t-h-i-g-h and b-r-e-a-s-t. Paradoxically, p-e-n-i-s was always acceptable, whereas v-a-g-i-n-a was not. While some talk show hosts seemed to think they were taking a risk in having us on the show, we saw conspiratorial smiles all around and knew we had started something. We couldn't wait to get back home and pick up where we had left off. Our typewriters and computers were humming. . .

Now more than ever we view our lives as erotic journeys. To give you a sense of the roller coaster thrills along the way, we offer these jottings from our personal scrapbooks and hope you will keep them as souvenirs.

The adage "love thyself" has been foremost in my mind over the last ten years of this erotic exploration. During evenings with the Kensington Ladies, I learned to appreciate the depth of my own feelings and to look at myself as a multilayered, even valiant, character.

I have an unwritten story yet to unfold about a "transformation place" where women learn to view themselves with reverence for the person and body they already are. In a way, the creative experience I have had as a member of this group has given me such a transformation place.

One of my many gifts from the group is a love letter written to me by one of the Ladies as part of a game on one of our retreats: to write loving words to ourselves and to each other. I offer it here. My stories celebrate love with sex. This letter celebrates love.

Beautiful, bountiful one,

I just want you to know how happy it makes me that you inhabit this planet and walk upon it in close proximity to me. As long as I have known you, you have been my touchstone for sanity. Your joy, your compassion, your elegance, your dedication to your own truth, your uncompromising commitment to making every moment count, in short, your marvelous life force has been the warm grasp of reassurance for my own shaky paws on countless occasions. I salute you and bless and praise the slender strength that bears your name. I love you and open my heart to you in the calm trust of one who knows she is accepted, warts and all, as another manifestation of the miracle of consciousness.

May your eyes always reflect the glow of your spirit and the winged creatures sing forever from your great heart. You renew my faith in human goodness. Your laughter gladdens all the world. When I'm with you, I feel all miracles are possible. You honor me by expecting magnificence from me. Please stay a long time in the world. It needs you as indeed do I.

Alice and the Phallus
in the Palace

My name is not Alice, but then it's not Susan either. What follows, however, is the pure and unadulterated truth.

I arrived in Germany full of our book, our bold, precarious adventures in the realm of erotica, and our gorgeously tinted dreams. The trip was a heedless, splurging lark, financed by my ill-got gains from *Ladies' Own Erotica*.

My son, Eric, left Heidelberg University early; meeting me at the airport to drive me to his favorite student eatery for a *Schweinebraten mit Knödel, gemütlichen* evening with his friends. Next morning, full of jet lag and a rich-food-and-wheat-beer hangover, I set out to explore this quaint Old World by visiting its castle ruin, the Schloss. It is an enormous chunk of hunkering rock that elaborately and ferociously dominates the wooded cliff, the medieval university town, and the River Neckar beneath it. Reeking picturesque, it is a major tourist attraction.

After crossing Heidelberg's stone bridge, I wandered through the cobbled streets and found a path leading upward to the fortress. The escarpment and countless steps had even sturdy teenagers huffing and puffing before they reached the top. As the castle loomed through the trees, its gigantic crumbling collection of stone halls, dungeons, porticos and walls was overwhelming.

I rested a moment to catch my breath. And there it was. Beyond the battlements, along the main tourist path lay what at first glance I took for an Indian dugout canoe. But this felt totally out of place here. When I approached the thirty-foot-long object, the "canoe" appeared to be a perfectly formed penis, quite badly charred at its root, but absolutely and incontrovertibly—with no detail missing—

a penis. Distrusting my eyes, I circled it warily to be sure I wasn't experiencing an erotic delusion. The German title, which I couldn't read, was no help. But there was no way to mistake its contours. The solid, slightly curved tree trunk, about three feet in diameter, carefully and lovingly carved, showed the engorged stalk, heart-shaped tip, and suggestion of veins of an enthusiastically distended male member. It appeared to have been circumcised. As the old Lucky Strike ad used to say, "So round, so firm, so fully packed, so free & easy . . ." The rest is too uncomfortable to contemplate.

Curiously I looked at the crowd of passing people for an explanation. Half of them were tourists; half of them were local school children. No one so much as glanced at it. By its charred state I surmised it to be an ancient Germanic totem which some affronted early Christians had tried to burn at the stake, and which had been exhumed by Heidelbrungian archeologists. In sheer magnitude it certainly beat anything our erotic imaginings might have fantasied. I wondered what its female counterpart would be like if I might accidentally stumble into it somewhere in the castle grounds. An abysmal prospect.

This was virgin culture to me. What was the point here? Did Nordic man use it in initiation rites to convince little boys that they had a big future? Or were they trying to awe their women into submission with it if they didn't behave? Yet what species could even pretend to such an appendage? It would take three Goliaths to get it off the ground, not to mention raise it to an appropriate position. The champion who sported it would almost immediately be crushed by its weight. Whoever had originally tried to burn it had only been able to create a blaze big enough to blacken one end.

I wish I could have sent postcards of it to my friends telling them about blasé Germans who keep such bizarre relics in their castles. When I questioned Eric about the penis in the palace, he gave me a blank look, assuming he had misunderstood his mother. Then I asked his girlfriend who replied casually: "Did you get a picture of yourself sitting on it? That's what all the girls did when it first came out."

First came out? Out of what?

Her answer explained the startling insouciance of the Germans. The phallus was part of an art show glorifying the uses of wood. It didn't fit into the local gallery and therefore was relegated to the palace grounds. It was conceived and carved by an American sculptor, who came, I was told, from California. Her name, I was told, is Alice.

On Truthful Answers
to Interview Questions and
the Nature of the Erotic

I've been asked this question when the Ladies were being interviewed:

Q. Would you say that life's best moments are erotic?

Quick answers are required, so mine has been, "Undoubtedly, yes." But there was always this qualifying thing I wanted to express to make my answer really truthful, and there was never time. So here's my real answer:

A. It's hard to categorize "best moments," but everyone remembers times of transient glory; some of them only a few seconds, some the length of a dawn or evening, and some were with that electric other person who, for a time, could make the galaxy spin. But for me, where there is enough joy and feeling, whether or not it is specifically sexual, there is the erotic.

For example: It is dawn of an autumn morning in a very high meadow of the Sierra, so cold that hoarfrost has formed on the sleeping bag, and I am awakened by my own shivering, even wrapped in gray goose down. In the sky I see, in the palest starting light, clouds perfectly formed in the shape of lenses, or vehicles from outer space, and the dawn has made them white on one curved surface and delicate pink and mauve on the other. No wind seems to move them, though wind surely formed them.

As I get up and try to start a fire with cold kindling and blue hands, I see, just across the tiny creek which has frozen on the surface during the night, a coyote—quite beautiful, with markings like those of an arctic dog's. He is motionless in a pounce position, ears forward, intently focused on a burrow entrance in the creek bank. As I get the fire burning, he looks across at me, but maintains his position. I am I and he is he, both going about the business of survival. Suddenly he springs on the burrow, swift as a cat, but comes up empty-jawed. His breakfast is deferred, but he has no resentment toward me, even though I stand less than thirty feet away, have an egg cooking now, and may have frightened his quarry. His patience has the quality of the strange clouds that never seem to change, and yet when you look again, they have.

He turns away and lopes silently across the frost-covered meadow to search out new prey. I watch him and feel a part of his universe, and, instead of feeling that he is a limited creature, I feel my own clumsy limitations. Coyote is the often despised hunter-scavenger, but I have seen the beauty of his foxy face and almond eyes and luxuriant fur, and I have seen that he works hard for a living.

I feel love both for the earth that set this scene and for the coyote. I would like to be the coyote's mate, mating under wintry moon and in lavender morning, and in whatever secret den supporting the cubs from hour to hour and day to day, suckling them and taking pride in their frisky play. I would like our landmark to be the granite butte which changes color with every stage of the sun's progress, washes to a gleaming dark in the rain, and emerges as a tapestry of white-delineated texture in the snow. Our water source would be the spring-fed tarn at the granite base, surrounded by miniature willows and inset with half-submerged boulders, where reeds stand in the shallows and only water skimmers disturb the evening's stillness. I would like to live by the earth's great cycles: when times are good, sleeping with my mate on the wild-flowered bank; when life turns harsh, wailing eerie music to each other under the falling stars.

But is this erotic? I don't think anyone would see it that way. You'd have to say that what I think of as peak experiences would not interest anyone directly seeking the sexual. So the answer to your question is, "No."

As a word person, almost as excited by romping through the dictionary as rolling in the hay, I have given some thought to what the word *erotic* means—to Webster, to me, and to you out there who have watched us blaze a midlife trail across the TV stations of these United States.

When I looked up *erotic* in Webster's *New Twentieth-Century Unabridged Second Edition*, I smiled to read "pertaining to or prompted by sexual feelings." And then my eye continued to scroll down the page where it landed on the noun form of the word whose meaning, to my stunned surprise, is quite a bit more lascivious: "a person abnormally sensitive to sexual stimulation."

I looked up from the dictionary, at no one and at nothing, and asked myself whether I was "abnormally sensitive to sexual stimulation." As if I were, indeed, two people, "Pseudonym" and "Realnym," Realnym winked at me and reminded me of my first experience flying a kite. I was in my thirties, she recalled for me, standing alone on a hillside, kite in hand, with instructions to start running as I let out the string. And so I ran as fast as I could, not knowing what to expect, when all of a sudden the wind whipped the kite from my hand and immediately began to play with me, provocatively releasing and holding back the tension on the remaining string, the kite reaching higher and higher into the sky as I first struggled against, then surrendered to, and finally controlled our movements with growing confidence. The wind, the kite, and I quickly and innocently formed a ménage à trois on that lonely hillside. As I vividly recalled the experience, I could see Noah and Sigmund folding their arms across their scholarly chests and nodding in smug satisfaction. (I could almost see the fine print: "a woman who is sexually stimulated by flying a kite, for example.")

Well, I soothed myself, even if I am both the adjective and the noun form of the word, neither they nor I have anything to do with that *other* word which we Kensington Ladies are asked about frequently, as if *pornography* were kissing cousin to *erotica*. It is not. Of that I am entirely sure. For one thing, the two words have different ancestors, one being Eros, the god of love, and the other being *porne* meaning *prostitute*. If Noah is to be trusted, *pornography* originally meant "a description of prostitutes and their trade." Actually, what sets pornography apart is precisely that it is *not* "prompted by sexual feelings" any more than a prostitute is. Those who participate in it are invariably prompted by *money*. Clearly, as with all words, it is not the strict dictionary definition that governs how we respond. Words have connotations for each of us, and, as elsewhere in life, one person's friend is another's enemy.

For me, the erotic is big, fat-cheeked cumulus clouds in the sky . . . it is exiting the freeway into San Francisco's financial district and being engulfed by a sudden skyscraper . . . it is a conversation that starts at ground zero and climbs quickly and effortlessly to exhilarating heights . . . it is the scent of Patchouli . . . it is Julio Iglesias reminding me in song of past (shamelessly romantic) liaisons . . . it is a déja vu (déja senti?) of the texture of an ex-lover's skin . . . it is fingers losing themselves in my hair . . . it is the feel of satin, silk, fur, or sun on my bare skin . . . it is an hour-long foot rub by firelight . . . it is a warm protective hand on my elbow as I cross the street . . . it is a trail of kitten-soft kisses on my neck . . . it is a hand that finds my best-kept secrets . . . it is a mouth a girl could die for . . . it is the smell of pipe smoke and the rough feel of tweed . . . it is a man's neck unafraid of scent . . . it is what makes me laugh from my belly and cry from my soul . . . it is what sweetens sleep and makes it possible to get up in the morning . . . it is smells, sounds, memories, sensations, colors, feelings, flowers, grass, sunlight, wind, rain, thoughts . . .

Just the other day I spoke with a woman from Switzerland who had read and loved *Ladies' Own Erotica*. She told me that she had approached the book in an unorthodox way. She read one Lady's autobiography and all her stories before going on to the next. In this way she felt as though she got to know each one of us personally. She loved the feeling of familiarity and confided that never could there be a group such as ours in Switzerland. She could hardly wait to read our next book and was interested to find out how our experiences of publishing and promoting the first book had affected our lives.

I told her that my private life has not changed much. My three teenagers are just older teenagers. My daughters, particularly, are proud of my participation in the books. I continue to have fantasies—enjoying them by myself or sharing them with my husband of twenty-five years. As Rose Solomon so aptly responded when asked if the book had an effect on her sex life, "Not particularly—erotica is just something I do on the side."

And so it has been for me—with the book-signing parties, women-in-writing seminars (suddenly we were all authorities on writing and sex), publicity tours, and finally getting down to work on the second book. All these activities were sandwiched in between working and shopping, feeding, and nurturing my family.

I must admit to a certain glow that came from the success of *Ladies' Own Erotica* and all the recognition and media attention. It's fun being even a little bit famous. Since I grew up in Hollywood, it was especially exciting to be chauffeured to television studios and escorted onto stages. I never dreamed of such things happening to me while I was growing up.

The glow from media attention fades fast, however. I'll always treasure the videotapes of our talk-show appearances, though; it'll give me something to amuse myself in my eighties and nineties. I'm sure I'll be a source of amusement to all my grandchildren and great-grandchildren when they see pictures of Naughty Nell in her heyday.

Erotica U.S.A.: An Interview

I've known Sabina all my life, but I refused to become a Lady when she invited me to join her gang of merry masquers. She sits across from me in her living room, which is cluttered with family mementos and well-worn antiques talking with missionary zeal about her erotic trip across the country.

"Flying will never be the same again. Everything looks different from an erotic perspective. From now on I'll look at a new city as a potential lover, somebody you may want to have a fling with, brief, but memorable. You know what I mean?"

I don't. She explains that every city has an erotic flavor, some stronger than others, some more to her taste, depending on her rapport with the people and the architecture. "There has to be water," she adds when I look skeptical.

"Take St. Louis, for instance. We arrived there at night. From our window I saw this stunning apparition, like a star or spaceship. First there was only a sliver of silver next to the full moon. Gradually a luminous slide revealed itself stretching further and further down toward us until it reached almost into our bedroom. We kept the curtain opened wide all night. Every time I woke up, I noticed that the arch had thickened at the base, but only one column was ever visible. In the morning we discovered that it was a portal to the Mississippi River behind it—a gigantic floodgate open to endless pleasures streaming westward. We ran across the street to take a closer look. Seen from below, it was even more erotic—like glancing up a pair of very long legs. It clearly showed the difference between male and female erotica. Most monuments are phallic symbols, right? But not this one. It may very well be the only monument to female orgasm in the world."

I fail to see the connection—gate versus tower yes, but orgasm?

"It rises from the ground," she says, "but not straight up like a tower. Instead of terminating abruptly it comes gradually to a peak and then almost maintains a plateau until it gently curves downward. The glide down is as exciting as the climax, don't you think? There is a train for spectators, much nicer than an elevator, although it makes some people dizzy. Anyway, we discussed the orgasmic qualities of the monument on the local radio show and our host, a very perceptive man, immediately got the point."

"And the people in St. Louis didn't call in to object?"

"Not at all. They loved the idea and wondered why nobody had mentioned it before. That's what makes it a truly erotic city, when the people are in tune with their architecture as well as with nature. We are, of course, partial to San Francisco because of all the bridges. Both are female cities, whereas Chicago and Seattle are male."

Sabina continues her rhapsody: Chicago impressed her with his elegance. She'd expected a gangster, but found a clean-cut gentleman, wearing a crystal white shirt of snow over the trim skyline. Seattle was very masculine, half fisherman, half pioneer in a seasoned wool sweater: "Upon closer look you can see that it has been lovingly mended everywhere." Portland was a younger man, a little self-conscious perhaps, but charmingly shy: "We met such a man actually at a book-signing. He told us he was the gardener in Rose Solomon's story. He was clutching a bunch of daffodils and our book. It was well read."

"What about our sex capitals," I ask, "like New York and Los Angeles?"

"Too tense. New York is like a lover who has to prove how good he is and blames you if anything goes wrong. The whole city has that worried frown: the shoppers, the receptionists, the talk-show hosts, except, of course, Dr. Ruth. And in L.A. they asked us questions like 'Has your book improved your sex life?' meaning, will it give readers an orgasm? It makes me feel self-conscious. I'm compelled to come up with something spectacular such as 'Sabina's Sex Life, New And Improved.' Whenever I've been there, I get this urge to redesign my living room and my sex life. I wear my mask on Rodeo Drive, because I feel so underdressed."

I can't imagine that this normal woman—who has the healthy glow of a backpacker—would cruise around Hollywood in a feather mask.

"In Boston they made me take it off. We had to confront the camera bare-faced. I wanted to talk about atomic waste instead of erotica. The mask brings out my playful, my creative side."

I ask her bluntly what makes the Ladies different from all the other writers of erotica. I mention a new book, *How to Write Erotica*, in which the Kensington ladies are listed with all the sleaze. Erotica is used interchangeably with pornography.

Sabina's face falls. "They've asked me to endorse that book. It's like asking Ronald Reagan to endorse Karl Marx. That book tells writers how to conform to the sex market, as if erotic literature for women was nothing but a fuck with a dinner thrown in. The reason why we came together in the first place was precisely because we found nothing on the shelves that appealed to us."

"Come off your high horse, Sabina," I interrupt. Her cheeks are flushed, her voice pitched unerotically high. "You are all writing about *it*, intercourse-related turn-ons."

"Yes, why not? It's about time that women get their own word in on the subject. I have nothing against explicit language, but words can be abused. The pornographers have cornered the verbal and visual market with their brand names. What upsets me most about *How to Write Erotica* is that it tells the writer to conform to the established sex market, to please the editor instead of herself, to fake orgasm to pleasure the customer. Our greatest satisfaction came from writing for ourselves before we ever realized that our book would be published. Writing erotica to us means writing about our own experience—real or fantasy—in a way that appeals to us and our very best friends, like you."

She looked at me and smiled: "I wish you'd been with us in St. Louis. Why don't you meet me there?"

Rose Solomon barged in upon my marriage eight years ago during a misunderstanding. If you have read our first book you might remember the story of her origin: During an intimate moment I had whispered to my husband that his ears smelled like roast almonds. "Rose Solomon?" he had cried out, backing off like a man accused. Rose continues to be the threatening Other Woman in our lives. Passionate and unpredictable, she shatters our domestic tranquility. She refuses to do housework (although she likes to garden), and she cannot tolerate routine. She says anything that comes into her head, blows everything out of proportion, and squeezes the most she can out of each moment. Her fascination with erotica, she claims, has been life-long, and now at midlife it is stronger than ever. She vows to "grow old erotically!" and regards herself as an Erotic Crusader: "What knights once did for chivalry, we Ladies must now do for erotica!" If she weren't so warm-hearted and entertaining, we would have asked her to leave long ago.

Our teenage children, wanting to monopolize the spotlight, complain when Rose takes over. They are open and direct with her, as she is with them. Frequently they ask to read her stories freshly hatched from the typewriter, and they are quick to alert Rose to anything they find "gross." In spite of their vociferous criticism, they usually like her stories because, as my fourteen-year-old son says, "they make sex believable." It is Rose's affinity for publicity, not her subject, that sometimes embarrasses them. Once, after a particularly sappy television interview in which Rose extolled the erotic potential inherent in the most commonplace tasks, she came home to find them writhing on the floor enacting a merciless parody: "Ohhh, see how the erotic permeates every aspect of my life! Just inhale the freshness of my laundry as it tumbles from the dryer into my waiting arms! Ahhhh, here—feel its warmth! How sensual is each sock and towel. Oh, let me press them to my lips, to my breasts . . ."

My husband is secretly in love with her. He never complains when she takes off and travels, and he tacitly encourages her writing. Recently he gave her a word processor (and me a food processor). I think he would prefer me to be more like her; she never asks him to take out the garbage, and she is always eager to jump into bed.

When Rose is around, we all become more playful and affectionate, and because she takes such a personal and confidential interest in me, I, too, welcome her. I express myself best in her presence. She encourages me to be more spontaneous and hedonistic, but lately this has become a source of argument. I find her scope too narrow. "Rose," I say, "it's time to realize your fixation with erotica limits your writing."

"Never!" she insists. "The erotic moment is the heart of every story. It's the part we all ache to experience. If it's denied, I feel cheated, and if it's missing, I feel dead. What better source of inspiration is there?"

I warn her that her passion blunts her judgment and blinds her to degrading realities. I point out, "Don't you realize that you are often presented on talk shows as if you are a sleaze queen? You are encouraged to titillate and shock. Sometimes you are even on programs with porn stars. Is this where you want your erotic crusade to take you?"

"I will go wherever I must to make the world safe for erotica!" declares Rose with a defiant bump and grind. "Home erotica is an antidote to pornography. I write it for love not money! And I write it with a key principle in mind: " 'No victims.' It is the rule we Kensington Ladies live by, and I will do whatever I must to get it across."

"Shut up, Sweethearts," my husband mutters. "Turn down the volume and come to bed."

Sparkle Polenta!

As an actress dedicated to the art of transformation, I am always on the lookout for someone to *be*. I love to observe and record that part which human beings casually expose to the world: body language, speech patterns, mannerisms of all kinds. I love to try these on like clothes, dressing from the inside out to ensure the fusion of my reality with that of the mysterious "other." It's magical, like an act of love.

Now, of all the *dramatis personae* I know as the Kensington Ladies, Nell is the part I would most like to play. To me she is the quintessential feminine: the Earth Goddess in odalisque pajamas, Venus in a French butcher's apron, Mother Goose in a designer suit, with all the children of the world nestled under her wing. What must it be like to be Nell?

She brought her cheese-polenta bread to one of our meetings recently, along with copies of her neatly typed recipe for those who would request it. When I decided to try my hand at it, I thought that this was my chance to attempt a transformation: I would bake cheese-polenta bread and study the part at the same time.

I looked over the recipe as though it were a script, thinking about what she had said on the subject of bread-making. It should be undertaken, she said, as part of a day spent luxuriating at home, preferably after a massage. Nobody can rush the rising of the dough, she said; ancient and sacred wisdom is at work. I began to feel excitement rising, a welling of desire to experience the elemental mystery in the chemistry she described: yeast moving through warm water to touch and change the grainy polenta, the cheese, the egg, the salt and flour. I could hardly wait!

First, though, I had to be sure that I included Bernadette in the process, otherwise the magic would not work; I would get only a caricature of Nell and possibly a leaden loaf. The first information was the fact that I, Bernadette, like to dance in the kitchen when I'm cooking. I really do. I dance whatever the mood dictates: jazz, tango, free-style rock-and-roll, a little Martha Graham technique, ballet. My favorites are the pas de deux from "Spartacus" as choreographed by the Bolshoi (I take both parts—no mean feat, let me say, while getting dinner for six) and the "Steam Heat" number that made Shirley MacLaine famous (I use a sauce pan lid as a derby hat. Tricky).

What would Nell dance, as the dough swelled under its linen veil? For some reason, "*Valse triste*" came to mind—not for its name, I'm sure, with its connotations of mourning. No doubt its voluptuous, swaying surges and its earthbound flight were the inspirations attendant on the choice. In any event, I believe that when the unconscious speaks, you listen. I knew that Nell's hair would float like a fragrant cloud around her face as she danced, wooden spoon aloft, apron billowing from her waist. I felt very connected and happy, creative juices flowing; I ran off to find my recording of the piece.

On the way I detoured into my closet to find something Nell-like to wear, something for "a day spent luxuriating at home." She would wear white pants, I decided, with a cotton shirt in sharp yellow, splashed with scarlet and green like paint strokes, espadrilles and bright earrings. I changed into my equivalent of this costume: black denims, blue shirt with black geometric shapes, white discs at my ears. I decided against shoes because I had painted my toenails shocking pink, and they looked festive against the kitchen floor tile. Also, bare feet keep me grounded: I was, after all, going to bake bread.

Now, delighted with my emerging Nell-ness, I put the record on the turntable, turned up the volume so that I could hear it in the kitchen, put on my reading glasses, and applied myself to the sheet of typed instructions . . .

Mix one package of dry yeast and one teaspoon (of the two tablespoons) sugar with one cup of warm water. Let it stand until it develops a marvelous foam.

I stood over the bowl, breathing in the love-odor of the yeast as it penetrated the warm, sticky liquid, watching the foam as, like a residue of receding tide, it frothed and muttered on its porcelain reef. Stealthily, furtively, I dipped my finger into it and licked the fertile solution. I shuddered at the potency of the flavor on my tongue and read on.

Combine half a pound of sharp cheddar cheese—cut in small cubes, 3¼ (of the 3½) cups of all-purpose flour, the remaining sugar, ½ cup of potenta or yellow cornmeal, and ½ teaspoon of salt. Mix until cheese crumbles.

Oh, this was the hands-on experience I adored! I remembered seeing Nell one time making pastry for a quiche. In the concentrated nurturing environment of the kitchen she was particularly fascinating and paradoxical to consider: so present, yet so remote, her shapely, manicured hands moving with supple insistence on the shortening, gently insisting on its union with the flour. I let my memory of her wrist movements inform my own. I rolled the rough polenta between my fingers, feeling the dusty, arid friction of the salt-sprinkled flour on my skin. As I rubbed the cubes of resilient cheese into granules to merge with the sugar and pressed the ingredients into soft submission, I could feel my throat growing dry as though I were walking through desert sand. The recipe called for one egg to be added. I cracked it, and the sight of the liquid gush, streaming in golden threads and gelatinous clumps over the dessication in the bowl was like stumbling into an oasis. On the stereo, Sibelius pleaded passionately with me to dance into his arms. Rapturously I closed my eyes, my hands, wrist-deep in dewy dough, flexing, relaxing, flexing, relaxing.

Pour in the yeast mixture in a steady, slow stream.

Now I knew how it felt to be Nell! Joyfully I squeezed the humid paste through my fingers, my pleasure as primitive and as innocent as a child's at the shore, making sandpies at the ocean's edge.

Dough should be slightly sticky. If too wet add some of the remaining flour, 1 tablespoon at a time. Plop dough onto a floured board, and knead with your own loving hands for a few minutes. Concentrate on the feel of the dough in your hands—smell it, taste it.

Ecstatic to learn that my physical connection with the dough would continue I followed the instructions, feeling the unmistakable sense of union with the character I was playing. How well I knew Nell! How well she knew me! I read on, conscious that now my head turned gracefully and precisely toward the typed page, an exact Nell-movement.

After your senses have been satisfied, form the dough into a smooth ball.

Weighing the dough in both hands, I shaped it exactly into a gleaming globe, turned it into a greased bowl, and covered it with snowy muslin. I now had about an hour and a half to wait before Nature in her implacable way caused it to double in volume. Staying carefully in character, I went outdoors to cut some flowers for the house, taking with me basket, clippers, the New Western Garden Book (for looking up the Latin names of plants), and a floppy hat. I weeded and watered and thought about landscape design, then returned to the kitchen to deliver a restrained but assertive punch to the upstart dough, now bulging under its flimsy chemise.

Knead briefly on a floured board to shape into a smooth ball. Place on a baking sheet made slippery with grease and flatten into a perfect circle. Cover it lightly and voila! After about an hour your loaf will be about two to three inches high and ready to bake. Sprinkle the top with a little flour and slide it into an oven at 375° until well browned, about 35 minutes. Let cool on a rack. Makes 1 loaf, about 2 lbs. Share with your lover or your family or very special friends. Love, Nell.

I completed the ritual of the bread and began easily to resume my own familiar persona, thinking about transformation as an act of love. Would Nell like to try on my Bernadette-ness sometime? I wondered. How would she wear me?

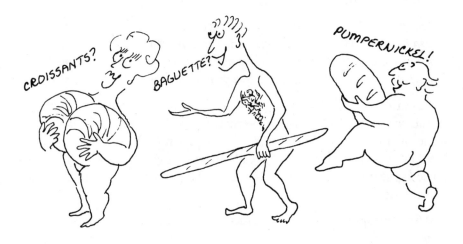

The Noah Griffin Show
—a Fantasy

It is four A.M. and the city sleeps.

My sisters-in-erotica, Bernadette, Emma, Susan and I park our car in front of the imposing KGO Radio Building. An unlikely group of people stand across the street, the blare of punk-rock music drifts through an open door. We wonder what is going on?

Clutching our coats and purses tightly, we lock the car and climb the long, Roman-style stairway to the main entrance. Entering the foyer, which is totally deserted, we see a night guard, who sits at a desk in the center of the large empty room. We tell him we are the Erotica Ladies. He nods and picks up his phone. "The guests for the Noah Griffin Show are here." He opens his register and asks us to sign in. I hestitate. Should I sign my real name or my pseudonym? I opt for the fake.

The guard accompanies us on a silent elevator ride to some unknown floor. As the door slides open, we dutifully follow him down long corridors, passing deserted rooms and countless empty cubicles. A portly, genial man suddenly appears around a corner. He explains that he is the engineer who will monitor the show.

"Where is the bathroom?" we ask in unison.

After a quick orientation, he disappears. We find the elegant bathroom and examine ourselves critically in the mirror. Emma is pale. "I look terrible at this hour," she laments. None of us has slept for fear of missing the alarm, and although our interview will be on radio, we take time to comb our hair and put on lipstick.

Leaving the safety of the bathroom, we voyage down mysterious, narrow hallways finally to enter a pleasantly furnished room with couches and chairs. A floor-to-ceiling window reveals the twinkling lights of San Francisco, halfway between night and day. A radio is on, and I hear a man talking. "That's Noah," someone says.

It is four-thirty A.M. and we are ready.

I look through a window in the room to see a man sitting on a high stool in the sound studio. He is very big and wears heavy earphones. He talks and swirls around, pushing knobs and clicking buttons. I watch his mouth, but it doesn't synch with the words on the radio.

The engineer reappears. "There is a five-second delay from the announcer to the airwaves," he explains. A young, attractive woman enters. She offers us a plate of cookies and tells us she is a rabbi, rehearsing for her early Sunday morning religious program, which will follow our interview. We are here to tell Noah about our book.

It is five A.M. and I am nervous.

Noah concludes his last commercial and ushers us into the studio. It is a fantasy of luxury and electronic jazz. Four black, leather-bound chairs face a long, wooden table; on top sit three big, imposing microphones, a tangle of earphones hang from them. We put on the earphones, Noah disappears. I see him across the room, sitting on his stool. His part of the studio is separated from ours by a glass barrier. Words begin to come over the earphones. "Good morning, this is the Noah Griffin show."

I concentrate on the words I hear and stare in fascination at the mike. It is so big, so hooded, so masculine . . . the voice asks questions. It is my turn. Staring hypnotically at the microphone, I answer the voice in my ears. I look up and realize, to my surprise, that I am talking to the man on the stool. It is his words I am hearing. He is nodding and looking at me encouragingly. He speaks in a soft, quick patter, his eyes on mine. I begin to feel lulled and seduced by his mellow tones.

"Tell me, Jenna, what do you find erotic?"

It is five-thirty A.M. and I am vulnerable.

I stare at his mouth. It moves and melts around his sensuous voice. I forget where I am. I feel a powerful need to get close to that mouth. I climb onto the table, never taking my eyes off the irresistible pair of lips and try to get through the glass barrier. It looms in front of me. There are gasps of horror and dismay from the Ladies. I hear Emma's disapproving voice, "Jenna, get down, for God's sake!" I hear Bernadette laugh in startled surprise. I see Susan wring her hands in confusion and disappear out the door.

Noah and I are staring at each other. He has moved his stool close to the table. Our faces are near, his voice is husky. "Yes, Jenna, how do you like your kisses?" "Moist and hot and sucking," I say.

Bernadette is climbing onto the table too. She kicks off her high-heeled shoes and swings her hips. I catch a glimpse of Emma's pale face. I see Susan enter the door, pulling the engineer along with her. He looks dumbfounded. He and Susan look at each other.

"When my husband left me . . ."

"When my wife left me . . ."

They have discovered each other. I see them in a close embrace.

Noah and I have discarded our earphones. We press hard against the glass, trying to kiss each other through the barrier. I stand on my tiptoes and strain to get my hand over the top of the frame. He has abandoned his stool and teeters precariously on a narrow ledge on the other side of the barrier.

Bernadette sidles back and forth on her runway, slowly discarding her clothing, throwing pieces recklessly about the room. Emma grips the mike with determination to fill the void Noah has left. "Yes," she tells the radio audience, "our book is a breakthrough, a cathartic experience." The rabbi appears at the door. She has been hearing the bumps and thumps and looks at the scene in amazement. Susan and the portly engineer thrash around on the floor. I hear Susan say, "Yes, I feel free to experiment with strange men."

Noah and I slide our tongues against the glass, up and down, and all around, small traces of moisture smear the surface.

The rabbi grabs a mike and gallantly interviews Emma. "Does your group always act like this?" Emma is loyal. "Yes," she answers, "we believe it is important to be erotic wherever you are."

Telephones are ringing in the empty desert of the engineer's office. No one answers or cares.

It is six A.M., KGO Radio, San Francisco. Weather clear today, ladies and gentlemen.